THE BIG RED ONE

SAMUEL FULLER

Introduction by
RICHARD SCHICKEL

THUNDER'S MOUTH PRESS
NEW YORK

THE BIG RED ONE

Published by
Thunder's Mouth Press
An Imprint of Avalon Publishing Group Inc.
245 West 17th Street, 11th Floor
New York, NY 10011

AVALON

Originally published by Bantam Books in 1980
First Thunder's Mouth Press edition September 2005

Library of Congress Cataloging-in-Publication Data is available.

ISBN-10: 1-56025-743-1
ISBN-13: 978-1-56025-743-1

Distributed by Publishers Group West

for Christa, my wife
and Samantha, our daughter

This is fictional life based
on factual death.
Any similarity the names have
to any person living, wounded,
missing, hospitalized, insane
or dead is coincidental.

INTRODUCTION

The book you are about to read was first published as a paperback original in the summer of 1980, coincident with the release of Samuel Fuller's movie of the same title. It was not a "novelization" of his screenplay. It would be more accurate to say that the film was an adaptation of the novel, which Sam wrote some time after 1959, when an early effort to make the movie—it was to have starred John Wayne—failed.

The critically unheralded publication of this book (surely based on a treatment or first draft screenplay of that aborted project) is an important way station in one of the remarkable odysseys—perhaps one should say, "obsessions"—of American cultural life in the twentieth century. The republication of Sam's novel, following shortly after release of the reconstructed version of his movie, which adds back to it almost an hour of material that was cut from it by the studio, brings that odyssey at last to a happy conclusion after almost sixty-four years.

That story begins the day after the Japanese attack on Pearl Harbor, December 7, 1941, when Sam Fuller, like thousands of other young American males, volunteered for service in the armed forces. Except that Sam was not so young. At twenty-nine, he was old for the combat duty he craved. But he was also a writer. He had begun working for newspapers—mostly tabloids—when he was a teenager and by this time had sold some screenplays and story ideas to the movies and had completed a novel, *The Dark Page*. He saw the war as an epic subject, about which he was consciously determined to gather firsthand experience, more likely for a book than for a movie. He always liked to say that his biggest thrill was not a screen credit, but a byline, even if it was only on a humble news story.

Assigned to the First Infantry Division—The Big Red One—he soldiered with it (in the Sixteenth Infantry Regiment) through all its campaigns. He landed with it in North Africa, in Sicily, and on D-Day on Omaha Beach in Normandy in 1944, where he won a Silver Star for bravery. He fought on through France, Belgium (including the Battle of the Bulge), Germany, and, at last, Czechoslovakia, where his unit was among those that liberated the concentration camp at Falkenau. He kept a rough diary of his experiences, illustrating it with cartoons, for which he also had a gift. These experiences form the spine of both his book and his movie. If you compare those works with his autobiography, *A Third Face*, published posthumously in 2002, you will see that he transferred many autobiographical incidents directly into his fictions. You will also see that he invented a great deal as well.

Except that I don't think *invented* is quite the word we want. To be sure, a major character, the brutal Nazi sergeant, Schroeder, who haunts the American squad on which Sam's fictions focus, is a purely imagined character (and much more fully realized in the novel than in the film). To a slightly lesser degree (he is given a little back story) so is the nameless sergeant who commands that squad. Both are, in effect, killing machines, symbolic (or, if you will, "literary") representations of the warrior spirit stripped of saving sentiment and explanatory psychological justifications. We "like" the American noncom because he saves lives for "our" side. We dislike the German because he is driven by the worst aspects of Nazi ideology. But we are, I think, obliged to recognize that they are two sides of the same coin.

Another fiction is less obviously present in Sam's work. That is the group of four young soldiers—Zab, who is based on Sam himself; Griff, the sharpshooter who cannot force himself to kill a man whose face he can see; Vinci, a street-smart Italian from New York; and Johnson, a southern hick, suffering from piles and from a familial link with the Ku Klux Klan, which he despises. These are "the four horsemen" who, under the sergeant's protection, improbably survive the war, unlike any of the replacements who briefly join their squad. These figures, like the sergeant himself, are obviously composite characters, and they are rather simply observed. But the point of the exercise is not characterization. It is to enforce—to quadruple if you will—the point of Sam's story, which is that the only glory in war is, finally, to survive. He once said to me that the only thing on a soldier's mind is "to live, live, live." By improbably doing so, while grudgingly doing their duty and even unwillingly achieving a few heroic moments, these men exemplify this theme.

But if you set aside these fictive conceits, *The Big Red One* must also, even perhaps most significantly, be read as a kind of oral history, into which Sam swept all the stories, all the rumors, that he heard in the course of the war. It is the relentless richness of this detail that makes both novel and film such compelling experiences. There are very few books or films about combat that so persuasively give the reader or the viewer such an intimate sense of what it is like to fight as a common soldier in a vast military enterprise, of the purely accidental ways the question of who shall live and who shall die is determined, the equally accidental ways in which moments of grace are dealt out to soldiers.

One can imagine Sam's head bursting with stories when he returned from the war. But determined though he was to shape all he had learned into some sort of coherent tale, he did not sit down and write his novel in the years immediately after the war as so many American writers—

Norman Mailer, Irwin Shaw, Gore Vidal, Alfred Hayes, John Horne Burns, among many others—did. He went into the movies full time instead, and some of his own World War II observations found their way into his two pictures about the Korean War, *The Steel Helmet* and *Fixed Bayonets* (both 1951). The former contains a rough sketch of *The Big Red One*'s American sergeant, the latter a portrait of a soldier who, like Griff, cannot shoot an enemy face-to-face. Obviously, it was in this period that Sam began to think of turning his wartime recollections into a screenplay instead of a novel. This was not necessarily an aesthetic mistake. But it was a practical one. War movies generally fall into two camps: there are those that use the movies' immediacy and vividness to capture the carnage of war and turn that imagery into antiwar statements (see *All Quiet on the Western Front, Platoon, Full Metal Jacket*) and there are those that simply use the topic as an occasion for heroic adventure. Sam was never interested in making either sort of film. He fully understood the brutality of war and the absurdist qualities of many "dogface" (as he nearly always called American soldiers) experiences. But he was not antiwar, not when it came to World War II. He was, after all, a secular Jew who thought it necessary to stamp out Nazism. On the other hand, having lived through the blood, mud, and shit of combat, he was not about to make *The Heroes of Telemark,* either. His story—and it is possible other factors were operating here—is that he turned down the 1959 opportunity to make *The Big Red One* because he was dubious about John Wayne as the sergeant. Wayne always carried an heroic promise on to the screen, an implication that he would lead his men to triumphant victory at the end of the story. Sam was after something much wearier and antiheroic.

It was not in Sam Fuller's nature to let obsessions fester. He kept busy after his first failure to get *The Big Red One* off the ground, making, under increasingly marginalized economic conditions, that series of films his devoted acolytes still rightly treasure. But he never gave up on *The Big Red One*. His script kept kicking around Hollywood and, finally, in the late '70s, Lorimar Pictures, well-heeled from prime-time television soap operas like *Dallas,* and starting up a movie division, agreed to make the picture.

The budget was tight—only $4 million—the schedule hectic, but the studio approved Sam's script and off he went to Israel and Ireland, to make his film. In the studio's eyes the best insurance on its investment was Lee Marvin, cast as the sergeant. Like Sam, he was a combat veteran—he had been a marine in the South Pacific theater—deeply haunted by his wartime experiences and with his gaunt face and lean frame he had about him the threat of death Sam wanted. The two veterans bonded, in effect becoming joint squad leaders to the group of young actors working on the production. In less than three months the company shot a movie that, when assembled, ran for over three hours.

That length alarmed the studio. It was so much more than it had bargained for. Yet there's a mystery here. If you examine Sam's shooting script and compare it to the footage he shot, he added nothing to the script in production. If anything, he appears to have cut a few sequences from it. But battle scenes that can be roughly described in a page or two of script tend to become much longer when they are shot. This is because details that may not even be mentioned in the script, but are vital to the work's effect, eat up screen time at an often alarming rate. More important, however, was the fact that the movie did not comfortably fit the studio's expectations: It was not an antiwar war movie and it was certainly not a triumphalist adventure. Nor was it a David Lean–style epic, something that might justify road show exhibition. It was what Sam always meant it to be—an intense, but quite modestly scaled, study in survival.

So the picture was taken away from Sam, and an editor, working independently of him, was brought in, ostensibly to shorten the picture, but really, I think, to make it a more conventional war movie. He cut at least an hour out of it, which Sam refused to criticize or disown. He went around promoting the film as if it were still entirely the one he had intended. And, in truth, it was not a bad movie. His intensions were so intrinsic to the material he had shot that they could not be entirely excised. I was one of the reviewers who, at the time, praised the film—even putting it on *Time* magazine's Ten Best list at the end of the year.

But once the film had played off in the theaters, Sam began talking in public about his disappointment with the movie, speaking wistfully about rescuing the lost footage and making a restored version of the film. No one—me included—read this novel, which at that point was the truest measure of his intent. Its humble status as a mass-market paperback pretty much assured its being ignored. As for Sam, he made one more important picture, the excellent *White Dog,* which another studio shelved in the face of protests from groups that, sight unseen, dubbed it racist, though, of course, it was quite the opposite. He then retreated to a more marginal filmmaking existence, directing only two more theatrical features, largely unseen in the United States.

But in the years before and after his death in 1997 his reputation among cinephiles and cineastes continually rose, while, incidentally, those of other more respectable contemporaries fell. In the Fuller films they most admired—*Shock Corridor, The Naked Kiss,* the aforementioned Korean war films—there was a kind of blunt, black irony that seemed more and more in tune with recent times. The same was true of their low-budget crudeness — Sam never had the time or money to explain delicate psychological nuances and wasn't much interested in them anyway. The tabloids had long ago taught him that life is ruled by chance, that human behavior is rarely as coherent, as rational, as conveniently explicable as we like to think it is.

In this period, too, people began to wonder anew about *The Big Red One*. When Lorimar failed financially its assets were sold to Warner Bros. and it was widely believed that the unused footage from the film now resided in the latter's vaults and, indeed, its computerized database listed many boxes labeled *The Big Red One* and stored in a vault in Kansas City. But no one had ever opened them to see what they contained, though several specialists in film restoration had, through the years, approached Warners with such a project in mind. Thanks to Brian Jamieson, a cinephile executive in the studio's home video division, for whom I made a documentary in 2003, I was the one who was finally given that opportunity.

I endured several anxious weeks as this material was unearthed. There were, as I recall, some 87 rolls of camera original negative and something like 112 reels of location sound in those boxes. But it was not organized at all. Studio technicians would print it up in the order that they found it. They delivered it to us in batches — a few shots from one scene, a few from another. Roughly 10,000 feet of film we are pretty sure Sam shot remains lost. But the roughly 70,000 feet we did recover was enough for us to reconstruct almost 50 minutes of the film. It is now, I believe, as close to Sam's original intentions as it is humanly possible to come.

Which statement is proved by reading this novel. It contains, of course, many characters and incidents that Sam did not include in his film. On the other hand, we were able to include in our reconstruction what seems to me every important scene in the novel that the 1980 version of the film eliminated. Among others, these include the brilliantly staged attack, by French-commanded Arab cavalry, on a German tank, parked in a Roman amphitheater in North Africa. There's the shooting of a little Sicilian girl by the evil Schroeder. There's an important romantic interlude between Griff and a Belgian resistance fighter (played by Stephane Audran) in the aftermath of an assault on an insane asylum the Nazis have commandeered as a fortress. There's the killing of a German infiltrator by a Belgian hotel keeper. There's a confrontation with a Hitler youth who has killed one of the squad members. Above all Schroeder becomes, in this revision, much less of a ghostly figure, much more of a living presence.

Altogether, we restored about fifteen scenes that were entirely eliminated from the original studio cut, all of which exist in this novel as well as in the shooting script. We also added significant shots to another twenty-seven sequences. What this material does, most simply, is restore narrative coherence to the film. More important, I think, it restores emotional coherence to it. Sam's antiheroic theme is now as clearly articulated as it is in his novel. But that said, I think the movie and the book work on us in diverse ways. The movie camera inevitably glamorizes the characters it focuses on, and these are, as well, very attractive actors, most notably Lee Marvin, whose minimalist performance — wry, knowing, fierce — is one of his masterpieces. We cannot help but take these men to heart, to empathize with their getting of wisdom, their developing relationships. As a result, the movie has a more immediate appeal than the novel.

On the other hand, the novel is no mean achievement. It may not have much to say about the hereditary factors determining human behavior, but in all other respects it is a naturalistic fiction, particularly in its detailed depiction of how the environment in which these soldier are trapped conditions their behavior. That's especially true of the combat sequences, in which death habitually appears (and disappears) with shocking abruptness and is dealt with casually, without sentiment. The writing is not fancy, but it is muscular and extraordinarily readable. Despite his raffish background in low-end journalism and movies, Sam Fuller was, we might say, a natural naturalist, and I cannot imagine anyone with a serious interest in the fictional depiction of war ignoring this book, despite its author's lack of literary credentials.

But, of course, I welcome its republication for extra-literary reasons. It required the passage of almost a quarter of a century for Sam Fuller's great film — surely one of the half-dozen best combat movies ever made — to appear in a form that is close to the one he envisioned for it so many decades ago. The republication of this novel, the writing of which so obviously influenced the final shape of that film, in an edition that will last longer than the casually produced first edition did, also completes a long overdue restitution. Between the restored film and the repackaged novel the viewer/reader can, at last, gain a full sense of what their auteur/author intended to accomplish, which was by no means inconsequential. Or, I think, easily forgettable. I think we can imagine Sam content at last, his vision finally realized and available to everyone. I can't tell you how proud I am to have been a part of the process that brought *The Big Red One* back to its intended form as a film and back into print in a format that should attract the attention of serious readers.

—RICHARD SCHICKEL
March 2005

WAR
DISTURBS SEX

—An old French peasant woman
to a young doughboy in 1918

PRELUDE

The shell-shocked horse ran toward the statue of Christ.

In the cold French mist, the horse zigzagged through the cratered no-man's-land that was loud with the silence of death. The crazed animal thundered over corpses of Yanks and Huns that were lying in grotesque positions.

American, German, and French telephone lines formed a crown of thorns above the bullet hole in Christ's brow. Worm-filled eyes. Fungi filled the half-opened mouth. Ants assaulted the beard. Reddish-brown nails from a fourteenth-century chest looked rusted in the left palm and feet. The arms and hands on the crossbar were intact in the grayish haze. The Cross supporting the towering figure loomed high on a mound that rose twenty feet.

The wooden Christ that had watched Joan of Arc lead her archers stared down at the lone Doughboy removing a dog tag from his faceless major in the eerie November afternoon of 1918.

Hooves stomped.

3

The Doughboy whirled. Hooves knocked his rifle to the ground and stomped and splintered the stock, on which was taped a five-round clip. The Doughboy dived into a big shell hole and landed on a Hun helmet. The horse jumped into the hole. The Doughboy sought refuge behind a dead Hun, the remains of the skull grinning at him. A shell had split open the Hun's belly. Busted bones stuck through the uniform like spikes. Hooves stomped, trampling the skull. The Doughboy rolled into the decomposed muck pile of the bodies of two Yanks.

The Doughboy clawed out of the hole, hurtled through the mist, and crashed into a body impaled on barbed wire. The entangled Doughboy saw the crazed horse charging, ripped himself free of the wire, and jumped as the horse's hooves demolished the impaled body. Bones flew, striking the Doughboy with shattering impact.

The Doughboy clawed his way up the high mound and drew his trench knife. It had a steel handguard, a steel spike on its heel, and steel spikes for four knuckles. Hooking his left arm around the wooden Cross to give his thrust all the strength of his body, he watched the horse ascend.

Hooves struck.

The Doughboy's seven-inch blade pierced the horny wall of the left foot, slashing the cushion. The Doughboy struck again, his knife deeply penetrating the horny sole. The horse felt the pain and hammered the Cross.

Christ shook.

The Cross swayed, creaked, groaned. The crown of thorns shook. The horse spat foam, blinding the Doughboy. He hung on. Hooves hammered the Cross, knocking the Doughboy off the mound. When he looked up he saw the horse hurtling over him.

The horse vanished.

"Ist vorbei—ist vorbei!"

The Doughboy turned toward the voice to see a gray ghost emerge through the mist without a weapon, his hands raised high. He wore a field cap. *"Der Krieg ist vorbei! Nicht Schiessen! Der Krieg ist—"*

4

The Doughboy lunged. His blade sunk into the startled Hun and killed him.

"*Alles kaput!*" the Hun said.

The Doughboy wiped the trench knife on his legging, then sheathed it. The red piping on the Hun's field cap was the only color on the gray corpse. The Doughboy shoved the Hun's cap in his cartridge belt and started to walk away when he sensed eyes piercing him. He turned his head and saw Christ looking down on him. The Doughboy grunted and walked through the mist over the corpses of men interred in mud.

He stopped only once to look back at Christ. The holes that were eyes were still watching him.

The Doughboy moved on until he reached the Yank listening post. It was deserted. That puzzled him. He moved on more cautiously and bellied down into the sandbagged Yank trench. A movement made him jump. It was the fluttering of torn long johns on a laundry line. He passed crude crosses propped against the damp dirt wall next to a sign "DON'T USE FOR FIRE-WOOD" and he went into the dugout where, to his relief, he found his Captain drinking cognac. The Captain had a long scar on his right alligator-skinned cheek. He was alone on an ammo box. A second box with a candle served as a table. He was shaving.

"Did you find the major?"

The Doughboy nodded and gave him the dog tag. "What happened to the Company, sir?"

"Moved out with Battalion. Drink?"

"Thank you, sir." The Doughboy drank. "Ever see a shell-shocked horse, Captain?"

"Can't say that I have. We go crazy in war, don't we? Why shouldn't a horse?"

"*I* did. He was loco; tried to kill me, stomped my piece to smithereens." The Doughboy returned the bottle, pulled out the Hun field cap, and began to cut off a three-inch strip of the red piping with his trench knife. The Captain watched. The Doughboy held the red strip against his left shoulder.

"What do you think, Captain? Like it?"

"What is it?"

"My idea for the Division patch. *First* Division.

Number *One*. Red *One*. Think General Pershing'll okay it?"

The Captain smiled. "Sure."

The Doughboy sheathed his trench knife. "I had to use this on that Hun to get his cap."

"When did this happen?"

"Oh, about an hour ago—near that Christ on the Cross."

"Did the Hun take a shot at you?"

"I jumped him before he could."

"Was he armed?"

"Why, sir?" The Doughboy began to feel sick.

"Did he yell out anything?"

"That same old war-is-over bullshit."

The Captain pushed the bottle at him. "Finish it."

The Doughboy did.

The Captain spoke quietly. "The Armistice was signed at eleven o'clock this morning." He looked at his wristwatch. "Four hours ago."

The Doughboy suddenly aged. He took on the pallor of a corpse as he stared at the red strip of piping in his hand.

"I murdered him," said the Doughboy.

"You didn't know the war was over."

"He did."

NORTH AFRICA

The camel does not see his hump.

—A blind Arab to a blind dogface

I

Cigarette and cigar ends glower. The Big Red One patch—worn on the left shoulder above an American flag armband—belonged to the Sergeant, the same Doughboy who had created it in 1918. Twenty-four years older, he pushed toward the picture of Churchill with his characteristic bowler derby and tweed jacket, British fighting planes above him, Montgomery's tanks fighting in the desert behind him, and below him: "LET US GO FORWARD TOGETHER." The Sergeant yanked the Royal Navy poster from the wall, brushed past a surprised but unprotesting British seaman, and moved through GIs wearing Stars and Stripes armbands and Big Red One patches. The cavernous smoke-filled hold of the British troopship, H.M.S. *Warwick Castle,* was jammed with Americans. A British voice boomed over the loudspeaker: *"First landing parties to deck stations in thirty minutes."*

The Sergeant reached his rifle squad in a corner of the hold and gave Griff the poster. Griff turned the face of Churchill to the floor. Sullivan moved his Browning automatic rifle to give Griff room. With his left hand, Griff began to draw on the blank side of the poster. Zab puffed his cigar. Vinci envied Griff's talent. Johnson leaned forward to watch, exposing a red inflated rubber doughnut under his aching ass.

Dempsey joined the Squad to watch Griff's pencil in action. Dempsey felt this squad was friendlier to him than the others. He was the chaplain's assistant, and part of his job would be to give the Grave Registration Bureau a hand collecting the dead in the padre's three-quarter-ton truck. He understood why his presence was never sought. He was a pallbearer.

Vinci moved to give Dempsey room. "What do you hear in officers' country, Demps?"

"The padre says there will be no resistance."

Sullivan leaned closer to Griff. "Will you draw a picture of me I can send home?"

Griff choked on Zab's cigar smoke. "Sure."

"Draw me as a fighter with boxing gloves."

"Fighter?" Zab grunted, blowing cigar smoke at Vinci. "I saw you run from a fight in Scotland."

Sullivan grinned. "I know. I'm lousy with my fists but my old man named me after John L. and I got to keep him happy." He scratched his head, watched Zab pick a soggy piece of cigar wrapper off his tongue. "We got a Dempsey and Sullivan in the Sixteenth. All we need is a Louis."

"Or a Benny Leonard or Lew Tendler or Battling Siki," said the Sergeant. "They were great fighters." He remembered with a smile. "Harry Greb, a one-eyed marvel."

"Hey, Zab," said Johnson shifting his ass on the doughnut, "you really a book writer?"

"Uh-huh."

"What book did you write?"

"The Dark Deadline."

"Never read it."

"Never heard of it," said Vinci.

"It's an unpublished mystery, left it with my mother. I'll polish it when I get back."

"Why's a *book* writer a rifleman?" asked Vinci.

Zab grinned. "To come out with a war book, what else? How about you, Griff? Still going to be a newspaper cartoonist after the war?"

10

"Yup . . . come up with a strip like Barney Google."

They sang "Barney Google and his goo—goo—googly eyes."

"I like Maggie and Jiggs."

"Prince Valiant."

"Skippy."

The same British voice announced, *"Your attention, please. A German radio broadcast reported that a submarine commanded by Senior Lieutenant von Richter yesterday sunk a British troopship in the Atlantic . . ."*

Griff stopped drawing. The coils around his stomach —and the stomach of every man in the hold— tightened. The men froze, eyes met eyes, blood pounded in their hearts.

"The Führer has awarded the Knight's Cross to Senior Lieutenant von Richter . . ."

The feeling of life in the hold collapsed like a rag doll. Death flooded the hold, each man in his private watery grave knowing a torpedo could hit their ship any time. The paralysis that spread was no longer fear of German bullets in their body but fear of a German sub stalking their ship. The dreaded moment had finally come to the men who had shut their minds to enemy subs, who had never spoken about it, who had anticipated the excitement of seeing North Africa and Algeria and belly dancers and sheikhs and the desert.

It had never baffled the Sergeant that, in the other war, he had escaped death. He attributed it to luck. He certainly had never given any thought of *drowning* in this war, but the British voice now made him think about it. He saw himself in the wet wreckage floating in a mass of gore, salt water, and blood.

Griff shared the same fear. He saw himself laid open, his innards eaten away by salt water.

Zab saw sharks fighting over what was left of his body.

Vinci saw his head splattered.

Johnson saw himself as pieces of bloody flesh floating in salt water.

"As Mark Twain would say, the report has been greatly exaggerated by Senior Lieutenant von Richter due to the fact that the British ship he claims to have

11

sunk was—H.M.S. Warwick Castle! *Adolf, take the medal back!"*

"Warwick Castle?" Johnson said. *"We're* on the *Warwick Castle,* ain't we?"

Relief swept the hold, laughter filled it. Their hearts stopped pounding with fear.

When Griff finished drawing, Johnson read the cartoon balloon aloud: "Watch out Vichy—here comes the Big Red One!" With confusion, Johnson stared at Griff. "I thought Vichy's a soda pop."

Zab spoke through cigar smoke. "Vichy is the French who are fighting on Hitler's side."

"If they open fire," said the Sergeant, "we'll have to kill them."

"I can't kill a Frenchman," said Johnson.

The British voice came on again: *"The officers and crew of His Majesty's Ship* Warwick Castle *wish the First U.S. Infantry Division Godspeed on the first amphibious invasion in the Mediterranean theater."*

The men were impressed. But not Vinci. "How come the limeys aren't getting their feet wet with us?" Vinci said.

The men looked to the Sergeant for the answer.

"Vichy's fighting them for hitting the French fleet," said the Sergeant. "We're counting on the French to swing over to our side." He tapped his flag brassard. "That's why we're wearing these. I don't think they'll shoot at Americans."

Vinci was persistent. "I *still* think the limeys—"

"Just think about them carrying the ball in Africa while you were playing with your prick in the can. Never sell a limey short." The Sergeant took out a small paper packet, broke it open, and fitted a condom over his rifle muzzle. "Put your rubbers on, it's going to be wet." He worked a rubber band firmly over it.

Every soldier slipped a rubber over his muzzle to protect the rifle from salt water. The Sergeant distributed rubber bands.

On deck, every face under a steel helmet stared at the distant lights on the Arzew beach. Johnson said,

12

"I thought we dropped 'em leaflets that we were coming, Sergeant."

"We did."

"Then all those lights means they're not going to fight."

"They left 'em on," said Zab, "so they can see what they're shooting at."

He thought he was funny. The other did not.

There was no small talk now. They stared at the lights and hoped Zab was wrong. They had trained hard for this moment. Forgotten were the stories of belly dancers and sheikhs and the desert. Soon they would be scampering down rope cargo nets into little boats that would take them to the beach. Soon they would be welcomed or shot at. They hunched at the rail, tense, rigid, waiting.

Zab chewed on his dead cigar.

Griff's helmet was giving him trouble. He tightened the strings in the liner.

Vinci kept his helmet on by stuffing balled paper in his liner.

Johnson's head seemed to have been molded to fit his helmet.

The Sergeant pushed his way through GIs and British seamen on deck until he reached the General who was studying the beach lights through his binocs. With the General was his staff.

"Those leaflets we dropped must've worked," said the General. "No blackout means no resistance—I hope."

The General lowered his binocs. Wind whipped at the long scar on his right cheek. He was the same Captain from the trench dugout in 1918. Now he commanded the First Division. A smile swept his leathery face when he saw the Sergeant.

"What've you got there, Sergeant?"

The Sergeant gave him the Churchill poster, turning it over. In the darkness it took a moment for the General to make out the caricature of himself with his Cyrano nose. That nose had caused him many fights at West Point. When he received his second star and was given command of the First Infantry Division in

13

early 1942, he told General Marshall that the enlisted men were really responsible for that second star. He was devoted to the infantryman. He respected and admired the Sergeant.

The two-star Cyrano in the cartoon was in an assault boat charging a French soldier who was standing with fixed bayonet under a lone palm tree on the Arzew beach. The balloon coming from Cyrano's mouth read: "Watch out Vichy—here comes the Big Red One!"

The General grinned. "Goddamn it, Sergeant, my schnozzle isn't *that* big, is it?"

The Sergeant smiled.

"Who's the Michelangelo?"

"A southpaw in my Squad. Wants to be a comic strip artist when the war's over."

"Draftee?"

"Yes, sir."

"Rifleman?"

"Expert, sir."

The General grunted. He smiled. "Not much difference between a volunteer and a draftee if both are expert riflemen. Can I keep the cartoon?"

"It's all yours, sir."

The General smiled again. Then his black eyes grew somber. "Remember that shell-shocked horse in France, Sergeant?"

"I remember that loco nag, sir."

"What's coming up is just as loco. Damn it, Sergeant, I just can't stomach the reality of facing French guns on that beach. If Pershing was on this transport, he'd blow his top."

"They got the leaflets we're coming. Their lights on the beach are a good sign."

"Or a welcoming bushwhack. All it takes is *one* shot and Lafayette will turn somersaults wherever he is." The General looked at the beach, but this time not through the binocs. "You're in the first wave?"

"Yes, sir."

"You firing that flare?"

"If there's no resistance, sir."

"I'll lay off that hard stuff for a year just to see that white star in the sky."

14

"I'd give my right ball to fire it, General."

"I'd give *both* my balls, Sergeant."

It was time for the Sergeant to leave. There was no farewell between them, no good luck nonsense. The Sergeant left. The General watched him swallowed up in the mass of uniforms. Brodie, a war correspondent wearing the green brassard, joined the General.

"Is that the Sergeant, General?"

The General nodded, grunting.

"Good story, the two of you in this same outfit in the other war. I'd like to know more about the Sergeant but he doesn't seem to have a personal side. He's just a soldier."

Father Deery, Roman Catholic chaplain of the Sixteenth Infantry, joined them. With the padre were the Protestant and Jewish chaplains.

"I'm counting on no resistance, not even token, padre," the General said. "The first church we find that has an organ, I want you to play on the god-box for the French."

The padre grunted, then smiled. "I'll play on the god-box for five minutes, General, then I've got to find a phonograph. I want to sit down with a bottle of bourbon and listen to Fats Waller's 'Minor Drag.'"

"I thought you played that record last night."

"That was 'Harlem Fuss.'" The padre cupped his cigarette and lighter to mask the flame. "Y'know, once a big-eyed young girl asked Fats Waller, 'What is swing?' and he told her, 'Lady, if you got to ask, you ain't got it.'"

They laughed. The General knew the panic and fear in them. It was good to hear them laugh. Even if they forced it.

"Know what I predict, General?" said the Jewish chaplain. "Tomorrow night the Arabs and the French will be jitterbugging with the GIs."

On the beach, Moullet, a *poilu,* sucked on his pipe as he passed French defense troops discussing the leaflets from the sky informing them that Americans were coming to North Africa to fight the Axis. He sat down on the ground next to Section Leader Broban of Colleville-sur-Mer, Normandy, who sat drinking

15

brandy as he stared at the leaflet in his hand. A battle was raging in his mind. Though he ate well, he was thin almost to the point of emaciation. His body was steel, his courage unquestioned, but his patriotism to France was very much questioned.

Broban was annoyed by the faint strains of radio music filtering down from the stone house atop the cliff behind him. He loathed that house, its occupants, the beach, the country—most of all himself. He shifted his gaze from the leaflet to his heavy Hotchkiss machine gun that was ready to kill for Hitler, for Pétain, and for Vichy France. It guaranteed many dead Americans, if they picked Arzew beach for the invasion of Algeria. But that guarantee was specifically up to Broban, and this fact was what really annoyed him. He remembered when, in 1917, he posed for a war poster with a Yank from the Bronx in New York. They were selected as models to sell camaraderie between France and the United States.

The bitter North African brandy filled him with pain as he remembered that every year after the war he would visit that American's grave in the small cemetery at Suresnes, near Paris, where under their flag rested 1,506 Americans.

Broban had not visited the grave of the American from the Bronx since 1940. Spitting out the brandy, he felt shame for defending Arzew for Adolf Hitler; shame for not having joined the Free French Army; shame for being a Pétain puppet on this miserable beach.

But Pétain was his God, and how could God betray France?

"I don't think I could kill an American," Broban said to Moullet.

In the stone house overlooking the beach, Vichy officers of the Arzew Coastal Defense Headquarters were listening to radio music and playing cards. Colonel Lourcelles and Major Baigneres held good hands. In a corner cavalryman Captain Chapier, wearing the ribbons of the *Croix de guerre* and *Légion d' honneur,* sipped *Côtes du Rhone,* his eyes fixed with contempt at the giant wall poster of Pétain, the man who sold out France to Hitler. The poster read:

16

"MARSHAL HENRI PÉTAIN HERO OF VERDUN 1916 SAVIOR OF FRANCE 1940."

Pétain was also Chapier's God. How could God betray France?

"God" did. And so did Chapier when he failed to join the Free French or the underground or to die fighting Hitler. Instead he chose to protect the North African coast for Hitler. He stared at Pétain's eyes. Once they glowed with dignity. Now they were furtive with treason. And the longer he stared at Pétain the more he knew that his own ribbons had become symbols of cowardice in the face of death. After the fall of France, he had tried to live with colleagues whom he knew were Jew haters, Hitler lovers, ass kissers of "Pope" Pétain. He had succeeded. He lived. He never knew how much afraid of death he was until France died. He had supported his decision with intelligent reasons. Why fight when all was lost? Why die for a country that was already dead? Why give up one's treasured life for nothing?

"Pétain, savior of France!" Chapier said with hate.

Colonel Lourcelles's tongue probed for that stubborn pellet from the couscous his Algerian cook had made. He found the tiny pellet of wheat, spit it out over his shoulder, and smiled. "Wine always makes Captain Chapier incoherent."

Chapier loathed Colonel Lourcelles. He pictured himself shooting him and then facing a firing squad. He waved a leaflet.

"Nothing incoherent about this leaflet!"

"Gangster propaganda."

A voice broke into the radio music: *"This is Franklin Delano Roosevelt, president of the United States. An American landing force is en route to fight the Axis in North Africa. Do not fire at us. We are Americans."*

Colonel Lourcelles turned off the radio.

"That Jew Rosenfeld is bluffing!"

Chapier knew that the Americans were coming. And he knew it was his last chance to restore honor to himself—and to France.

17

2

Slowly, sipping his wine, Colonel Lourcelles studied the big wall map of the Oran-Arzew beach defenses. He smiled. Unsmiling, silently engrossed, his officers stared at the map. Next to it was a caricature of de Gaulle.

"However," said Colonel Lourcelles, "if that crippled rabbi in Washington is *not* bluffing and his Communists do land at Arzew, we'll slaughter every one of them on the beaches."

"The hell we will!" Chapier ripped the picture of Pétain off the wall. "Even with German bayonets at our backs, this is our chance to stop kissing Hitler's ass to save our own! If we kill Americans then we're *really* traitors like Marshal Pétain!"

"You've had too much to drink!"

"You've had too much Hitler!" Chapier flung Pétain to the floor.

The stunned officers were aware that Chapier's act could lead to chaos and revolt if not smashed at once. Colonel Lourcelles also knew this as he suddenly flung his wine in Chapier's face. Swiftly, Chapier was relieved of his double-action 8-mm revolver by Major Baigneres.

"In there for the firing squad." Colonel Lourcelles pointed.

Chapier was shoved roughly into a small bedroom with a barred window. The door was slammed. Major Baigneres turned the key. Colonel Lourcelles ordered his officers to join their sections on the beach. Major Baigneres remained. Colonel Lourcelles refilled his glass and sipped between sentences.

"Inform General Tavernier that Captain Chapier is a traitor. Prepare the charge sheet and court-martial papers. Put Marshall Pétain back on the wall. I'm going down to the beach to make sure that no more turncoats are behind French guns."

He finished his drink and left.

As Major Baigneres picked up the poster of **Pétain,**

18

·assault boat 1 was carrying the Sergeant and his Squad toward Arzew.

3

Broban wept. He turned his head so that Moullet would not see the tears in the half-light of the lamp. He had given up the fight for the French way of life; to him that meant the humane way of life. Muffling his sobs so he wouldn't be heard, he remembered with pain de Gaulle's words coming to France in 1940 from the BBC in London: *France has lost a battle. But France has not lost the war.*

"Me," said Moullet, "I don't think Americans'll come here. What'll they find in Arzew? In Oran? What do *you* think, Broban?"

Broban was thinking of the way he had scoffed at de Gaulle's stubbornness to prove that France was still a power.

"*You* know Americans," Moullet went on. "You know how they fight. You think they'll be stupid enough to land here?"

Broban was in agony. Even when the Resistance was rallying to de Gaulle, Broban had scoffed at the re-birth of his country. Now he wept. He was a traitor. He could have been a hero in the Resistance.

Moullet shook him. "Do you think Americans'll land here?" he asked again.

"Tell me, Moullet, if they landed here, would you kill Americans?"

Moullet sucked on his empty pipe. "Yes."

"They are not the enemy."

"To Pétain, anybody that's against Germans is the enemy."

"If you kill an American you'll never be able to face yourself."

"That's better than facing Pétain's firing squad."

Broban turned and stared at Moullet. "We're shit. You and I."

"But we're *live* shit."

19

The sound of a voice came from the black Mediterranean. Broban and Moullet stiffened and stared at the sea. They could see nothing. The faint voice came closer: "Frenchmen—do not fire!"

On the beach, Algerian soldiers in Broban's section also heard the voice, also stared at the black sea.

"We come to help you fight Hitler!"

The voice was very clear now. Broban slowly rose to his feet.

"Do not shoot! Do not shoot! We are not British! We are Americans!"

Now a second voice overlapped the first, repeating the same words. Then a third voice. And a fourth.

"Hold your fire! We are Americans! We come to help you restore your honor. We come to help you fight Hitler!"

An electric tension charged through Broban. He strained his eyes; he was tense with confusion and excitement. Then the confusion vanished. They had dropped leaflets that they were coming. Now they were here. He stared at the black waters and wondered how many Americans were out there. Broban knew his night of reckoning was at hand.

Broban was the first to see assault boat 1 touch down. He was the first to see the Sergeant and his Squad hit Z White Beach on their bellies. He was the first to see the Sergeant turn toward a man who was not moving, waist-high in water; and he was the first to hear the Sergeant shout, "Minox, move your ass!"

Broban glanced at Moullet. Then their eyes turned to Minox, who did not move. He was evidently too frightened. They watched the Sergeant drag Minox out of the water to the Squad.

The pfc's voice continued: "Do not fire! We are Americans! We come to help you fight the Germans!"

Broban suddenly found himself angry with the Americans. They had put him into an impossible situation. His section waited for his command to open fire, and all he could do was stand like a child watching a circus.

One word from him, he knew, and those Americans would be slaughtered. Just one word. *Fire!* Yet he also knew that, if he gave the order to hold fire and the Americans lost (and he knew that they would), he would end up facing Pétain's firing squad.

Moullet shook Broban. "Broban! What the hell's the matter with you? Give the order to open fire!"

French and Algerian soldiers, hunched behind their weapons, watched the enemy on the beach and waited for Broban's command. Sixty seconds had passed since Broban had seen assault boat 1 touch down.

"Hold your fire!" Broban shouted. "Pass the word! Hold your fire! Hold your fire!"

The word was passed from one French defender to another. Some were relieved; others furious.

"I should've been a priest," Broban said to the astonished Moullet. Then, suddenly feeling good, he clapped Moullet on the shoulder and grinned. "Goddamn it. I feel as holy as any goddamn priest in France!"

The belly of the Sergeant felt like a stone on the beach. He waited for the first shot to be fired by the French. He did not pray. He knew prayers never changed the trajectory of bullets fired by trigger-happy defenders.

Fear froze the Squad as they waited for the first shot from the French. Griff did not feel the sand on his hands and in his mouth. He stared at the lamps flickering on the dunes and knew that soon those lights would guide the French bullets and show them the way to shoot off arms and legs, to tear away faces, to destroy bodies. He saw himself hit. He saw himself dead. He saw the condom. It was still on his muzzle. He forced himself to move and he pulled off the rubber. He had heard that some men in the Pacific were sent home with self-inflicted wounds. He didn't have the guts to shoot himself. The million-dollar wound was what he wanted. It would take him out of combat. It would send him home. He wondered how long he'd have to stay like this on his belly on the beach. He felt he'd been there an hour. He didn't know that only ten seconds had passed since the instant he threw himself down.

Zab tried to force the fear out of himself by thinking of other things. He had been close to finishing his mystery novel when Pearl Harbor happened. He couldn't miss the biggest story in the world. But he wanted to finish the book, so he didn't volunteer, and finally he had to ask the draft board to give him time to finish the novel: he was his mother's sole support and if the book sold she would have money. They gave him time. He finished *The Dark Deadline,* and he wound up in the Seventy-eighth Lightning Division, Camp Butner, North Carolina, for basic and from there found himself in Scotland in the First Division with a Red One on his helmet. But the book was never published. He consoled himself, knowing it was only a first draft. He told his mother he'd polish it when he came home from Camp Butner. Now he looked at the lights on the dunes. Camp Butner seemed a million years ago. If the French opened fire and if he lived to be taken prisoner he knew how he would describe those lights in his next book. As a reporter he had covered murders, worked in the morgue, seen death. Now he was about to cover his own.

Vinci's courage faded. He blamed it on the long wait. If the French fired a shot he would be all right; he would be in action. But the wait sapped his guts. He hated being in such a sweat. He pictured a Frenchman behind a light with eyes fixed only on one man: himself. He felt the Frenchman waiting for him to make one move—just *one* goddamn move. He aimed and began to squeeze, but his finger froze. The Sergeant wouldn't like it if *he* started the fireworks. He had heard that Italian soldiers were in North Africa. He wondered if there were any Italians with the French behind those lamps. He could speak Italian. He should shout in Italian and tell them to throw down their rifles and surrender.

Waiting in fear for the French to open fire, Johnson found that Jesus was far away from him now that he really needed him. A "born-again" Tennessee Baptist who once distributed fundamentalist pamphlets for his father, Johnson now wished for an evangelical miracle to transfer him back to the safe hold of that British ship. He wished the preacher back home was on the beach to prove that all that stuff about a personal relationship with Jesus Christ was not a lot of bullshit.

Johnson never gave living much thought because he took it for granted—until now. Now if he stopped a French bullet he would be nothing—as if he had never been born. Maybe he had been nothing all the time. The more he thought about this the more depressed he became and the more depressed the angrier. He wondered how much guts he had. Could he kill a Frenchman who was trying to kill him?

The wait for the first shot slowly suffocated the fear in the men. They became cocky now that it was apparent that their baptism of fire would not be on this beach. The Sergeant read their minds: infantrymen were always eager to fight the moment they knew there would be no battle.

The Sergeant slowly raised himself up on one knee, making himself a target. He stood up and waited another sixty seconds. Then he fired his flare pistol. The white star exploded in the black sky.

Standing on deck of the ship the General saw the "no resistance" flare in the sky. His prayers had been answered. He would not lose any of his men at Arzew. And they would not have to kill any Frenchmen.

"Thank God!" said the General.

4

Dialects infuriated Colonel Lourcelles. The dark-skinned Algerians under his command infuriated him. He was sure more light was available than he had now as he descended the steep dark dirt path from the stone house to the beach. He had counted four lanterns that had burned out. When this annoying invasion scare was over he would deal with the man responsible for those lanterns. He would deprive him of leave in Oran or Algiers for sixty days.

Captain Chapier was a fool! Colonel Lourcelles knew that in the morning Captain Chapier would apologize, but it would be too late to ask for mercy. In the morning Captain Chapier would be taken to the turncoat cells, would be charged, found guilty of treason, and shot.

Colonel Lourcelles stopped. He was sure he heard a faint voice coming from the sea. He shrugged. The men on the beach were talking. He continued the annoying descent. Tomorrow he would order steps built from the beach to the stone house.

In fourteen days he would be fifty-two years old. He was aware that his staff planned a surprise party for him on November 22 in Oran. There would be a bullfight in his honor and gypsies to dance.

A pity Captain Chapier would not be alive to attend the party. Chapier infuriated him. Chapier made him think of Charles de Gaulle. Colonel Lourcelles and de Gaulle were born on the same day in the same year. Both attended Saint-Cyr. Both graduated in 1911. He loathed de Gaulle's haughtiness. He really envied the giant from Lille. Since the fall of France the giant was determined to make himself the lord of a dead France. He had the perfect name for such a dream. Every French schoolchild was familiar with *les Gaulois,* the early inhabitants of *la Gaule.* Gaulle. De Gaulle. The sound of France. What a perfect name. And what an imperfect dream! To gather Frenchmen to fight for the rebirth of France was suicidal. Yes, he envied the name Charles was making for himself, but it was a name that would be short-lived. Any day England would be invaded. And that would be the end of de Gaulle. Colonel Lourcelles envied de Gaulle because he was a rebel. In his day Pétain was also a rebel. But there comes a time in the life of every man, especially a rebel, when he must face facts. Pétain did the right thing for France.

Lourcelles stopped again. He was sure that the voice he heard did not come from the beach but from the sea. He listened. Yes. It *was* coming from the sea! He quickened his descent, tripped, and when he angrily rose to his feet saw the white star in the black sky. He ran. He froze. He saw Americans spilling from small assault boats. He saw Americans on the beach. *His* beach! He heard the voice, then the many voices asking the French to hold their fire, announcing they were Americans, not British, filling the air with plans to fight Hitler!

24

Aghast, Colonel Lourcelles reached Broban and Moullet who were *watching* the enemy land!

"Broban!" shouted the red-faced, outraged Colonel Lourcelles, "open fire!"

"Not at Americans!"

Colonel Lourcelles shot Broban.

The Sergeant threw himself down on his face.

Colonel Lourcelles manned the machine gun himself. Moullet, still sucking on his empty pipe, began firing his rifle. Colonel Lourcelles fell backward, his finger hooked on the trigger. The machine gun exploded with life as the dead Vichy colonel raked the beach. Algerian time it was 1:05 A.M., November 8, 1942. The battle of North Africa was on.

5

Griff stared at the first American killed by the French machine gun. He felt strange, almost immoral, the way it fascinated him to watch the bullet-shredded eyes, the cheeks, nose, mouth, neck, shoulders, and body turning into a blur of dust. Instead of burying his head into his helmet, Griff's eyes with astonishing coolness pierced the dust until the blur came into sharp focus.

"Follow my tracers!" The Sergeant aimed at the machine-gun bursts and fired. From his rifle, red-nosed bullets traced their own course through the blackness with a trail of fire, giving the Squad something to aim at. The Squad fired. The only targets were the red tracers. Griff aimed at the red streaks and fired. The recoil was a tremendous hammerblow, but he kept on firing. He couldn't see where the bullets landed. He didn't feel he was hitting, let alone killing, anyone. For Zab and Vinci the Sergeant's order to fire was a relief. The wait had drained them. The noise was exciting. Johnson forgot about whether he would be able to kill a Frenchman. He saw no Frenchman.

Colonel Lourcelles's finger—stubbornly hooked in the trigger guard—kept firing. The machine gun shook and jumped uncontrollably.

With his fixed bayonet, still being missed by red tracers and bullets, Moullet chopped Lourcelles's hand. The finger unclenched. The machine gun stopped firing, and a red tracer hit Moullet, burning through his mouth. He was dead before his shattered pipe fell on the American leaflet lying next to Broban.

6

The Vichy mortar shells blasted the beach. Anything moving on the beach was instantly dead or wounded by Pétain's defenders who, some with tears, unenthusiastically raked the invaders, knowing that Colonel Lourcelles's morning report of "resisted invasion of Arzew, American casualties heavy" would bring them medals and furlough for the slaughters. Killing Americans, to many, was like killing their brothers.

Two heavy German mortars, manned by Frenchmen, concentrated on the First Platoon of I Company. Staggering fire, the French lobbed in HE shells twenty to twenty-five per minute. Each shell weighed 9.6 pounds, had five charges, gave maximum range of five thousand yards. The muzzle-loaded weapons fired by percussion the instant a shell dropped down the barrel. Supporting the two mortars were riflemen and machine gunners.

The Frenchman in command of this mortar section recoiled as his shells chewed up the American platoon. The bastard son of a French mother and an American soldier who had returned to his wife in Texas after the war, he had always been proud that the Germans were stopped at Château-Thierry with the help of God and a few marines. His father was one of those marines. But he could not switch his loyalty. The enemy was the American. Perhaps his own father was out there on that beach.

Commanding the First Platoon, the West Point

Lieutenant was angry because the bazooka team was late or lost or dead. When the team showed up he barked an order and pointed.

The bazooka team set up shop fifty feet in front of Griff.

Griff watched them. One man held the 2.36-inch rocket launcher—equipped with a shoulder stock and fittingly named bazooka after Bob Burns's gas-pipe horn—on his shoulder. In his handgrip, operated by the trigger, was nested an electric primer to spark off the rocket, actually a Fort Henry rocket brought up to date with twentieth-century power to be baptized in North Africa. The tube was wide open at both ends. Griff watched the second man load the rocket. The first man fired. A tremendous burst of flame shot out through the end of the rear opening. Griff felt the heat.

It was a direct hit for mortar one.

Mortar two also scored a direct hit. Griff watched the bazooka team and the bazookas demolished like cork into a thousand pieces. Skin and bones of men struck him. He took a dive through the air and plunged into a splattered Second Squad corpse. Griff gasped for air. Grilled entrails blinded him, burned his nostrils, scorched his mouth. He crawled backwards and bellied blindly until he crashed into a dune. There he opened his canteen, washed his eyes, took a big swig of water, and spat.

He emptied his canteen all over his face, but he could not rub hard enough.

He vomited. His helmet fell off. He put it back on.

Then through the black, gray, and white smoke he caught a flash of his Lieutenant and the Sergeant. The Lieutenant was pointing at mortar two. Under Platoon fire cover the Sergeant zigzagged among his men, gathered up his Squad. His shouts brought his men to life. Griff remained frozen. The Sergeant told him to move. Griff couldn't. The Sergeant kicked him. Griff moved, trailing the Squad as the Sergeant, leap-frogging, led them inland toward the mortar commanded by the bastard son of a United States Marine.

When the Platoon cover fire was slowed down by mortars, the Sergeant herded his men behind dunes. French rifles and machine guns drenched the area.

The Sergeant and Squad returned small-arms fire. An ejected clip from the Sergeant's rifle bounced off Griff's helmet. Griff was on the wrong side of the Sergeant. As the Sergeant jammed in a fresh clip, Griff bellied past him to get on the Sergeant's left only to find himself on Zab's right. Another empty clip zinged off Griff's helmet. He crawled into Johnson who was grunting because the recoil was shattering his shoulder. Johnson rearranged his shoulder padding. Vinci glared at Griff, who was not firing. Griff aimed at enemy rifle bursts and squeezed. The rifle did not fire. His safety was off; he had a full clip in the chamber. He squeezed again. It did not fire. He could not understand what caused the mechanical nonfunction. Then he realized it was his own mental nonfunction. He had *imagined* he squeezed the trigger. This time he stopped imagining and squeezed. His rifle fired. He emptied two clips, firing into the darkness. His helmet kept falling off. He adjusted the liner. He dared not fasten his chin straps; concussion from those shells could rip his head off if the blast lifted his helmet.

Bullets drove Griff to a low mound. Sullivan's BAR was firing; his ammo carrier was being treated by a medic. From the flank, rifle fire killed a man near Griff. He turned. The Sergeant turned at the same time. Another man in the Squad was hit. Griff and the Sergeant saw a dogface from the Third Squad shooting at men in the First Squad. The dogface had blown his top. With every shot he shouted, "Goddamn krauts!"

The Sergeant killed the dogface.

Griff gasped. The Sergeant yelled for the Squad to follow him. Griff found himself running with the men.

The Colonel of the Sixteenth Infantry Regiment ran past the beachmaster bellowing through his bullhorn at incoming assault boats. The Colonel reached an officer.

"They think we're British, goddamn it!" shouted the Colonel. "Show 'em we're *not!*"

The officer fired an enormous heavy mortar. The bomb burst in the sky, displaying gigantic pyrotechnics of the American flag in brilliant colors. The Fourth of July fireworks illuminated the running Squad, making them easy targets. Furious, the Sergeant caromed from man to man, slamming each one behind a mound. Hypnotized by the flag, Minox stood under its blinding glare. He had never seen anything so beautiful.

"Minox!" yelled the Sergeant. "Move your big fat ass!"

The last thing Minox saw before a French bullet tore his heart out was Old Glory sparkling in the night sky.

7

The Sergeant dived alongside Minox and dragged the corpse like a shield across exposed ground toward the path leading up to the mortar. A French rifleman spotted the moving corpse and fired. Horrified, Griff watched bullets thud into the dead flesh. He remembered how proud Minox was of his body; his dream was to compete at the Olympic Games.

Griff had to stop this. He spotted the French rifleman, aimed, squeezed, uncontrollably raised his barrel, fired, and missed. Guilt shook him. Again he fired. Again he deliberately missed.

"Where is he?" Zab shouted. "I don't see him. Who're you shooting at?"

Griff's hands twitched. His head was on fire in his steaming, heavy helmet. The fearful truth staggered him.

He could not kill a man he could see.

But he was a rifleman. He had to kill. Once more he had the Frenchman in his sights. He would not raise the barrel this time. He would hold it steady. He would squeeze without affecting his aim. The head of the Frenchman was in his sights. Don't jerk the trigger! Don't flinch! Don't move before the bullet leaves the barrel! Don't anticipate the recoil! He did. Don't! If you flinch you'll miss! He began to squeeze very very slowly, so he wouldn't know the instant the hammer fell. *Hold it!* He stopped squeezing. Wrong. Wrong breathing. The muzzle tipped. He held his breath. He knew that the instant his hammer fell he would squeeze again. Two seconds per shot. Eight rounds. Eight chances to kill that Frenchman who was mutilating Minox's corpse. His eyes blurred. He focused on the target.

The target was Private Maurice Ronet, Second Regiment Zouaves. That morning his wife had given birth to a 9½-pound boy. Only twenty, Ronet had his whole life ahead of him. But Griff was determined to shatter that life. Ronet was confused. He fired many bullets and still the man kept moving toward the path. The man was such an easy target, illuminated by the glaring red, white, and blue flag in the sky.

Ronet kept firing at the moving corpse.

Griff drew in an ordinary breath, let it out a little, and closed his throat. Without tightening the muscles of his diaphragm he held his breath, raised his barrel at Private Ronet, and squeezed.

And missed.

Zab looked at the American and French soldiers running to their deaths. Unlike the others, he had a special reason for being in the infantry and for being here at this moment. He planned to write about it. To him a rifleman was not a rifle, not a man. Zab knew that a rifleman was just a number: 745. Now it was time to stop playing the writer, the observer; he had to fall into the killing lockstep of the 745s. His belt and his two bandoliers, clasped with black diaper pins, sagged with death.

"Who the hell're you shooting at?" Zab yelled.

Griff pointed. Zab saw nothing. Griff aimed. Zab maneuvered behind Griff and got a fix on Griff's piece.

"I see him!" Zab focused on Private Ronet, centered, and squeezed. The bullet from Zab's 9½-pound rifle promptly made Private Ronet's 9½-pound son fatherless.

Zab had killed his first man. A man he actually could see before firing. The act did not bother Zab. What impressed him more than anything else was that the fear of death never crossed his mind. He had only one fear: his cock being shot off.

Still dragging Minox's corpse for cover, the Sergeant closed the distance and grenaded the machine gun, but he wasn't close enough to grenade the mortar that had the Squad pinned down.

Sullivan, the BAR man, was blown into four sections by a direct hit. His head landed in front of Griff who was lying there on his belly. Sullivan's left ear touched Griff's right hand. Griff snatched his hand away. It took a while for him to realize that Sullivan's head had been severed from the body. Sullivan's lids were gone and in his bulging open eyes was still the shock of surprise.

Zab crawled away from the head.

Griff was hypnotized by Sullivan's eyes. He became deaf to the shell bursts. He thought it strange that he and Sullivan heard nothing. The silence was weird. Stones and sand and smoke covered them like a shroud. Their eyes remained opened, still staring eyeball to eyeball.

Slowly Griff unclenched his teeth. "I'll go out and find the rest of you, Sully."

Griff saw a movement. A red movement illuminated by the American flag in the sky. The beach wind ruffled Sullivan's red hair. Griff did not move. He forgot about going out to find the rest of Sullivan.

8

Vichy General Tavernier, who sided with Pétain, resented the expression "collaborating" with the enemy. He believed a captive government was in no position to fight Hitler's steamroller. General Tavernier was scholarly, a widower with two daughters and three grandchildren. What he did in 1940 was to save them from being taken to a concentration camp. Behind his desk at French Army Headquarters in the Oran barracks he was nervous, impatient. His nose reddened. The shock of Americans twenty-five miles away at Arzew changed the purple blotches of his cheeks to red.

General Tavernier turned to one of the many officers in the noisy, confused office. "What about Major Baigneres?"

"The Arzew line is being repaired, sir."

General Tavernier sighed and in that sigh was the question he had been avoiding for a long time. Had he sided with Pétain for France's so-called survival, or had he secretly agreed with Hitler's grand plan of the extermination?

Unlike his colleagues, he was sure that if the Americans ever entered the war, events would turn against him. He was ready for that. He kept a tiny blue glass vial of poison on him at all times in case of capture. He knew he would be officially treated as a Nazi, and rightly so. He didn't have the stomach to face the gallows. A military firing squad? Yes. But never the gallows.

He kept hearing Pétain's words to the French Council in 1940: "The armistice is the only guarantee of the survival of eternal France." Pétain did not fly to England. Pétain remained to face Hitler's music. Pétain had said he would "stay with the French people to share their miseries."

"Contact with Arzew is made, general." The officer held out the phone. "Major Baigneres."

General Tavernier took the phone and sighed because he was fond of Chapier. "Is Captain Chapier still under guard?"

"Yes, sir, general," replied Major Baigneres.

"Shoot him."

Major Baigneres slowly put the phone down, stared at the Pétain poster on the wall, drew his pistol, and then changed his mind and holstered it. He went to Colonel Lourcelles's desk, opened the top drawer, and took out Captain Chapier's pistol. As he unlocked the door and opened it, Captain Chapier caved his head in with a chair.

Captain Chapier grabbed his pistol from the floor, ripped the Pétain poster from the wall, ran out of the stone house on the cliff overlooking the beach of Arzew, and dashed down the dirt path. It wasn't too dark.

He reached mortar two and ordered it to cease fire. The bastard son of the United States Marine refused. He would only take such a command from Colonel Lourcelles. Captain Chapier shot the bastard. The crew stopped firing. Under the sputtering American flag in the sky, Captain Chapier ran toward the beach.

The Sergeant, surprised that the mortar stopped, peered over the mound and saw a French officer waving a white poster. The Sergeant yelled to hold fire. His men obeyed him as they watched the French officer coming closer with Pétain.

The Sergeant dashed to another mound, moving toward Captain Chapier. They met and huddled low behind the mound. The Sergeant listened to the Frenchman's plan delivered in simple English. The plan could stop the Vichy forces from firing. Would the Sergeant be the guinea pig?

The Sergeant turned away and shouted to his Squad, "Fight with the Second Squad!"

9

The Oran Barracks beam, aimed from the high tower of the 700-year-old Moorish Mediterranean fortress, blinded the Sergeant who was advancing with his hands on his helmet, prodded with his own rifle by Captain Chapier. The Sergeant was a "prisoner" and Captain Chapier was his "captor." They were picked up by another beam that was aimed across the parade ground. As they passed, a silhouetted French machine-gun crew watched them. The Sergeant hoped Captain Chapier's plan would work. In the Vichy colonel's command car, seized by Captain Chapier at the cost of the Vichy driver's life, the French cavalry officer had convinced the Sergeant, during the wild ride from Arzew to Oran, that this was the only way to halt the battle at Arzew.

Captain Chapier marched the Sergeant past Vichy field pieces and Vichy mortar sections and Vichy riflemen and roughly pushed him forward with the rifle into the fortress.

"Enemy prisoner," Captain Chapier announced to two armed guards who stared at the Sergeant, at his American flag brassard. The guards then preceded them

33

down the stone steps through the damp wet tunnel that was dimly lit by kerosene lamps. Guards were stationed every fifty feet.

The fortress was honeycombed with underground barred cells that held anti-Vichy French soldiers, Algerian thieves, deserters, sodomists. The prisoners faced execution or life imprisonment. The two armed guards led the Sergeant and Captain Chapier past four Vichy noncoms playing cards by candlelight on a small table in a circular connecting passage. A Pétain poster was on the wall. The guards led them down a long corridor, and halted in front of a filthy cell holding three prisoners who were listening with contempt to the voice of Pétain that was being piped throughout the barracks. His voice boomed out: *"Soldiers of the French Army, this is Marshal Pétain speaking to you for your Vichy government. If France is attacked in North Africa, I command every French soldier and officer to defend North Africa. France and her honor are at stake. We are not puppets of Germany. We are Frenchmen and every Frenchman's allegiance is only to France."*

The first guard, unlocking the iron door, was promptly felled by the rifle in Captain Chapier's hands. The Sergeant killed the second guard with his trench knife. The three astonished French prisoners stared.

Captain Chapier tossed the rifle. The Sergeant caught it. Captain Chapier drew his pistol, pointed it at the American flag armband under the Sergeant's Big Red One shoulder patch. "He's American! They are fighting Vichy on the beach at Arzew! They've come to North Africa to fight Hitler and liberate France!"

Pétain's voice echoed through the tunnel: *"Beware of treason that festers among you. There are traitors to Vichy in Casablanca, in Algiers, in Oran, and in Arzew."*

With a shout the three prisoners followed Captain Chapier and the Sergeant through the tunnel, killing Vichy guards, opening the cell doors, and with a roar the three soon became thirty, then fifty, then over one hundred liberated Frenchmen. As the tidal wave of revolt swelled through the tunnel, the Frenchmen

34

yelled, "Americans are fighting Vichy at Arzew!" They chanted "Down with Pétain, kill Hitler! Down with Pétain! Kill Hitler! Fight! Fight! Fight!"

The voice of Pétain fought the chant: *"Any military assistance to the American invaders violates the armistice that France signed with Germany. Soldiers of France, beware of treason that festers among you in North Africa. Beware of the traitor in French uniform."*

Captain Chapier, the Sergeant, and the liberated "traitors" burst into General Tavernier's office and overpowered the stunned staff.

The sudden silence was broken by Pétain's voice: *"When you face a soldier dishonoring the French uniform, show him no mercy. He is your enemy. He is France's enemy."*

Born to soldiering, cradled to combat, General Tavernier showed no fear. He had only contempt for the traitor Chapier.

"Shoot the traitor!" the Pétain voice boomed.

"General Tavernier," said Captain Chapier, "order your men at Arzew to cease fire at once!"

General Tavernier drew his pistol.

The Sergeant fired. His rifle bullet slammed the pistol out of General Tavernier's hand.

"Long live France!" the Pétain voice boomed.

The Sergeant aimed his rifle at General Tavernier's head. "You have five seconds to give that order, General."

"Liberty!" boomed Pétain.

"Four seconds!"

"Equality!"

"Three seconds!"

"Fraternity!"

"Two seconds!"

"We die for France!"

"One second!"

The stirring music of *"La Marseillaise"* came over the loudspeaker as General Tavernier stared into the muzzle of the Sergeant's rifle.

The muzzle of a French rifle on the beach spat bullets. Defense accelerated. The Vichy troops were no

35

longer fighting for Pétain, they were fighting to stay alive as the Americans advanced, tossing smoke grenades to mask themselves and firing through the smoke at the unseen enemy. Zab, Vinci, and Johnson advanced with Second Squad. They missed the Sergeant —and Griff.

"Cease fire! Cease all fire!" boomed a French voice through a loudspeaker. The battle drowned out the words.

The voice repeated the order for thirty seconds before it was heard. The order was passed down the French line from section to section. The French ceased firing.

Twelve French soldiers carrying twelve big crudely fashioned white flags emerged through the smoke and advanced toward the beach.

Seeing them, the American Colonel seized his bullhorn. "Cease fire! Cease fire! Cease fire!"

His command was relayed from company to company. The assault stopped. The Americans ceased firing. Zab, Vinci, and Johnson stared at the approaching flags that could mean either an ultimatum or surrender.

"Americans!" The French voice boomed over the loudspeaker. *"We have been ordered by General Tavernier to surrender!"*

The words, spoken in English with French accent, reminded Johnson of Maurice Chevalier. Zab wished he had a camera. Vinci suspected a trap.

"Frenchmen," the American Colonel said into his bullhorn, "we do not accept your surrender!"

He had spoken in French with a Missouri accent. The twelve white flags stopped advancing. Tension swept the bewildered French soldiers. The Americans had no idea what their Colonel said. The Americans checked their weapons and waited for his command to resume the attack.

"You surrender only to the enemy," the American Colonel said into his bullhorn. "We are not your enemy. We are your allies. We are Americans. The hell with Vichy! We are talking only to Frenchmen! If you are French, join us. Fight Hitler. *Vive la France!"*

He repeated his words in English for the benefit of his dogfaces. Not one moved. Not a Frenchman moved. Wind hummed from the sea. Then the dam burst. With an enthusiastic roar French troops swarmed toward the beach, many in tears. The Americans rushed to meet them.

Griff was still staring at Sullivan's eyes. Neither he nor Sullivan saw the men embracing. And they didn't hear the Frenchmen singing *"La Marseillaise."* Griff lay there, out of the war, his mind wounded—perhaps fatally.

10

Weary medics in shadowy slow motion unclogged tubes in the shock tent. The tent was being battered by rain. Blood slowly dripped from suspended plasma bottles. Mental shock cases were hidden by canvas partitions.

In his cubicle, gaunt, red-lidded Griff said, "Sully hates the sound of my voice so he keeps his eyes open to bug me."

Griff was not alone in the cubicle.

"His eyes are closed now," said the psychiatrist.

"They *are?*"

"Yes. Know who I am?"

"The doctor."

"What kind of doctor?"

"Section Eight."

"Right."

"Psychiatrist."

"Right. Do you remember Zab?"

Griff smiled. "I like Zab."

"He found you on the beach talking to Sullivan's head."

"I blew my top. I'm okay now. On the level." Griff smiled. "I'd better get back to the Sergeant before he gets a replacement for me." His red eyes twinkled. He rubbed his beard. "I better shave."

"Something we've got to straighten out, Griff. You

37

told me you had the enemy in your sights, you fired, and yet you missed."

Griff studied the Medical Captain. "Nobody can score all the time, sir."

"A *sharpshooter* can, and you qualified the best in Company I."

"Hitting a target on the firing range isn't like shooting at a man." He sighed. "This killing business. It's all wrong, Doc. Makes you explode inside, gets you sick. It's abnormal."

"You're not a Columbus on that subject, Griff. War's always been wrong, it always will be, but not this war."

"Doc, they must've handed out that line ever since cavemen got to clubbing each other over the head."

"Of course they handed out that line, but there'll never be another war like this one because of the healthy unity behind it to kill the enemy."

"Healthy unity to kill? That's a lulu. You sound like *you* belong in Section Eight." Griff grinned nervously.

"Griff, countries that can't see eye-to-eye on *anything* have banded together into one big fist to fight one big enemy and *that's* what makes this a right war. It's a war for survival even if you get killed to survive. Why didn't you kill that Frenchman?"

No response.

"Because he was *French?*"

No response.

"Would you kill an Italian?"

No response.

"Would you kill a German?"

"There was enough light on the beach to see his face," Griff said quietly, eerily. "He was an easy bull's-eye and I squeezed the trigger when his eyes looked at me and I fired and I missed on purpose."

"Buck fever."

Griff shook his head. "Buck fever's for hunters who feel guilt when they aim at a deer and see its big beautiful eyes." He broke out in a fit of perspiration. "You think I'm chicken, don't you?"

"No, Griff. Chickens don't invade North Africa. I'm shipping you to England as a clerk."

38

"The hell you are, Doc! I'm part of a team. A combat team!"

"You can hit a bull's-eye throwing darts in a London pub."

Griff stood up. "I'm going back to my Squad and nobody's going to stop me! Nobody!"

He turned to gather up his rifle and gear. The doctor smiled, proud of himself, pleased with the way he cured this blowtop so easily.

II

The fly on Zab's grimy hand was smashed. The crushed body left a red smear. The day was hot. The medic distributed Atabrine to the Squad for malaria. The "veteran" combat men and the replacements popped the yellow pills into their mouths with water chasers. Zab tossed his pill to the ground. An Arab kid scooped it up, bit it, made a sour face, spat. He held out his little brown hand.

"Smoky-smoky for zigzag?"

The men ignored him, munching hot chow on the outskirts of a North African village. Nobody knew the name of the place. Nobody really cared. A hundred yards away I Company's kitchen was flanked by a fifth-century trading post and giant olive trees.

"What's zigzag?" asked a new man. He was Sullivan's replacement.

"A drink," said Johnson. "They'll swap you a bottle of *rooje* or *blank* wine for cigarettes, but they piss in it." He watched Zab smash another fly.

"Zigzig?" The Arab kid held up four fingers. Smoky-smoky for zigzig?"

"What's zigzig?" asked the new man.

"A fuck," said Vinci.

"Only four cigarettes for a fuck?" The new man grinned. "Hell—that makes fifty lays in every carton."

"You'd be spittin' crabs," said another wetnose. "Back at the repple depple a warrant officer told me these Ay-rab women are loaded with crabs."

"You going to take a warrant officer's word about

39

pussy?" Zab pulled a small book out of his pocket. "Find out for yourself. It's like combat. A guy can't tell you what it's like. You've got to find out for yourself. The same goes for screwing an Ay-rab."

Several Arab kids moved close to the Squad and watched the men eat. Zab put his mess kit down. The kids fought over it. The men kept eating. Zab took his time lighting a cigar.

The Sergeant joined them. Johnson shifted the rubber doughnut under his ass to make room. The Sergeant sat and began to eat, ignoring the kids staring at his chow.

Sullivan's replacement looked at the Sergeant. "Sergeant, what did they feed you guys in the other war so's you wouldn't get a hard-on?"

"Saltpeter."

"Why'd they call you doughboys? Were you paid a lot of dough? More than fifty bucks a month?"

"Nothing to do with money. In the Mexican War when the infantry got caked with white adobe dust the cavalry called 'em *adobes,* after Mexican huts." The Sergeant chewed slowly. "Then they were called *dobies* and finally *doughboys.*"

"Were you wounded in that war?"

"I wasn't in that war."

The Sergeant spotted Griff sitting alone in the rubble near the dusty road, not eating. The Sergeant joined Griff, sat, went on eating. Arabs led goats and sheep past kids playing in the road. Griff was clean-shaven but gaunt. He was watching worms in the rubble. He seemed very different, remote, after coming out of Section Eight.

"How do you feel, Griff?"

Griff nodded.

"Glad you got a clean bill of health. Be tough finding a replacement who draws cartoons."

Griff looked up at the death-pale sun, death-pale clouds, death-pale sky, and they were not friendly. His thoughts floundered. Americans blessed to kill by priests and ministers and rabbis. Germans blessed to kill by priests and ministers. In the clouds he saw a crucifix and a Star of David and a swastika and the Big Red One shoulder patch.

40

Emblems, he told himself, mean that we are good, they are bad. We are right, they are wrong. We will live, they will die. We will go to heaven, they will go to hell.

Griff could not escape the smell of death. A dead enemy was supposed to smell good, but Griff couldn't tell the difference between the smell of a dead enemy and the smell of a dead GI. The smell of blackened bloated bodies was always the same to him. No one had ever told him that the smell of cooked meat back home was not the same smell as cooked soldier meat.

Through the dust a very little Arab girl appeared, perhaps five years old. She was standing in front of the Sergeant, her sick black bloodshot eyes devouring the lukewarm chow in his mess kit. Griff stared at the child and at the Sergeant eating.

"I can't murder anybody," Griff said quietly.

The Sergeant stopped eating. He envisioned Christ on the Cross and he saw again the startled look in the dying Hun's eyes. "We don't murder. We kill."

"Same thing."

"The hell it is!" The Sergeant lost his appetite. He held out his mess kit. The child shoveled chow into her mouth with her fingers. "We don't murder animals. We *kill* 'em."

"Zigzig?"

Griff turned. A boy of about eight seized Griff's hand. The dirty little face was covered with tiny pimples. The eyes were old. He wore only filthy ragged trousers. He smelled of death.

"Zigzig *ma soeur? Zigzag ma mère?*"

Griff was shattered. The boy was pimping for his sister and his mother. The little procurer gently rubbed Griff's hand across the pimples on his cheek. He kissed the hand.

"Zigzig *moi?*"

The sun grew darker, matching the boy's skin. His hollow eyes filled with a lustful invitation. Griff wrenched his hand free and walked down the dusty road, his eyes fixed on his shoes. Walking that way made him dizzy. He stopped looking at his shoes. The boy followed him, but Griff did not look back, and the boy went up to another soldier.

41

The wadi was like any dried riverbed in the States.

Through it the Sergeant led his six-man recon patrol into enemy country. Every djebel had an Arabic name, but on his map they were Hill 276, Hill 253, Hill 380, according to their height in meters. Behind him, feet sweltering in leather, leggings baking legs, plodded the radioman and the Four Horsemen: Griff, Zab, Vinci, Johnson. The Captain had branded them the Four Horsemen because after five weeks of fire fights there was never a request for their replacements in the Company morning report. The four riflemen survived every fight.

Rumor had it that the Sergeant sacrificed wetnoses to keep his four friends alive. Nobody had the guts to accuse the Sergeant to his face of this dangerous favoritism.

But two replacements complained to the platoon sergeant, who advised them not too gently to go fuck themselves. They went to the Lieutenant and finally even to the Captain. Both officers listened, shrugged, and said the Sergeant hadn't broken any code of ethics. After all, the Sergeant was the Squad whip, and his job was to kill the enemy. He killed the enemy not in spite of but with the help of the Four Horsemen. The Four Horsemen stayed alive because they were fast, they were good, and they were killers. Of course, if the two replacements had any specific charge to bring—

One had such a charge: he saw the Sergeant deliberately send a new man across a field to see if there were any mines. There were. The new man was killed. Why hadn't the Sergeant sent one of his four favorites?

The Captain said, "You men and the Four Horsemen all have to stay alive. If you're slow or stupid or if you freeze, you're dead. Ape the Four Horsemen and you'll stay alive."

"What about the minefield, sir?"

"Stay out of them."

For weeks the men in the Sergeant's Squad did their job like robots because robots made the best infantrymen. They were pack mules carrying the healthy backbreaking gripe: why are *we* doing all the fighting?

The Sergeant himself had been the same kind of pack mule carrying the same backbreaking gripe back in 1918. Since war was born, every infantryman felt that he and a small group of beetle-crushers did all the fighting in every battle. It would never change.

The Sergeant smiled. The First Squad did all the scrapping for the First Platoon. The First Platoon did all the scrapping for I Company. I Company did all the scrapping for the Third Battalion. The Third Battalion did all the scrapping for the Sixteenth Infantry Regiment. The Sixteenth did all the scrapping for the First Division. And the First Division—? Brodie, the war correspondent, had covered it simply: "Any man wearing the Big Red One knows that the United States Army is made up of the First Division and ten million replacements."

The Sergeant stopped for a breather. The men pissed. Each man carried two canteens. The water was hot. The Sergeant was mildly optimistic about the possibility of finding any Germans.

They heard the sound.

They jumped for cover. The sound came closer.

Loudly scratching the brush with oversized hind legs, using its long tufted tail for balance to make enormous leaps with large whiskered feet, the kangaroo rat stopped short. It stared at the strange men, then like a shot zigzagged through them and vanished.

The men followed the Sergeant through the wadi. Zab inched up until he was alongside the Sergeant.

"I heard," Zab said, "that sometimes wounded guys are buried alive. Y'know, snap judgments by medics."

"Tell it to the chaplain."

Zab grunted. "A lot of good *he* does when you're dead."

"It does *him* some good."

Zab pulled a stethoscope from his shirt. "Will you use this in case I stop one? I don't want to wake up six feet deep."

"Don't let the regimental surgeon catch you with that."

"I gave him a Luger for it."

The Sergeant smiled. "All right, Zab, but what if I stop one first?"

"*You?*"

"Yes. Me."

"Hell, you'll be around for the next war."

"I'll be too old."

"You're in this one, aren't you?"

The Sergeant stopped. The men stopped. The Sergeant smelled coffee.

Fifth Panzer Grenadier Schoen, twenty-seven, wore a camouflaged uniform that was old, stinking, tattered, and itchy. Paid 360 reichsmarks annually to radio-report enemy activity to the panzer major, Schoen was unhappy.

He wondered how far Franz had penetrated to spot any sign of the Americans. He decided not to wait for Franz before having his coffee. Let Franz make his own coffee. There was a special bonus of one reichsmark a day for front duty and a further special bonus for service in North Africa.

Schoen wanted less special bonuses and more pay. He deserved more pay. He was exhausted, and the Americans were fresh. He had heard that they raped children, drank whiskey from German skulls, and were all millionaires. Schoen was certainly worth more than 360 reichsmarks to risk his skin against fresh troops. Next to the ersatz coffee that was percolating on a portable stove the size of a cigarette case was his two-man pack transmitter with fourteen bands. He could take that transmitter apart and put it together blind-folded. No American radio operator would risk *his* skin for less than one thousand reichsmarks a month.

Wearing his peaked cap at a rakish angle, Schoen shifted on the flat rock and cursed his ass. It ached more than ever. He sipped the hot coffee, squeezed yellow cheese out of a fat silver tin tube onto black rye bread, and began to eat. He heard Franz returning.

Schoen had not counted on death before lunch.

Without turning he said, "Coffee's hot, Franz. Did you see any Amer—?"

The seven-inch blade of the Sergeant's 1½-pound trench knife—the same one that was used on the Hun in 1918—drove into Schoen's broad back as a hand covered his mouth, muffling his cry.

On Schoen's body the Sergeant found what he was looking for: a four-by-five-inch brown book. A black eagle perched on a swastika was on the cover. There was one word: *Soldbuch.* The service book, frayed, aged, still warm from body heat, gave Schoen's name, unit, and all the information desired by the enemy.

The Sergeant glanced at Griff who unlike the others appeared sad as he watched buzzing flies already feasting on the fluid discharging from Schoen's eyes and more flies banqueting on the food in Schoen's open mouth.

Schoen made Griff think of Sully's head.

The Sergeant picked up faint thuds of running footsteps, waved his men behind rocks, propped Schoen's body in a sitting position against the flat rock, and took cover as the out-of-breath Franz dashed around the bend. Franz Canaris, no relation to the admiral, was twenty-five. He had worked for Krupp in Essen since he was sixteen.

"American infantry!" Franz shouted. "Looks like battalion strength! Get the major—"

Griff watched Franz's body slip away from the blade of the trench knife. He watched the Sergeant sheathe his trench knife, smash the radio with his rifle butt, and check the map in Franz's blood-smeared map case.

Griff stared up at the blue sky. The sky was beautiful. He stared at Franz's open eyes. He wondered what those eyes were seeing now.

"Dutch cheese!" Zab picked up a tin. "Danish butter!" He searched both bodies. "No cigars!"

Griff bridled. "That's looting," he said, feeling ridiculous the moment he said it.

Zab chuckled. "How do you think *they* got this stuff?" He caught Griff staring at him. "Looting's living, Griff."

Johnson found Franz's shaving kit.

Vinci found the stockings from Schoen's grandmother.

The lizard heard the sound, stopped eating the ants, and darted under a rock. It watched the Sergeant sling his rifle across his back and start up Hill 607. It watched the radioman follow the Sergeant. It watched the four remaining soldiers move out of the broiling sun to the shade of the rock.

Griff, Zab, Vinci, and Johnson rested in silence. A horned viper moved past them. Zab smashed it with his rifle butt. Griff watched ants attack the dead viper.

The two men were near the top of Hill 607. The lizard fled. The long shadows of the Sergeant and his radioman slanted down the hill. The radioman's heart burned painfully. Frightened, he halted. The Sergeant, more than twice his age, kept climbing until he reached the top, automatically flattening to keep off the skyline. Spasms shot through his body and, unable to control the tremors, he collapsed. But for only a moment. His instinct for survival revived him. He crawled to the reverse slope and studied the area below through his binocs, seeing nothing but a cluster of palms disturbing the wasteland of arid hills, brush, rocks.

He hooked his helmet chin straps and began to work down Hill 607 over huge boulders and jagged rocks that were fried by the sun. He needed to get a closer look at what was under those palms. He heard a sound and stopped. A wild sheep climbed past him.

Then the Sergeant spotted a movement below.

Walking away from the palms toward Hill 607 was a German.

13

The German was Schröder. Infantry. Eagle above swastika on the left of his helmet; black, red, and white shield on the right. His baggy field-gray uniform housed the most fanatical fighting machine in the Wehrmacht.

Iron Cross First Class. Wound medal. Three potato

mashers in his belt. One in his boot. Field glasses and compass around his neck swung on his chest.

Two black leather holders for six clips for his slung nine-pound Schmeisser burp gun, deadliest submachine pistol in war. The magazine held thirty-five cartridges; caliber: 9 mm.

For best and proven results he loaded twenty-eight cartridges.

The Schmeisser was Schröder's bible. He lived by it. He would die by it.

He stopped to look through his binocs. He had seen something. It had moved too fast. A flash. But the flash was red. He knew that red did not belong on Hill 607. He kept walking toward the hill. He had to get closer to identify that red flash. The anger within him increased. An hour ago he was happy and free. An hour ago he was leading his four-man patrol on the hunt for Americans. An hour ago he was in his element; he was his own boss.

"*Schröder!*"

He stopped walking and strode back to the palms. He reached the enraged panzer major who was standing under the palms. There was no love between them and Schröder made no effort to mask his open contempt for the tank officer. A panzer operator put his black tin cup on his radio and smiled. Behind him were three Mark VI tanks. Jutting from the three Tigers were 88-mm guns that looked like telephone poles, their graceful lines slightly marred by the flash hiders on the muzzles. Their crews enjoyed the personality duel between their major and the belligerent foot soldier. Three helmeted infantrymen were also amused as their patrol leader locked horns with the tank major.

"Damn it, Schröder, I told you not to expose our position!"

"I spotted a movement on that hill, major."

"I saw it, too! A wild sheep!"

"I saw the color of red."

"You saw one of my observers!"

"On *this* side of the hill, major?"

The major felt the men behind him smiling.

"Schröder, you've been a pain in the ass ever since we found you lost out here!"

47

The major had stepped on Schröder's sensitive toes.

"We were never lost!" Schröder responded, controlling his anger.

"I've had a bellyful of your insolence!"

"And I've had a bellyful of hiding under these palms with you! My job's to find Americans. I can't find them waiting here. I'm taking my patrol to the other side of that hill."

"You take one step toward that hill and you're dead!"

The panzer major glanced at one of his machine gunners who promptly lowered himself into the fourth tank, a Mark IV, and traversed the barrel of the machine gun to aim at Hill 607.

"Schröder, your presence is demoralizing. Take your damn patrol back to your own company right now!"

Schröder knew the major would shoot to prove his authority. Schröder studied Hill 607. He no longer saw the color of red. He walked through the palms away from Hill 607. With relief the three infantrymen followed him.

"Damned infantry!" said the panzer major.

On Hill 607 the Sergeant, having misjudged a sharp incline, was sliding with jarring momentum, his palms slashed open, bruised face bleeding, body mauled, arms and legs crashing against rocks. He blacked out.

A big rock stopped the Sergeant's fall. He waited in the scorching North African sun for the bullet. Nothing hit him. He slowly moved his head around a rock.

He saw the German moving back toward the palms.

The Sergeant tasted warm blood. A tooth had been jarred. He worked it back and forth, pulled it out, and started down the hill again, but he couldn't move. The weariness in his body, the stiffening of his bones, the same goddamn frustration of getting old—all of it enraged him. The fear of not being able to keep up with the other men had been with him day in, day out. He gave the illusion that he was physically fit. It was a myth. But he had always had the strength to make that myth a fact. Until now. He was too exhausted to move. He needed all his strength to make the descent to a point where he could see what was under those palms.

On guts alone, he forced himself to continue.

He swabbed his bleeding sandpapered face, started down, slid, was stopped by a rock, and began to black out again. Coming to, he worked down and reached the edge of a straight drop. He wanted sleep. He bellied along the drop. He had to get low enough—low enough—suddenly he realized he was not moving. He had imagined it all. Furious, he pushed himself to his limit and descended and halted and moved his binocs to his eyes. The blur blinded him. He adjusted focus under the palm trees . . .

And saw four German tanks.

Griff's cartoon of the General, tacked on the big situation map at Danger Forward, watched G-2 study the enemy and G-3 study friendly units on acetate. The First Division command post was carrying on business as usual.

The General was on the phone. The patrol report from the Sixteenth tensed his muscles. His voice was calm.

"Freeze your Regiment, George." The General paused. "Has the Sergeant pulled out with his men?"

"Yes, sir."

"Give him a cigar." The General hung up.

The intelligence officer and the operations officer stepped back to give the General room as he looked at the map and then grimly fingered Hill 607. "Four German tanks are waiting under palms to sandbag the Third Battalion of the Sixteenth Infantry." He re-adjusted the rubber stocking under his shirt. It supported his bad back.

G-3 selected a more detailed map of the Hill 607 sector. It showed exactly where the palms stood. "I'll alert our 155s to move up within range."

"It'll take too long." The General tightened the rubber stocking. "Get me Air Base Three."

"They're hitting troop-carrying Junkers from Sardinia, sir."

"Base Six."

"After tankers from Sicily."

"Base Eleven."

"Running cargo carriers from Naples."

"Goddamn it, get me the British 225th Squadron!"

I'll run into him again, catch him alone, blow his goddamn head off! The thought kept lingering in Schröder's head as he led his patrol back to company. Walking close to him was Gefreiter Armin, the acting corporal who knew and understood Schröder better than any man in the company. He glanced at Schröder's face and read it.

"You'd like to get that major alone, wouldn't you?"

Schröder nodded. "I will."

To Schröder, the Nazi party was a force that could not be stopped, a force he killed for and would die for; soldiers like that panzer major were not Nazis, they were selfish bastards fighting for medals, promotions, publicity. No real Nazi would have prevented an infantry patrol from doing its job of seeking out the enemy of Hitler.

Schröder rejected nothing Hitler stood for. Nothing.

Schröder loved being a combat infantryman. He hated the SS troops. They were political soldiers. He felt at home in the Wehrmacht. He fought in Poland. He fought in France. He was among the first to fight in North Africa. He did not like Rommel because Rommel meant tanks and he hated tanks. He hated their fumes. He hated the arrogance of Rommel's soldiers and their loyalty to Rommel. A German's loyalty should be to Hitler and Hitler only. Rommel was a good panzer commander but a poor follower of Hitler. Schröder did not trust Rommel.

He did not trust any of the brass. They were *Junkers*. He did not trust any man with a *von* in his name. To him the German general staff meant a group of ambitious Prussians who secretly fought Hitler's military intuitions and secretly hated Hitler's party followers.

Schröder also hated the Italians. He killed four of

them when they froze in an attack against the British. The French confused him. He thought they were smart when they kissed Hitler's ass to remain alive, but why did they jump the fence in North Africa? Why did they drop their weapons at Arzew and rush to meet the American invaders with embraces and kisses? Didn't the French know that sooner or later they would lose? Didn't they know that within weeks they and the Americans would end up like the Jews in camps or in gas chambers or in ovens?

He disagreed with Hitler's policy on only one thing: Jews. He didn't think any of them should be spared to end up in slave labor camps or brothels for German officers. They should all be liquidated.

He looked forward to killing Americans. They were all Communists and gangsters—except for the anti-Semites.

The explosions were bombs.

Schröder and his men turned and stared at the distant puffs. Through his field glasses Schröder saw RAF bombers demolish the panzer major, his tankers, and the four tanks hidden under the palms. With a grunt Schröder smiled; that red flash on Hill 607 *was* an American! Schröder was puzzled. He was told to hunt for Americans; no British were reported beyond 607. He knew British aircraft.

Those bombers were not American.

They watched the distant smoke and flames.

Armin grinned. "Goes to prove that insolence to a panzer major can save your ass from being burned."

Schröder grunted. "If that son of a bitch major had let me go about my business I'd have found that American and he'd never have radioed what was under those palms." He opened his fly. "Let's cross swords in honor of that stupid panzer major."

They pissed, crisscrossing their streams of urine.

14

Rain battered Big Red One insignia on steel helmets as the men moved through the gorge on the forced march, for Battalion the shortest route to the desert. The cold rain numbed them. War correspondent Brodie sloshed alongside the Squad in icy silence. Packing his portable and cameras, he envied Ernie Pyle's homespun coverage. Pyle was smart; he never wrote about the big picture, only about the average guy with the rifle.

Brodie decided to do the same. Pyle proved that readers back home didn't give a damn about tactics and strategy. They wanted to know about the guy doing the actual fighting.

Brodie would concentrate on a rifle squad. He picked the Sergeant's because Brodie knew there was one hell of a story in that man. In 1916 the Sergeant, then a private, crossed the Mexican border under General Pershing commanding the Punitive Expedition to capture Pancho Villa and his Villistas after their raid on Columbus, New Mexico.

The Sergeant had pretty good stories about the war but he wouldn't share them with Brodie. He never discussed his ideas or his personal life with anyone.

The General had told Brodie whatever he knew about the Sergeant. The facts only skimmed the surface. The Sergeant was among the first to fight in World War I and among the last to leave the occupation of Germany in 1919. His record from 1919 to 1942 wasn't exciting; it could fit any gravel pounder in the First Division. The Sergeant returned to the States with the Sixteenth Infantry Regiment and back to his home: Fort Jay, Governor's Island. The Regiment was called "New York's Own"—furnishing guards of honor for VIPs, playing watchdog over the transportation of gold from the East Coast to Fort Knox, Kentucky. End of the record.

Brodie had to get inside the Sergeant, learn why he never married. Or had he? Why he never talked

52

about his infant days, parents, school; his work before joining the army in 1916. Brodie wanted to know the real reason why the Sergeant had turned down a field commission. The General told Brodie that the Sergeant was capable of fighting a company. But he preferred to fight a squad.

Why?

Brodie wanted to get inside the head of the creator of the Big Red One patch. He wanted to learn why there were no listings of anything in the Sergeant's service record before he donned the khaki uniform. The Sergeant's home address was given only as APO 1, New York. APO 1—Army Post Office Number 1— meant the First U.S. Infantry Division. The Sergeant's private life was a blank. His nearest relative was listed as *none,* and the designation of beneficiary was the First Division. For military qualifications, his army specialty said simply *rifleman.* Brodie wondered if the Sergeant ever had a life outside of the army.

Brodie shifted his portable. He watched the weary but easy gait of the Division's most famous foot soldier and wondered what was going on in the Sergeant's mind.

What was going on in the Sergeant's mind was his lost tooth. He brooded over it. His dental record had always been up to snuff. It was marred now.

He also brooded about the rain.

Griff, Zab, Vinci, and Johnson more than brooded; they were ready to throw their pieces into the mud and fall down and sleep. Dwarfed by the giant inaccessible rock and unimpressed by the sandstone massif from which loose stones and gravel—flushed by violent sheets of rain—kept hitting them, they couldn't understand this weather. They were being stabbed by wind filled with icy moisture that froze their eyelashes and ears, even their balls.

Thunder cracked like artillery. Lightning flashes seemed to bounce off their helmets. They sloshed along, their slung rifles barrels down, the muzzles condom-covered. Packs grew heavier. Bandoliers weighed a ton. The men were not conscious that they were putting one sodden foot in front of the other. They did this as if their legs belonged to someone else's body. They had no idea how far they had marched. The sky grew darker, the wind stronger, the cold colder. The men were too weary to appreciate that the Sergeant's cadence made them take on a regular pattern of breathing, of balancing their heavy weight to save their strength from being completely sapped.

The rumble they heard was not thunder.

The roaring avalanche from the massif fell with full force on I Company.

There in the rain, medics gave sulfa, penicillin, and blood. The Captain led the grim work of searching for bodies. Litter bearers moved like phantoms.

The Sergeant was missing.

Brodie was shoved aside as more men plunged to help find the Sergeant. Brodie looked at the corpses among the rocks. Brodie wondered if they would be listed KIA by an avalanche. People back home thought all soldiers were killed by the enemy.

"I found him!" cried Griff.

He, Zab, Vinci, and Johnson pulled out the body and stared at the Sergeant. Zab applied his stethoscope. Thunder made it hard to hear the heart. Zab listened harder.

A medic examined the Sergeant. "He's dead."

Zab still listened.

The Lieutenant bent over the Sergeant. The Captain appeared. He, too, bent over. They confirmed the medic's statement just by the way they straightened up and looked at each other.

Brodie looked at the story he would never get. Rain drenched the Sergeant's face.

The box score was brought to the Captain.

"Fifteen dead, sir, twenty-eight injured, five in shock."

The Captain looked at the Sergeant in the rain. "Make that sixteen dead."

"Fifteen!" yelled Zab. "He'll be buried alive!"

"He's dead, Zab."

"I heard something!"

"His heart stopped."

Zab listened again. Maybe the Captain was right.

But Zab wasn't finished yet with the Sergeant. He applied mouth-to-mouth resuscitation on the Sergeant. When Zab tired, Griff took over. Then Vinci. Then Johnson. The reality of the Four Horsemen came back to Zab.

Again he listened on the stethoscope.

Zab looked up and grinned. "Fifteen dead, Captain!"

The Captain listened on the stethoscope. "I'll be a son of a bitch!"

Griff picked up the Sergeant's helmet and held it over the Sergeant's face, protecting him from the rain. The medic checked for broken bones.

"Nothing feels busted," said the medic.

The Sergeant opened his eyes.

The men pissed. Johnson did not. Zab's numbed fingers finally managed to open his fly. Panic shook Zab.

"I can't find my cock!" Zab shouted.

Johnson grunted. "I sure as hell ain't going to pull it out for you."

"It's shriveled!"

"Piss in your pants like I'm doing."

Zab put his arm around Johnson and with increasing relief in his face he announced, "I am pissing . . . now."

They laughed. The Sergeant was alive. It meant that they *all* had a better chance at staying alive.

15

The sun was the only witness to the massacre.

The new man in the Squad, twenty-three-year-old Kollin, had never had so much fun. He felt a strange power of authority. The rifle made him feel superior, like a god, a destroyer of everything anti-American, a protector of the American flag and white women.

Kollin came from a heroic line. Members of his family had died in every war America had fought.

Approaching the nomad tent in the desert, Kollin

55

saw two goats and five Arabs. Two men and three women. The Arabs nodded. One woman was breast-feeding her baby.

Kolling got a hard-on and fired. The bullet splattered the baby's cheek and found a home in the left breast of the mother. The goats went wild. Kollin was in ecstasy. He came in his pants. He felt like he just had the greatest fuck in his life.

Exhausted behind a dune, the Sergeant, his Squad, and Brodie heard the rifle shot. The Sergeant clicked off his safety and ran, trailed by the others. They heard the crack of four more rifle shots, the echoes chasing each other across the desert. Kollin was in trouble. As the Sergeant ran he got madder and madder with himself for having sent Kollin out alone to probe for the enemy, but it had been Kollin's turn, goddamn it. The Sergeant was really angry because he had no idea where they were. Six hours ago his radioman had been hit and the radio knocked out of action when seven German tanks and panzer grenadiers sandbagged I Company. The Third Battalion had nothing that could penetrate eight-inch frontal armor. Shells from American tanks bounced off the King Tigers that spit back everything thrown at them by the American artillery.

He felt better when he saw Kollin emerging from the tent in one piece.

Kollin was happy. "No other Ay-rabs in there, Sergeant."

The Sergeant stared at the dead Arabs. The men in the Squad felt sick. Brodie was thunderstruck.

Kollin grinned. "It was no sweat."

The Sergeant pointed his rifle at the corpses.

"You did this all by yourself, Kollin?"

"Sure did." Kollin was proud.

"Any of 'em open fire at you?"

"Didn't give 'em a chance."

The Sergeant reeled. He remembered the Hun he had murdered after the Armistice had been declared. He shuddered, shoved the memory back into its dark corner, and spoke as quietly as he could. "Did they pull a knife on you?"

"On *me?*" Kollin laughed. He looked like a happy hyena. "You should've seen 'em flippin' like chickens." The eyes of the Sergeant were blank. "You really gave it to them, didn't you?"

"Sure did, Sergeant."

"You get your gun off killing, don't you?"

"Better than some lays I've had."

"Which one made you come? Which one, Kollin?"

"I don't know. Guess all of 'em did."

"That why you massacred them?"

"You told me to wipe out the enemy, didn't you?"

The Sergeant handed his rifle to Griff, lifted the red, wet tiny ten pounds of murdered humanity, and looked at the naked dark bloody remains. He held out the baby, weightless as smoke, to Kollin.

"You call *this* the enemy?"

"Anybody ain't American's the enemy," Kollin said and then made the most valuable mistake in his life. He smiled.

The Sergeant saw in the smile mankind depraved by total war. He saw himself sharing Kollin's lust for death, wearing his skin, feeling his emotion—an emotion he had never been able to conquer or even explain.

He and Kollin were both guilty of war's greatest indignity—the murder of an unarmed innocent life. One bullet and the Sergeant knew he would be able to finally seize that emotion, shake it, destroy it, and cleanse himself of his nightmares.

The Sergeant laid the baby on the wool rug near the opening of the tent, just behind the slaughtered bodies. He swaddled it in red robes to protect it against the sun that beat down on the goat-hair cloth stretched over the lightweight poles of the bedouin shelter. Washing the blood off his hands with water from his canteen, he put the canteen back, stood there, and focused his eyes on the distant expanse of pink dunes rolling to warped horizons. He heard his own breathing. He watched flies attack the baby's bloody face.

Every man in the Squad was silent, horrified, frozen.

Griff saw himself eventually reduced to a Kollin. Zab saw a chapter for his book. Brodie saw a scene from a Greek tragedy.

The Sergeant took his rifle from Griff and point-blank destroyed two cancers—his and Kollin's. Kollin's surprised eyes asked the Sergeant *Why?* The echo raced across the desert and died with Kollin. The silence was disturbed by the rifle being clicked back on safety.

But the Sergeant didn't feel his search was over because killing Kollin didn't bring that Hun back alive.

16

Wearing pigtails, the bearded goums rode their Arabian thoroughbreds through clouds of dust up and down the steep slopes of sand dunes, their ancient French helmets glittering in the baking sun, their long French rifles bouncing on the backs of their gray burnouses. Dirty bandoliers danced crisscrossed on their chests, and their long clean knives rolled in goatskin-toughened scabbards.

Leading the one hundred Berber horsemen who had come out of the Atlas Mountains in Morocco, Captain Chapier of Arzew felt like the U.S. Cavalry riding to the rescue. It had taken his goums forty-seven hard-riding minutes to finally locate the Sergeant's lost Squad hugging a towering pink dune that was being attacked by 110 German infantrymen who were supported by a six-barreled *Nebelwerfer* mortar.

A *Nebelwerfer* in this deserted area? Captain Chapier was baffled.

To Captain Chapier, the appalling thing about war was that it killed men he grew fond of, and he had grown fond of the Sergeant. He hoped the Sergeant was still alive, and he looked forward to their reunion. Riding behind him was the bugler. The bugler typi-fied every goum that Captain Chapier knew. The Bugler's legendary ancestors, known as superior horse-men long before the Arabs came, passed down their skill to their descendants so that in the twentieth century the proud Berbers still had contempt for the Arabs, wouldn't fraternize with them, wouldn't eat with them, and wanted to exterminate them.

The bugler stood up in his stirrups and passed wind. His bugle hung on a gnarled leather cord clamped to his battered belt. He missed his wife and three children and he waited for the war to end to rejoin them. He liked Captain Chapier and had respect for the Frenchman's courage and felt comfortable with him. All the goums did. None felt that the color of their skin was a barrier between them and Captain Chapier. None felt superior to the French infidel, but they looked down at all other pale-skinned Christians as an inferior race of trespassers. The goums fought for France to get the war over quickly and get the French and other trespassers out of their country.

The six barrels of the *Nebelwerfer,* arranged in a manner similar to the chambers of a revolver, were mounted on wheels. The barrels opened at both ends and the projectiles were HE rocket type. Because of boredom, the crew guarding the outer perimeter of the ammo dump—listed on the panzer map as Rommel Blood 9—had grown lazy. Now every man worked the fat off his bones as they fired electrically, from a distance, so as not to be burned alive by the powerful flames. They enjoyed peppering the high pink dune.

Leading the foot assault was Oberleutnant Willy Stork who had been guarding dummy petrol stations and dummy reservoirs in the desert for eight months. Now assigned to a rear ammunition dump, he couldn't understand why the enemy had probed this far into remote country. The dump was a secret, the area camouflaged and far off the route. He was sure the enemy squad was lost and their radio destroyed.

Willy Stork cursed the mortarmen as he and his infantrymen hit the ground. The shells were falling short. Correction was swiftly made and he continued his attack, knowing that, if anything still moved by the time his men reached the pink dune, their bullets and bayonets would finish the job.

Hugging the grilled pink dune, Brodie forgot all about getting sentimental stories about GIs for the folks back home. He was no longer a reporter. He was a target for the Nazi's "secret weapon" he had heard about: the ugly smoke-throwing *Nebelwerfer*'s rocket-propelled mortar dubbed Screaming Meemie by the Eighteenth Infantry. He waited for the long hot fingers of metal, knowing he should be back at the press camp swapping stories with colleagues. He *could* have been drinking with the boys at the National Press Club in Washington. Instead, he would be killed in the desert hugging a pink sand dune. Unidentified pieces of him would eventually be found. He looked at the men in the Squad. Their faces were dry. His eyes clamped shut. The shell burst behind him. Ernie Pyle! Ernie was in a class by himself. Why try to be like him? Brodie knew down deep he was a hypocrite. Unlike Ernie, he didn't give a damn how the American soldier felt, whether his socks were warm enough, how he fought, or how he died. All he wanted was a Pulitzer Prize.

Griff couldn't move his left hand. He had heard that fear could paralyze the hands. Vigorously he rubbed it. If he lost its use he would never draw again. A mortar fragment nicked his rifle stock, and slivers flew through the air.

Zab lay at the base of the pink dune and saw himself blown apart. His great war novel would be written by some rear-echelon clerk using company morning reports, regimental history, and division history to record heroic garbage, to camouflage foul-ups with military textbook flag-waving lies, to soft-pedal death, and to make killing a romantic pastime. The mortar shell exploded. He buried his head into the sand, heard the fragments whistle all around him, and waited for one to pierce his back.

Vinci wondered why he jumped. Fragments would find him anywhere. His thoughts paralyzed him. What was he thinking about? His rifle? It lay five feet from him, covered with pink dust. No. He had been thinking about something else before he jumped. He reached for his rifle and wondered how many people were attacking. More than fifty, he figured. His thoughts took him back to Little Italy, just north of Chinatown; to dancing in the streets, sidewalk booths, Italian sausage, ziti, lobsters, olives, and Fascists. He remembered his father shouting, "The Fascists are not Italians!" He remembered the shame of being an Italian in New York City and his own pride in the culture of Italy, and he wondered how many Italians he had killed in North Africa and if any of them were relatives.

Johnson gripped pink sand, held his breath, and prayed for the mortar shell to keep on going. It did not. He waited for hot fragments to rip his flesh to the bones. They did not. He turned slowly, leaning on his left elbow, and felt his rubber doughnut folded inside his shirt, the one housed to ease his aching ass. He looked at his wristwatch and was shocked. The glass was shattered. He couldn't remember it being hit by a fragment. A million years ago his father gave him the watch at the Chattanooga National Military Park. His father had been filling his young ears with KKK speeches. He looked at the busted wristwatch. It was 12:40.

The Sergeant watched the German fixed bayonets trailing the mortar bursts. He ran his dry tongue over his cracked, blistered lips. His canteen was dry. Breathing was painful. His nostrils were clogged with sand. He estimated that there were about a hundred bayonets coming. Thoughts clashed in his mind. What was that kind of mortar doing out here among the dunes? What was it defending? How long had he been lost? How long had he been out of contact with Platoon? It seemed so long ago when his radio man took a direct mortar hit while taking a crap. How had he managed to get his Squad to this dune? It had been an exposed run. He had chanced it. They had made it. Now they were pinned down, waiting for the German bayonets.

He bellied to a higher position. The crawl was in quicksand. He had to fight to keep from sinking. Then he saw it, through two dunes. A goddamn miracle! Rubble. A good 400 yards away, but rubble! The remains of a Biblical village? Rubble could not save them from that mortar, but could give them cover to fight from. From rubble his men could pick off the advancing Germans.

He looked down. His men were helpless, waiting to be killed. They were all going to die, all right, but they were going to die running.

He rolled down to the base and ran. They followed him, running. If there was one chance in a million to put up some kind of fight, the Sergeant had found it.

Brodie ran, following their heels.

The German mortar man spotted the two-legged ants running and his shells began to fall, the bursts landing beyond the running targets. Even with readjustment, the mortar never had a chance to spot the fleeting figures for longer than a couple of seconds.

The Sergeant led the zigzag dash through the dunes, the last hundred yards in a straight line. The shells came closer. He hurtled into a stone passageway, positioned his men, checked his rifle, ammo, grenades, untaped his extra clip from his stock, placed it on a stone in front of him, then he turned and saw that his men were also checking their rifles, ammo and grenades.

Brodie, huddling behind a huge block of stone, was halfway through writing his own obituary.

17

Oberleutnant Willy Stork had fought the boredom of the desert by giving the infantry protectors of the dump a sense of high adventure. He was a one-man morale booster who stirred them with military tales of pounding hooves and inspired them with the history of the cavalry, going back to the Asiatic horsemen fighting European foot soldiers. His thousand and one Arabian Nights stories filled the isolated men with vicarious courage and with envy, and they forgot they were unglamorous foot soldiers as Willy Stork took them on historic charges. Willy Stork's most satisfying battle, because the Germans won it, was the suicidal French cavalry charge at Sedan against Prussian cannon.

He was a frustrated cavalryman. He loved horses.

He, too, saw the fleeting enemy dart into the rubble

and, when the *Nebelwerfer* stopped firing, Willy Stork was grateful.

Although on foot, he imagined himself in the saddle as he led the charge against the pitifully outnumbered enemy infantry.

The truth amused him. Shells for the *Nebelwerfer* cost money. Lives of German infantrymen cost nothing. Why waste mortar shells on an enemy squad? The report would not look good.

A volley of rifle shots from behind the rubble brought down several of his men, but he coolly continued his gutty advance, determined to lead the charge right into the rubble. He could picture his bayonets plunging into the enemy. He was impatient to hear the shrieks of punctured men that would soon fill the air.

But the rubble turned into a maze for Willy Stork and his Germans. Dozens of ancient passageways, some interlocking, some vanishing behind more rubble, became a haven for the retreating enemy. He found himself admiring the way the leader of the enemy squad utilized every inch of cover while pulling back, with every foot costing more German casualties. Willy Stork was really not worried. He knew that soon his mass of men would overrun the enemy.

He approached the high stone arch silhouetted above the narrow passageway, flanked by high stone walls, and he knew that at the end of the long passageway the enemy would be demolished. The poor bastards were retreating into a shock that would give them heart attacks before their bodies were blown all over the rubble.

Captain Chapier split his column, sending fifty goums to attack the *Nebelwerfer* and, with the bugler, he led the other fifty goums toward the German infantry swarming through the rubble in pursuit of the trapped American squad.

During the gallop Captain Chapier again wondered about the *Nebelwerfer*. And what were 100 German infantrymen doing in this area? Setting up a command post for the German General Staff? A captured Panzer grenadier had blurted something about Rommel having a rendezvous with several members of the General

Staff. The prisoner had also spoken about the Afrika Korps's hunger for more tanks, petrol, ammunition; about the hell breaking loose in high echelons; about Rommel demanding a showdown with the Staff.

Captain Chapier discounted the gossip. That was all it was reduced to. Gossip. False stories from a prisoner anxious to live, anxious to make friends with his captors, anxious to eat. It was ridiculous for a grenadier to know Rommel's plans or problems.

Suddenly Rommel was forgotten. The rubble! Of course! More than once Captain Chapier had visited what still remained in superb condition behind the rubble: one of the largest Roman coliseums in North Africa. The circular stone benches were in excellent shape. Beneath the arena was a labyrinth of underground corridors, chambers, stables, and cellars. Even the big lion pit was intact.

He could hear the fire fight and pictured the outnumbered Squad retreating inch by inch through the passageway. Captain Chapier prayed that the Sergeant, by a small miracle, would dive through the breach at the spot where the floor had sunk in the sand. The breach, fifty yards from the stone arch, would protect the Squad in the chamber where two thousand years ago naked women gladiators with their swords had waited to be summoned to fight naked dwarfs for the Emperor. From this chamber the pursued Americans would be in position to chop down the Germans.

But if the Sergeant retreated beyond the passageway, his Squad would find quick death in the exposed arena from which the Germans could lay down fire from all points of the compass.

18

The Sergeant's pullback was adroit. He deployed his men shrewdly, retreating piecemeal as dogfaces covered dogfaces and then, in turn, were covered. Halfway down the passageway, his spirits soared. His men were cutting down the attacking Germans. It was a long way to even the odds, but the enemy casualty rate gave every man in the Squad a glimmer of survival. The Sergeant figured the boxscore a good twenty-five dead Germans, two dead Americans, one wounded. A blowtop dogface halted in the middle of the passageway, shouting at the Germans. He swiftly brought the boxscore to three dead Americans.

For a flash the Sergeant thought of Minox on the Arzew beach. Griff also thought of Minox, and Sullivan's head on the beach. During the flash, Zab caught a brief glimpse of the dead dogface whose name he couldn't remember; Vinci and Johnson could not share any emotion about the third casualty who picked a hell of a time to lose his marbles.

The Sergeant pulled back to the end of the passageway, making every shot count as he positioned his men behind rubble flanking him. Through chinks in the ancient stones, the dogfaces picked off Germans charging through the suicidal corridor.

Willy Stork halted the assault, motioned. The Germans darted into passageway openings, waited. Like Willy Stork, every German knew that the Americans hiding in stones beyond the passageway would be buried in those stones. And without any German infantrymen firing another shot.

Suddenly the Sergeant's small, safe world of cover collapsed when, from behind him, there was an ear-shattering crack of a 75 gun. The shell's instant burst momentarily blinded him, its concussion slamming him behind a rubble mound. He saw a dogface and a chunk of a stone column blown to pieces; stone, flesh, bones showered the Squad.

The Sergeant looked behind him. In the middle of the arena a German tank, cloaked under a camouflage net blending with the terrain, fired again. The shell demolished a wall. The Sergeant lost ten pounds; he had backed his men into the nose of a 75 mounted on a Mark IV tank. To remain meant the quick finish by the tank; to run meant facing the German infantry.

The Sergeant swiftly improvised a satchel charge, lashing four grenades together with a bandolier. He sent a dogafce dashing along the stone benches to the left of the tank. The 75 swung left, its nose no longer pointing at the passageway. The Squad hurled grenades to force closure of apertures. The Sergeant jumped to his feet with his satchel charge and ran toward the tank. A chance hurl was out. The bunched grenades had to be placed, not thrown, in order to blow the guts of the thickskin.

The dogface and a stone bench were obliterated by the 75's shell. The tank was not blinded by the thrown grenades, the apertures remaining open. The tank's machine gun drove the Sergeant back to his rubble.

Twenty feet from him, his face bleeding as he dug it deeper into rubble, Brodie finished his own obituary. Blended into rubble, Griff, Zab, Vinci and Johnson became their own pallbearers, each man waiting for the 75 to swing back and fire.

The Sergeant knew that the North African campaign for his Squad was to end in this goddamn coliseum. He felt like a shit; he had led them into this bushwhack. He should have looked behind him during the pullback, but he hadn't. And even if he had, what the hell good would it have done? As a squad leader, he had fucked up. An amateur. A goddamn amateur. From that moment when he knew he had lost his bearings, he should have retraced his steps. Instantly. But he hadn't. He was sure he'd find his way back to Platoon taking that goddamn shortcut. What shortcut? Who the hell would be amateurish enough to determine what a shortcut was in this kind of terrain? One landmark looked like another.

He took a deep breath and prepared to chance the run. Even wounded, if he could place the satchel charge in the gut, and blow it with a grenade . . . He heard the thunder rumbling from his rear and he turned. He saw *horses* beyond the long passageway and he heard rifle shots. Above the din he was sure he heard a trumpet blowing a cavalry charge.

19

The soothing crack of the 75 hurtled Willy Stork from the Franco-Prussian War to the 1943 goum cavalry assault. The bugler was sounding the same

French charge that was trumpeted in the Battle of Sedan. Willy Stork saw the determined French officer leading his bearded cavalrymen. Willy Stork fired. His bullet missed the French officer, but tore through the right eye of the goum riding behind him.

"Don't hit the horses!" Willy Stork yelled.

The hooves' thunder reverberated through the passageway, echoing with his shout, bouncing off the stone walls, throwing the astonished Germans into panic.

German infantrymen fired pointblank, hitting horses and goums. Horses fell dead. Blinded by dust, the terrified Germans shot Germans. Horses stomped Germans and goums. Blinded by dust, goum smashed into goum. The bottleneck of humans and horses grew bloodier, the dust thicker, the trumpeting louder. A riderless horse squashed the head of a German, kicked the head of a dragged goum caught in the stirrup. Hooves split German skulls from crown to chin. Hooves split the skulls of fallen horses. Horses hurdled dead animals, dead men, wounded animals, wounded men, dying animals, dying men. Goums fired their long rifles from the saddle, and when fallen ones slammed on men they used their long knives. In the dust of chaos the groaning, shrieking animals reared, stomped and were stomped by horses trying to hurdle them.

Willy Stork saw goums charging, towering, firing their rifles. Willy Stork threw up his arms and crouched. The French officer's mount struck. Willy Stork fell and saw hooves stomp his shoulder bone. That's all he saw before he died. The hooves tossed him into the dust like a rag doll. Just before his brains were splattered, the French officer's horse and the bugler's horse played a grisly game of soccer with what was left of the German who had loved them.

After his astonished horse struck the German officer who threw up his arms around his head and crouched, Captain Chapier was in his element—a Frenchman in the saddle leading a horse charge. The stench of once having been a Vichy bastard was gone. Gone also were the ghosts of Frenchmen who had died for France instead of living with Pétain under Hitler's jackboot. Captain Chapier was going to make up for those dead Frenchmen; he was going to keep fighting Nazis until they were all dead or he was dead. His determination made him feel good. Reborn.

Leading his galloping goums past the Squad, Captain Chapier charged the tank, circling it like Indians around a wagon, building up a thick wall of sand dust. The 75 and the machine gun fired wildly and blindly as horses attacked frontal armor. Captain Chapier led his mount straight at the tank. The horse reared, tried to climb up on the Mark IV. Inside the tank the astonished gunner saw through the aperture the teeth of the horse smashing the glass. The Sergeant ran through dust with his satchel charge. He was caught between horses. He was knocked down. Close behind him, Griff seized the satchel charge, ran, was slammed by wild-eyed horses, saw one receive a direct hit by the 75. From behind rubble, Brodie watched the anachronistic battle. In the coliseum where once man fought man, and man fought animal, now man and animal fought steel.

Griff reached the blinded tank that was still firing wildly, planted the satchel charge in the sprockets, pulled the pin of his last grenade, dropped the grenade on the satchel charge and dashed through galloping horses. The explosion shook the arena. The turret top flew into the air. Chain reaction from 75 shells hit the camouflaged ammo dump.

Pieces of horses and goums were part of debris blown 100 feet in the air. Zab, Vinci, and Johnson carried the Sergeant through smoke and dust to safety at the far end of the arena.

20

The German infantry prisoners watched the bearded goums bending over dead Germans, knives flashing in the bright sun. One of Hitler's defeated supermen opened his mouth to protest. But he changed his mind.

The Sergeant checked Captain Chapier's bandage. The survivors of the Squad watched the goums. Brodie, his eyes still inflamed, joined them. He had gotten what he wanted: he had witnessed an extraordinary battle between horses and a tank. And he was still alive. He could write about it.

Zab pulled a cigar from his pocket. "Why do those goums wear pigtails, captain?"

"When one of them dies, his pigtail is seized by Allah who pulls him up to heaven."

The men watched goum knives glinting over German corpses.

"They go in for scalping, too," said Zab.

Captain Chapier didn't understand. "Scalping?"

"American Indians used to cut off the back of the head of the man they killed to collect his hair."

"That is absolutely barbaric. Goums are civilized."

Zab punctured the cigar with the match, struck the match across his helmet, and gently turned the cigar over the flame. The operation over, he puffed slowly.

"They sure as hell look like they're carving *something*." Zab's face disappeared in smoke. "Are they castrating 'em for Allah?"

"That is also barbaric," smiled Captain Chapier.

"Then what are they doing with those butcher knives?"

"Cutting off German ears to trade for cigarettes."

The men were shocked. Shocked at the act and also because Captain Chapier did not seem to think it barbaric to mutilate men for a few cigarettes. But the Sergeant was not shocked. Nothing shocked him. He had seen too much. His feelings had been burned out by the war—all his feelings except one: the guilt, the remorse he felt for killing that Hun after the Armistice in the First World War. It still haunted him. And that memory was his last link with humanity, with being a man instead of a death machine. He could only remember but he could not weep. Not for himself. Not for anyone.

21

Drunken flies lapped the cognac trickling down Schröder's chin stubble. But he didn't feel the flies. He was drunk and in an ugly mood. Sitting with Schröder against a dune was Armin. He was also drunk. But Armin was not too drunk to read the dangerous thoughts of the man he admired more than any other soldier in the Wehrmacht.

Armin seized the bottle from Schröder's hand. "If you tell the battalion CO he's a disgrace to the German uniform he'll stand you up against the wall." He drank. The cognac was hot.

Schröder grunted. His words came thickly. "At Sidi Resegh in Libya I shot a German captain when he ran from the British."

"You shot a German captain?"

"I blew a hole in his back big enough to march a company through—packing full field equipment."

"How did you beat the court-martial?"

"Court-martial? They decorated me for shooting the son of a bitch." Schröder seized the bottle and drank.

"Well the battalion CO isn't running like that captain."

"Running, retreating, withdrawing—it's all the same shit, Armin. The battalion CO's a horse's ass if he pulls back from the dunes." Schröder laughed and held out the bottle.

Armin drank, then leaned closer. "Want to know *my* secret for staying alive?"

"Yes."

"When you see a bullet coming right at you, wait till it's close enough to read."

"To *read?*"

"Sure, if you can read your name on it, tell it to find another target." Armin felt silly as he laughed.

Armin returned the bottle and suddenly exploded, "When the hell do we go on furlough?"

"With Americans breathing on our hides?" Schröder laughed. Then his eyes flashed angrily. "No Nazi pulls back. Ever. If the battalion CO was a Nazi he'd stay in those dunes and fight!"

"He *is* a Nazi."

"He's a shit!"

"He's a shit that goes back to the early days when the party was formed."

"Who told you that garbage?"

70

"Everybody knows he was a close friend of Ernst Roehm."

"*Roehm?*" Schröder hurled the bottle. "Roehm was a goddamn homo! He was in bed with a young private when Hitler shot him!"

"That's not the way *I* heard it."

Schröder seized Armin. "You calling me a liar?"

"I guess I heard wrong."

"Right now," Schröder said, "morale's lower than a whore's kiss." He spat, aiming at the patch of gray stocking seen through the sole of Armin's boot. It was a bull's-eye.

"It's low, all right."

"You saw those men in the First Company. None of them are doing their homework. None of them think of killing the Americans. They only think of how many American cigarettes the goums are getting for one German ear."

"Don't you think about that?"

"Never!"

"The goums scare the shit out of me."

"Propaganda, Armin! Just Bolshevik propaganda to scare us. That Jew Roosevelt in Washington is good at propaganda!"

Armin laughed. "I'd give a year's pay to see you murder him."

"*Murder?*" Schröder seized him again. "In war, when what you're fighting for is right, you kill. You don't murder the enemy. You kill him. You don't. murder animals. You kill them. If what you're fighting for is wrong, *then* it's murder. I kill for Hitler because he's right. I do not murder!"

22

"The first Americans killed in France during the First World War were in the First Division," said the General, sipping his hot coffee. "Corporal Gresham, Private Enright, and Private Hay. Sixteenth Infantry. Next to them in the muddy trench was the Sergeant with a grenade splinter in his heart."

"In his heart?" asked Brodie.

"In it." The General understood Brodie's doubt. "He's been shot, shelled, bayoneted, gassed—and he's still alive. I've seen him move with an assurance that no other combat man ever equaled. And all the time he was frightening. Not just to the enemy. To us."

"How?"

"The emotion he stirred up in us and—yes, the lack of emotion. The Sergeant and war are one. Both go on forever. The Sergeant is unkillable, if there is such a word."

Brodie stared, deaf to the barrage of buzzing phones, voices, movement of uniforms, unrolling of maps, and exchange of reports in the Danger Forward CP. The Sergeant and war are one, he repeated to himself, seeing the lead for his story.

"What about his private life, General?"

"Ask *him.*"

"He makes the sphinx sound like a nonstop talker. His record's a big zero before he joined up. A blank."

"That's because he lives just to fight. Friends, family, women—they just don't count. They aren't real to him. He doesn't relate to them. Friends die in battle or go off and fight in other divisions. His family never meant much to him. He probably ran away from them— if he ever knew them. Most likely he was a foundling, raised in an orphanage. I don't know. And he won't say. As for women—when all they are to you are one-night stands, you don't think about them ten seconds after you use their bodies. The Sergeant never had affairs or relationships. He's always known he could die in the next battle and he couldn't afford to get involved in anything but staying alive. Love would probably throw him off-balance, make him think when he should act."

It was a long speech for the General to make. But Brodie had touched off something in him, his feelings about the Sergeant. It was not a topic he often thought about, but he had lived with and almost died with the Sergeant through two wars almost a quarter of a century apart. He knew that no one cared about the Sergeant as deeply as he did. And he knew that he was the one friend the Sergeant had. It bound them together, like brothers almost, certainly like comrades. The General knew he loved the Sergeant, but he couldn't—wouldn't—put it that way. The General rose and squeezed his way among the men, moving across the big tent to his map with Griff's cartoon tacked on it. "Get me Dagwood 6." A moment later he was on the phone with the Sixteenth Infantry Colonel. "How does it shape up, George?"

"They're on their way, General."

"Who's the workhorse?"

"Third Battalion, sir."

The Colonel asked the General about his back condition, hung up, adjusted his binoculars to the dusk, and from his high ground command post focused on the orange, yellow, and blue pastels dwarfing the olive drab antlike trudgers and goum horses that were crossing the blank wasteland rolling to enemy horizons. It was a wasteland unmarked on earth, but now it was Reference Point 43 on the Sixteenth Infantry Regiment map. The Colonel shuddered, watching the ants of the Third Battalion vanish. He lowered his binoculars and spoke aloud to himself: "I hope the goums pull it off."

The new men in the Third Battalion knew that Sahara meant desert and desert meant deserted. There had been no sign of the enemy, yet every one of the 800 two-legged ants knew that this wasteland was crowded with Germans. The ants knew that where they were going to fight didn't even have a name and that their victory and their identities would sink without trace into the sands. What irked them was how little military value this wasteland would have when it was seized and held. Held for what? For Ike to move his pins on his map to show that the wasteland was now inhabited by the First Division? And why did the Germans inhabit it? What good did it do *them?* Did Hitler really want to hang onto this wasteland?

Why did the Colonel pick such a place? There was no airfield to capture, no ammo dump, no petrol dump —nothing of vital military value except people. And hell! They could kill people *anywhere.*

The Battalion halted for a break.

Goums slid from their saddles, ants with their packs sagging to the ground. Horses sneezed, blew their lungs, and were given water. The Lieutenant Colonel commanding Battalion, nicknamed Batshit, had wrenched a knee. No one called him Batshit—the cussword he used constantly—to his face, but they all loved and respected him because he had proved himself a fighting dogface many times. Under his helmet he wore a neck-protector against the scorching sun. He had gotten the piece of striped cloth from an Arab. He was never without it. When the wind flapped it, it gave him the exotic look of a sheikh. Batshit was no amateur in killing. His dream was to one day command Regiment. He was proud that the Sergeant was in his Battalion.

The Captain of I Company reread the letter from his kid brother who had lost both legs in the Pacific. The Lieutenant commanding the First Platoon was hoping that the replacements would not let his Platoon down. He had twenty-seven wetnoses. The Sergeant lay on his back using his helmet for a pillow. Griff watched Zab examine a human ear. The more Griff got to know what went on inside Zab's head the more he was confused. Zab wasn't like the others. Zab was sensitive, literate, and yet . . .

Johnson said, "You really going to put us in your book?"

"I sure am," Zab said.

"*If* you make it," said Vinci.

"I'll make it all right." Zab dropped the German ear into a small chamois bag. "The four of us'll make it."

"How do you know?" Griff demanded.

"Replacements."

The Sergeant smiled. His Squad was up to full strength now and it made the so-called veterans feel that their chances to survive would continue.

Zab leaned over so he wouldn't be overheard by the new men. "As long as *they* keep getting it, we'll come out of this."

"Yeah," said Johnson, "we been lucky so far."

"Lucky my ass," said Zab. "It's predestination."

"Is that what it is?"

74

"Sure. It's been ordained by divine decree."

"Don't cloud the air with that intellectual gas," said Vinci. "Why will we four make it?"

"Cause virgins get killed, not veterans. The Sergeant is proof. That right, Sergeant?"

"That's right, Zab. You four are veterans now."

Griff, Vinci, and Johnson *wanted* to believe Zab; it made them feel protected; it made them feel that God had handpicked the four of them to survive the war.

Captain Chapier and the bugler, who was smoking an American cigarette, walked their horses up to Zab. He smiled. "The bugler considers you his friend forever, Zab."

"I like him, too." Zab grinned. "He's not pretty, but I like him."

"Because of your generosity, tonight he will honor you with the ears of a German officer—if he finds an officer."

"Tell him I'm loaded with ears."

"It would be unfortunate if you refuse them."

"Why, sir?"

"To refuse a gift from a goum may cost you *your* ears."

"You're kidding!"

"The captain's right," said the Sergeant. "I heard that a man in the Twenty-sixth turned down some ears and that night lost his own."

Johnson laughed. "Hey, captain, tell the bugler I'll give him a whole pack of smokes for one of Zab's ears."

Vinci held up two packs. "I'll give him *two* packs!"

Zab stared at the bugler. "Tell him I'll be honored to accept the officer's ears, captain."

Captain Chapier did. The goum muttered several words.

"Tonight," said Captain Chapier, "he will give you the honor of cutting off the *second* ear."

23

Griff was stretched out on his back, staring up at the blackest of skies. It had more stars in it than he had ever seen. Yet all he could see was death's glittering eyes. And death made him think of Zab's prediction. Griff wasn't sure. He didn't want to be sure. All that stuff about the four of them predestined to come out alive—yes—it *was* a miracle that he, Zab, Vinci, and Johnson were the only ones alive of the original Squad that hit Arzew—not counting the Sergeant, who was a legend, and everyone knew that nothing could kill a legend.

Zab wanted to reach up to touch the stars because they seemed so near. He wondered why the Sergeant was still alive and wondered how much time he himself had left.

No sooner had he closed his eyes than Vinci was awake. The stars kept him from sleeping. There were too many of them and they made him dizzy as he lay on his back. He knew that he couldn't sleep because of Zab's mystic prediction. Vinci knew it was stupid to swallow such hogwash. Listen to Zab and you get to feel too secure, you relax and get careless and stop being alert, and you make yourself very, very vulnerable. Still, it did seem goddamn funny that he, Zab, Griff, and Johnson were not in coffins or in the psycho ward or at Walter Reed Hospital learning to use artificial limbs. There was no doubt that, even with all his bullshitting, Zab made sense.

You killed Christians! Jesus shouted. You're no Christian! Johnson awoke from his dream in frigid sweat. The night was cold, but what really made him cold was the face of Jesus in every star in that black sky. It made him think he was in church and the stars were painted on stained-glass windows. An aura of guilt lingered over his nightmare. After the war he would explain to Jesus that he killed the enemy, not Christians. *After the war?* Why was he so sure he would be alive to talk to Jesus after the war? He knew

76

why. Zab. Zab made sense. Somebody up there in all those stars was looking out for the four of them. Johnson fell asleep believing Zab's prophesy.

The flame made the Sergeant knock Zab's match and cigar to the ground.

"No lights at night, Zab!"

Zab groped for his cigar, found it, and cursed. The wrapper was loose. He licked it. It did no good. But he didn't throw it away. He dug his back in deeper behind the snoring Johnson and fell asleep, his cigar in his mouth. He dreamed of success, the success of his best-selling war novel, *The Big Red One*, hailed as an authority on war. His face was on the cover of *Life, Time,* and *Newsweek* with the grin of a Pulitzer winner.

A woman's voice came from somewhere: *"Hello suckers of the Big Red One!"*

The woman's voice was louder: *"Wake up, suckers of the Big Red One!"*

Zab opened his eyes. The stars dazzled him.

"This is Axis Sally," the woman's voice went on, *"ready to tuck you in for the night with the latest war news."*

The eyes of every man opened. Her familiar bedroom voice filled the night. *"Don't look for the loudspeaker—other GIs have tried and are now deader than Kelsey's nuts."*

The Sergeant smiled grudgingly. True. No one had yet been able to locate that loudspeaker in the desert.

"Churchill is enjoying his cigar because the British Army is fighting to the last American in North Africa."

"I wonder what she looks like," said Johnson.

Vinci licked his lips. "If she looks the way she sounds I'd fuck her right in Hitler's bed."

"Just relax in your graves for the next few minutes."

The men shared Johnson's curiosity. What did Axis Sally look like? How old was she? Blonde? Brunette? Redhead?

"In a few days German soldiers will be washing down fish eggs with vodka in Moscow. In the Pacific the Japanese are slaughtering the U.S. Marines. In North Africa the conference between President Roosevelt, drunk on martinis, and Prime Minister

77

Churchill, drunk on brandy, turned sour because the two rear-echelon drunks could not agree on how to surrender gracefully to Hitler."

Zab grinned. "The meathead who writes her copy should be writing for the comic strips."

"You can say that again," said Griff.

"Rommel's sixty-two-ton Tiger tanks are whipping the bejesus out of Montgomery's demoralized Eighth Army, and our well-fed, victorious Luftwaffe owns the skies over you suckers, so wise up and throw down your rifles. Don't be ashamed to cry uncle. Your Uncle Sam doesn't give a good goddamn about any of you dying in your prime of life. You're young. You've got a right to live. Hitler has nothing against Americans. His beef is with England. You dogfaces should be on our side."

"Come on, Sally," Zab said, "quit the bratwurst bullshit and get to the music."

"And now for news from the home front. Great news, suckers. Great! In the United States, instead of supporting you, those patriotic civilians are on strike at all major defense plants. You dead pigeons want a break, away from the fighting, and the civilians back home a million miles away from the bullets are striking for more pay. You suckers are dying while back home they're demanding shorter hours. You poor slobs are being fed red, white, and blue bullshit by Eisenhower, who was never in combat, who hasn't the goddamnedest idea of what it means to dodge bullets and bombs and shells. He never tells you about the food shortage back home, the petrol rationing, and the low morale while war profiteers are riding high."

"Get to the song!" yelled Zab.

"Before I sing you suckers to sleep I want to tell you we just got word that about an hour ago the Third Battalion of the Sixteenth Infantry of the First Division was clobbered by our tanks. I Company was practically wiped out."

I Company laughed.

"All right—keep your hands on your cocks and think of your wives and sisters and sweethearts getting fucked by draft dodgers and deserters and those lucky, lucky 4-Fs."

A haunting harmonica accompanied the voice of Axis Sally. The voice made the men horny. They thought of their women as she sang "Lili Marlene."

The Sergeant heard the German bomber, shouted "Bedcheck Charlie," and every man covered his face with his helmet so their reflection wouldn't be seen from the air. The plane was in labor carrying a bellyload of bombs. Perhaps Bedcheck Charlie was right behind: a plane that came every night to strafe the area. The pregnant bomber was now overhead, drowning out the song. Sucking in hot air from inside his helmet the Sergeant thought of Axis Sally's accent, and it brought to mind that Scottish girl's accent and he remembered she had red hair but he forgot her name. She was the last person, and the only one, who bid him farewell and good luck before he shipped out of Scotland for North Africa.

The Sergeant remembered the way the Scottish redhead turned cold in his arms and he asked her what was wrong and she told him it was no use, even naked he smelled of the uniform and she hated any kind of uniform especially the uniform of a soldier because it made her freeze. But he had answered her angrily, "If Nazi thugs marched down this street, you'd be the first to yell for the army." And he kissed her breasts to make up for his anger, but she said, "Sergeant, I feel you were breast-fed on a grenade." Her nipple tasted bitter but more bitter were her words: "I just can't fuck a soldier." He kissed her belly to change her mind. The urge to sink his teeth into her soft flesh was strong but instead he kept on kissing her all over and she became warm and full of life and told him, "Keep kissing it, Sergeant, don't stop, don't stop . . ." But suddenly she pulled away and his fingers dug into the mattress instead of her thighs and she got out of bed. "I'm sorry, Sergeant, I tried but I can't—keep thinking you're going to put a bayonet in me instead of your cock."

The German bomber was returning to base. No longer in labor, she had dropped her load on some poor bastards. The Sergeant lifted his helmet.

His mouth was parched with the memory of that

Scottish redhead. He washed her out with one swig from his canteen. He realized he had not been listening to Axis Sally until he heard her sign off.

"This is Axis Sally saying good night and sleep tight because tomorrow you'll all be vulture food."

The men could not sleep. They were all aroused. Johnson whispered without turning, "Zab—"

"Hm?"

"Quit poking me with your rifle."

"That's not my rifle."

Johnson grinned and moved away. Zab fell asleep with a smile on his face and his hand on his crotch.

24

Four hours later, twenty-six patrols were on the move with the goums. It was a special mission: psychological warfare. The goums supplied the "psychological" factor; the dogfaces were to handle the "warfare." Twenty-six listening posts were pinpointed on the perimeter of the German-held territory.

The Sergeant picked his Four Horsemen. With the addition of the Bugler, patrol strength was up to six.

The dunes were endless and agonizing. Halfway up one dune, Johnson fell to his knees. The Sergeant descended and found Johnson on his stomach. Forcing strength from his own exhausted body, the Sergeant helped Johnson to his feet.

"Level ground soon," he said.

But there was no level ground. The men pushed down on their thighs with their hands to climb the sandhills. The Bugler did not halt to examine the blisters on his heels. The Sergeant knew he was in agony: cavalrymen had tender feet. The Sergeant did not halt to give him a breather and the Bugler understood. Every patrol had a timetable to keep. It was essential that the "psychological" blow was struck simultaneously on all twenty-six listening posts.

Without calling for a break, the Sergeant checked his watch and compass and forced from his men a second and even a third wind until he reached the high dune. They studied the area. Below and far beyond were more dunes. The Sergeant was as disappointed and as angry as his men. He tobogganed down the slope. They rolled down after him.

The Squad knew what needed to be done, but they did not know how to do it, a grim fact the Sergeant had to face with every step he took. A search had been made for a goum that knew these dunes. Division had come up empty-handed. Masters of the desert at night, not a single goum was familiar with this terrain. The chance of getting lost dominated the thoughts of every dogface. Not knowing where they were, or the exact place of the listening post they were assigned to, increased their fear and drained their morale.

The men were sure that the senseless patrol invented by goums and imposed on the men by Regiment would turn out to be an experiment in failure. The Sergeant was not. He had faith in the mission and faith in his strength to keep his patrol moving. If the mission succeeded, it would cost a lot of German lives and save a lot of American lives. He knew that somewhere out there were thousands of Germans—waiting, camouflaged, eager. Perhaps they were on the other side of the last of the dunes. Perhaps they were only several hundred yards away. The Sergeant's patrol was not isolated. On the flanks were other patrols thinking the same thoughts, fearing the same isolation, facing the same desperation of being lost.

Suddenly the Sergeant reached level ground.

The men did not know how he managed to find it. The Sergeant slowly lowered himself onto his stomach. The men aped him. He studied the small oasis that was illuminated by stars. Then he began to crawl, followed by the Bugler and the four creeping figures. Inch by inch they moved closer and closer to the stand of palms, a relief from the desolation they had left behind.

From the palms two Germans could be heard talking.

The Sergeant checked his watch. He was three minutes late. He studied the palms. The stars were both a help and a hindrance. He could make out two Germans near a palm. He wondered if they were looking at him. If he could see them, they could see him. He studied the top of the palms, searching for any sign of a tree house. The I and R had reported two people, but he had to make sure. He lay motionless. The enemy voices stopped talking. Even the silence menaced them.

And then Johnson farted.

25

"Hear that?" The lean German seized his machine pistol and stared across the starlit level wasteland that looked like a drawing of the moon.

"Hear what?" The stocky German was bored.

"A fart."

"Last night it was a cough, the night before a sneeze."

"I know a fart when I hear one." The lean German strained his eyes at what he thought was a movement. Was it possible for a mirage to take place under the stars? "See if anybody is out there."

"You heard the fart. *You* go."

"Listen!"

"To what?"

"Shhh!"

They heard the wind as it swept up sand in eerie patterns, forming semihuman shapes.

"They look like ghosts," said the lean German.

"First you hear a fart, now you see ghosts."

"The goums say that shapes made by the sand are ghosts of their ancestors."

"You afraid of ghosts?"

"If they're goums I am!"

"Why? Because they cut off our ears?" The stocky German pissed. "What the hell good are ears to a dead man?"

He never completed his piss. His throat was slashed from ear to ear by the Bugler's knife as the Sergeant drove his trench knife into the back of the lean German. The Sergeant whistled. The patrol appeared. Zab watched the Bugler examine both dead men, looking for an officer. The Bugler grunted with disgust and then cut off the ears of the two Germans and dropped them into his pouch.

The Sergeant checked his compass and moved through the oasis toward the ruins, followed by the Bugler and the Squad, leaving behind them the smashed radio of the German listening post.

Exactly forty-three minutes later, the Sergeant led them to within a hundred yards of the inner-perimeter outpost. He checked his watch. He was on schedule.

Sitting against one of the two remaining walls of the crumbling ninth-century Arab fort, Lieutenant Kleink of Berchtesgaden was enjoying his pipe. Relaxed by the starry night, he was soaking his left foot in his water-filled helmet. He didn't care how precious water was, his feet came first. He sighed. He would trade his rank right now to be a technical sergeant pilot in the Luftwaffe.

Fifteen yards to his direct front the operator was hunched asleep over the radio. Twenty-five yards from him three men slept on blankets below date palms.

The man in the middle, nineteen-year-old Obergefreiter Kollmann, who came from the apple and pear orchards of the valley slopes of Hesse, was having an agonizing nightmare. Kollmann sat up quaking and cold and glanced down at the two men in deep sleep on each side of him. He walked briskly, sucking in the air, hoping to forget his nightmare, when he came upon Lieutenant Kleink—his throat slashed, his left foot still in the water-filled helmet, and his ears gone. Kollmann pulled his Mauser from its wooden holster, unfastened the catch stud as his eyes searched for the dreaded goums. He attached the pistol to the holster, making it the stock, when he noticed the grotesque angle of the operator drooped over the radio and, upon examination, found his throat had also been slashed. His ears were also gone. Kollmann ran back to his two sleeping comrades and shouted, shaking them, only to discover that they, too, had slashed throats and missing ears. He shit in his pants. He had been sleeping between them!

He had been spared. Why? Why did they let *him* live? Why did they let him keep his ears?

Terror suddenly wrenched open the door of sanity and rushed in, engulfing him with spasms. He vomited. Panic forced open his fingers, and his Mauser dropped to the ground.

With an insane shriek Kollmann fled. Reverberations of his shriek pursued him through the OP.

Kollmann kept on running and kept on screaming. His nightmare was not over. He was awake now and it had just begun.

26

Schröder stepped over sleeping Germans. He had been awakened by an invisible hand and ordered to report to the battalion message center at once. His head heavy with a hangover, he crouched near a battery lantern. It was 1:15 A.M. Shifting the Schmeisser on his shoulder, he moved past members of the security guard, stumbling over cases of ammunition. Finally, he reported to Oberleutnant Jedele. Through the half-open trapdoor above, Schröder glanced up at the sky.

"Come over here, Schröder."

"Yes, sir."

By a dim corner lantern that stood on a big case of armor-piercing ammunition for antitank rifles, Oberleutnant Jedele's finger traced a route on the map acetate. "One of our recon patrols reported enemy activity in that area—213.9—southeast of the dunes." He spoke softly in a bored voice.

Schröder studied the map. The light was muddy. "What kind of activity, oberleutnant?"

"That's when their radio died." Jedele yawned. "Take six men. I've alerted a radio team, two of our best."

"Password?"

"Göring Richthofen." Jedele took the tin cup off the switchboard and sipped the cold coffee but offered none to Schröder. "Schröder, it's important that you learn what's going on there without getting into a fight."

"I need just one man for that job."

"You'll take the number of men I told you to take."

"Yes, sir." Schröder did not mask his contempt.

"We don't want all hell to break out with the Americans until *we* call the shot, the time and the place."

Schröder thought, you and the CO are full of shit. The way we've been pulling back, the Americans will call the shots, the time and the place. But he said, "Yes, sir."

Jedele smiled. "By this time tomorrow the Americans will be fertilizing the dunes."

Schröder thought, by this time tomorrow the Americans will be playing baseball and using our bones as bats. But he said, "I'll meet the radio team near the main arch, sir."

He left.

Oberleutnant Jedele raged silently, unable to suppress his deep antagonism toward Schröder. Not only did he envy Schröder's courage and combat record, he was afraid of the man. Schröder was a fanatic and that made Jedele uncomfortable. He had heard about Schröder shooting a German officer who ran from the British during a fire fight. He knew that Schröder would shoot him, too, if he discovered how frightened he was of death and dying. His father knew what a coward he was and his father's look of contempt for him was the same expression Schröder had on his face when they confronted each other.

On the way back Schröder tried to understand why he instinctively had contempt for Jedele. He couldn't pinpoint any specific reason. He shook six sleeping men, among them Armin, told them about the patrol, ignored their cursing, and checked his Schmeisser and extra magazines.

"Let's go. No packs."

Fifteen minutes later, Schröder's sleepy, disgruntled, rebellious patrol was on the move. Even Armin's humor soured. Only Schröder felt good. They heard a distant scream. Their eyes strained in the direction from which the weird sound came.

"What the hell kind of animal is that?" asked Armin.

"Oberleutnant Jedele," Schröder said dryly, "just discovered he's got a cock between his legs."

The men found themselves laughing. Armin was surprised that Schröder actually had a sense of humor. They followed Schröder toward the dunes. Schröder had surprised himself by his dry words, but he knew why he said them: he despised Jedele. The bastard was a coward. It was suddenly clear now. Jedele acted as if the Americans were already defeated. He talked with arrogance, certainty, bravery. Because he felt safe. Because he dared not go into battle.

Not only was he a coward, he was a stupid coward.

27

Kollmann's scream tore through the area. Sleepy Germans saw Kollmann, minus his weapon, running. They pursued him.

Kollmann looked back as he ran, seeing goums bearing down on him. The pursuers found Kollmann huddling in a corner, his hands were glued against his ears. He screamed at them not to cut off his ears.

The battalion commander lay on a creaky cot, his exhausted body wrapped in a gray woolen blanket covering even his head, like a mummy. He was smiling in his sleep, dreaming of his Holsteins. Awakened by the shouts of men, he cursed, turned up the low-burning battery lantern on the dirt floor, and was told by his aide about Kollmann.

Fuming because his dream was interrupted, the CO went to see the madman for himself. Kollmann, hands to his ears, was still screaming.

"Get him to his feet!"

Kollmann was roughly jerked up but he kept both hands covering his ears. His scream made the CO sick. Pulling Kollmann's hands away from his head, the CO struck him brutally with his fist. Kollmann fell. The blow stopped the screaming.

"Stand up!"

Kollmann stared up at the CO.

"Stand up!"

Kollmann obeyed.

"Now," the CO said gently, "what frightened you?"

"Goums!"

The color the men had from the sun left their faces. The CO did not miss the change. Their faces froze, taut with one thought: desertion. The babble of panic pouring out of Kollmann's bleeding mouth was swiftly relayed from man to man until every German was aware of what had happened at the outpost.

Each German pictured his ears dangling on the belt of a goum.

The CO did not share their fear, but he understood it. Their morale was low because the war was not going well. Whatever morale was left now plunged to rock bottom because the goums had cleverly allowed Kollmann to survive so he could report what happened. The CO was angry. This kind of terror robbed his men of the will to fight because the "psychological" horror of losing their ears held more horror than losing their lives.

Terror created rout. The words burned in his brain. He must not let anything like that happen in his command post. He knew that he was in command of a powder keg, and that only one frightened man could ignite a stampede. He also knew that it was easy for terrified soldiers to run away at night.

He took his time lighting a cigarette; he must show calmness. His immediate task was to control his security guard before the goum panic reached the companies in his battalion by radio. In the morning the Luftwaffe would bomb the dunes before he led his infantry attack. He would find hundreds of dead and wounded Americans and with ease round up survivors as prisoners.

He fought for greater self-control, a more convincing display of serenity.

He did not know that at that very moment twenty-five hysterical German observation post survivors were reporting to their twenty-five section leaders of waking up to find their sleeping comrades with slashed throats and ears cut off. He did not know that in his companies terror was spreading along with rumors that five hundred goums had infiltrated to collect ears. The figure increased from section to platoon to company: seven hundred goums. Fifteen hundred goums. Two thousand goums. Five thousand goums. He did not know that eight enlisted men in the First Company were shot by their officer when they fled in panic. He did not know that three enlisted men in the Second Company were shot by their officer when they joined the rout. He did not know that riflemen were throwing away their weapons and packs to increase their speed and widen the distance between themselves and the goums.

Even as he groped desperately at his next move to retain control in the coliseum, a man 150 feet away shouted. The CO knew that that shout robbed him of control. He pushed through stunned officers and men to stare down at a German whose throat had been slashed and whose ears had been cut off.

The goums were in the command post!

Every German felt a bearded shadow behind him. Even the CO felt the closeness of those goums. A veteran standing next to him was the first to break.

"I'm not staying here to lose my ears!" he shouted.

He ran.

The CO aimed and squeezed the trigger of his Luger 9 mm. The bullet, traveling fifteen hundred feet per second, smashed the spinal column of the fleeing veteran.

At that instant the CO knew he had lost command. He and his officers tried but could not stop the avalanche of Germans pouring out of the arena.

Joining the stampede of terror, the whimpering, bewildered Kollmann ran into the CO. The CO shot him in the face. An instant later the CO was knocked down by a wave of hysterical German uniforms and trampled to death by German boots. The rout charged across the desert.

28

With a razor-edged alertness, Schröder led his patrol through the dunes. Whatever the Americans planned, it was evident that they didn't attack because they were understrength. He was sure that sometime tomorrow they would hit in regimental, if not division strength. It all finally came down, he had to admit to himself, to the Luftwaffe. The enemy planes were no match for the ME-109s and JU-87s. He could not understand why the Americans, with their great factories, didn't darken the sky with planes to support their infantry.

He suddenly threw himself down at the foot of a dune. He listened tensely. The sound came from behind. He bellied past his men who swiftly flattened out. Whispering, they asked him what he saw, but they got no response. He stopped alongside Armin, who was pointing his rifle at the gray darkness. Schröder was baffled. No American would make all that noise. The thudding sound came closer, and, as Armin aimed at the figure dashing toward them, Schröder pushed down Armin's barrel. "German."

The figure crashed into Schröder and gasped as if shot. It was Oberleutnant Jedele. He blurted the story of the goums, the ears, the mass rout from the command post, the rout of the battalion.

"Did the CO run?" Schröder asked him.

"Terrible—it was terrible—terrible—men running and crashing into each other—everybody running, running—"

Schröder cracked Jedele across the face. Armin and the astonished men waited for Jedele to shoot Schröder for striking an officer. But they saw that he had no weapon. They also saw that he had no guts, no authority.

"*Did the battalion commander run?*" asked Schröder.

"I saw him trampled to death by his own men!"

89

"Good!"

The word snapped Jedele out of his confusion and panic. "What did you say, Schröder?"

"I said *good!*"

Jedele stared, said nothing.

"Where were you running, Jedele?" ·

The fact that Schröder had not addressed him by rank or with a "sir" made Armin and the men ashamed.

"To—to—" Jedele stammered, "to the regimental combat post."

"In the dunes?"

"I—I—" Shame gave Jedele lockjaw.

"You were scared."

Jedele nodded.

"*Say* it, goddamn it!"

But all Jedele could do was weep.

Throughout the German battalion sector, eight hundred terror-stricken Germans fled under the stars to save their sanity and their ears. Crazed with fear, they ran in three different directions. Their progress was constantly reported to the Sixteenth Infantry by I and R patrols. The three-pronged rout stampeded into three Big Red One mousetraps rigged with machine-gun mortars and rifles. Each trap was sprung by mass panic. Even after 200 Germans were killed, 100 wounded, and 450 captured, small scattered groups of Hitler's gladiators were still running.

At the crack of dawn, GIs had German ears, goums had American cigarettes, and the Bugler had suffered disillusionment.

Zab did not have the stomach to cut off one of Lieutenant Kleink's ears. It was the end of the Bugler's friendship for Zab.

29

Replacement Swain, resting with the Squad at the oasis in reserve six miles from the fighting, was sorry for himself.

Born lonely, he grew up lonely, and even in the army he found himself shunned. There was something about Swain that kept the others away from him. He wished he knew why. But he didn't. He wished he could do something about it. But he couldn't.

He envied men talking and laughing as they pissed.

He always pissed alone.

Swain and the other goggle-eyed wetnoses at the replacement depot were assigned to the First, Ninth, and Thirty-fourth infantry divisions. During the ordeal of learning in what division he would be killed, he knew that finally he would have a home and make some friends.

He was marched with other replacements to the First Platoon and found himself a member of the Sergeant's Squad.

That was two weeks ago.

He still felt the outsider even though he now proudly wore the famous Big Red One patch. He was desperate to become friends with the Sergeant's Squad of veterans: Griff, Zab, Vinci, and Johnson. But they ignored him, looking through him as if he did not exist. And because rank scared him, he kept his distance from the Sergeant.

For the last three days at the field hospital rest area, he thought of how he could break the ice with the Squad. Finally, he hit on something that would force them to sit up and take notice of him.

"My brother's an FBI man," Swain said.

"Guess he deals directly with Hoover himself," Zab said.

"He's a fairy," stated Swain, delighted to have gotten a response from someone at last.

"I didn't know J. Edgar Hoover likes it in the ass."

"Not Hoover. My brother."

"Oh, your *brother* likes it in the ass."

"That's why he's got the goddamnedest job in the FBI. He turns tricks in a male whorehouse."

Zab's eyes opened slowly. He enjoyed anything sexual or scatological about the FBI, the OSS, the Secret Service, or any government agency. The humor of an FBI agent being a homo in a male whorehouse appealed to his imagination.

"Does he give it in the guy's ass?" asked Zab.

"Sure."

"He never fucks women?"

"Never. He fucks sailors. Foreign sailors."

Johnson forgot his aching rump and turned to stare at Swain. The minds of the other men jumped to alertness as they regarded Swain with interest. He met the inquisitive stares. Up to this moment he had been a nonentity filling the shoes of a dead rifleman, his existence totally ignored. Now, flushed with pride, he reveled in their attention. The Sergeant and the Four Horsemen were impressed.

Zab chewed his cigar. "Does the FBI know what he's doing on the job?"

"Know it? They're *paying* him to fuck enemy sailors!"

"German sailors?" asked the Sergeant.

"That's right, Sergeant!"

Zab choked on the cigar juice. "Now why in the hell would J. Edgar Hoover pay your brother to screw kraut asses?"

"To get military information out of 'em."

"He's a male Mata Hari, Swain," said the Sergeant.

Swain was in heaven. The Sergeant knew he was alive, had actually called him by name.

Zab lighted his dead cigar, ignoring the ash falling on his face. "What some guys won't do for their country. Where is this male brothel?"

"Germany."

"Where in Germany?"

"Military secret."

In the strange silence, interrupted only by the batteries firing, the Squad pictured with uncomfortable amusement the FBI agent extracting information for Uncle Sam from blue-eyed blond Aryan Nazi seamen.

Zab's words pierced clouds of cigar smoke. "Was he drafted?"

Swain looked at Zab in astonishment. "The Federal Bureau of Investigation is a volunteer organization, Zab. No agent can be *drafted* to fuck German sailors!"

The Squad paid scant attention to the six Arabs until their camels halted at the water hole. Wearing

92

blue traveling robes and white veils over their mouths and nostrils, the Arabs pinched the necks of their mounts with their toes. The camels promptly crouched. The Arabs dismounted, their eyes friendly through the slits. With blue-tinted hands they rubbed the palms of every man in the Squad, then turned to the task of filling their big goatskins with water. The camels drank.

"One hump's got to be hard on the ass," said Johnson. "I haven't seen any two-humped camels yet."

"One hump here," Zab enlightened him. "Two humps in Asia. These Arabian camels can put away twenty-five gallons of water."

"How do you know that?" asked Johnson.

"Captain Chapier. He told me they go five days without needing a drink." Zab pointed with a smile. "The one on the far right has his pecker pointing toward the rear."

They looked.

Johnson laughed. "It sure *is* pointing the wrong way."

"Maybe it'll point the right way when he gets a hard-on." Zab grunted. "The Division ought to have camp followers. Did they have any in your war, Sergeant?"

"Nope. Just whores in the big towns."

"Good-looking?"

"All French girls are beautiful. They worked fifty to sixty tricks round the clock, and to speed up the lines the doughboys carried their clodhoppers around their necks with the laces tied."

"I bet you sweated out a hell of a lot of lines," said Zab.

"Nope. Not because I'm against whores. I'm just wary of syph and clap. VD knocked more men out of action than Hun bullets."

Vinci looked serious. "If you get hospitalized with syph, is it listed under line of duty?"

"Sure it is," said Johnson. "They shove a Purple Heart up your cock."

"I heard you wrote a book, Zab," said Swain, trying to remind them he was still there.

"You heard right."

"When do I get to read it?"

93

"You a smart-ass?"

Swain paled. "No, Zab, I ain't no smart-ass."

"It hasn't been published yet."

"Ho!" cried Vinci. "Zab says he left it with his little old mother, but he never had a mother."

Swain waited for Zab to hit Vinci. Instead, Zab grinned and tossed sand in Vinci's face. They laughed. The others laughed. Swain laughed. *This* was the camaraderie he had hungered for all his life.

"Sergeant," said Swain, "when a tough job comes up, let me handle it, will you?"

"Why?"

"To show my brother I got as much guts as he's got."

"How old are you?"

"Eighteen."

"You won't see nineteen if you start volunteering."

Captain Chapier had galloped up to them and was now waiting for the dust to settle.

"It is okay, Sergeant," said Captain Chapier, "but the adjutant demands a signed statement by your officer that the camel corps will not be held responsible for broken heads and backs."

"I'll ask the General to sign it."

"Excellent."

"How many camels did you get, sir?"

"Sixteen."

"What kind of a deal, captain?" asked Zab.

"Four packs of American cigarettes for each camel."

"Not bad. Well, I better get my idea into action."

30

Zab approached some bullet-riddled, dust-covered ambulances that were unloading bandaged casualties. He trailed stretcher-bearers into the gloomy over-crowded field hospital and asked for a medic called Sam Wilson. He was directed to a shapely, slim nurse with big brown bloodshot eyes. She sipped cocoa as she cleaned surgical instruments.

"Sam Wilson?" She wiped her cocoa-smeared lips

94

with her rubber-gloved hand. "He took some DDT powder to the lice squad. Down the hall, last door on the left." He thanked her and turned to leave when she caught a flash of his Big Red One patch. "I hear you men have had it rough."

"Not as rough as what you've got to see every day."

In the lice squad room, two medics were discussing infantrymen living in filth among squashed rats.

The medic smiled at Zab. "Looking for a wounded buddy?"

"I'm looking for Sam Wilson. He's a medic here."

"Outside in the back."

Behind the barracks Zab found men burning blood-soaked bandages and scrubbing blood off stretchers. One of them pointed out Wilson. Zab found him burying amputated feet and parts of hands he took out of buckets.

"Sam Wilson?"

"That's me."

"You making bets on the casualties they bring in?"

"Yeah. You bet on what hit him. I give good odds." Sam Wilson kept on burying. "Two to one on a rifle or machine-gun bullet. Three to two on mortar or artillery. Four to one on a mine. How much you wanna bet on the load coming in now?"

Zab lighted a cigar. "I'm banking a race. You want to cover the hospital?"

"A race, huh? I should've thought of that myself."

Zab watched him toss in a leg. "Well, you've got a lot on your mind, Sam, you can't think of everything."

"Those goums are attached to you guys, aren't they?"

"Yup."

"Arabian horses are fast. They'll draw."

"Not horses. Camels."

"*Camels?*"

"Yup."

"Christ, that'll *really* draw a crowd. How many in the field?"

"Sixteen."

"Where?"

"Here."

"When?"

95

"Late this afternoon."

"Those Ay-rabs are great riders."

"The jockeys'll be men from the First Platoon, four from each squad."

"Did those guys ever ride camels?"

"We'll sure as hell find out this afternoon."

"Did you have to lay out any loot for the camels?"

"Four packs of cigarettes for each camel."

"Smart. Can we rig the race?"

"Not a prayer."

"Tough."

"Yeah."

"What's your name?"

"Zab."

"How'd you hear about me?"

"Artillery. Want to divvy the bank?"

"Sure. I figure an eighteen-hundred-buck war chest. Can you come up with half?"

"Yup."

"Who sits on the cash?"

"The chaplain."

"Yours or ours?"

"Ours."

"Who'll watch *him?*"

"The pope."

"What's his cut?"

"Two bottles of bourbon."

"Fair enough."

"I need a typewriter, paper, carbon sheets."

"What for?"

"Racing tips, odds, favorites, background of jockeys and camels."

"Great! You bank the infantry, Zab. I'll bank the hospital and the artillery on a fifty-fifty split. Deal?"

Zab thrust his hand out. "Deal."

Sam Wilson shifted the amputated foot to his left hand. Zab knew this handshake would be in his novel. Ten minutes later, walled in by plasma, penicillin, morphine, and tetanus toxoid, Zab was at home in the corner of the supply room smoking a cigar and typing. He glanced up at the rust-colored wall plaque above the big crate of sulfa drugs. It proclaimed that Colonel

Picquart, the defender of Dreyfus, had lived in this room after his demotion in France.

Zab typed numbers for the jockeys. He decided to give the camels names and he began with Dreyfus, Picquart, Zola . . .

31

Extra ack-ack guns were placed in case German planes spotted an exposed battalion watching a camel race. Zab's racing sheets, distributed to all companies, quickly filled the vast track area. The afternoon was hot and the excitement made every man in the Third Battalion forget combat. They thrust their money at Zab. He thrust back the tickets across medical supply cases that had been converted into an improvised betting table. On it, nailed to several large boxes, was the tote board, with odds on each camel and the number of the jockey. Zab kept the cash flowing to the chaplain who dumped the money into a big ammo box. The tickets were made from cut-up wound tags. A V-mail censor stamp authenticated each ticket.

As trucks delivered more men, Zab announced over the bullhorn: "Twenty-five minutes before post time. Place your bets right over here. The odds are on the tote board. We'll take Algerian and Tunisian francs if you're out of dollars. We'll even take Moroccan francs. I'll cover all bets. There's no limit."

The men charged the tote board. Sam Wilson ran up to Zab to report that he had sold all his tickets. "The only guys who didn't place any bets are dead. I'll give you a hand." Together they shoved money to the padre and shoved tickets to the men. The average bet was five dollars.

A S/Sergeant elbowed through to Zab. "What are the latest odds on Esterhazy to win?"

"Still ten to one."

The S/Sergeant held up a helmet loaded with money. "One thousand bucks on Esterhazy to win!"

Zab paled.

"You said you'll cover all bets. No limit!"

"I got to count it." Zab counted the money, gave the one thousand in twenties and francs to the padre. Sam Wilson gave the S/Sergeant his ticket.

The S/Sergeant leaned over the supply cases and pointed his big grubby finger at Zab. "If my camel wins on the nose you better have ten thousand bucks ready for me."

He left.

"Who's riding Esterhazy?" Sam Wilson asked Zab.

"Swain. A replacement."

"Most of my bets are on Esterhazy."

"Mine, too."

"How do we stand if he wins?"

"Horizontally."

"Christ!"

Zab slaked his parched throat with water from his canteen. "I counted on Esterhazy as an also-ran."

Sam Wilson saw hope. "Then you *did* rig something?"

"I picked the oldest camel for the ten-to-one long shot. I was told he's a bum. That's why I named him Esterhazy, after the French officer who framed Dreyfus. My big mistake was giving Swain number one to wear. I didn't know most of the guys would bet on number one."

"But if he's a bum, what're we sweating about? A bum can't win. Can he?"

Zab had no answer.

Sam Wilson was desperate. "You're a rifleman! Shoot him! Shoot the son of a bitch during the race!"

Zab's grin was weak. "I've got to have a reason."

"Reason? Our lives are two reasons."

"If some krauts showed up, that'd be the reason. I would open fire and accidentally kill the bum."

"Scratch him!"

The Bugler trumpeted the approach.

"Too late!" Zab pointed.

The sixteen purebred mehari racing camels were led by three veiled, uniformed crack riders of the camel corps whose long, straight double-edged swords dangled at their hips. The camels walked with bent-kneed gait and drunken swinging of fetlock toward the starting line where the I Company Captain and First Platoon leader waited.

Bed sheet strips with large numbers drawn on them were lashed on the sides of the camels and stitched on the chests and backs of the jockeys. The GIs were thrilled. It was like being back home at the track. The Bugler kept blowing. Shepherds with goats and sheep, and kids with strings of donkeys joined the audience and were just as excited as the American soldiers.

As the Bugler hit the stirring notes, ambulances pulled up to the field hospital two hundred yards away. Wounded were carried on stretchers into the barracks. Patients who could manage shared windows with off-duty hospital technicians. Artillerymen focused attention on the sixteen camels even as the batteries were being fired. The men on antiaircraft guns watched the sixteen camels through their binocs. A handful of disgruntled motor pool men serviced ambulances, but their eyes were on the sixteen camels.

Jockeys from the Sergeant's Squad were Swain, No. 1 on Esterhazy. Griff, No. 2 on Zola. Vinci, No. 3 on Dreyfus. Johnson, No. 4 on Picquart. They were selected by Zab, the originator of the Division's first camel race. Every one of the sixteen jockeys carried a four-foot whip contributed by the camel corps.

A roar of boos came from the holders of tickets on Esterhazy. Swain knew the boos were for him because his old milk-white soft-faced weary animal was sleepwalking. In contrast, the other camels—large-boned bad-tempered half-wild impatient beasts—jigged along with high noses and wind-stirred hair in an uneasy dance, busting to race against each other.

The boos and angry shouts made Zab and Sam Wilson smile.

Swain desperately urged his slow poke camel to keep up with the others, but Esterhazy was falling behind even in the approach to the starting line. Swain's whip brought no change of pace. Zab had brilliantly selected the right camel for the ten-to-one long shot. Esterhazy was bored, tired, and on the verge of going to sleep.

Looking down from their great swaying height, Griff and Vinci regretted having been talked into this race by Zab. As they rocked back and forth in their wooden saddles, their asses on fire, each one wondered, What the hell am I doing up here?

Strangely enough, Johnson felt at home. It was magic. The ache in his ass was gone. He attributed it to the pleasant motion of the rocking chair on his porch back home. He grinned as he watched Griff and Vinci in agony, their bodies and heads jerking and snapping back and forth like puppets. He looked at the other jockeys, all of them in agony. His camel was named Picquart.

Fifty yards from the tote board were the goums who were attached to Battalion. They huddled around small fires, brewing mint tea and smoking American cigarettes. Their unsaddled, hobbled Arabian horses ignored the excitement.

Standing at attention atop the high-domed Sherman tank, with its five-man crew holding tickets, was the bugler—his sharp notes continuing to stir the GIs. Standing next to him were the Sergeant and Captain Chapier. Both had ten dollars on Esterhazy to win. Behind him on another tank were GIs with the tank crew.

Zab walked past men and officers booing Esterhazy and climbed up on the Sherman with his bullhorn to join the Sergeant and Captain Chapier. They looked at him for an explanation. Their eyes asked, What's the matter with Esterhazy?

A hundred yards from the Sherman a camel caravan had halted. The Arabs were glad to enjoy the rest and eager to watch the race. Their pack camels, unlike the fleet-footed riding mehari, were sluggish and mean as they rested beside their baggage on the ground.

The sixteen racing camels had enough room now to line up abreast at the starting line, a difficult feat for the three camel corps riders, borrowed from the French XIX Corps camel brigade, because the American jockeys didn't know how to handle their animals. The three camel corps riders moved up and down, waving back the thoroughbreds, trying to get them in line for a good getaway and to make sure no rider got a head start. After much shouting, cursing, and whip-cracking, the GIs finally managed to get their mounts abreast.

They had to wait until the three camel corps riders maneuvered Esterhazy into his starting position. The moment this happened, the platoon leader raised his hand and brought it down. Captain Chapier fired his .45. A split second later the artillery guns let loose with deafening salvos.

The jockeys shouted, their whips cracked, the crowd roared, and the entire group plunged ahead, reaching top speed in a few strides.

Taking the lead was Esterhazy.

Zab held the bullhorn to his mouth, tongue-tied. Then he snapped out of it. "And they're off an' running! Esterhazy taking the lead! Zola slipping between Joan of Arc and Dreyfus! Napoleon moving forward. Zola and Dreyfus fighting for second place! Napoleon is third trailed by Lafayette coming up fast! Esterhazy is still up front!"

The roar of enthusiasm drowned out his words and drowned out the crack of batteries firing. The pack of caravan camels were becoming irritated. It was rutting season. The females were disturbed by the clamor of Long Toms and voices. A new member of the caravan called Khayin (meaning treacherous) was big and horny as he eased his way to his target, his pecker definitely pointing in the right direction. He reached the restless couched female from behind, then spread his forelegs over her back.

The male leader of the pack camels, called Dalil because once he had been a guide, had always serviced the she-camels. He bared his teeth, got to his feet, snarling and growling, and with jealous fury attacked Khayin.

The female was pleased as the two males bit each other, trying for a grip on each other's testicles. The battle carried Khayin and Dalil away from the caravan and to the field in front of the sixteen camels. Khayin threw Dalil and trampled him. Kicked in the testicles, Dalil sprang up in pain and at that moment blindly crashed into Esterhazy. The racing camels piled up in the dust. Jockeys were thrown. Khayin kept after Dalil's testicles`despite the pandemonium. Racing camels bit and kicked one another, running berserk. Unable to control his camel, Griff, on Zola, charged into the crowd. GIs ran for their lives. Vinci on Dreyfus demolished tents. Johnson on Picquart assaulted the artillery guns that stopped firing as men fled. Swain on Esterhazy, in sudden reverse, galloped past parked ambulances, scattering men in the motor pool, and in seconds the white camel charged into the barracks.

The race now a shambles, angry GIs stormed Zab on the Sherman and demanded their money back. When he announced over the bullhorn that as soon as the racing camels were gathered by the camel corps the race would start from scratch once again, he was met by dogfaces climbing up the tank for him. He swiftly announced that all money would be returned at once. And as the padre, Zab, and Sam Wilson shoved cash back to the GIs in exchange for their tickets, the Colonel pulled into the jammed area and stopped. The Colonel stood up, holding a bullhorn. At first his words could not be heard. He had to fire his .45 three times before the GIs began to quiet down.

"Let me have your attention!" the Colonel announced.

It became deathly quiet. Now and then the batteries' firing again invaded the silence. The men knew they were either going back to fight or they were facing a counterattack.

"The goums," said the Colonel, "have been cutting off American ears!"

Every man in the Battalion turned pale.

The goums continued to calmly sip their tea and smoke their American cigarettes.

"I know," said the Colonel, "that you can't tell the difference between a German ear and an American ear, so from now on there will be no more swapping cigarettes for *any* kind of ear!"

32

Brodie missed the beautiful Swede, their golf games, their wrestling in bed, their breakfast talks. They never mentioned war in their letters because she believed her country was right, and he believed Sweden was wrong to remain neutral while Nazis occupied Norway.

Thinking of the Swede made him forget the back-breaking jeep ride he was taking from Second Battalion to Division headquarters. Lately everything bushed Brodie. Facing another day had become an ordeal of physical agony. It was the war. He needed a full month of rest to regain his strength.

He felt so goddamn old. He was only forty, but he felt eighty. And he knew it wasn't just the war.

It was the Sergeant. The goddamn Sergeant made Brodie feel eighty years old. The Sergeant was forty-five—five years older! How did the Sergeant keep up with his Squad of young men? What did he do to stay young, to renew his strength?

Brodie was sick with envy. He did not have to fight. He did not patrol and march and run and kill. He did not have the constant responsibility of the lives of eleven men in his hands. Yet the Sergeant made Brodie feel old.

The Sergeant was in superb condition because he was regular army. Years of keeping fit. Marches. Running. Healthy chow. Early in the sack. Early to rise and suck in clean air. More exercise. Training. Discipline. Then war. Forced to be alert. Forced to keep up with the fuzzy-cheeked kids.

"You know the General pretty good, don't you, Mr. Brodie?" the young jeep driver asked.

"Pretty good."

"I mean you're kinda close to him, aren't you?"

"Do me a favor."

"What's that, sir?"

"Don't look at me when you talk. Keep your eyes on the goddamn road."

"Sorry, Mr. Brodie."

Sorry, Brodie, the regimental surgeon had told him after the last physical, *no mistake about your age. You're around forty all right. You feel twice as old because you're going haywire trying to keep up with a rifle squad. You've got to be a kid to stand that pace. Over twenty-five you become a straggler. Over thirty you're ready to throw in the towel.*

"Yes, I'm close to the General, as close as anybody can get to a division two-star. Why?"

"Well, I'm wondering if he ever said anything about us fighting under the British flag."

The Sergeant at forty-five didn't even know what the towel looked like.

"I guess because we're Johnny-come-lately out here," said Brodie. "The British have been scrapping here for a long time. Must be a reason for them running the crap table."

"Can't the General run his own crap table?"

"He's got to have more than two stars to call the shots."

"Jesus Christ!"

That was it! Jesus Christ! It had always chilled Brodie that the Sergeant reminded him of Jesus Christ. Christ with a rifle. It was insane, of course, but that was the picture the Sergeant brought to mind.

"Jesus Christ can't do the General any good. Only Ike and Winston Churchill can give the General the green light to call his own shots." He hoped the driver wouldn't keep on talking.

Twenty minutes later Brodie joined officers jamming the lean-to at Danger Forward. He nodded to several, exchanged a few words about the Second Battalion's action, and moved over to the General who was studying the big map. Griff's cartoon was tacked on the side. The General looked worried. "Kill a little time, will you, Brodie?"

Brodie wondered what was coming up that was not for his ears. "Of course, General."

The General managed a smile but he seemed concerned. It was Brodie's pale, drawn face. "You look a hundred years old, Brodie. Better rev down."

Brodie left.

The General tightened with dread as Brodie, out of

104

earshot, joined the other correspondents having coffee with the half-track crew. The dread was a familiar emotion. The General had experience with enemy maps before. Now his thought centered on one particularly suspicious enemy map that had been captured by a Big Red One corporal in the Twenty-sixth Infantry and promptly forwarded to corps.

The General turned to the officers. All talk stopped.

The General spoke quietly. "Ever since Rommel got shellacked at El Alamein he's been looking for a knockout blow to square himself with Hitler. That captured map says his blow will be struck at Sbiba. That map is about as secret and subtle as a front-page headline, and I don't buy it. Sbiba doesn't seem like the main event to me."

"It does to me, sir." G-2 tapped the dry tobacco in his pipe with his stubby finger.

"Why?"

"I think Rommel's aim is to hook up the Afrika Korps with the German army in Tunis."

"I think you're right, but I don't buy Rommel trusting an Arab courier with such restricted information. I know *I* wouldn't."

"Well, General, we *have* been intercepting, so it stands to reason he couldn't chance contacting them by radio."

"Contacting them?"

G-2 tapped the map with his pipe. "His camouflaged tanks between Thala and Sbiba."

"You didn't tell me there were German panzers there."

"I'm assuming—"

"Of course, of course, and you've done a hell of a good job with your assumptions of what the Germans will do—and when and how, but I need confirmation. How many patrols have you got between Thala and Sbiba?"

"Sixty, sir."

"And so far negative?"

"Yes, sir."

"What about the Ninth and Thirty-fourth divisions?"

"Their patrols report negative, sir."

The worried General paced back and forth. The

105

phone buzzed. It was corps asking for Danger Six. The General took the phone, grunted into it, listened for a few seconds, said "Yes, sir," and hung up. He did not look at the map. He did not look at the officers.

"Corps," said the General, "decoded two intercepted German reports—both confirming that captured map's information. Rommel *is* preparing an all-out thrust at Sbibà. Orders are being cut for us to join the British and French at Sbiba."

"Is the whole Division committed, sir?" asked G-3.

"I still think that map was a plant. I still think Rommel's too goddamn foxy to dump his last shot on an Arab courier."

"Is the whole Division committed, sir?" repeated G-3.

The General turned. "Two regiments." He walked to the map. "In 1918 the Hun launched a similar last-ditch knockout blow in the Meuse-Argonne. I was with the Sixteenth then. While the Hun hit the division head on, our regiment swung around his rear and whipped him."

Every officer was worried because the General was worried.

He stepped closer to the map. "There's an old road between those two mountains that was used by the Roman legions." He held his finger at a spot on the map. "I'll send one regiment through it to swing east and ream Rommel's ass while he's at Sbiba throwing everything he's got at us and the British and the French."

G-3 said, "What regiment, General?"

"Sixteenth."

"What's the name of the road, General?"

"Kasserine Pass."

A gust of wind blew Griff's cartoon off the map.

33

Schröder jumped from the rumbling Mark III tank and started up the steep slope of the high sand dune. Halfway up he shifted his slung Schmeisser, reviewing in his mind the news he had learned from an old comrade at regimental headquarters. The situation upstairs had become a political soccer ball—kicked back and forth by German and Italian brass fighting each other for power in Africa. Schröder was furious. He disliked the Italians as a people and resented their military inefficiency.

Schröder felt the sand give under his boots. He slipped back at least eight feet and recovered his balance. Hearing music coming from above, he continued to climb, delighted that in the coming attack Mussolini's soldiers would remain on the sidelines. Schröder did not like Rommel's overpublicized panzers, but as long as they killed for Hitler he tolerated them. When he reached the top of the dune, his section, mostly filled with new faces, was enjoying music from a small hand-crank phonograph.

"Did you get any cigars at regiment?" asked Armin.

Schröder gave Armin a handful of cigars as he kept his eyes on the phonograph.

"Communication center got hit," said Armin. "I found the phonograph and record undamaged."

Feldwebel Gerd, a big, husky Schleswig-Holstein combat veteran, laughed. "Look at the faces of these baby masturbators, Schröder. To them the 'Horst Wessel' song is holy."

A young masturbator said, "It *is!*"

The hard-bitten Gerd was amused. "You're old enough to know the facts. Horst Wessel was no hero. He was a shit. And he didn't die for Schicklgruber."

Schröder saw the stunned youthful faces trying to recover.

The young masturbator bristled. "His name is Adolf Hitler, not Schicklgruber!"

Gerd laughed. "I bet you wet cocks didn't know that Horst Wessel was killed in a fight over a whore."

The desert wind came to life. Grains of sand were blown up to the crest of the dune to sting the faces of the stunned youths. Their belief in Horst Wessel was being undermined.

"You got diarrhea of the mouth, Gerd," said Armin.

Gerd ignored him. "I knew a whore named Erna Jaenicke in Berlin. Every time I paid Erna she gave the money to her pimp, Ali Hoehler. Until she met Horst Wessel." He laughed as he remembered. "She dropped Ali, and Horst became her pimp."

"That's a lie!" shouted a young soldier.

Gerd smiled. "And for money Horst also supplied Hitler's brownshirts with fat little boys who had tight little assholes like yours." He laughed at their shock. "To get his whore back Ali shot Horst Wessel through the mouth. Goebbels had Ali murdered, then he personally built up Horst Wessel as a heroic storm trooper who was killed by the Jews because he was a Nazi. Goebbels turned the pimp's funeral into a big Nazi demonstration and ordered all the idiots in Germany to sink the 'Horst Wessel' song." His red eyes twinkled. "Tell them, Schröder, tell these baby replacements that is how it happened. Tell them that's how a pimp's poem became the holy hymn of Hitler's party."

Armin watched Schröder's face. It was vacant.

"Let's go," Schröder told the young faces. "We're going to kiss panzer asses through Kasserine Pass."

"Not *me*," said Gerd. "I'm no grenadier. I'm Wehrmacht. I'm not choking anymore on their stinking petrol fumes."

Schröder spoke quietly. "Rommel ordered—"

"Rommel couldn't order a stein of beer right now," said Gerd. "I'm glad he got whipped at El Alamein. I never wanted no part of this stinking war. I'm no Nazi."

I'm no Nazi!

The three words drained the blood from Schröder's face. He controlled his nausea. He was face-to-face with the most dangerous enemy of the Third Reich: an Aryan who had lost faith in Hitler.

Schröder heard himself saying, "I didn't know you had Jew blood in you, Gerd."

"I don't, Schröder! But if I did I'd have put Hitler on a spit a long time ago and cooked him slowly on all sides and fed him as slop to that pig Göring."

"You didn't sing that tune when we were winning."

"Goddamn right I didn't! Nobody sings that tune when we're winning. But we lost!"

"What made you join up, Gerd? You could've run away."

"What for? Hitler came in handy. He served a purpose for the morons and the unemployed and the perverts and the ex-convicts like me. But now he's finished. The war caught up with him. When the Americans capture him they'll parade him in a cage like a freak. He'll be a joke! He'll be Charlie Chaplin fucking a swastika!"

Schröder opened fire at close range.

The bursts from his Schmeisser sent Gerd's buttons flying. The bullets, with 800-per-minute rate of fire and 2250 feet-per-second muzzle velocity, slammed Gerd back to the time when he was a little boy playing pranks with his playmates, tumbling from the fountain of Tyll Eulenspiegel to frighten little girls, rolling down the green grass hill to terrify a baby in a carriage. Bullets gored his flesh and smashed his bones. Lightning and thunder burst behind his eyeballs. An electrifying explosion of red and white and yellow burst inside his skull, and the convulsions of his headless body increased as bullets sent it dancing, twisting, kicking in clouds of dust all the way down the steep slope to the bottom of the dune.

Schröder stopped firing. Gerd's body was a sieve.

When the dust settled, the only thing moving was Gerd's blood gushing through the sieve into the sandy sponge.

34

When the British Dr. Condom introduced the thin rubber sheath to be worn over the penis to prevent conception or VD, he guaranteed that his brainstorm would resist any and all pressure and punishment during sexual intercourse. From his eighteenth-century vantage point he never imagined that some two hundred years later his condoms would be worn over the Squad's rifle muzzles to protect them from the savage sand particles scudding through Kasserine Pass. He would have been disappointed to see his rubbers demolished in the storm.

The GI scarf-covered faces of the Sergeant's Squad would have been slashed to their cheekbones had he not ordered them to dig their noses into their steel helmets. Before the gut of the sandstorm struck, their eyes, mouths, and ears were filled with powdery abrasive dust; it was hard for them to catch their breath and they sneezed regularly. But now, if they halted and dug in, there was the danger of being buried alive. They kept marching blindly, moving single file through whirling sand, each man with an iron grip on the shoulder of the man in front of him, their bent bodies buffeted by howling waves of millions of razor-blade grains hitting them like buckshot.

The Sergeant led them, using both his hands to keep his face covered. Blinded, he led the blind. When he lifted the brim of his helmet to see where he was going, his face was stabbed by flying needles. His eyes were on fire. To close them was agony. He tripped and fell. The men piled up like dominoes, scrambling for their fallen helmets. The Sergeant felt the obstacle with one hand. A fallen petrified tree. He crouched behind the big fossil for temporary cover. The men flattened against it, every face jammed into a helmet.

The Sergeant got madder and madder. *Somebody* at Regiment should've warned them about the sandstorm before any men were sent to find the lost recon car. Communication with the recon car had ceased abruptly. It had to be located; it was the eyes of the Regiment. The Squad was the fourth group out hunting for it. Holding his helmet while wind tried to whip it away, the Sergeant felt each man for a count. He had not lost a man. He rested for a moment, wondering if they had passed the recon car in the storm. Perhaps the crew was buried alive in it. A helmet slammed into his, clinking. He lifted his brim. He saw Zab plunging. Zab's hands grabbed his helmet and covered his face with it. The Sergeant wondered if Zab would ever live to write that book.

Zab's blood- and sand-caked scarred hands dug his face deep inside his helmet and for no reason he thought about the three-minute hourglass his mother used to use to time two eggs for him and how he used to watch the magic grains of sand trickling. In each grain he had pictured camels, Arabs, belly dancers. His hot breath in the helmet liner stank. He felt the weight of sand on his back. It was piling up. He was going to die at the bottom of that hourglass.

Griff's bloody face was glued to his helmet liner. He could see himself drawing a cartoon of the Squad killing Germans in the desert and Germans killing the Squad. His eyes burned with the stiletto stabs and his cartoon slowly broke into crazy lines and then vanished.

Johnson was blinded by sand and philosophy. He hated philosophers because they never answered their questions. Now he found himself philosophizing as he kept his face pressed into his helmet. His fingers were numbed. He choked on sand as he calmly asked himself what he had accomplished in life. He had never questioned himself before. He felt smart. Perhaps some of Zab's stories about books and emotion had rubbed off on him.

Vinci had his head buried into his steel helmet. His salty tears reminded him of Lachryma Christi, his father's favorite wine. He felt the sand heavy on him. The wind screamed, his body shook, his nostrils stung with grit, his mouth with sand.

Swain had finally found a home and friends; he was now part of the organism called the Squad. He was no longer an orphan with a rifle, but he knew he would never live to use that rifle, never live to see and kill the Germans, never live to be the wearer of the Silver Star. He wondered, when and if they found his body, whether he would get a Purple Heart. He moved closer to the fossil, but sand attacked him and tore the back of his neck with shards of glass.

35

Mengershausen, age twenty-four, commanding the lead Afrika Korps tank in the Kasserine Pass sandstorm, was an intellectual, an ex-Marxist, and the murderer of his father and mother. Sand slashed the skull and crossbones on his cap and on his lapels and attacked his major's shoulder strap as he stood in the turret, his face protected by a thick scarf and thick goggles.

He only exposed himself for a moment, but in that moment, to show the crew he was fully in command, his foot guided the driver. The driver thought Mengershausen was insane to lead the thrust in the Mark VI mounted with an 88-mm gun. The point should be a Ram-Tiger created by Hitler to ram tanks and walls of sand.

But Mengershausen had insisted on a Mark VI for a damned good reason, when he volunteered for point in the assault. He did the same in Russia, in the snow, and steamrolled his way to an Iron Cross First Class. Suicidal job then. Suicidal job now. There was no reason why his division commander could refuse Mengershausen the honor.

Mengershausen soon found what he was looking for. In the swirling sand he passed a Lobster field howitzer buried under an avalanche of rocks and sand. He felt nothing for the dead crew. He had five more Hornet 88s on self-propelled Panzer IV chassis. So far, without a fight, he had lost a Panzer II with armor-plated sheet aprons, and another was out of radio contact. He didn't care. He had three more with aprons lumbering loose about the flanks and rear to deflect antitank shells when the storm was over and contact with Americans was made.

He closed the hatch. The storm was a nuisance but it didn't really annoy him.

Mengershausen sliced off a piece of cheese from a giant wheel, cut it in half and gave half to a machine gunner, and ate it, chewing slowly. His mind was not on the sandstorm but on the face of Rommel, a face he would never forget.

He remembered that windy day when he had accompanied his tank division commander; a day never to be forgotten. All that morning he had looked forward to seeing Rommel. That magnificent line of tanks had made Mengershausen so proud to be part of the panzers.

Rommel's sand-colored command car—bearing the

112

palm-tree marking of the Afrika Korps—had pulled up in clouds of dust. When the dust settled, a score of top-ranking officers ringed the car. Mengershausen had joined his division commander and stood twenty-five feet from Rommel, whose words and plan had been electrifying.

Rommel had planted a map on an Arab courier who was instructed to be captured by the First United States Infantry Division. Rommel had also dispatched messages designed to be intercepted by the Americans.

Riding in the Tiger, Rommel's words still burned in Mengershausen's memory: "The Americans have joined the British and French at Sbiba as I planned. I'm going to send a token display to put up a battle at Sbiba, but our main thrust will be through those two mountains, an old road once used by the Roman legions. Kasserine Pass. It opens into the broad flat bowl that leads to Tébessa. Perfect terrain for our panzers. I'll pick a cloudy day when enemy planes are grounded. After Tébessa, our objective is Eisenhower's headquarters in Constantine, Algeria."

Mengershausen planned to win the Knight's Cross in this drive through Kasserine Pass to Tébessa, where he would be the first to smash into Constantine, capture General Eisenhower and his staff, and get the Grand Cross from the Führer himself. Only one man wore it. Göring. The Grand Cross would make Mengershausen a national hero overnight.

36

The sandstorm died very slowly. The Sergeant began thinking of the first man he had ever killed, in 1916, at Babicora, William Randolph Hearst's ranch in Mexico. The fire fight had a zero result. Pancho Villa had galloped off to San Geronimo. The Sixteenth's first casualties were two guides, a Mormon and a Carranzista Mexican. There was no formal state of war between the U.S. and Mexico, but that was not the Sergeant's business. He was not in Mexico as a tourist. He was a groundfucker infantry private with a Springfield to be used to kill or capture Pancho Villa and his Villistas for their Columbus atrocity. Behind the Hearst barn the Sergeant had come face-to-face with a young Villista. The Springfield jumped to life first. The young Villista's brandy-colored hands flew to his bleeding groin and the Sergeant just stood there, hypnotized, watching the first man he ever shot take a damned long time dying. "Viva Villa!" the young Villista had said and finally died. The Sergeant never forgot him. All the men the Sergeant killed looked like the young Villista. But the Hun he murdered did not have the face of the young Villista. That face was unique and unforgettable.

A still wind came up after the raging storm. The Sergeant led his Squad into a dry sand swamp. When the wind died completely every man was like a lost balloon going nowhere. Finally, with the dry mire behind them, they walked in the sand prints of the Roman legions. Their needle-clogged, bloodred eyes saw the blur of the Sergeant leading them through the defile, flanked by mountain walls that once flanked chariots.

The Sergeant dragged his baked, stinging feet across hot stones. The sun was fighting to burst through the dark clouds, but not a ray of light appeared to give him hope for any air support. Sick with the failure of his hunt, exhausted by the heat and the pain that knifed him with every step he took, he slumped down on a projecting rock and rested. He didn't have the stomach to radio the Lieutenant that they hadn't found the recon car. The men rested. Their water was hot, muggy, metallic. Every man ached.

Johnson was too beat to even inflate his rubber doughnut.

After a short rest, the Sergeant got to his feet and moved out. They got to their feet and followed him. He glanced back for stragglers. None. He stopped before every bend and, while they waited, he investigated what was behind the bend. He hated the whole thing. Either it was one more hill or one more bend. Hills sapped him, bends scared him. He approached one that appeared more ominous than the others and halted. He felt strange. The men were puzzled. The Sergeant seemed to be in a trance. The shape of this bend looked strangely familiar to him. He stared at it for a long time. The men looked at each other. Then the Sergeant knew why it was familiar. During the First World War, he had seen a bend in France just like the one he was staring at. He had poked his head around that bend into mustard gas.

He bellied along the wall until his eyes could see around the bend. Bile filled his mouth. The area was vast; in the distance were more hills. In the road was the scorched crippled recon car he was sent to find. Vultures were fighting to get through the open hatch.

The Sergeant hated heroics. He knew if he followed the obvious direction of the wheels, he would reach the car. He wasn't sure if the car had been hit by a shell or had hit a mine, and he was taking no chances. Slowly, hesitantly, he lifted one foot and put it down very, very gently, then took another step and another. He could have shot up the area to trigger mines, if there were any, but he couldn't chance waking up any people if any were behind those mounds. He could've radioed the Lieutenant that he found the knocked-out car, but he didn't want to make contact until he could come up with a full report. His left shoe froze an inch above the ground. He lowered it. He wasn't worried about AT mines. It was the Bouncing Betty that made him sweat. He didn't want to have his balls blown off. The Bouncing Betty, when tripped, would jump in the air before exploding a waist-high spray of shrapnel.

He reached the car. The frightened vultures took off. He carefully checked the damage, found what he suspected, climbed to the open turret, and looked down into the car. A vulture with a bloody hooked beak was tearing at human flesh. The Sergeant placed the radio on the car and dropped through the hatch. The vulture's only defense was to puke decayed meat at the Sergeant, who checked the bodies knowing he wouldn't find a dying one. The vulture refused to abandon its feast.

The Sergeant climbed up, closed the turret hatch, and checked his map. A moment later he was in contact with his Platoon.

"Found the recon car Point 76, hit a mine, crew dead."

"Hole up," said the Lieutenant. "I'll send a detonator squad. Did you lose anyone in the sandstorm?"

"Not a man, sir."

"I and R reported moving dust near 254 an hour ago."

"Can't our plane identify?"

"Two Pipers slammed into djebels. Nothing's flying in the soup."

"That dust could be another storm coming up."

"Or British tanks."

"British?"

"We got a report three Valentines were lost in the storm heading vicinity 254."

The Sergeant checked his map, then looked through his binocs. He must remember to give that goddamn bird an exit. "I see some kind of movement vicinity 265."

"Holding."

"It's moving."

"Which way?"

"Toward me."

"Holding."

"They're tanks Lieutenant!"

"Markings?"

"Too far, sir."

A shell exploded a half mile in front of the Sergeant. Two mines erupted. Then in zigzag chain reaction seven more mines blew.

The Sergeant said, "Do the British know we're in the pass?"

"Yes."

"They're Valentines!"

"Are you sure?"

"They're blowing up the minefield for us!"

"*If* they're Valentines!" The same fear struck them both at the same time. The Lieutenant added, "If they're Germans they haven't time to dig up their own mines. How about markings now?"

116

"Still too far to identify."

"Holding."

The Sergeant strained his eyes through his binocs. Now he clearly could see four ghost tanks firing. More mines burst. A daisy chain dominoed. Each mine explosion overtook another and another. Then the Sergeant made out the markings on the lead tank.

"Tiger tanks!" he said. "Can see four German thickskins!"

"We're on the way with Shermans!" The Lieutenant's voice was calm as he added, "Dig in. Let 'em pass."

"We sure as hell aren't going to try to stop 'em."

The Sergeant opened the turret hatch, jumped off the car with the radio, and ran back to the bend to join the Squad who were staring at the advancing clouds of dust and the mines being blown up.

"Dig in!" said the Sergeant.

Griff's stomach became a fist. "To fight *tanks?*"

"Ours'll fight 'em."

Zab's cigar juice flooded his mouth. "I'm getting my ass out of here."

Vinci's voice cracked. "Let's *go!*"

Johnson cried, "Let's go, Sergeant!"

"Their lead tank'll spot you."

The men ducked behind rocks.

"Their grenadiers poke behind rocks for AT guns." The Sergeant walked off, selected an area he figured viable, and began to dig.

Without a word the men joined him, and began to dig.

37

Mengershausen's binoculars were fixed on Kasserine Pass. He was pleased that the dark skies would keep enemy planes grounded; it was exactly what Rommel had counted on. The area in front of him narrowed to a bend. As his Tiger roared toward the bend, he made out what looked like a vehicle. He smiled. An American recon car or half-track had hit a mine. He had no time to send out detonating teams to clear the field. He knew where the mines were and he had to blow them up. He watched nine more mines blown in zigzag chain reaction. He directed three panzers behind him to chew up the minefields. He was delighted as a staggered daisy chain dominoed. Then he saw a movement on the American vehicle. A man carrying a radio jumped from the vehicle and ran to the bend and vanished.

Mengershausen assumed the man was a member of the crew. But assumptions were dangerous. The man could have been a scout for an infantry patrol. There was a good chance that around the bend were Americans, perhaps company strength. Perhaps AT guns. Perhaps even tanks. He knew that the major striking force of the American First Infantry Division was at Sbiba to amass strength with the British and French against what they had been led to believe was Rommel's main thrust. He came to the conclusion that any enemy he encountered around the bend would be lightweight —just a probing company. It was his responsibility to be quick, to see what he could and could not do. He could halt after blowing up the German minefield, or he could wait for his grenadiers, supported by the Wehrmacht, to investigate by foot around the bend for AT guns. He was impatient. What the hell! Even if he ran into American tanks, their 75s were no match for his 88s. If he halted his panzers this side of the bend, the rest of his division would be halted. Rommel himself would show up and raise hell with him for throwing the attack plan off its timetable.

The minefield was completely destroyed.

Mengershausen's Tiger reached the bend and halted.

To test any delay, always a nuisance, he would waste only one man. His panzer grenadiers, too valuable to sacrifice, should be saved for mop-up in the major attack. He smiled, knowing how much the Wehrmacht hated eating panzer petrol fumes. He decided to give one of the infantrymen the chance to inhale clean fresh air.

Schröder slogged close behind the lumbering, deafening tank, choking, fighting the toxic fumes, blinded by dust, and filled with anger. Being roasted alive in a

118

steel coffin didn't appeal to him. Neither did the Luft-waffe. If he were hit he would still have thousands of feet to fall. He preferred to fight on the ground.

Head bent, his helmet crashed into the tank ahead of him that halted suddenly. When the dust settled, Schröder saw that all tanks had halted. He moved away from the heat waves coming from the hated tank and slumped to the ground. The young soldiers moved away from the tanks they had been following and also collapsed on the ground for a breather. Their rest did not last long.

"On your feet!" the Wehrmacht oberleutnant shouted.

Schröder, Armin, and the thirty-five grumbling young faces of the Wehrmacht attached to the advance panzer group rose to their feet, prepared to kiss panzer asses. Instead, their oberleutnant told them to follow him. They marched past stopped tanks and panzer grenadiers in parked personnel carriers, and it took a few minutes for the German infantrymen to realize that they were the only ones on the move toward the bend.

Armin caught up with Schröder. "What's happening?"

"See that bend up there?"

"Uh-huh."

"We're going to poke round it for AT guns."

They passed more grenadiers in halted carriers.

"Why *us?*" said Armin angrily. "Why not their goddamn grenadiers?"

"They're Rommel's boys. We're not." Schröder jerked his thumb behind him. "Rommel's back there somewhere. Ask him, not me."

They followed the oberleutnant through the chewed-up minefield.

"What if we walk into American tanks?" asked Armin.

"We'll be potato pancakes." Schröder shifted his Schmeisser and grinned.

Armin forced a smile. He respected Schröder and in a strange way felt affection for him, but he also feared him.

They marched past the American recon car and

waited as the oberleutnant advanced to the point Mark VI to huddle with Major Mengershausen. The eyes of the thirty-five Wehrmacht were fixed on the bend.

"Schröder," the oberleutnant called out, "see what's around that bend."

38

The Sergeant had trained himself to never show the fatigue in his body. He was admired by the Squad for his physical endurance. But now the stabbing pain in his side outraged him, the weariness in his bones outraged him, the difficulty of breathing outraged him. Yet he showed no sign of exhaustion as he went from hole to hole, checking, rearranging the surface to blend with the terrain. He saw in his Squad's tense faces the fear of being crushed under the tanks. He made sure that the tops of their helmets were three feet from the surface.

He grunted final approval of the camouflaged holes and made his way back to his own hole and sat down on the edge with his legs dangling. He looked at the bend, then lowered himself into his grave. It was shoulder width and six feet deep. As he reached the floor with his ass and brought his legs to jackknife position, his rib was pierced by the brass knuckles of his trench knife. *Shit!* He shifted, made it worse, and fought its scabbard into the wall. Now the brass knuckles just grazed his rib. His thighs began to burn against his chest. Soon his legs would be asleep. His rifle pressed so hard and close against him it appeared that the two of them were poured into the same barrel. He was silent as he listened to the idling tanks waiting for their panzer grenadiers to check the bend for AT guns. He gambled on them making a fast survey before motioning for the mechanized coffins to advance. If his Squad did not panic when the tracks roared over them, they would live. If they got out of their holes and ran, they would be killed. His impatience made him stand just high enough to squint at the fine mist of sand blowing through the bend.

Schröder appeared around the bend with his Schmeisser.

The Sergeant was puzzled. The color of the one kraut's collar braid edging was not panzer-grenadier grass but Wehrmacht white. Schröder shifted his Schmeisser. The Sergeant watched the way the kraut held his weapon and the way he moved and it was like watching a tiger. Every step the kraut took filled the Sergeant with grudging admiration. The Sergeant knew—by the way he executed his investigation and rejection of every foot of ground—that this man was not going to settle for a cursory sweep. He was impressive, deadly, expert at his trade. It was exciting to observe a professional destroyer at work. He himself would have been just as careful as the German. When Schröder glanced toward Griff's hole, the Sergeant stiffened, strangely aware that his intense desire to shoot before Griff was killed was as intense as his respect for the kraut. This one had style, the kind the Sergeant would have liked in his own Squad. He felt a strange kinship with this kraut; they seemed so alike in their dedication to professionalism.

Watching Schröder, the Sergeant suddenly felt the chill of watching himself. Every movement was his; only the uniform was different. It was unreal.

Abruptly Schröder wheeled and vanished around the bend.

The Sergeant was disappointed. The man who had advanced with such exquisite skill should have completed his security check. That was where Schröder and the Sergeant differed.

The Sergeant took a long deep breath. His plan had worked. Suddenly he had the sickening feeling that Schröder had spotted Griff.

❖ ❖ ❖

Schröder had.

He had also spotted Zab, Vinci, and Johnson. He was sure there were more, perhaps five or six Americans. Squad strength. He admired the artistic skill taken to blend their pits with the terrain. He would have liked such a high caliber of combat men in his section instead of his young unskilled replacements.

121

He approached the oberleutnant and was about to give his report when the harsh impatient voice of Major Mengershausen barked with contempt.

"Well, you idiot, what do you have to report?"

Schröder's eyes shifted slightly to Mengershausen who stood ramrod straight in the Tiger turret showing the same arrogance every panzer officer had toward the Wehrmacht. It was a face Schröder hated. He could not control his rage.

"I am *not* an idiot, sir!"

"Report, damn it!"

Schröder thought, how pleasant it would be to shoot this bastard. No. Let the Americans do it. Since the Afrika Korps believed the propaganda that they were doing all the fighting in North Africa, let *them* fight. They were the elite. Schröder's brutal sense of warped humor made him feel good. Let the superior panzer grenadiers discover the Americans in the holes and shoot it out with them. It was *their* job to support panzers. Not his.

"No AT guns around the bend, major," Schröder reported. "Nothing out there to stop you, sir."

He did not lie. A few soldiers couldn't stop panzers.

"The man I saw must be running his legs off," Major Mengershausen said to the oberleutnant. "He and whoever's with him." He readjusted his goggles. "When I spot them I'll have a little target practice with my 88."

In his snake pit, Griff waited, jackknifed in terror, with weird images of his skull being ground into his kneecaps. His numbed thighs shook against his chest. What am I doing here? he thought. Why? Why did I let the Sergeant talk me into digging my own grave and waiting in it to be flattened paper-thin? I am making myself a corpse. I'm waiting here to end up nothing. Just waiting to be crushed, smashed, annihilated, a squashed gnat called Griff with no head, no flesh, no bones, nothing. Jesus Christ, what am I doing in this hole? Why did I put on this damn uniform? Why didn't I desert before they shipped me out?

Zab waited and thought about the most important chapter in his book: fear. He had hypnotized himself to stand away from fear so he could weigh it, observe it, attack it objectively. He was surprised by the way he had shut out the thought that whatever would be left of him could be soaked up with a blotter and identified under a microscope. He thought of FDR's *the only thing we have to fear is fear itself,* but FDR never dug himself a foxhole for a German tank to crush him, so how in hell would *he* know real fear?

Vinci was brought up to believe that fear of the Lord meant true religion. He never feared God and neither had he ever sought true religion. He was not afraid of death. He was afraid of how he was going to die. Few people knew exactly how they would go. He knew it would be in his snake pit, waiting for the German tanks. If he ever felt like praying it was now; if he were guaranteed he'd be alive before darkness came, he would pray. But he knew that thinking of such a guarantee was as foolish as praying. Twice before, he had tried, even saying the words aloud that he said as a child, but the stupidity of those words almost choked him. He knew what really mattered. Luck. Where the Germans drove their tanks was what counted. Vinci began to pray for the tanks to bypass his hole.

To Johnson, war was no longer a necessary adventure of kill or be killed. It had suddenly deteriorated into a self-destructive act as he waited in his grave to be destroyed. He found himself thinking of a red-neck back home who ate snakes washed down with red-eye then tossed a tied-up hound into a hole in the ground and ran over it with a tractor. The hound had no choice. Johnson did. He could have and should have fled. Now it was too late to run. Now he was that hound waiting for the tanks.

In his cocoon Griff listened to the idling tank engine. Suddenly he heard the grinding, clanking noise that became an advancing roar. Gritting his teeth, keeping his helmeted head bowed, he imagined the driver looking through the slit and aiming the tank toward his hole. Griff shuddered as he prayed for the middle of the tank to pass over him. But behind his prayer was the picture of a track dropping into his grave.

The hole shuddered; the roar seemed close enough for him to touch. He looked up and saw the sky and knew it was his last look. It was an ugly dark gray sky but from his grave it was blue and beautiful—the same sky that looked down on men in safe areas.

The Mark IV belly blotted out the sky.

Griff's scream was a whisper in the overhead thunder. Toxic fumes filled his black hole. Panic made him swallow them. Deafening waves in the dirt echo chamber bounced off the walls, crashed into each other, tore at his ears, drowned his mouth with spit, and shattered his tear-filled burning eyes.

Then he heard nothing.

The ass of the tank passed over him, and through the settling dust he saw the sky. And the top of his hole. *It had sunk!* He knew that one or two more tanks would level it. He shit in his pants. He knew he was deaf. The silence was short-lived bliss. He heard *another* tank coming and he leaped out like a bolt of lightning and ran, leaving his rifle and helmet and his grave.

"Tanks!" Griff shouted.

The astonished Sergeant looked up. Griff looked old, his face immobile, his eyes lifeless. *"Tanks!"* He repeated and vanished. The Sergeant jumped out from his hole. The Mark IV had passed and Griff was running from hole to hole shouting the word. The men popped up. Angrily the Sergeant hurtled toward them, trying to drive them back into their graves, grateful that thick clouds of tank-churned dust masked their flight from the second tank. But Griff's act was contagious. The men ran as Schröder, Armin, and the Wehrmacht came at them.

Schröder caught a flash of fleeing figures and squeezed off bursts of fire, but the dust grew thicker and he couldn't see a target.

❖ ❖ ❖

. . . Griff ran without shame. He would stop running when he reached Battalion.

In the Mark VI, Mengershausen spoke to his machine gunner. "Give him a burst." He watched Griff zigzagging through the dust clouds. The machine gun fired into the dust. A mound made the Mark VI swerve. Waves of dust and sand filled the air. Mengershausen was fascinated. The lone American was still running, streaking past a high mound and up it and over it, and then he vanished. Catching a flash of the top of Griff's head dashing behind the mound, Mengershausen knew the helmetless enemy was a shock case and knew that he, too, would have run from tanks like an insane man. He decided the Wehrmacht would take care of that crazy American out there when he got tired of running. Mengershausen spoke into the mike. "Forget him." Then three more Americans darted past his tank, followed by two more. It amused him to watch men running who did not know they were dead.

. . . Griff was going to make it. He knew it. He would be treated for shock, end up in Section Eight. He was not a shock case, but why tell Battalion? They wouldn't understand that it was normal for a man to run from tanks without shame.

Swain ran past him.

Swain was not zigzagging! It horrified Griff. Swain was hit by a machine gun. When Griff raced by him he knew why Swain was dead. Replacements always got killed first. Poor Swain would never see his nineteenth birthday.

Griff heard footsteps on his heels but did not look round. The footsteps were closer. He knew. Zab. Vinci. Johnson. Veterans never got killed—not if they zigzagged. He began to feel cold. He was sweating, burning up. He should be hot but he was cold and hungry and his vision blurred and he blinked and his left knee caved in and numbness crawled up his right leg. Hot air burned his open mouth.

125

What if Battalion did not put him in Section Eight? Desertion meant the firing squad. No! Not for deserters. For murder or rape but not for deserters. He'd live out the war in the stockade. That would be great.

He felt sick. He thought of the Sergeant. If he ever saw him again he knew what would happen. The Sergeant would tear his guts out for running . . . but they would be living guts.

The Sergeant stopped one of Schröder's bullets and tumbled into a shell crater that was showered with dirt by a shell burst. Tank after tank rumbled over the Sergeant in the crater, a hole five feet deep and wide enough to hold two men if their bodies interlocked. He remained lying in a grotesque position. His face was rigid. Blood gushed over his chest. He looked up at the dust sky. Tanks rumbled over him. He held his breath as fumes filled the crater. He closed his eyes, and when he opened them it was dark for a few seconds. A tank passed over him. He should be angry with Griff for triggering the run but he felt sorry for him, felt sorry for Zab and Vinci and Johnson. He did not feel anything for the others because they were green, they didn't know any better than to make themselves targets for a tank. He knew that soon the top of the hole would be leveled . . .

Deafened by an 88 blasting ten feet from him, Schröder was brushed by a Mark III. He jumped. He couldn't see the enemy in the dust. He knew he had killed three, possibly four of them. Suddenly Schröder was hit by a Mark VI machine gun. He fell in front of the advancing tank. The driver saw nothing but dust.

Armin spotted Schröder only because he stumbled over him. Dropping his rifle, Armin dragged Schröder out from under the moving tracks that demolished the rifle.

A Mark V bore down on them. Armin used every

ounce of strength to pull Schröder out of its path. Moving panzers were all around them.

❖ ❖ ❖

"*Tanks!*"

Griff's shout spine-froze every man in the advancing three platoons of I Company. Their march stopped. The Captain seized Griff, who wrenched himself free and kept on running, closely followed by Zab, Vinci, Johnson, and the rest of the First Platoon. The Captain's command was drowned out by shell bursts. The Company whirled and ran. Three men were blown up by an 88. The Captain was helpless. More shells landed. He ran. Everybody ran—away from certain death toward a chance at a few more moments of life.

39

The lizard was watching a fly investigate the corner of the Sergeant's closed eye; the rest of his face was under dirt and dust. The foul odor under the dirt didn't bother the lizard as its tongue gathered up the fly. Now the lizard investigated the eye, its tongue darting out again. The red-streaked eye opened. The lizard's tongue struck. The Sergeant's head moved under dirt. The lizard stood its ground. The head moved a little more and dirt on it tumbled. The Sergeant smelled his own stench and it was awful. He felt a stab in his breastbone, sucked in air, shuddered with pain. The fire inside him increased, the flow of blood stopped, and he felt he had turned to stone. He forced himself to suck in more oxygen and he looked up. Above him was about three feet of dirt. He felt the change of rhythm in his heart, moved his hand, and slowly it emerged through the dirt. He raised his hand. The lizard made a short scurry, stopped, stared. The Sergeant brushed the dirt away and the putrid odor from his blood-caked chest burned his nostrils and made him gag.

His hand moved more dirt, found his kit, and unclasped the cover. He could not move his other hand. With his teeth he tore open the envelope and sprinkled sulfa on his wound. He tossed a tablet in his mouth and fought for long minutes before he could get his canteen out. He drank. He clawed through the dirt and seized his other hand and pulled it up, then winced. He could not move the arm. He ground his body from side to side until he freed himself enough to make an effort to move his body out of the crater. He had no strength to stand up. He slowly began to belly up when a bullet flashed across his face.

The bullet was the lizard.

The Sergeant's weak breath went in a drawn-out gasp. Gradually, he felt the shock subside. He was not hit again. It was a goddamn lizard. He felt relief. Now he had to get out and get some plasma. He didn't know where he'd find any but he had to get it. He knew he had lost a lot of blood.

The lizard jerkily inched closer until their eyes were a few inches apart. With his fingertips the Sergeant gently pushed it aside, not wanting to hurt it, and again painfully he began to crawl up the dirt-sand wall. He shuddered after a few seconds and rested, his face flattened sideways on his hand. He sucked in strength, began to move up inch by inch.

The lizard charged, slammed his cheek, and blinded him with dirt. The Sergeant gasped, lost his grip, and slid down. His face tilted. Above was the murky sky. His heart pounded against the soft earth. Somewhere out there was plasma. The word made him forget the lizard and gave him the strength to try again and he gripped sand again and dragged himself up. The lizard struck. The Sergeant slipped down again. The goddamn lizard was beginning to annoy him. He struck out to frighten it off but he struck air. The lizard stared. Once more the Sergeant began his ascent. Once more he was attacked. Once more he slipped back. Annoyance turned into anger.

He seized a handful of sand and tossed it at the lizard to blind it. But even as he moved his hand, the lizard darted away in lightning turnabout. The sand fell on its back. The lizard turned and stared, its expression remaining unmoved. Mentally they stalked each other. The Sergeant held his breath. So did the lizard. The Sergeant could kill it with one blow. He tried. The lizard wasn't where the fist struck. Pulling his fist out of sand and earth, the Sergeant's anger turned into fury.

Again he raised his fist and brought it down, but this time he stopped it in midair to trick the lizard. The lizard hadn't moved. It simply stared at the fist in midair as if it knew the Sergeant was trying to trick it. The Sergeant slowly moved his fist in midair from left to right. The lizard's eyes moved from left to right, following the fist. The Sergeant suddenly brought the fist down, but a blur streaked past his cheek, almost knocking his eye out with the impact.

When the lizard started its own ascent, the Sergeant struck and did not miss. The blow sent the lizard back into the hole. The Sergeant was not going to let a goddamn lizard get out of the hole before *him*. The strange duel began as they each fought to be first. Slowly, without realizing it, the Sergeant deteriorated to the mental level of the lizard. Their battle in the crater became a contest of wits.

Deflated, exhausted, the killer instinct in the Sergeant hung on. His eye had been gouged but he had stunned the lizard with a blow. They were now two lizards taking a breather, each trying to figure out the next move to kill and to get out of the hole. They stared at each other. With a startling lunge the lizard attacked the red chest again and again, assaulted the face, then darted up the dirt wall and vanished.

The lizard's victory brought a grunt of pain from the Sergeant. He waited for strength to return and slowly began to pull himself up. Every inch he gained increased his agony.

Above him a human hand was waiting to help him up. He seized the hand, but it collapsed in ashes. The Sergeant groaned and bellied to the top. The owner of the hand was in the way. The Sergeant didn't have the strength to bypass it. The Sergeant couldn't move. He glanced up. Perched on a busted rib, staring at him, was the lizard. The Sergeant was trapped by a burned-out corpse.

Then he passed out.

Wearing dark blue with the Arabic number of their army medical pack, two German medics whistled, one echoing the other, as they treated Wehrmacht survivors who had been run down by Mengershausen's tanks. The first medic neatly completed a head bandage, leaving a triangular window for the soldier's vision and enough mouth room for food and a cigarette, then hunted among the dead for the dying. He spotted a big lizard perched on a busted rib staring at a body impaled on the ribs of a burned German. The medic kicked the lizard away, examined the Sergeant, and called for his co-worker who grunted when he looked at the enemy uniform and the Big Red One patch.

"American," said the second medic.

"Still alive. We're supposed to haul back *all* wounded."

"Pull your wings off. We evacuate only those who have a chance."

"How do you *know* he has no chance?"

"I know."

"The hell you do!" The first medic called for litter bearers.

They extricated the Sergeant and carried him past dead Wehrmacht and past two dead dogfaces of the First Squad and placed him in the German ambulance alongside the unconscious, bandaged Schröder.

40

The frail male nurse with clipped golden hair stroked the hand of the Sergeant as he slept under a Hitler victory poster. It was the fourth day of stroking and the seventeenth day after surgery. For the first time the Sergeant opened his eyes. They were still red-streaked. His mind was a shifting darkness, but clear enough to know where he was as he gradually inhaled the nauseating aroma of medicine, drugs, alcohol, disinfectants, and decay. A slight breeze carried the sickly stench of burning bandages and uniforms into the ward. He could make out German words spoken miles away. A tattoo of a naked man on the hairless chest of the male nurse caught his eye.

"How do you feel, Sergeant?"

Recoiling at the clammy fingers stroking his hand, the Sergeant said nothing, but he was impressed. The male nurse had a slight accent but his English was damned good.

The nurse read the Sergeant's eyes. "I speak excellent English, Sergeant. I went to Columbia University in New York City."

The Sergeant thought the nurse's neck looked like a long banana with a golf ball protruding from his throat. The ball jumped up and down with every word.

"For you the war is over, Sergeant."

The Sergeant wondered how long he could control himself.

"Your indestructibility is the talk of the hospital, Sergeant. Twice you were pronounced dead. Our surgeons can't understand what is keeping you alive." The male nurse brushed the Sergeant's cheek with his sweaty fingertips. "I adore supermen." His fingertips moved back and forth on the Sergeant's cracked and swollen dry lips. "How could a land half Judaized and the other half Negrified produce such a magnificent soldier as you?" He kissed the Sergeant on the cheek. "America is such a decayed country." He kissed the Sergeant on the mouth. "But you are a beautiful man."

The pale male nurse turned red, his eyes popping. He gurgled. The Sergeant's grip was steel. The thumb pressed deeper into his Adam's apple and he heard his own death rattle.

"I can understand you being horny, Fritz," said the Sergeant, "but you've got bad breath."

He released his grip. The gagging, frightened nurse staggered away from the bed, gasping, weaving past bandaged remnants of war-scarred Germans.

Among them was the sleeping Schröder.

A laugh made the Sergeant turn. The laughing casualty in the next bed was a young tanned German. He said, "He *does* have bad breath."

131

"You went to Columbia University, too?"

"No. I also speak French, Italian, and Spanish. We are more educated than you. All Germans are. The nurse was right. The doctors call you a medical freak, Sergeant."

"My rank got round here fast."

"Your stripes and uniform were burned, but your Big Red One patch was taken by one of the doctors."

"Why?"

"He collects them. He has the American Ninth Division, the Thirty-fourth, First Armored, Second Armored—he said your division was the best."

"Why?"

"Rommel said it was."

The Sergeant remembered Griff, Zab, Vinci, and Johnson running from Rommel's tanks. He wondered where he would be sent. He took a long pull of breath. The pain almost knocked him out.

The Sergeant had heard of dogfaces successfully making breaks from prison trains. He hoped it would be a train. Trucks could wait while Germans hunted for an escaped prisoner. But trains had to keep on the move.

There could also be a PW camp here—and that would make it tough if they marched or carried him there under heavy guard.

The Sergeant lay in the bed and learned nothing of the war, only that the Germans were taking every objective. One day he was wheel-chaired into a room where a battery of surgeons examined his healing chest wound and treated him as the prize patient. The male nurse never bothered him again. One night he was given a loose-fitting jellaba and ordered to put it on because there was nothing else for him to wear. He stood unsteadily and by himself slipped the long-hooded white tunic over his head and his chest bandage. Manacled and in sandals, he was marched out of the hospital to a half-track. He had only one possession: his dog tags.

Under heavy guard he was transported through the blacked-out Tunis to a heavily fortified school that was boxed in by electric barbed wire. He was marched into

132

a big stuffy room. Through unbarred windows the moon illuminated a blackboard chalked with cartoons and names of British outfits. He heard the unsteady breathing and snoring of many men. He slept on the floor.

Morning found him the only American among twenty-seven British and French voices arguing about their chance for escape. Each PW felt he was in command of the escape plot. But the hope of escape grew fainter as they discussed the thirty heavy machine guns, supported by one hundred Wehrmacht, surrounding the school. The Sergeant learned that areas checkering the ground were mined; that all together there were about a hundred and fifty PWs in the building; that classrooms were cells. He learned he would eat where he lived, in this classroom. Exercise was out. Bathing was out.

He lost track of time. Three men shared one loaf of bread, fifteen shared one tin of tobacco, each was given a dipper of peas, and at 1400 hours the French Red Cross brought macaroni, date bars, and one bottle of vino.

When a new batch of PWs shuffled in, the kommandant announced with a Bavarian accent, "All of you will be shipped to Sicily. Volunteers for work battalions will get extra rations."

The kommandant left.

Hoping to find friends, the new PWs called out the names of their outfits. An American voice shouted, "Anybody here from the Big Red One?"

Sitting on the floor, his back against the wall, the bearded Sergeant came to life. "Sixteenth Infantry."

The Big Red One patch pushed through British and French PWs, saw an Arab sitting on the floor, and looked around. "Who's the Sixteenth?"

"Me."

The American stared at the bearded Arab in the dirty jellaba. "You?"

"Yes."

"Twenty-sixth Infantry." He sat down by the Sergeant. "What the hell you doing in that Ay-rab blanket?"

"What happened at the pass?"

"Huh?"

"Kasserine Pass."

"We took it."

"We *did?*"

"Yeah. The whole Division counterattacked. We took Gafsa and El-Guettar and Tunis and chased Rommel right out of Africa."

"We took Tunis?"

"We sure as hell did."

The Sergeant laughed. It hurt to laugh. "I'm going to let you in on a military secret. *This* is Tunis! You understand? We—are—in—Tu—nis—*now!*"

41

Through his glasses, the Italian seaman in the crow's nest of the freighter *Garibaldi* watched the battle smoke on land two miles away. It did not impress him. Very little of what took place on land impressed Giovanni Lattuada. Even as a boy, when he was told by his gondolier father that the Lattuadas descended from the Goths who settled the lagoon a few hundred years after the death of Christ, it did not impress him.

The sea was his love. He saw nothing exciting about his unimaginative father with one oar at the stern hauling silly tourists under the Bridge of Sighs.

In 1915, on his fifteenth birthday, he ran away from the boredom of gondolas to sign on the freighter *Garibaldi*. Completely apolitical, when Italy declared war against Germany in 1916, seaman Lattuada's only interest was cheap *grappa* near Trieste. Twice, the *Garibaldi* came under Austrian fire on the Adriatic, and the war became a very annoying interruption to Lattuada. In his world of adventure on the high seas he couldn't understand why men found pleasure in the killing of other men. And his world was the *Garibaldi*.

Lattuada was happiest when in the crow's nest. In the crow's nest he was high, alone, part of the sea.

He didn't like the Germans manning the ack-ack and machine guns on *Garibaldi*. He especially didn't like the German gun officer Reichert who made no secret of his contempt for the "macaroni mariners"; who hungered for action on a destroyer; who hated playing nursemaid on a POW ship. Lattuada felt sorry for the *Garibaldi*'s Italian captain who never challenged Reichert's constant insults.

Through his glasses Lattuada saw the planes appear. When he was sure they were British Spitfires, he rang the alarm bell six times, then alerted the bridge by phone. The alarm was relayed to Reichert's ack-ack batteries and MGs.

Lattuada shrugged. He knew there was no reason for alarm because the three giant white letters—*P O W* —on the deck had always saved *Garibaldi* from Allied bombing and strafing.

But this time Lattuada was surprised to see German Messerschmitts intercept the Spitfires. Suddenly a dogfight was raging above the *Garibaldi*. Three planes fell. Lattuada watched a Spitfire eating the tail of a Messerschmitt diving at the freighter. Reichert also saw the pursuit and opened fire. Bullets sang past Lattuada. One of them hit him.

Bleeding in the crow's nest, Lattuada watched the crippled Spitfire arc, then streak down like an arrow, its smoking nose pointed at the *Garibaldi*. Lattuada felt no pain. He didn't mind dying in the crow's nest, but when he saw that the blazing Spitfire was coming down to wound the *Garibaldi*, Lattuada cried "No!" and died as the meteor roared past him and crashed on the deck.

Jammed in lower hold number two near the engine-room bulkheads, the Sergeant and the PWs heard the explosion at the very instant the hull shuddered. They didn't know the *Garibaldi* was a tinderbox.

Fire devoured the old freighter as more explosions rocked her. The Italians raced to get their lifeboats turned out only to be fired at by Germans who made up their minds to get into the lifeboats first. Flames engulfed Italians and Germans in battle. The Italian captain was cremated. The chief, a running human torch, jumped overboard. The *Garibaldi* was collapsing like a dynamited wall. She began to heel over.

Trapped in the flaming hold, the Sergeant and PWs busted through the burning door and clawed and fought their way to the deck. Reaching it, the Sergeant found men half blinded by flames. Ripping off his jellaba,

135

shedding his sandals, naked but for dog tags over chest bandage, he jumped overboard and struck the water just as another explosion shook the sea like a quake. The shock of cold oil numbed his arms, legs, chest. He was dashed against an overturning lifeboat that was filled with Italians and Germans. He was dashed against dead men, dying men, men with burned-away faces, men screaming. He had to get away from the burning *Garibaldi*. PWs jumped. The Sergeant was hit by a man. The Sergeant went down.

The dogfight continued in the blazing sky.

The Sergeant bobbed to the surface and forced himself to swim away from the sinking ship. The last thing he saw before the *Garibaldi* shuddered and vanished, sucking Italians and Germans down with her, was a dead Italian in the crow's nest.

Oil and water loosened his bandage. He stopped for a breather. He could see battle smoke on land in the distance. He breast-stroked like a robot, using every bit of his energy, and made slow progress. Ahead he could see the death plunge of a burning Messerschmitt. Five hundred yards from him the plane plowed into the sea. His spent body became warm. The heaving movement of breathing was gone and he knew he was losing blood. Part of the Messerschmitt beckoned. He saw no life around the debris. He sank, complete exhaustion corkscrewing him lazily, until instinct made him kick his legs and move his arms. He felt no movement, but he knew his legs were thrashing only because his mind willed them to thrash.

He surfaced, swallowing air with a death gasp. He didn't know if he made the fuselage on his own or if it had been battered by waves to him, but he clung to the big black white-bordered cross.

Something prodded him. A mine! Hanging onto Göring's broken bird, the Sergeant paddled with one arm. Two ominous eyes stared at him. The face was monstrous. The neck was puckered. It prodded him again and he kicked at it. He saw the armor plate as the turtle lunged at him violently, butting his wound again and again, busting it wide open.

The Sergeant laughed. Sapped of all physical and

136

mental energy, he was going to be killed by a goddamn turtle in the middle of the Mediterranean.

42

Tank Commander Gibbs, Second Battalion, Royal Tank Regiment, was riding point in his Valentine. Low-geared creaking Valentines followed him. He feared encountering Tigers with 88-mm guns in their snouts that could and did knock out Valentines at three thousand yards.

Moving through the ruins, he came upon a group of nomadic women and children. They ran from the British tanks in panic. Watching them, he recalled the story he heard about Kasserine Pass, when American infantrymen ran from Tigers. It was a disgrace, he was told. Such a rout had never besmirched the American army in its history. To Gibbs it was no disgrace. It was natural. *He* would have run from Tigers, and he was not infantry. He was in a tank. He had some protection. Not much from an 88. But some.

Since Crete he had had four Valentines knocked out from under him. This was the fifth. Yet to him they were one and the same tank. If he had been born in Germany he was sure he'd fight for Rommel as he fought for Monty. Or would he? The thought haunted him often. Four hours ago his squadron had run into several Valentine tanks only to learn, too late, that they were Trojan horses captured and manned by Germans leading panzers.

It was weird. Valentine versus Valentine. Gibbs and the squadron held the panzers long enough for Shermans to attack the right flank of the Afrika Korps.

Now he poked through the ruins of buildings and hunted for the enemy, moving down streets, crossing the Avenue Gambetta to the Esplanade. He halted. Two Arab kids were rifling a body on the beach. Gibbs jumped down from the Valentine and ran toward them. They fled. He overtook one kid and yanked dog tags from him. American! Then Gibbs walked to the body. He saw a dead naked Yank whose chest wound was wide open.

Then Gibbs saw movement of the man's eyelashes.

The Sergeant was still alive.

The medical team in the British hospital studied the X ray and stared at each other. What kept the Sergeant alive? Seven hours later a dead British soldier was covered with a blanket and carried out of the ward. A sister pointed at the warm bed. The unconscious Sergeant was placed in it. The next morning when he opened his eyes the sister was holding his hand and stroking it. "You are in a British hospital," she said. "The North Africa campaign is over. With God's help and a little help from men like you, we won."

Two British walking wounded came to say good-bye. "Well, sister," said one, "now that we've finally booted Rommel out of Africa, we'll be on our way home."

"You're Canadians?"

"Yes, sister."

"Where's home?"

"First Canadian Division, Eighth Army." He glanced at the Sergeant. "That the Yank who's supposed to be dead?"

"Yes."

Wearing British army shirt, Bermuda shorts, British high hose and shoes, and American dog tags, the Sergeant slowly walked among the Arabs in the crowded noisy street. He was suddenly seized by drunken French soldiers. Celebrating the victory, they all kissed him on his cheeks and forced him to drink from their bottle of wine.

"I speak English," said one to the Sergeant, "and with respect to all you British desert rats, we French were the ones that kicked Rommel out of North Africa."

"You're bloody right." The grinning Sergeant disentangled himself from them and moved on, passing whores inviting him into their cribs despite the Off Limits sign right next to another sign with an arrow: VD-Pro Station. A few doors away was the sign he was hunting: U.S. Military Police, Tunis.

The MP M/Sergeant looked up from his paper work and couldn't suppress his grin as he stared at the Sergeant's bare kneecaps. "British MP down the street at Place Bab-Souika. Reason I grinned is that your knobby kneecaps remind me of my wife's dimples."

The Sergeant grinned. "Those dimples belong to my outfit."

"Jesus H. Christ! A goddamn dogface! What the hell you doing in that limey getup?"

"It's all the limey hospital had. Where's the Big Red One?"

The MP stiffened with respect. "First Division?"

"Yes."

"Not in Tunis."

"Where?"

"Is that your outfit?"

"Yes."

"Then you ought to know they don't go round advertising their movements. It's an *amphibious* division."

"Where's the AGHQ?"

"What's your rank?"

"Sergeant."

"You landed at Arzew?"

"With the Sixteenth Infantry."

"I wouldn't let the AG know that if I was you."

"Why not?"

"Any beetle-crusher with combat know-how is shanghaied for cadre in the repple depple here, and there's no way you can get out of it. No way at all."

"Well, my General's—"

"His two stars pack no muscle here, Sergeant. There's a shortage of veterans. Ike ordered everyone not with his division to train wetnoses how to piss without getting wet."

The Sergeant sighed. "Thanks for the tip."

"No sweat. My cousin's a clerk at army. He'll find out where your outfit is. Say, were you at the Kasserine rout?"

"Yes."

"I don't get it."

"Get what?"

"No real American would run scared like that."

139

"Ever play with yourself in a hole waiting for a German tank to drive over you?"

The MP thought for a moment, then decided not to pursue the matter.

"Will you call your cousin for me right now?"

"No can do, Sergeant. He's on a trip to the coliseum at El-Djem. He took a couple Ay-rab guides with big tits. He'll be back in the morning."

"I've got to dump these clothes."

"Uh-uh."

"Hell, you can get me a uniform from QM."

"You better stay in that boy scout suit if you don't want to be stopped for papers. This is Limeytown." He gave the Sergeant some money. "Here's enough to cover drinks while you kill time. Café Balzac's round the corner to your left. I'm off duty at seven. Wait for me."

The Sergeant thanked him with a look.

"Forget it," said the MP. "Shit! After the war my kid'll ask me what I did in North Africa. Shit!"

"You feel the resentment?"

"From guys like you? Twenty-four hours round the clock."

"Makes you feel guilty."

"I *am* guilty. I'm nothing but a goddamn rear-echelon son of a bitch. A lucky son of a bitch."

"At Saint-Cloud my Squad was out on patrol. The point man was about thirty feet in front of me, scouting. He stopped and looked back at me and said, 'Hey, you rear-area echelon, what're you doing back there?' " The Sergeant smiled. "Anybody behind *anybody* is rear-echelon. I bet that's what you think of the men in London. And what do you think they say about the men in the Pentagon? There are about seven to ten men to back up each infantryman in the line. He's dead without that backup."

The MP felt better. He smiled. "You guys ain't as cocky as I heard."

"What did you hear?"

"I heard a Big Red One man say the U.S. Army was made up of the First Infantry Division and ten million replacements."

The Sergeant smiled. "He was right."

The glistening black bare-breasted barmaid brought the Sergeant a glass of red wine and in broken English told him how much she hated Germans and how much she loved the British. He paid her in Tunisian francs, told her to bring him a bottle. The wine was warm piss. He waited at a marble-topped round table in the corner of the small, dark Café Balzac, keeping his back to a group of British soldiers. He had nothing to worry about. They weren't interested in the stranger wearing one of their uniforms. The barmaid brought the bottle. He refilled his glass as three American replacements sat down at the next table. They were excited to be in North Africa, sad they missed the fighting, anxious to be placed in fighting outfits so they could kill Germans. They were young and loud. In less than fifteen minutes, they were drunk.

The MP joined the Sergeant.

"Your cock's been in mothballs. I got a rubber for you." The MP grinned. "I'm taking you to a house I own a piece of."

The Sergeant was impressed. "You're going to come out of this war a rich man."

"There's a Krupp in every outfit, Sergeant." He drank from the Sergeant's bottle. "You don't have to manufacture tanks and guns to turn a buck in war."

The MP's brothel, a three-story building in a narrow noisy street jammed with stalls, had a selection room reeking of sweat and incense, and there were twelve girls of all colors. They each wore the same blank look, the same jasmine flower over the right ear, the same transparent red blouse. But the panties were not the same. They were made from different flags.

"Meet my patriotic pussies." The MP playfully cracked the British flag on the girl's crotch. "Miss John Bull gives the best British head in North Africa." He slapped the Japanese flag. "Miss Tokyo made the raw-fish eaters back home commit hari-kari because they couldn't satisfy her." He brushed the French flag. "Miss Paris is the deadliest nympho in the stable." He patted the Italian flag. "Miss Rome'll take you on a trip that'll make you walk on your knees for the next twenty years."

The Sergeant looked at the American flag. Tall, white, blonde, twenty-five. "What did you wear for the Germans?"

"The swastika," said Miss America indifferently. "All cocks look the same to me. They salute the same, they shrink the same. You're no limey."

"Canadian."

"Bullshit. You're an American."

The MP grunted. "If he says he's a Canadian, goddamn it, he's a Canadian!"

"Okay with me, Charlie, so he's a Canadian."

"Where are you from?" asked the Sergeant.

"West Fifty-second Street, New York."

The Sergeant turned to study the Tunisian flag: a five-starred green Solomon's seal on a red field. The girl's dark flesh looked so soft. He wanted to touch something soft. He figured she was about nineteen.

"Oh," said Miss America, following his glance and noting his interest, "so you want to change your luck." She put her arm around Miss Tunisia. "This local will blow you to kingdom come with twenty-nine zigzig positions as a starter. And she speaks pretty good King's English. Read the sands for him, Calf Eyes."

The MP saw that the Sergeant was ready to go.

"And give my pal here some of that hashish to smoke," he told Calf Eyes, then turned to the Sergeant. "That stuff puts you on a magic carpet."

"Okay," said the Sergeant.

Calf Eyes took his hand and led him through a dimly lighted hallway into a red-rugged sitting room where, pushing back a multicolored beaded curtain, she invited him into her jasmine-scented crib. The corner lamp was weak, the floor pillowed wall to wall. She showed the Sergeant the toilet, a half-darkened perfumed closet with a hanging red bulb revealing a disk drain on the floor.

When he joined her, Calf Eyes was Buddha-squatting on the floor, preparing a hookah with cocoa brown hashish. He liked the sweet smell and minty cool taste as he drew the smoke through water.

"I'll read your future." She placed a red crock on the floor and sifted the sands in it. He watched her fingers make shapes, circles, figures, and before long he was on the flying magic carpet soaring through shadowland.

"You are going on a long journey."

He shifted his eyes from the hookah to her fingers in the sands.

"The snow will turn red with the blood from your heart," Calf Eyes continued softly. "Ah—I see you with a woman in a thick forest and you are making zigzig with her." She stirred, then suddenly stopped. She stared at the sand and pulled her hand away with a start. She looked up and her face filled with sympathy for the Sergeant. "The woman is a corpse."

43

The Sergeant dozed as he rode in the lulling sun, covered by dust, deaf to the rattling sidecar, deaf to the coughing of the motorcycle, deaf to the French driver who was cursing each time a bump almost made him lose control. The Sergeant was daydreaming about facing green troops and making a speech. The sin is to think you can buy your luck, he told them. You can't. Luck has nothing to do with killing or getting killed. Experience gives you 99 percent chance to make it. Nothing but experience. When you come face-to-face with a German, don't think. Shoot. And shoot again and again until you are sure he's dead and to make sure shoot him again.

He was being shaken by the French driver. It took a moment for the Sergeant to open his eyes. The sidecar he had squeezed himself into had stopped moving. Wearily the Sergeant climbed out, muttering, *"Merci beaucoup."* He watched the motorcycle's dust blot out a small side road.

He was in Algeria, a hundred miles from Tunis and about seven hundred miles from Oran where the MP's cousin reported the Big Red One in bivouac. The Sixteenth couldn't be pinpointed, but finding the First was all the Sergeant wanted. He felt good. He had beaten the cadre shanghai.

He began to walk west very slowly to regain the strength that Calf Eyes and hashish had drained out of his body. Still in Montgomery's boy scout short pants, he wondered if he'd made a mistake passing as a British soldier. No. He hadn't. Seeing combat-seasoned men was the best propaganda for green troops. It made sense for repple depples to snare veterans.

He lost track of time and distance as he walked. He got a lift in a U.S. 2½ ton sardined with GIs returning from Bône, learned they were en route to Philippe-ville, mumbled thanks with a British accent, and fell asleep again only to awaken in a replacement depot.

Moving past the motor pool, among GIs headed toward their tents, he was about three hundred yards from the road, dreading being stopped by an American officer to answer questions. Approaching the guard, the Sergeant heard a voice coming from his right flank. "You with the Second New Zealand?"

The Sergeant stopped walking, turned. Leaning against a jeep was a husky dogface. On his right shoulder was the "Red Bull" patch. The Sergeant had run into Thirty-fourth Division men, National Guardsmen from Minnesota, Iowa, and the Dakotas. From the MP he learned the Red Bull was badly hit at Faïd Pass.

"First Canadian," said the Sergeant. "Eighth Army."

"Where's your outfit?" asked Red Bull.

"Oran."

"You'll rejoin 'em in a few days."

"They said I can go now."

"They *did?*"

The Sergeant was in trouble. In a moment he would be asked to produce the papers. "Yes."

"Where's your transportation?"

The Sergeant kicked a stone with his British shoe.

"Hey, Collura," yelled Red Bull, "give this Canadian a ride." He turned to the Sergeant. "He's going to Bougie. Not much of a lift but it'll cut down your bunions."

The Sergeant smiled gratefully as he watched Collura leave a cluster of GIs.

The Sergeant was grateful that Collura was not a talkative man as the jeep took him to Bougie. From there a half-track gave him a lift to Bhada. He spent the night in a vineyard and, at sunrise, a truck hauling French foreign legionnaires to Sidi-bel-Abbès dropped

144

him off at the crossroads. He waved thanks. The tall, lean black soldiers wearing World War I khaki leggings tossed him a bottle of wine. He started walking toward Mostaganem. Again he lost track of time and distance. His feet were on fire and he felt winds blowing in from the open sea when a British tank slowed down for him. He took no chances so close to Oran and waved the tank on. He walked. A cart with empty wine barrels hauled him to eight kilometers from Oran, and he walked the five miles to find two young American MPs near the Sacré-Coeur Cathedral. He abandoned his masquerade.

"Where's the First Division?"

They reacted to the British uniform and the American accent. "Let me see your pass," demanded one.

"Better take me to your HQ."

The Sergeant was jeeped to MPHQ next to the neo-Spanish railway station where he was questioned. His story and dog tags got him transportation to the AGHQ where in a big office in Boulevard Clemenceau he found a sympathetic major and an unsympathetic captain listening to his tale.

After a long silence, the major said, "Your Division sailed from Mers-el-Kebir for Algiers."

The Sergeant reeled.

"We'll see you're issued an American uniform," said the major. "Your rank is Sergeant?"

The Sergeant was still reeling.

"Sergeant?"

"Yes, sir. Sergeant."

The captain spoke up. "I'll see that his Division gets the report that he's been assigned to cadre to train replacements, sir."

The Sergeant's face showed his despair.

The major saw the Sergeant dying. "Give him a shot, captain."

The captain gave the Sergeant a belt of cognac.

"Any man who covered more than eight hundred miles to rejoin his outfit," said the major, "deserves to rejoin it. Don't you agree, captain?"

After showering with soap that lathered, the Sergeant was given an ill-fitting American uniform without stripes or patch. He was fed hot chow. The major arranged transportation on an LST from Oran to Algiers, where the Sergeant learned that the Sixteenth was in the vicinity of Staouéli, about thirty miles from Algiers.

He walked.

An ammo convoy forced him off the narrow road. Speaking to an old Arab herding scrawny goats, the Sergeant followed the brown bony finger pointing to Staouéli. It was getting dark. A sudden swift wind raced past him driving dust clouds. He was hungry, weakening, his feet swollen as he walked on the rocky footpath. Twice he twisted his ankles. He sat down on a rock. The air was warm and dry. Another swift wind and the air grew cold.

He stretched out, angry that he had followed the Arab's directions. He was lost. Tomorrow he would make his way back to the convoy road. He brushed insects off his face, squashed a spider, but he couldn't sleep. What if the Sixteenth had pulled out of Staouéli?

He dozed, the thought keeping him from sinking into restful slumber. If the Sixteenth had pulled out, some-one had his Squad. He heard the soft voice of a woman singing "Lili Marlene" in German. He sat up, peering into the darkness, then found himself on his feet, making his way through a wadi toward the voice. He came upon a black woman singing to several children gathered round a dying fire near a tent. When he reached them, she stopped singing. They stared at him, frightened.

In broken French, he told them he meant no harm to them; he was lost, looking for Staouéli. With a ges-ture the woman invited him to join them. He squatted. The children stared at him. He looked at the woman. She was still, silent, like beautiful black marble. She gave him mutton and a bottle of red wine. The children watched him eat.

"You sing good," he said.

"Many nights I heard the Germans play it for Americans."

When he finished, she led him into the tent. The children followed. They huddled in a corner. There was no lamp. Moonlight lit three little faces. The woman pulled the Sergeant down on the ground and gave him the bottle. They finished it. She opened another. They got drunk. The children were asleep.

"No men here?"

She shook her head.

"Your children?"

She nodded.

"How do you live?"

"We steal."

They finished the second bottle. He went out and pissed. She pissed a dozen feet away from him. They kicked sand over the urine and went back into the tent and stretched out.

She spoke first. "You killed many Germans?"

"Yes."

"Are you sick of killing?"

"Yes."

"Live with me." She pressed closer. "Soldiers desert from the German army—American army—French army—Italian army—they wear jellabas and live with women in Algiers and Tunis and Oran and in the hills and in the Sahara."

"They will get shot."

"They are never caught."

"They *will* get caught."

"A German deserter lived with me. He called me Negre. I left him. I am not Negre. Feel my nose." She guided his hand to it. "Is it flat with big nostrils? Feel my lips." He did. "Are they thick?" She kissed him, her face buried in his. "You smell good."

The Sergeant fell asleep in the moonlight.

The Sergeant awakened to feel her lips running up his thigh. She had stripped him naked. He felt the sand in his toes . . . the rising excitement in his body. Her tongue flicked closer and closer to his stiffening sex.

The Sergeant felt the avalanche shoot through his body and he fell asleep again with the black woman sprawled across him.

The Sergeant found himself hard again. The woman was awake. The tent was fogged with animal sweat and hard breathing. The three little faces in the moonlight were still asleep. When he entered her he felt her teeth

147

sink into his flesh. But the pain was not from the bite. It was his left leg. He had a charley horse.

The Sergeant knew the black woman was in great spirits the way she took it for granted that he would stay with her. He was alone, resting, when he smelled the stench. He looked out of the tent and saw her trying to burn his uniform. He stopped her. She pleaded. She would make a jellaba for him in the morning . . .

But by the morning he was gone.

Hot water poured on men under the shower. Staouéli kids bunched together to watch the American soldiers' horseplay. I Company was naked. Arab women pounded uniforms on stones, ignoring their bodies. Under the shower, Griff stopped lathering as he caught a flash of a man approaching from the distance. He slowly thrust his head forward. Water scalded his back. He was transfixed. He didn't show astonishment. He didn't show delight. He could feel his body tremble and an emotion he could not quite identify. The man walking toward the more than one hundred naked GIs had a curious effect on Griff although Griff couldn't see the man's face. But there was no mistaking the way that soldier walked, the easy gait, the relaxed, swaying shoulders. He moved out from the line of men under the water pipes and walked, still holding the soap, toward the man.

Still under the showers, Zab, Vinci, and Johnson also saw the man. Like Griff, they stared without expression and like Griff they moved out from the line, still holding their bars of soap. There was no mistake. Led by Griff, the four wet naked riflemen passed the giggling Arab kids and the Arab women. Their pace quickened very gradually. Then the four riflemen reached the Sergeant and their naked bodies surrounded him. He was alive. He had come back. They all knew they would live to fight again, they would live because they fought with him, for him.

SICILY

Kiss my hand or cut it off.

—*An armless Italian to an armless dogface*

44

Leaving a gray trail from his cigar, Zab carried a scabbarded trench knife as he walked among Big Red One patches in the sweaty hold of the American transport. Not one of the chain-smoking veterans had honestly enjoyed the two-month respite. To them, the verdict had been rendered the day the campaign ended: somewhere the fatal bullet that missed them in North Africa was waiting for them in Sicily. The absent dead were envied by the survivors sitting at their own wake.

Replacements, on the other hand, were eagerly looking forward to action. To them the process of meeting the enemy seemed achingly slow. Their innocent adolescent toughness sustained them. Fueled by the belief that they would be heroes parading down the Main Streets of the U.S.A., they discussed the Silver Star, the D.S.C. and the Medal of Honor with optimism. They were too green to be disillusioned. The bravado and confidence that flowed at the repple depples now spilled over. One played "Colonel Boogie" on his harmonica. Four sang: "Hitler has only got one ball, Göring has two but very small, Himmler's are very similar, but Goebbels has no balls at all."

Pushing past the green faces, Zab knew exactly how he would describe these untried warriors in his book. He would devote one chapter to the "oatmeal invaders," amused with the observation that, to them, being in this hole was as natural as having cereal for breakfast. They had no reason to fear death by violence. They were young. He grinned. So was he. Once he too was an oatmeal invader.

A shoulder accidentally brushed the cigar out of his mouth. He crashed on his knees hunting for it. The search took place beneath a wall poster of an island shaped like a jagged arrowhead with its broken point to the west between the tip of Tunisia and the Italian mainland. Under the island was the face of Mussolini with one of his boasting quotes: "Sicily is so well defended it would be a nameless folly for anyone to try to invade it. *Mussolini.*"

Zab found the cigar casualty, licked the wrapper, revived it, and made his way over to Griff who was drawing a V-mail cartoon of Johnson posing with his rubber doughnut. Vinci was reading *Soldier's Guide to SICILY;* on the booklet's cover was a finger pointing at the island. The Sergeant, in a new uniform with stripes and Big Red One patch, was asleep, his helmet the pillow. Zab dropped the trench knife on the Sergeant's belly. Grunting, the Sergeant opened his eyes, saw the scabbard, and pulled out the trench knife.

Zab grinned. "Gave the supply sergeant a Luger for it."

There was no camouflaging the fact that the surprised Sergeant was pleased. He scabbarded the trench knife, closed his eyes, and smiled. The smile made his gums hurt. Not as bad as when he went to the regimental dentist. It was not an abscessed tooth. It was a long-standing pain that flared up sporadically. Periodontal infection, the dentist called it. One day, the Sergeant was warned, his lower jaw would appear out of line.

Then he frowned. He had paid little attention to the new faces, to their names, to their potential. The re-supply effort was adequate. He was full strength. It would be a waste of time to remember the name of each new replacement. To him they were all wrapped up into one dogface wearing the same patch. And most of the replacements would soon be killed.

All that really mattered was that his Four Horsemen were still alive. He never brought up the Kasserine Pass because the rout was triggered by shock and one didn't chew out the ass of a shock case.

They never talked to him about Kasserine.

A new face in the Squad, Denno, was struggling to make space in his bulging pack, trying to fit in a civilian roll of toilet paper. He was twenty-one, small and wiry.

Zab plucked the toilet paper from Denno's hand and examined it gently.

"Where'd you lift this?" Zab held up the toilet paper.

"From Eisenhower's personal toilet at the Saint George Hotel in Algiers," said Denno.

"I'll carry it for you."

"I'll find room."

Zab stared at the roll. "This is the closest Ike's ass will get to the fireworks." He tossed it back to Denno. "How'd you get into the Saint George?"

"I was a clerk at Allied Forces HQ."

"You mean you had hot chow every day and slept in a bed with clean sheets?"

"I sure did."

"What're you doing *here?*"

"I volunteered."

"Horse's ass."

Shep, another new face, shifted his 190 pounds and glared at Vinci. "Hey, Vinci, how come they let a wop like you in this outfit?" All you spaghetti eaters are for Mussolini, ain't that right, Vinci? What's a matta, Vinci, you no gotta the tongue?"

Vinci did not look up but kept reading to himself.

The Sergeant felt a familiar angry wave surging through him. *His* damn luck to have a Shep in his Squad. The twisted ailments of all the Sheps in the army created tensions and setbacks in every squad. Their prejudices planted distrust and confused morale. Tongue-whipping Shep would only kindle more hatred and bring revolt. Revolt brought lack of concentration

153

on the job coming up. The backbone of this invasion was the riflemen, and Shep was a rifleman. The Sergeant needed him.

Griff stopped drawing. Zab bit his cigar, waiting for Vinci to chop Shep's Adam's apple. Johnson pictured Shep on the floor with a dislocated jaw. But Vinci sat like a stone.

"Goddamn dagos!" Shep boiled hotter because Vinci ignored him. "I'm going to kill every garlic eater I see, no matter what uniform he's wearing!"

Shep was weaned on hatred of Catholics. At twelve he played finger-finger with a nine-year-old girl and hit her when he learned her sister was a nun. At sixteen he mugged a priest. At eighteen he vandalized Catholic churches. He showed such a remarkable talent for hating Catholics that he outdid his proud father, surpassing him on every count of overt bigotry. The legacy was a disease.

"You're right, Shep," said the Sergeant. "That's your name, isn't it? Shep?"

"Yeah. Shep."

Shep was startled. He stared at the crow's-feet crinkling at the corner of the campaigner's eyes, at the grim mouth that appeared friendly. Suddenly the Sergeant did not look old. He became, to Shep, a young ally who also hated the pope.

"You just kill every garlic eater you see when we hit the beach," said the Sergeant. "And forget Vinci."

Shep was disappointed. "He's a wop, Sergeant!"

"That's right."

"You think a wop's going to kill wops?"

The Sergeant's eyes blazed at Vinci. "If Vinci makes one wrong shot it'll be his last shot as sure as this is Saturday."

Shep grinned. "Okay. I'll leave that altar boy to you, Sergeant."

The Sergeant's angry wave receded temporarily. He closed his eyes. Griff resumed drawing Johnson. Zab's grin vanished in a thick cloud of cigar smoke. Vinci smiled as he turned a page. Denno was surprised that the Sergeant hadn't backed up Vinci. Denno had heard that Vinci was one of the Sergeant's Four Horsemen. The Squad remained silent.

"First chance I get," Shep announced to the Squad, "I'm layin' a wop with big tits no matter how old she is and make her sing, 'O Sole Mio.' "

Vinci thrust his rifle muzzle into Shep's laughing mouth and clicked the safety off. Shep gagged. Vinci spoke almost in a whisper. "I got a relative in Sicily and if I catch a bigmouth like you a thousand yards from her I'll blow your bigmouth head off." Then quietly he sang "O Sole Mio." Griff, Zab, and Johnson sang it with him. Vinci clicked the safety on, withdrew the muzzle from Shep's pain frozen, bleeding mouth, picked up his booklet, and continued reading to himself.

Shep's switch from a threatening bigot to a scared child was awesome. He was the only one that knew he had just shit in his pants.

"The first four assault waves will report to their boat stations," piped the Yankee voice through the ship's speaker.

The atmosphere changed. The men gathered up their equipment. Shep did not move; his balloon had been punctured by the fear that an Italian Catholic named Vinci masquerading as an American soldier was going to shoot him in the back the first chance he got.

"Put your rubbers on," said the Sergeant.

The wetnoses watched him slip a condom over his rifle muzzle.

Denno asked, "Won't covering it make it sweat?"

Griff replied, "Better sweat than dead."

The Sergeant grinned.

By the time the Squad reached their boat station, the motion of the ship had become violent, the Mediterranean angry. The wind shrieked at forty miles an hour. The night, thundering with navy guns, brightened the hostile horizon with crimson splotches. The quarter-moon sky vibrated with the roar of planes. The Sergeant slung his rifle across his back, muzzle down, and welcomed the gale that helped keep the invasion secret. The men, except for the BAR man, backslung their weapons. A navy searchlight blinded a plane. A navy gunner opened fire. The plane was hit. A navy officer shouted to hold fire—they were

C-478s—*American* troop carriers! The 504th of the 82nd Airborne!

Dogfaces and sailors were stunned.

Griff looked up. Figures silhouetted against the blazing plane were falling. The Sergeant looked up. A fiery engine was hurling down directly at him. He made a flying twenty-foot leap, flattening himself behind a shell storage next to the ack-ack gun. Men slammed into each other diving for cover. The engine plummeted into the sea.

The Sergeant got to his feet and saw fires along the Sicilian coast.

Griff got to his feet and saw bursts of tracers streaking through the blackness.

Zab got to his feet and saw crisscrossing coastal searchlight beams hunting for the navy.

Vinci got to his feet and saw the enemy searchlights doused by navy guns.

Little Denno was halfway up when he was knocked down by men running to their boat stations. Johnson helped him up. Shep was still on his face, hugging the deck.

From the plane, those paratroopers who could make it, hit the silk. The dead tumbled through the sky. One of them crashed headfirst on deck. In the glare of rockets, Griff stared at the charred skull. The eyes, hair, flesh were burned away. The skull hurtled Griff back to Sully's head in North Africa and Sully and the paratrooper melted into one another.

The Sergeant brushed past Griff, jerked Shep to his feet, and turned and saw Griff looking at the skull. The Sergeant knew what was happening to Griff. Determined not to lose Griff to Section Eight again, the Sergeant pivoted him roughly, slamming him back to the rail.

Griff saw small rocket crafts lowered. They smashed when they struck water. He watched their crews sink. Still haunted by the specter of Sully's head on the deck, he felt nothing as he stared at the drowning men.

When the navy guns stopped firing, the Sergeant knew that paratroopers were jumping in pitch-darkness to gain the high ground behind the beaches. He

156

wondered how that poor navy gunner who hit the plane was going to sleep for the rest of his life.

"First waves to your boats!"

Deaf to everything, Griff didn't hear the voice coming through the ship's speaker. Slowly he turned and looked at the skull. Suddenly jerked up and hoisted over the rail by the Sergeant, Griff found himself hanging onto the swinging cargo net. He was smashed against the side of the rolling ship, his dangling feet struggling to get a grip on the slippery wet rope rung. A face under a helmet was visible for a flash next to him. Denno. In one hand was his toilet paper. A giant shudder through the cargo net broke Denno's one-handed grip. Griff watched him fall into the heaving assault boat below. The boat looked miles away and so damned tiny. Griff became aware of I Company clambering down into boats that were bobbing alongside the ship. His shoes found the rung. The Sergeant climbed down past him. Sully vanished. Griff was back in business, a veteran invader now. He descended with seasoned agility, keeping abreast with the Sergeant. They both dropped the last five feet into the boat as it surged up to meet them. The coxswain was examining the stunned Denno, who got to his feet, unhurt. The coxswain turned his attention to the scout boat that was darting back and forth like a mother hen, checking her little assault chicks as they were swallowing men dropping down from the nets.

The Sergeant and Griff plunged to assist two sailors clutching the ends of the lashing net, and the four of them held the net taut for the rest of the Squad coming down. There were flashes of color. Green lights blinked at red lights and yellow lights with messages. Men on the nets swayed, their knuckles bashed against the ship. Voices barked commands through bullhorns. The Sergeant checked men and weapons in his Squad. The boat filled fast with men from the Second and Third squads. Heavier stuff came down the net with the Fourth Squad. Over the whoosh of rockets the Sergeant heard the familiar scream, yelled "Incoming mail!" and flattened. Men fell on men. The incoming mail was a shell from a coastal gun. It made a direct hit on an

157

ammunition truck. The truck was on an LST. The truck exploded. Chain reaction set off explosions. The LST mushroomed sheets of fire, illuminating crammed assault boats awash in rifles, machine guns, and bazookas eager to beat the drums of night. But their eagerness died. Men were shot up without getting hit. Vomit ambushed and demolished every invader; there was no way for any of them to fight back. They all knew that if their boats started the charge, the sickness would subside. It was staying put there, cramped, tossing and bucking and smashing against the side of the big ship, that was draining them.

Still the coxswain waited, his eyes on the scout boat.

The assault boats were racehorses. Their jockeys were coxswains waiting for the signal to lunge forward. During the agonizing wait, more rocket boats were firing on the beaches. The scout boat kept checking, speeding back and forth in circles. Suddenly it roared away from the ship and guided the assault waves to the beaches.

Griff felt for his life belt. He had it on. He checked his bandoliers, felt the ammo clips in the pockets. Each clip had eight rounds. Eight dead Italians. Would he be able to kill an Italian? Someone had asked him that once. Why kill someone who had no stomach for fighting? Griff looked at Denno pressed close, holding up his roll of toilet paper.

Denno watched Zab staring at the toilet paper and knew that Zab was waiting for him to get killed so he could have the luxury of using Ike's own roll.

Zab saw the toilet paper but wasn't thinking about it. He was thinking about his book and wondering how the hell he would describe a night invasion where, other than the familiar fireworks in the sky, there was so little he could observe. Zab glanced at Shep two helmets away from his. Shep would be in the book. Zab enjoyed Shep's fear; he knew that Shep was more worried about Vinci than about the enemy.

Shep was terrified as nose-to-nose he faced Vinci. Shep's manhood had been insulted by Vinci in front of the Squad. Shep read Vinci's face and knew that

Vinci was planning to shoot him in the back when they hit the beach, and Shep knew he could do nothing to protect himself.

Vinci didn't even see Shep although they were almost kissing. Vinci was sick because he knew his luck would run out on this night. Six months' combat in North Africa without a scratch. Right now, on the beach, Italians were conspiring to assure his death. He was not going to face Germans. He was not going to face the Vichy French. He was going to face *Italians*. He glanced at Johnson and envied the assurance in Johnson's face.

Johnson was assured of only one fact: his death within the hour. It was a miracle he had survived North Africa without being stabbed by a bayonet. He had gotten so used to new faces in the Squad turnover that they had become one face. By morning or in the afternoon a new face would replace his. He was going to drown or be splattered on the beach. Zab's prediction that the Four Horsemen would live was to be proven wrong tonight. There would be only three Horsemen left. Johnson saw his own grave and looked at the Sergeant and knew that the Sergeant was including him in the casualty count he figured before every action. Johnson was partially right.

The Sergeant figured 60 percent casualties. He was usually right.

The General of the First Division stood on the bridge of the transport. The assault boats were gone, but he imagined he could still see them in the blackness of the sea. This was his second time up at bat to spearhead an amphibious invasion. *His* battle of Africa had become history; but it was *their* graves in a clearing of El-Guettar, at Béja, in the valley of the Medjerda, and at Kasserine Pass that put him on *Time*'s cover. *They* had made him. No matter how much he talked about them, the article was always about him. Now, standing on the bridge, he imagined he could see the little assault boats heading toward the beaches. His men had been trained well. All he could do was what all generals did: wait.

Deep inland, north of Gela, near the ruins of Grecian temples, 416 German first-line tanks were parked, the brigade part of the High German Division. The command post was in a church where nets protected the German general and his staff against malaria-bearing mosquitoes. Phones were ringing, men were punching typewriters, officers were huddling over maps and reports. The German general listened on the phone, put it down, and turned to a noncom.

"I want the following to be distributed to every man and officer in my command." He began to dictate as the noncom typed. "A number of coastal areas have been shelled by enemy navy. It is evident that a landing will be made at more than one point on this island. We are just off the bomb-stubbed toe of the Italian boot. We are a stepping-stone to Italy. If Sicily falls, Italy will be invaded. If Italy falls, Germany will be invaded and your homes in the Fatherland will be overrun by enemy infantry. I am not going to let that happen. *You* are not going to let that happen. Wherever we are called, we will drive the enemy back into the sea. During the last days in North Africa I had the bitter experience to watch scenes that were not worthy of German soldiers. Panic and the spreading of rumors are to be eliminated. Withdrawal without orders and cowardice are to be punished on the spot. I shall apply the severest measures of courts-martial against such saboteurs of the fight for freedom of our nation, and I shall not hesitate to give death sentences in serious cases. I expect that all officers will use their influence to suppress any such undignified attitudes. I will personally shoot any officer running from the enemy. Conrath, Commanding General, Hermann Göring Panzer Division."

The nine Second Sicilian Grenadiers were obviously baffled. The tenth man, an officer, kept his bafflement to himself. They had been bombed by air and shelled from the sea. That made sense to these untried Italian soldiers. Their searchlights were knocked out by enemy navy guns. That made sense. But when more enemy planes passed over without dropping bombs, that didn't make sense. Why? Why hadn't the planes bombed them? One of the men voiced his thought: the planes were carrying enemy paratroops. British or American. Another man said that such talk was crazy. No army ever dropped parachutists at *night*. Not even the Germans. "Nobody ever dropped into Sicily from the sky and nobody ever will."

"Daedalus did," said Capitano Dante softly.

"Who, sir?"

"Daedalus—from Crete."

"When was that, capitano?"

Capitano Dante smiled. "It's just a Greek legend." He paused, hoping to amuse them and help them in their fear. "He was an inventor. He made wings for himself and dropped into Sicily."

The men smiled. They understood their capitano's thoughtfulness and his reverence for kindness. They were proud that in this Sicilian outfit was a man better educated than all those rich landowning bastards on the mainland. The men in the company didn't understand Capitano Dante's intellectual convictions, but they admired the way their fragile capitano survived the monotonous punishment of keeping physically fit. They felt secure under his command because he wasn't like the other noisy martinets who ran their companies brutally hard. *Their* capitano was quiet and intelligent, and intelligence in combat, they were convinced, meant more than just knowing how to shoot a gun. The men in the company would fight when the time came, but fighting men should be led by a *thinking* capitano and they had the best thinker in the Second Grenadiers.

Born of peasant stock, Capitano Dante was handsome and blond with a small soft golden beard. The thirty-two-year-old schoolteacher from Messina never showed any sign of hot Sicilian temper. He didn't act like a Sicilian; he never spoke with hand gestures.

He wore his brown-green camouflaged shelter half as a poncho on this hot July night, but the men never joked about it because they knew he was cold. They were worried about his cough. And he was pitifully underweight.

There was a long silence as the men pictured thousands of professional killers dropping out of the black sky to kill them.

161

"I hope Hitler's assassinated tonight," said one man. The others grunted, agreeing. Then he said, "But we have to fight for him."

Capitano Dante despised himself for fighting with the Nazis. He understood the seeds of German contempt for Italians. To the Germans, Italy "defected" in 1915 from the Kaiser to the Allies and luckily ended up on the winning side in 1918. The Germans never forgave the Italians.

But Mussolini! Capitano Dante couldn't understand Benito Mussolini. How did the one-time Milan socialist editor who loathed dictators become an ally of Adolf Hitler? How?

"Well," said a hawk-eyed man, "there's one good thing to look forward to. If paratroops drop in Rome they'll surely kill all our absentee landlords."

The men spat. Like all Sicilians, Capitano Dante had envious contempt for the rich mainland Italians who owned the island and wallowed in Dom Perignon on the Riviera.

Capitano Dante found the army a nightmare. The low level of the professional military mind shocked him. His commanding officers were all virgins in combat fighting. They fought the war from an officers' club in Palermo. Ant-brained, rigid disciplinarians, they were unimaginative toy officers who obtained their rank the way he did: through a friend. The disrespect he had for them was really for himself.

"Capitano—" said the gunner.

"Yes?"

"In May, didn't Field Marshal von Rundstedt visit Sicily?"

"Yes."

"He said that a hundred German bombers were being shifted here from Norway, didn't he, sir?"

"Yes."

"Where are they, sir?"

Capitano Dante shook his head.

The gunner blanched. Everywhere things had gone wrong for Italy: the army was inept, the air force was obsolete, the fleet was a phantom navy. He thought of his young brother on the battleship *Roma,* hiding for three years with the rest of the Italian fleet in their

162

rear bases, afraid to tangle with British warships. Three years of hiding! How humiliating! The gunner wondered if *he* would hide at the sound of the first British or American shot. Quickly he removed the question from his thoughts.

A frightened soldier poked his head in through a swarm of flies and shouted, "Capitano, we are being invaded!"

Commanding a coastal defense company, Capitano Dante was expected to give a dramatic order. But *what* order?

Self-doubt struck terror among them. How would they face the enemy in combat? The immediacy of the question aged every man. Rommel himself had said that, if the time came, the Italians wouldn't even have the stomach to fight for their own land.

The time *had* come. The men looked at Capitano Dante.

"Send up a flare," said Capitano Dante, knowing he could not kill a human being for *any* reason. His birth as a killer was going to be a miscarriage.

45

Blackness burst into blinding daylight. Assault boats became glaring targets charging toward their touchdown areas. The scout boat spewed up waves as it wheeled round on its return to the ship to guide in more invaders. The flare in the sky also illuminated the faces of the defenders of Sicily. It revealed their three-inch *femme fatale* firing through the big aperture in the pillbox. At the same time, Breda heavy machine guns fired through the slits. From dug-in positions, mortars, submachine guns, and rifles fired. The deafening crack of Italian weapons reverberated with confidence. Tonight the Italians would overcome their poor reputations as fighting men.

Through a slit, Capitano Dante watched the Sergeant's lead assault boat suddenly lurch upward and stop, stuck on a sandbar. Capitano Dante knew the contest was unfair. The German flares stockpiled by the Second Grenadiers would decide the outcome of the invasion. The flares were the best shield against the enemy in the water who had no chance against the Very signal pistol cartridges that burned for six seconds from a height of approximately 250 feet. Dante's crafty gunner concentrated on spewing shells on moving boats.

"The one stuck on the sandbar," said the gunner, "isn't going anywhere." He was *enjoying* this. "Not until I blow it off."

With sickening fascination Capitano Dante saw a giant swell slam the bow of the boat on the sandbar. The boat shuddered but remained stuck. He saw machine guns spatter bullets at the boat. With horror he saw a speeding craft explode. Pieces of the craft and pieces of the men flew into the air. He pictured them hitting the sea floor, trapped, drowning, and he saw them later, washed ashore in rag doll postures and the Second Grenadiers celebrating with vino in the sun. He felt like throwing up because he was a part of this massacre. He glanced at his watch. It was 2:40 A.M.

"We won't need those German bombers now, capitano!" The cocky gunner fired. The echo of the blast ricocheted off the walls of the pillbox.

The Sergeant's boat shook with reverberations from the close shell burst. He timed the flares. Every ten seconds the sky was filled with a blinding hot light for six seconds. He had ten seconds of darkness to make any kind of progress. When a flare directly above him began to weaken, he shouted *"Now!"* and the two sailors lowered the heavy creaking ramp. The bottom of the ramp was three feet above the water. In the darkness the Squad, holding rifles, their helmet chin straps hooked, trailed the Sergeant down the ramp and jumped and fell into water six feet deep. The coxswain and two sailors, knowing their boat would be hit any second, decided to abandon her and they followed the rest of the dogfaces down the ramp.

The men advanced slowly. Machine guns blazed away furiously.

Pint-sized Denno held both arms high above his sub-

164

merged helmet. His hands were all that could reach the surface. Shell detonations hit him like an earthquake. He stumbled, gulped water, was struck by another undersea avalanche, and saw shadowy apparitions made visible by flare light. He lowered his hand, clutching the toilet paper in the waterproof bag so that he could inflate his life belt, but the release clasp failed and the life belt slipped away from him.

He thrust his toilet paper above the water.

In the 2:43 A.M. flare on July 10, 1943, the first casualty in the Squad's invasion of Sicily on the beach at Gela was the roll of toilet paper that was shot out of Denno's hand. Zab grabbed the toilet paper, sank his teeth into the plastic bag, kept his rifle above water, and with his other hand probed, found dead weight underwater, and seized and dragged Denno through the darkness. In the 2:44 A.M. flare a bullet zinged the toilet paper out of Zab's mouth. With Vinci's help, Zab pulled Denno to breathing height. The toilet paper was lost. And so was Shep, moving away from the beach, panicky, scared, no longer obsessed with killing wops. Johnson grabbed him, froze him, and waited till the flare fizzled out. He turned him round toward the beach and for ten blessed seconds of darkness the Squad labored against the waves, freezing in the flares, every eye on the back of the Sergeant.

At 2:45 A.M. the Sergeant and his Squad hit the beach, shed their life belts exactly when and where scheduled to shed them, and hugged the sands. They felt alone. Not a man believed that more assault waves were landing alive. Not a man gave a damn that Operation Husky, the largest triphibious effort undertaken by the Allies, or in world history, was perfectly timed. Not a man gave a damn that somewhere the Third Division and the Forty-fifth Division were touching down, that somewhere the British were touching down. The feeling of being alone, the Sergeant understood, was typical in a wet invasion. And though he was aware that they were not alone, he too felt isolated and abandoned.

As another boat touched down, two new men in the Squad were hit. They flanked the Sergeant. He shouted for a medic. A bowlegged medic waddled to

165

the two casualties who were being relieved of their bandoliers and grenades by the Sergeant. The medic checked their wounds. The Sergeant pinned their bandoliers and grenades on himself. The flare began to die. The medic turned away from the two men. They died with the flare. The Sergeant grunted. His Squad was down to ten now.

The stunned tough Lieutenant, reeling from the hot mortar fragment that tore off part of his mouth, gathered up the rest of his Platoon. The flare died. His task was to build up enough fire to get the bazooka close to the pillbox. With slurred speech, spitting blood, he gave the Sergeant a D-day present: the pillbox. Then the Lieutenant deployed the rest of the men to tackle enemy submachine gunners and riflemen. A hot fragment from the same mortar had bounced off the Sergeant's helmet and burned the hand of his bazooka loader. The Sergeant studied the pillbox in the glare of the flare. Situated two hundred yards inland, the gradual rise to it gave scant cover. He gave brief orders to his Squad, pointed, then waited for the flare to die. The six seconds seemed like sixty.

"Now!"

Zab and a pale-faced replacement pants-presser from Albany, New York, fired at the big gun aperture. Johnson and Denno emptied clips at the left machine-gun slit covering the advancing two-man bazooka team. Griff, Vinci, and Shep zinged bullets at the right machine-gun slit covering the Sergeant's zigzag grenading of a mortar and a submachine gunner.

When a flare appeared the men froze. When the flare died the men resumed. In interrupted darkness the Sergeant and his Squad leapfrogged like threads of a web toward the pillbox, covering one another, clawing a path for the bazooka through the defenses fronting the pillbox. They paused only in the light of the flares.

Griff maneuvered closer to the Sergeant, even passing him, firing at the slit. There was no emotion, no hesitancy because he couldn't see the enemy faces in the pillbox.

Zab thought about his novel. How many ways could

166

he describe blackness? Johnson decided no more wet touchdowns. Never! He hated water behind him, there was no place to pull back. Vinci wondered how many Sicilians had relatives in the States. Shep's courage returned and he wondered who'd be the first in the Squad to kill a wop. Denno wondered what Eisenhower was doing to kill time while he risked his life every second.

The bazooka team advanced, one man carrying the tube that was open at both ends, the second man hauling the rockets. The launcher weighed ten pounds and the rocket could punch a hole in armor plate one inch in diameter and ten inches deep. The team felt nothing for the men in the pillbox.

The Sergeant was pleased with the replacements. They were moving with precision. He was sure that after the pillbox was knocked out, he would have a well-oiled Squad. But he wasn't 100 percent pleased with Shep. There was no doubt in the Sergeant's mind that his Squad would be better off if Shep got killed on the beach.

Second Grenadier Vito Ariosto, twenty-year-old tarantella dancer who won last year's tarantella whirl contest in Marsala with his nineteen-year-old sweetheart, was a hundred yards in front of the pillbox. His ambition was to go to America and be a cowboy. More than anything else in the world he hated his Mannlicher-Carcano rifle. It weighed nine pounds but it felt like ninety.

In the glare of the flare he saw frozen targets of men. He fired his rifle at every statue.

As the flare sputtered out he caught a flash of Griff zigzagging toward the pillbox. Ariosto waited ten seconds. When a flare made Griff freeze into a prone target less than twenty feet away, Ariosto squeezed the trigger. His rifle jammed. In the falling brightness he and Griff stared at each other. It was only for a second, but in that second Griff could have but did not shoot the man he was aiming at. Griff saw the face of Ariosto too clearly. Ariosto, in that same second, knew he was dead if he didn't use the six-shooter he always carried. He reached for his gun fast, like a Western movie hero, when the Sergeant's bullet shattered Ariosto's collarbone.

The stunned Ariosto raised his six-shooter that now weighed a ton. He was covered with blood when he pulled the trigger and blew off half of his own face.

46

Slowly lowering his binoculars, Capitano Dante turned away from the slit. He had identified the Americans by the shape of their scattered helmets. He shivered. The poncho didn't help. He'd had enough. He could no longer watch more of the smashed, smoldering little boats sacrificing more Americans to be blown up. In the deadly light of the flares he had seen their Red One shoulder patches. Every little brown mound asleep in blood was a dead American.

He walked slowly to one of the four cots and sat down. On the floor was a depressingly dim glow from the lantern. On the walls were graffiti, Italian slogans, drawings, pictures of Jesus, and nudes from magazines. Why didn't the Americans show the white flag? They were being amputated, mauled, confused, and beaten. Their invasion was a failure.

He sadly looked up at the exhilaration of his men. Each one burst with pride as the noisy killing went on and on. They feasted on American blood like wolves. Wolves? A wolf will not make war against another wolf. How did the will to kill a human begin? He had never found the answer. He was one of the assassins with rank. No matter that he was not personally firing the big gun or the machine gun. He was an assassin. And he would have to live with this stink of victory for the rest of his life.

"Capitano!"

The first casualty from a ricochet in the pillbox staggered toward Capitano Dante when an explosive quake busted the eardrums of every man. Chunks of flying concrete knocked them off their feet. A second explosion rocked the pillbox. The blast blew the gunner ten feet. He crashed on Capitano Dante. A chunk of concrete exploded the back of a man's head. Hot metal tore a big blood vessel in the brain of the big gun's loader. A third rocket plowed past the big gun, blowing a hole in the domed roof. Then, in the smoking debris of the wounded pillbox, there was silence.

Unwinding, snakelike, Capitano Dante rose from the dead and stood in the dust and smoke. He saw an arm, a leg, a head in the flare light. He saw a body with a piece of metal driven into its back, both hands missing, its arms around the gunner whose torn face dangled on a giant chest hole gushing blood, breastbone sticking out. Through the smoke, Capitano Dante stared at the big silent gun. The world was silent outside the pillbox. All firing had ceased. It was as quiet as a tomb. He was bleeding from his ears. He was deaf.

The flare died.

In darkness, twenty-five yards from the pillbox, the bazookaman held the tube on his shoulder. The loader reached for another rocket.

"Save it," said the Sergeant; then, "Shep, check the front. Vinci, Johnson, check the rear."

Shep was himself again as he eagerly crawled up over chunks of concrete. Vinci and Johnson maneuvered to the back of the pillbox.

Capitano Dante, standing there in the dying smoke, didn't hear Shep climbing up to the remains of the big gun's aperture. Neither did he hear Vinci and Johnson moving through the rubble behind him. In the flare, Capitano Dante saw Shep looking down at him from the big gun.

"Tutto finisce," said Capitano Dante.

Shep fired.

Capitano Dante's instant corpse crashed on its back, its legs splayed. Three feet from him were Vinci and Johnson.

"What'd he say?" Johnson asked.

"Tutto finisce," said Vinci, staring at the grinning Shep.

"What's it mean, Vinci?"

"Everything finishes."

The flare died.

Vinci's voice filled the darkness. "Shep."

169

"Yeah?"

"He was surrendering."

"He was a wop."

Silence in the darkness. Shep waited for Vinci to shoot him. Only in the dark would Vinci have the guts.

A flare showed Shep and Vinci staring at each other.

The Sergeant pushed through the debris. "All dead?"

Shep, still staring at Vinci, said, "Every goddamn dago."

"Move out. Battalion's touching down. Six pillboxes been blown. K Company's taking care of the flare shooters. We've got to give muscle at an airfield."

Shep and Vinci moved out. Johnson remained, his eyes fixed on Capitano Dante's handsome face in the glare.

"Let's go, Johnson."

Johnson didn't move.

"What're you staring at?" The Sergeant was impatient.

"He reminds me of somebody." Johnson pointed at the face as the flare died. "The son of a bitch looks just like Leslie Howard."

Two Messerschmitt fighters had turned into burning black cigars. A Heinkel exploded. Paratroopers fired grenade launchers and rifles and submachine guns. Others threw grenades. Flaming planes and explosions were the background for the streaking silhouettes of the Sergeant and Squad running with the Lieutenant and his understrength First Platoon. The platoon sergeant was next to the radioman. The Platoon reached paratroopers who were fire-fighting enemy infantry, defending the airdrome.

The paratroop captain, relieved to see support, stopped firing his carbine. "Eighty-second Airborne."

"First Division," said the Lieutenant. "My Company's moving in on your right."

"They'll run into a lot of people. How many bazookas with you?"

"One."

The paratroop captain pointed, his finger almost poking out Denno's eye. "Horse-drawn 150 howitzer."

"By the hangar?"

"Left of it."

"How many people in the hangar?"

"Don't know. Two heavy MGs there."

"Kraut or Italian?"

"Don't know."

"How're things on the beach?"

"Third Division hit Licata, Forty-fifth hit Scoglitti."

"Where are we?"

"Near Gela."

"We've been lost since we jumped."

"See you, captain."

The Lieutenant led his Platoon across the landing strips that had been cut out of wheat fields. He spotted the howitzer firing at paratroopers on the far side of the field. Buildings were blown up. The sky was on fire. Three planes, side by side, made a bonfire explosion illuminating a Junkers 88 long-range twin-engine loaded bomber that was lumbering across the field for takeoff, its machine guns firing at running men.

Every belly in the Platoon hit hard and flat, firing rifles at the bomber. In its direct path were three men: the bazookaman, his loader, and Denno. The bazookaman raised himself on one knee, lifted the tube on his shoulder, and was hit three feet from Denno. The bomber, four hundred yards away, picked up speed.

Denno picked up the tube and held it on his shoulder, balancing himself and the bazooka on one knee. The loader shoved in a rocket and slapped Denno's helmet. The bomber was three hundred yards away, its machine guns firing. Denno's half-paralyzed finger numbly felt the trigger in the sweaty handgrip. He hoped he knew what he was doing. The bomber was two hundred yards away. Denno pulled the trigger. The electrical primer sparked off the rocket. There was no recoil.

Denno missed. The rocket hit a burning building.

The loader shoved in another rocket and cracked Denno on the helmet. The bomber was a hundred yards away, its wheels lifting, when Denno fired. The engine exploded. The Junkers 88 gasped and shuddered.

171

A second explosion and a third and a fourth turned the entire airfield into a brilliant blinding inferno as pieces of the blazing bomber showered the fleeing Lieutenant and his Platoon. He led them toward a big repair shed a hundred feet from the hangar.

They reached the shed. The men checked their ammo and grenades.

"Who fired that bazooka?" said the Lieutenant.

"A little guy in the First Squad," said the platoon sergeant.

"Denno," said the Sergeant.

Above him on the shed was a poster of Mussolini and Hitler standing side by side. They were smiling.

"Denno!" the Lieutenant shouted.

Denno pushed through carrying the bazooka. His rifle was backslung. Behind him was the rocket loader.

"Yes, sir! I'm Private Denno, sir!"

The Lieutenant pointed at the active howitzer. "It's about two hundred yards away. Can you hit it?"

"No sweat, sir."

"Okay, hit it."

"No, sir."

"What?"

"I won't kill no horses, sir!"

The Sergeant smiled.

"I'll fire it, Lieutenant!" Shep arrogantly grabbed the bazooka, dropped down on one knee, held the stovepipe on his shoulder, and aimed at the howitzer. The loader shoved in a rocket. The Sergeant pushed men away from the rear of the tube. The loader cracked Shep on the helmet. Shep fired.

He missed the howitzer. The rocket exploded behind the gun. Horses ran berserk across the airfield. Denno watched the horses in agony.

The two heavy machine guns opened fire at the shed from the hangar's entrance. Twenty feet on their flank a plane was burning. The howitzer lobbed in a 150-mm shell that wailed over the heads of the Platoon and detonated a stockpile of petrol tanks 150 yards behind the shed. Smoke from clouds of exploding fire reached the Platoon.

"Only one rocket left, sir," said the loader.

Denno seized the bazooka from Shep.

"Give him noise," said the Lieutenant.

The Platoon opened fire, pinning down the two heavy machine guns at the hangar as Denno moved into an exposed position and dropped on one knee. The loader shoved in the last rocket, slapped Denno's helmet, and dived back behind the shed. The noise of the Platoon firing over his head and on each side of his head drove Denno crazy, but he forced himself to take his time aiming. Another 150-mm shell from the howitzer screamed over the shed and burst a hundred yards from the men, and they knew the third shell would get them as they kept up their covering fire for the bazooka.

Denno fired.

A direct hit on hundreds of 150-mm heavy explosives that were neatly stacked by the howitzer obliterated everything in a furnace of red and white and black explosions. The Platoon stopped firing and took cover behind the shed. Hypnotized, Denno stared at the result of his aim. The loader ran to him and pulled him back to the shed and enthusiastically kissed the embarrassed Denno on both cheeks. The men smiled. Their smiles died as they saw a human torch running from the holocaust.

The human torch was screaming as he fell.

An insane horse emerged through the smoke and galloped over the human torch, kicking the man into the air. The horse was struck down by an incendiary shell fragment. The horse shrieked as smoke rose from its body.

Denno, watching in horror, unslung his rifle, but he couldn't shoot.

The Sergeant looked at Griff. Griff fired his rifle. The horse stopped shrieking.

The Lieutenant waited for the men to check their ammo again. *"Now!"* he shouted. They fired at the two machine guns, covering the Sergeant and Squad as they zigzagged toward the hangar hurling grenades on the charge. The machine-gun crews were dead when the Sergeant and the Squad reached the side of the hangar ten feet from its entrance. Above them on the wall was a thirty-foot face of the helmeted Mussolini, jaws clamped shut in heroic expression, Italian words painted below him.

The bazooka loader poked his head inside the hangar and was killed by one rifle shot. The hollow echoes reverberated throughout the hangar as a small blue egg-shaped grenade was hurled out of the hangar. The concussion grenade burst. The men spread out. Denno, staring at the dead loader, blew his top, ran to the entrance, and fired into the hangar. He was cut down by a fusillade.

The Sergeant told Vinci to make it behind the burning plane. He lobbed two grenades into the hangar. Their explosions covered Vinci's run past the entrance. He dived behind the burning plane. From his position he could make out many figures in the hangar. A blue concussion grenade slammed Vinci to the ground. After a moment of collecting his balance, he found his left hand in pain, useless. He tried but could not pull the pin grenade with one hand.

"Throw me a live one!" Vinci shouted.

The Sergeant discovered the men were out of grenades. All but Griff. The Sergeant took in the positions of Zab, Johnson, and Griff.

"Griff!" the Sergeant yelled, "throw live ones to Zab!"

"*Live* ones?" Griff stiffened. The short fuse would explode in five seconds.

"*Throw 'em!*"

Griff unhooked a fragmentary grenade from his bandolier, pulled the ring, and threw the pineapple to Zab. Zab threw it to Johnson who threw it to the Sergeant who threw it to Vinci who fumbled the catch. He hit the ground, rolled as the grenade burst.

"Throw 'em!" yelled Vinci, getting back into position. A "live" one was thrown. This time he caught it and grenaded the enemy with forty metal slugs bursting in all directions. The live grenade relay was repeated, split-second timed so that a hot grenade was always in the air. When Vinci dropped the last grenade by fumble he scooped it up and hurled it. It burst in mid air but demolished the last of the enemy infantry a few feet from the entrance.

The fighting stopped suddenly on the airfield.

Cries of "Medic!" filled the air.

Shep went into the hangar. Stunned to find so many dead enemy, he emerged and eyed Vinci with admiration. "Jesus Christ, Vinci!" said Shep. "You sure killed a lot of krauts! I never saw so many dead krauts!"

Vinci walked past him, picked up a green-plumed pith helmet near the entrance, and held it up in front of Shep.

"They're wops," said Vinci.

Shep took the pith helmet and stared at the green plume. Shame filled his face. "I'm sorry, Vinci—"

A wounded Italian lifted his head, lifted his weapon, and aimed at Shep standing ten feet away fom him.

"I'm really sorry," Shep said chokingly.

The Italian fired. Shep fell with the green-plumed pith helmet still in his hand. Griff shuddered at the squishing noise of Vinci's rifle butt smashing the head of the Italian.

Vinci dropped down on one knee, seized Shep by his shirt front, and pulled him up to a sitting position. Shep was dead. Vinci whispered to the dead man.

"You died a long time ago, you bastard."

47

The Sergeant lay flat on his back off the narrow dirt road. He was snoring. Nearby slept his exhausted Squad. The tension of nine hours of fighting was behind them as they replenished their strength.

The Sergeant's head was on his helmet.

An ant crawling across his face awoke the Sergeant. He brushed off the ant, felt more of them, brushed them off, and as he sat up discovered an army of large foraging harvester ants carrying seeds to their mound. He moved away and settled back to sleep when he heard a barking cough coming from his Company's area. He turned his head and saw the three-quarter-ton truck rattling up to the tree. It stopped. Dempsey, the chaplain's assistant, switched off the engine and jumped out of the truck.

"How long they keeping you in reserve?"

"Long as K Company's out there." The Sergeant looked at the truck that was empty of corpses. "No audience?"

The men began to stir as Dempsey pointed at a winding lane leading to some hills. "Got to pick up four men out there from L Company."

A copper butterfly flew past the Sergeant. "What's the matter with the Grave Registration Bureau?"

"Busy with Second Battalion," said Dempsey.

Zab reached for his cigar. A grasshopper next to him almost had a heart attack as it jumped. "Four men, eh? Is *that* all they lost?"

"Yeah."

Vinci felt his pinched ear. "You going to chew out the stiffs in front of the padre like you always do, Demps?"

"Yeah."

Griff scratched his itching hand. "He's bound to get wise to you."

Dempsey's eyes twinkled. "The hell he is. As long as I keep up my screwball act it'll only make him leery of me, that's all. Oh, it'll take maybe another couple dozen truckloads of dead guys to make him get rid of me and transfer me to London." He sighed. "It ain't fun to talk to dead guys."

They heard the braying of a donkey and the creaking of cartwheels, and they turned, but a dead tree's hanging talons blocked their view of the road. When the donkey and cart skirted the dropping claws, they saw the girl. She saw them at the same instant. She jumped off the cart and ran. The Sergeant jumped to his feet, overtook her, and struggled with her as he shouted, "Check for weapons!"

Vinci found no weapons in the cart as the Sergeant hauled the girl back. She clawed and kicked, but he held her tight. Vinci spoke to her in Italian. She didn't have to be afraid of them, he said. They were not going to gang-rape her. He told her to take a good look at their uniforms. She stopped struggling when she learned they were Americans. She spoke rapidly with gestures.

176

"She thought we were Germans," said Vinci.

Zab sized her up for his book: about eighteen, five feet four inches, 120 pounds, big-bosomed, narrow waist. Her bra was visible through a transparent salmon-pink blouse. Skirt dirty, dusty, brown. She wore sandals, had black hair on her legs. Unusually pretty. Hair black and long. Her eyes were dark.

"Find out where she came from," said the Sergeant.

Vinci asked her.

"Niscemi," said the girl.

"Did she see any Germans?"

Vinci asked her. She shook her head, muttering.

"She kept to the hills. Didn't see any *Tedeschi*. That's Germans in Italian."

"Tell her to move on."

"It's a mistake."

"Why?"

"She's lying."

As if she understood Vinci, the girl spat a venomous torrent of profanities at him. Her anger came as a shock to the men. The Sergeant waited for the translation of the sudden explosion of hate.

"She wants us to burn Mussolini and bury alive every goddamn motherfucking Fascist in Sicily. She wants to drown 'em with her piss."

The girl opened her blouse, exposing not a bra but a sweat-stained medical bandage covering her breasts. The bandage was taped with soiled, thumb-smudged adhesive. She spoke quietly now. Her eyes filled with tears as her words became a whisper.

"Was she hit in the breast?" asked the Sergeant.

"No. A Fascist raped her and bit off her nipples."

The men shifted uncomfortably. Dempsey unpeeled a stick of gum and offered it to her. She took it and began to chew.

"She's lying," said Vinci. "Next she'll tell us her old man and her ten brothers were killed fighting Fascists. Then she'll expect us to give her a medal and some chow."

"You don't buy her story?"

"Hell, no! I know these ass kissers. When Mussolini was riding high they all killed for the son of a bitch.

177

Now that they figure he's licked, everybody here hates him and always hated him. We won't find one Fascist in Sicily. *Not one!* I'll prove this cunt's a liar!"

He ripped off her bandage. She screamed. The men paled as they stared at the teeth marks on her mutilated breasts. In place of nipples were two ugly red-blue-black dents.

"So I was wrong," growled Vinci.

"Give her a temp patch," said the Sergeant.

Still growling. Vinci unclasped his kit and went to work with bandage and adhesive, angry with himself as she talked. She understood his doubt, his suspicions. She didn't blame him. Many Fascists changed their politics when they heard the rumor that Americans landed in Sicily last night. But it was almost impossible to find a Sicilian who was anti-Mussolini. Those against him were executed or in prison. She herself had been an admirer. She knew no better. She was too young to understand. She had believed the Fascists were good for Italy. Until that Fascist raped her. Her voice comforted Vinci. Touching her breasts with his fingers made him excited. He wondered what it would be like—a girl whose nipples had been bitten off in rape? The thought made him ashamed of himself.

"Take her to battalion aid," said the Sergeant.

Vinci helped her up in the cart and led the donkey down the dusty road. The men dropped to comfort under the tree.

Dempsey climbed behind the wheel of his truck and started the engine. It coughed. He started off toward the hills.

Shortly after two o'clock they were back in the line with two canteens of chlorine-spiked water for every man, two bandoliers, six grenades, eight grenades for the Springfield launcher. I Company inherited three miles, two fire fights, thirty-six casualties. The Italians lost seventy-three men. Like an idiot, Zab had filled his canteens with cocoa and ended up begging Johnson for water at dusk.

The quarter moon found the Squad glumly forcing C rations down their throats. They tried to sleep on the ground near an olive grove but insects kept them awake.

178

"The hell with Company posting extra security," said Zab. "They should concentrate more on getting us mosquito nets."

Griff scratched his hand. "I got one hell of a bite."

"Y' took your Atabrine, didn't you?" asked Johnson.

"I'm living on it."

Zab carefully unpeeled the cellophane and cursed to himself because the cigar was so dry. He began to light up when the match and the cigar were roughly knocked to the ground by the Sergeant.

From nowhere the Lieutenant appeared.

"Who the hell struck that match?"

"Must've been a firefly," said the Sergeant.

"I told you men *never* to show a light at night!" The Lieutenant squatted by the Sergeant. "Remember that graveyard?"

"Yes, sir."

The men listened for the bad news.

"I and R heard people there."

"When do you want me to go?"

"Go at 0500. You hit head on. Second Squad on your left, Third on your right. I'll be with heavy weapons on the hill on your left. People've been reported there, too."

"What about my replacements, sir?"

"They're at Battalion. You'll get yours in time."

"I need—"

"I know what you need, Sergeant. You'll get what you asked for." The Lieutenant rose. In the darkness the men could feel his glare. "Next joker who shows a light at night I *personally* will make him eat whatever he's smoking in front of the entire Platoon—even if it costs me my gold bar. And if he's *not* a smoker I'll make him eat one of Zab's cigars." He left.

Griff looked at the quarter moon and thought about the girl's nipples. The thought still made him sick.

Zab found his cigar. Hiding the flare under his helmet, with his back to the Sergeant, he lighted up and settled back and looked at the quarter moon. He smiled. He was sure the Lieutenant knew he had struck that match.

Vinci looked at the quarter moon and felt no guilt.

179

The girl had even thanked him for being so gentle with her when they made love under the cart after they left battalion aid.

Johnson looked at the quarter moon and thought how nice it would be to have an ass that never ached.

The Sergeant looked at the quarter moon and thought about the graveyard.

❖ ❖ ❖

Schröder looked at the quarter moon and thought about the American beachhead in the south of Sicily. If German troops had been there, not an American would have reached the beaches alive. In the hospital in Tunis, when he had heard of their Kasserine counterattack and subsequent victory, the explanation was obvious! The Americans had more planes, more tanks, more guns, more money.

He was sitting next to Armin against a knocked-out Italian tank near a high-arching bridge over a river south of Syracuse, the shelled 75-mm howitzer jutting above their heads.

"What do you think, Schröder?" Armin asked. "Is the end of the war in sight?"

"Well—" said Schröder, his mind running off in pursuit of past events from the day he was shipped to Sicily with his battalion before the fall of Tunis, "no and yes."

"What kind of an answer is that?"

"In North Africa the Italians never had any real heart in fighting, did they?"

"Never."

"They said if their homeland was invaded they would fight like tigers."

"Like tigers."

"Well, here we are in their homeland, holding this bridge that *they* lost to the British and that *we* had to take back." He paused. "That is the *no* to your question."

"What is the *yes?*"

"When Mussolini disbands all his forces and lets us do all the fighting, the war'll be over in two months,

180

and then we can concentrate on wiping out Ivan and end up in the Kremlin washing down fish eggs with vodka." His voice began to show anger. "Why should *we* take orders from a damn Blackshirt militia officer who belongs behind a barber chair? Why the hell should *German* soldiers be attached to Italians? It's degrading! Our battalion should be here with us—or we should be with our battalion!"

"You're right, Schröder! We're hampered by macaronis who do their best fighting in opera!"

Schröder laughed. The pain shot through his back. He grunted.

"Still hurts?"

Schröder grunted that it did.

"I thought that Englishman busted your back with his rifle."

"So did I." Schröder shifted his position slowly. It did not ease the pain.

"You should've killed him."

"I was ordered to bring in a Churchill salesman for interrogation."

"He was a cocky bastard."

"All British officers are cocky bastards, especially those that hit the beaches here."

"But that one was intelligent." Armin grimaced as he drank from his canteen. The chlorine in the water almost made him retch. "I was at his interrogation when you were at battalion aid station. He was damn intelligent. He quoted Alcibiades."

"Who?"

"Alcibiades—the Athenian general."

"*Athenian?*"

"About 400 years B.C."

Schröder laughed, even though it hurt. His back burned as if a bayonet had just been driven through it. "That's British humor for you—giving his name, rank, and a two thousand-year-old military report!"

Armin did not laugh. "That military report may have a long white beard, Schröder, but it was about us."

"Us?"

"Us! Right here! Right where we're sitting near that goddamn bridge!"

"What is in that canteen?"

Armin smiled. "Piss." Then the smile died. "I'm serious, Schröder. That general said that if Syracuse falls, all Sicily falls also, and Italy immediately afterward. The man you captured said that before morning the British will smash through us, join up with the Americans, take all of Sicily, and invade Italy."

There was silence. Schröder and the other soldiers stared at Armin.

"And it's a spit's throw from Italy to Germany," Armin went on. "*Closer* than spit with British paratroops and American paratroops!"

Schröder smiled. "You know nobody but a German soldier will ever set foot on German soil."

"I know that POW thinks we'd be smart to surrender right now and let them take Syracuse before we're all killed."

"I don't care what he thinks! Every soldier we killed in Poland and France and Norway and Russia thought he was going to win. We don't have to *think* it! We *know* we're going to win!"

"What about North Africa?"

"Ah-h—just a temporary setback."

"*Temporary?* There are more British and American troops than Arabs in North Africa!"

Schröder turned to stone on the subject, and Armin let it drop before he got his own jaw smashed. They heard Germans around them bitching, sharing their resentment over serving under Italians. Then the voices stopped, and the darkness grew heavy with the angry silence of men fighting under a flag not their own. A slight wind brushed the faces of Schröder and Armin. When the wind dropped, they felt the heat again.

The rifle shot came from the other side of the bridge.

"That's a Lee Metford," said Armin uneasily.

"The hell it is," said Schröder. "It's a Canadian number 4 Mark I rifle."

They heard the second shot.

"You're right," said Armin, getting to his feet with his weapon.

They heard British Bren machine guns firing. Every man was on his feet now, peering into the darkness at the distant bursts.

"How many Italians are on the other side of the bridge?" asked Armin.

Schröder slowly rose. "Not enough to hold back a charge of ten year olds with brooms."

"We're going to be overrun."

"Yes."

"Let's pull back!"

"To *where?* They'll start plastering this area with heavy stuff." Schröder hurled himself flat on the ground as he heard the incoming scream in the sky. Every man hit the dirt. The shell burst landed several hundred yards behind them. Two British flares illuminated Italian troops fleeing across the bridge under small-arms fire. Several fell as they approached the Germans.

Six more British shells fell, expertly missing the bridge, bursting closer to the Germans who were running for cover that did not exist. A third flare revealed British troops storming across the bridge as the Italians melted away. The company of Germans fired at the advancing British. Italians running in panic made themselves target risks for Schröder's Schmeisser. Shells landed closer to the Germans.

Outnumbered by British storming toward them, Schröder hurled his burp gun to the ground and flung his hands up, urging his men to surrender. Armin was stunned, but he threw his weapon away and raised his hands. The demoralized Italians and whipped Germans were swallowed up by the superior-numbered British and herded to an old Greek theater. The semicircular structure was in a miraculous state of preservation, and so were the fortunate prisoners.

Armin was confused. Schröder, of all people, was the first to surrender. Armin didn't have the courage to bring up that subject to his fallen idol. He was aware that from the moment they were marched to the theater, Schröder hadn't uttered a word to him. Perhaps, Armin feared, the shock of seeing the overwhelming number of British in assault had made Schröder lose his courage, if not his reason.

Schröder's contempt for the other prisoners exploded. They had become cowed oxen. The only reason he surrendered was to save their lives because they were outnumbered. Now they must find their battalion and

183

continue to kill the British bastards. He figured that Group Schmalz was with the Napoli Division in the north on the Catania Plain.

His "We must escape" shocked the men.

"Not *me!*" said one German. "At least now I won't end up a legless beggar in Berlin like my father!"

"You're right," Schröder said quietly. "You ended up a dead traitor in Syracuse."

Schröder strangled the German as the stunned men looked on without making a move to stop him. Armin was pleased. His faith in Schröder was restored. Schröder summoned one of the many guards who surrounded the theater, pointed at the dead German, and told the guard the man died of a heart attack. The guard called his sergeant, who spoke German, and the dead man was carried out of the theater.

Before dawn Schröder's company was herded into ten captured open Italian trucks. Followed closely by Armin, Schröder maneuvered toward the British soldier standing in the front of the truck with a Lancaster submachine gun. Behind him was the driver. Next to him another man with a Lancaster. The truck packed sixteen POWs. They were commanded to sit. They did. Schröder observed a third Lancaster held by a British soldier who was standing in the rear of the truck. When the sweating British completed the loading of the enemy cargo, the trucks pulled out in the darkness. British cars and military trucks whizzed past the POW trucks at breakneck speeds. Schröder observed that buildings were shuttered. British infantry filled the streets. Benumbed residents were told by a bullhorn on a small truck to keep off the streets. Armin saw children lingering in doorways, saw pressed faces against windows.

Schröder's truck passed prowling groups of British choking off a side street, hunting for die-hard snipers. A last-ditch Fascist fired and ran. Schröder saw bursts from British guns kill the man.

Schröder could not wait for dawn. He had to act now. He stared at the bleak squatting prisoners in his truck and slowly angled his body around so that his pain-stabbed back was firmly jammed against Armin and a solid wall of men. Armin's heart beat like a trip-hammer. He knew that Schröder was about to act.

Schröder waited until the British troops began to thin out. Suddenly he drew his leg back until his knee caved in his chest, then he thrust his boot out, ramming the back of the British soldier above him. The man grunted in agony. Schröder ripped the Lancaster from his hand and, hurling himself forward, he swung the weapon, crushing in the face of the British soldier beside the driver.

Two seconds had passed.

Whirling, Schröder kicked aside a prisoner and shot the British soldier standing in the back of the truck. The shot made the driver stop the truck and turn. His head was blown off by Schröder who jumped, followed by two men. One of them was Armin.

The rest remained. They wanted to live.

The three escaped prisoners ran down a dark street and turned off into an alley. A truck pulled up to the alley. Two British submachine guns opened fire. A German fell. Schröder and Armin ran along the river, British guns firing at them. They ran through growths of papyrus and into an ancient quarry. They moved through the black labyrinths until forced to halt to catch their breath.

"Did you grab one of those Lancasters?" asked Schröder.

"Yes."

Schröder grunted that he was satisfied. They heard the echo of feet running. They ran below street level, slamming into walls, falling, leaping to their feet. Dawn came and Armin and Schröder were no longer pursued. It was quiet. They rested behind gravestones in the graveyard.

Dawn found the Sergeant and Squad in a fire fight in a terraced graveyard on the side of a hill. Not a man could be seen. Only bullet-chipped gravestones witnessed the action.

Then there was quiet.

Slowly the Sergeant rose and checked the enemy dead. He found no wounded. Then he counted his own men.

"Griff," said the Sergeant.

"Yeah?"

"You shot over their heads."

"The hell he did." Vinci pointed at a dead German sprawled against a gravestone. "He got *that* one."

"Sergeant," said a new face, *"I* got him."

"Who're *you?"*

"Smitty. I joined you last night with the others."

Griff was relieved.

"We didn't get a scratch, Lieutenant," the Sergeant reported on the radio. "Seven dead Germans in the graveyard and no wounded. Yes, sir. Germans. What? Okay." He tossed the phone to the radioman. "A war correspondent's joining us, going to watch us set up an OP for tanks."

"Tanks?" Griff felt the fist turn in his stomach.

"Supposed to be out there somewhere." The Sergeant waved his arm. "The Lieutenant said S-2 thinks they're the Hermann Göring Panzer Division."

Zab struck a match across a Berman helmet and puffed at his cigar. "Who's the correspondent? Ernie Pyle?"

"Brodie."

Vinci grinned. *"He* still alive?"

Resting against gravestones, the men ate C rations in silence as they realized they had come out of the fight without a scratch. They steered clear of thinking about the Hermann Göring Panzer Division. Still trembling over how close the Sergeant had come to finding out that he couldn't shoot a man he could see, Griff glanced at Smitty, grateful that the new face had spoken up. Griff felt guilty. He *had* fired over the heads of the Germans.

"'More villages in Sicily are on hills," said Vinci. "Houses on one side, graveyards on the other. My old man was brought up here. He told me that from a distance it's hard to tell the houses from the grave-stones."

"Your old man Sicilian?" said Smitty.

"Sure, but he voted for FDR."

"I know a girl whose folks come from here. Syracuse." Smitty enjoyed his C rations. "My folks like her folks a lot. We're going to be married when I get back."

"She'll want a battalion of kids."

Smitty laughed. "I know! So do *I!*"

They raised their heads to the hum. Johnson pointed. The white-bordered black cross was visible on the plane.

"Germans scouting for our tanks," said the Sergeant.

Smitty raised his rifle and aimed.

"Put it down," said the Sergeant.

"I don't get it."

"If he spots your bursts he'll have artillery on us by the time you've emptied your clip."

Confused, Smitty lowered his rifle as the Sergeant kept his eyes on the jeep that was pulling up to the base of their hill. He watched Brodie and a corporal get out and climb up to the graveyard. Brodie lugged a bulging bag of film. Two cameras were slung round his neck. He carried his portable, waving as he reached them.

Zab said, "Vinci wants to know if you're in one piece."

"Take a look," grinned Brodie. "Hi, Vinci. Zab. Griff. Johnson." He paused. "Sergeant."

The Sergeant nodded.

The corporal hunted among the dead Germans like a surgeon looking for the right vein. "How about it, Mr. Brodie? Will you take one before I get my ass back?"

"Sure?"

"You'll really send it to my folks?"

"Sure. You gave me the address."

Griff's reaction was numb disbelief as the corporal rearranged a German corpse to pose with in front of a gravestone that marked the remains of a man who fought with Garibaldi. Brodie aimed his camera. The corporal produced a toothy grin, one foot on the dead German.

Three hours later Brodie, accompanying the Squad under a pink sky, marveled at how the Sergeant

187

approached a cave on the flat rock-strewn plain. The Sergeant moved effortlessly in the way he deployed his men.

Brodie observed that the new faces were sent up ahead; that the Four Horsemen were bringing up the rear for cover. Brodie chilled. His camera shook as it clicked confirmation of rumors he heard that the Sergeant sacrificed new faces to keep the invincibility of his four veterans intact.

But the Sergeant always led.

When Brodie clicked Smitty in his camera there was an explosion. Smitty fell in a burst of fire and smoke. The Sergeant flattened first, the men hitting dirt a second later. Brodie fell and flattened his belly to the earth. Then the Sergeant ran toward the cave under cover fire bursting from the Squad. He ran into the cave. They stopped firing. He found the big cave empty, hurried back, and checked Smitty's blood-splashed groin. The men gathered round Smitty who stared at his bloody hands.

"You stepped on a mine they forgot to undig," the Sergeant told Smitty whose hand was now feeling the blood round his crotch.

"Oh, no!" cried Smitty.

The loss of his cock snapped his mind. He stared like a madman. The Sergeant knew that stare well and he began to search the area close to Smitty. When he was sure that Smitty's eyes shifted from the sky to watch him, he grunted.

"Found it," said the Sergeant, picking up something bloody from the ground.

A tremor shook Smitty. His complexion turned pasty gray. The flicker in his eyes staring at the Sergeant's hand increased. "It's mine!" yelled Smitty. "Give it back to me!"

The Sergeant flung it behind a cluster of small rocks.

"You son of a bitch!" cried Smitty.

"Just one of your balls," said the Sergeant casually. "You can have a kid without it. That's why they gave you two balls."

"Are you *sure?*"

"Feel."

Hesitantly Smitty probed his crotch. The glaze in his

eyes vanished. Relief shone on his face, then ecstasy. He laughed the strange hysterical laughter of sanity.

"I still got it!" Smitty yelled. "I still got my cock! I still got my cock!"

48

In the heat, Brodie hunched over his portable, pecking at keys, balancing the battered typewriter on his lap. His back was pasted against the entrance to the cave. The men rested, their eyes on the Sergeant who was looking through his binocs at the plain.

"Ten German tanks and infantry twelve hundred yards northeast of the Gela-Niscemi intersection," the Sergeant said on the radio. "Headed toward our position."

Brodie's fingers froze on the keys. The men rose and looked across the plain at the distant dust.

"Confirm coordinates you gave me," answered the Lieutenant.

"559–308."

"559–308," the Lieutenant repeated. "I'll get Regiment to ask for a TOT. Make corrections direct with artillery and be ready for stuff to fall on that cave."

The Sergeant glanced over his shoulder past the men to study the earth and rocks above the cave. "We've got good cover, sir. Out." He looked at the men. "We're getting a TOT."

"What's that?" said Brodie.

"Time on target. All our big guns'll fire at the same time."

Griff felt good. The men grunted with satisfaction.

"We've got front-row seats," grinned Zab.

Brodie was white-faced as he spoke. "When I left the General he was raising hell because our big guns were still on the ship."

"They've been unloaded by this time," said the Sergeant.

"Maybe."

"Anyway, Patton's got tanks."

"*They* were still on the ship, too!"

189

"Holy Christ!" said Zab. "Another Kasserine!"

"Get in the cave, all of you," said the Sergeant. "Check your weapons. Stack all ammo for rapid reach."

Like zombies they went into the cave, followed by Brodie packing his gear. Griff remained outside the cave with the Sergeant. The Sergeant read Griff's thoughts and couldn't blame him for wanting to run.

"We're far enough away to make an easy withdrawal," said Griff.

"That's right."

"And only one man's needed here to direct artillery fire."

The Sergeant looked through his binocs as he spoke. "One man can't handle their infantry."

"They'll be killed or burn their asses running from the shells."

"Figure on the opposite of what could happen, Griff. That's what this war, any war, is all about."

"If any of them get through that TOT they'll be wiped out by Battalion."

"And kill our men while getting killed."

"That's what this is all about," Griff said bitterly.

Lowering the binocs slowly the Sergeant looked at Griff for a long, long moment. "All right, Griff, you can take off. I'm not stopping you. Tell the Lieutenant malaria hit you again."

"It *did!*" Griff went into the cave.

The Sergeant wasn't surprised as he lifted his binocs.

Griff sat by Zab and waited in silence with the men. Brodie had decided to finish his story later. The wait began to strain Griff.

The men were too busy thinking about the tanks to pay any attention to Griff.

Brooding, he felt sorry for the vacant-eyed, grimy-faced men, their expressions as cold as wet stone, and he knew that these hunched warriors faced the oldest situation in the world: the time and the place—not of their own choosing—of their own death. He knew they and millions like them killing and being killed were beyond any emotion except fear. He knew they were not survivors. These almost fragile-looking young men were, in fact, dead already.

"I think the artillery's been unloaded," said Brodie.

"After all, when I heard the General raising hell it was quite some time ago." He was trying to raise the men's hopes.

"Sure," said Vinci, stacking his bandolier clips in front of him. "Wouldn't surprise me if, after our 155s send 'em running, Patton and his tanks follow up in the chase."

An older soldier named Baldy watched the Four Horsemen stack their ammo and their grenades. "You four guys been with the First since North Africa, right?"

"Right," said Vinci.

"Is that what kept you from getting killed? That bullshit optimism?"

"Nope," said Zab. "Wetnoses like you kept us in one piece. That's the way it goes, Baldy. In war some guys always get it. We don't."

Brodie observed the faces of the new men staring at the Four Horsemen.

Baldy pointed at the ammo clips on the ground. "What good'll they do against tanks? Even if they're shelled, you know damn well some tanks'll get through. What good'll that pea-shooting ammo do against tanks?"

"They'll have footsloggers with 'em." Zab unhooked his grenades.

"And if they poke their heads in her for a look—" said Johnson.

"It'll be their last look," said Vinci.

"Or ours!" said Baldy.

"That's right, Baldy," said Zab. "Just do what we do. We faced tanks before."

"So I heard at the repple depple. You guys ran."

"Did you hear about El-Guettar?" asked Zab through his cigar. "We slugged it out for four days and nights with the Tenth Panzer," he went on without waiting for a response. "Three times they counterattacked but we stood up against a hundred mothers, all Tigers, until our artillery blasted 'em."

"*Who* stood up against a hundred tanks?" Baldy challenged Zab. "Your *Squad?*"

Zab grinned. "That's right. The Squad—and the First Division."

"Goddamn right the Division!" echoed Vinci.

The drone of the tanks crept closer. The men caught garbled snatches of the Sergeant's voice on the radio and waited for the first shell burst from artillery. Their wait became agonizing. The silence and tension in the cave was heavy.

Still they heard no shell hit a tank.

"I hope," muttered Zab through a cloud of smoke, "those jokers in Division Artillery don't lob in any short rounds. There's nothing more humiliating than having a Division short round give you a haircut."

"There won't be any short rounds."

The men turned. Standing at the entrance, the Sergeant had overheard. "There won't be *any* rounds."

Zab spat a piece of tobacco. "Meaning Brodie was right."

"Right. Our heavy guns and tanks are still on the water. Who's got a smoke?" The Sergeant watched his words cut apart their guts as Griff shakily gave him a cigarette and Zab held up his trembling cigar. The Sergeant was fighting back his own anxiety as he steadied Zab's wrist and drew a light from the cigar. "All we do is wait for 'em to pass."

"There's nothing back of us to stop 'em," said Vinci.

"Right."

"Hell, they could bust through Battalion."

"They could bust through Regiment and Division and chase any survivor back into the Mediterranean."

"Where's Cannon Company?" asked Griff.

"Division's hounding the beachmaster for news on 'em."

Vinci tried to sound calm, as if asking for the time. "What about our bombers? They sure as hell aren't on ships."

"Fighting off planes. The Germans and Italians got anything that can fly going after our ships."

Johnson blurted, "Didn't Company send *any* kind of muscle?"

"Bazookas. Four teams."

"To stop an armored division?" cried Baldy. He turned on the men. "I'm getting out of here!"

"They're close enough to spot you," said the Sergeant.

"I'll take my chances!"

"Fifty yards from here they'll stop you from drawing your pay."

"It's *my* pay!" Baldy started out.

The Sergeant stopped him. "It's our pay, too. After blowing you up they'll fill this cave with 88s."

"That's *your* funeral!" Baldy ran out.

The Sergeant shot him. Baldy tumbled five feet outside the cave. An instant later a tank fired. The shell burst behind the cave.

"Drag him in, Griff. Check his leg." The Sergeant moved to a viewing position as the men pulled Baldy into the cave. The Sergeant saw the lead tank fire again and watched the shell miss a three-quarter-ton weapons carrier that was racing toward the cave from the rear. The truck came to a stop when the third shell from the lead tank landed close by. From the truck jumped four bazooka teams. They opened fire with their rockets at once.

One tank began to burn after a direct hit. Six tanks fired. The four bazooka teams were blown, the truck exploded, and the tanks never stopped advancing.

"How's he doing, Griff?" shouted the Sergeant.

"I can see the bone."

"Broken?"

"Can't tell."

The Sergeant ran into the cave and checked Baldy's bone. "Just torn flesh. Patch him up."

"What for?" asked Zab. "The next shell will zero in on us."

"They didn't spot him."

"Who the hell're they shelling?"

"The bazookas."

"Wiped out?"

"All four teams. I saw infantry eating tank fumes."

A pimply faced kid, aged twenty years, said, "Let's t-t-throw in the t-t-towel, Sergeant."

"Tanks don't feed prisoners."

The drone grew to a deafening roar of engines and clanking tracks as tanks and men passed and smoke and dust began to fill the cave. The noise was so shattering that every man was sure he had concussion of the brain.

Zab stiffened, finger on trigger, as he saw through the dust a tall grenadier peel off from the column to advance toward the Squad. The tall grenadier stopped. Behind him passed his comrades and tanks. The grenadier pulled aside one end of the machine-gun belt draped around his neck, fumbled with his fly, pissed. Then he turned and vanished into the dust.

A phantom German hobbled into the cave, balanced his machine pistol against the wall, removed his right jackboot, and began to hammer it upside down against the wall to dump out the painful stones. Behind him tanks rumbled and two-legged ghosts walked.

The German saw Griff.

In the billowing dust, Griff, finished with bandaging Baldy's leg wound, saw the German staring at him, holding his jackboot. The eyes of the German drove nails into Griff's hands as Griff aimed point-blank. His hang-up froze his trigger finger. The freeze was enough to give the German life. He dropped his jackboot and picked up his weapon.

Griff aimed but did not fire. The eyes had paralyzed him.

Before the German could squeeze off a burst, his face twisted. He grunted in surprise and fell. The Sergeant loomed out of the dust with his wet trench knife.

The floor shook.

The yowling of gears reverberated like wildcats at rutting time and the clanking swelled to the rattle of a thousand bones in a hollow chamber. The Sergeant and his men inhaled the burning, asphyxiating fumes. The stutterer and Baldy and the other new men were in their first and last combat without having fired a shot. The men choked and coughed. Their terrible choice was slow suffocation inside or a fast finish outside. Either way the certainty was that the Squad would have twelve replacements by nightfall.

A tank stopped with a dead engine in front of the cave. The driver of the seventy-ton King Tiger angrily tried to revive it. The stationary tank was the ultimate terror to the Squad.

The Sergeant, refusing to weaken, hung onto his last shreds of courage and sanity. Finally the engine came to life. But not to the driver's satisfaction. The Tiger

194

blasted fumes and dust into the cave and suddenly burst into flames.

The Sergeant heard another shell explode beyond the blazing tank. He saw the driver climb out through the escape hatch. The driver's screams were inaudible as more shells pounded the plain. The driver stopped screaming. The Sergeant watched him burn to death. Shells burst on the roof of the cave. Shells burst outside the cave.

The TOT was on!

To escape the shells, a German infantryman dashed past the burning tank, jumped over the cremated driver, and burst into the cave. He thought he would be safe in the dust. He was shot by the Sergeant. Four more panicky Germans rushed in for cover. The Sergeant shot them. Three more Germans ran in. He shot two of them, crushed in the face of the third with his rifle barrel, and gathered up his Four Horsemen. "Stack 'em in the rear, make room for more!"

The Four Horsemen dragged the bodies from the entrance.

The Sergeant jammed in a fresh clip, gave the other men flank-fire positions and instructions to drag bodies as they dropped.

Brodie fumbled with his camera.

The shelling increased. Again the cave roof was hit. Stones and dirt showered the Squad. The men forgot the fumes and the danger from the crumbling ceiling. They were unafraid of being buried alive now that they tasted the possibility of survival. Finally the big guns were clobbering the tanks.

More Germans ran in and met instant death.

Griff couldn't see enemy eyes. He shot startled ghosts in the dust. Detonations outside mushroomed. The dead began to pile up around Baldy.

Brodie's flashbulbs popped. His camera caught the Sergeant directing his Squad in the art of wholesale killing. The crack of rifles was drowned out by shell bursts and by tanks running for their lives. In the flashes from the bulbs, the cave appeared to be a crowded charnel house. German blood splattered the walls. The number of piled bodies increased.

Brodie took pictures of the precision of killing that

seemed more horrible than killing itself. His camera caught Germans rushing into the cave to live—only to die suddenly.

The rush of Germans entering, being killed, and being stacked became a mad dance of death choreographed by the Sergeant.

Suddenly the artillery shelling stopped.

A plane was heard.

Dragging the radio, the Sergeant climbed over corpses and found the Gela Plain pock-holed with burning tanks, burning men, and hundreds of scattered pieces of dead infantrymen.

Nothing moved.

He looked up at the U.S. Navy plane that was flying away and then he got his Lieutenant on the radio.

The Sergeant left the burning tank in front of the cave and poked through dust to bring the news from Platoon. "Know who knocked out those tanks? The Navy. The *Savannah*—a cruiser— laying out there a few miles—shelled those thickskins. Well, I'll be damned. The United States Navy saved our asses!"

There was no reaction from the exhausted, glassy-eyed, blood-covered victors sitting on stacks of dead Germans.

49

The fat woman at the railroad switch crossed herself and cautiously tasted the scrambled eggs in the GI mess kit. She wore a clean yellow straw sombrero, freshly laundered tent-large blue overalls, a brilliant red bandanna around her bull neck, and a crucifix.

"How do you like it?" asked Vinci.

"In a shell." The fat woman spat out the eggs.

"With salt they taste like eggs," said Vinci.

"Nothing can make them taste like eggs," she said.

"Americans," philosophized her small, moustached husband, swinging gently in the frayed hammock slung between two poles trackside, "will win the war with powdered food."

The woman returned the mess kit to Vinci. "You also eat powdered butter?"

"Yes." Vinci struck out. He had hoped she'd swap real eggs for his powdered ones. Sweat rolled down his face. His rifle was slung. He wore no pack.

"You also drink powdered milk?"

"Yes."

"You get drunk on powdered vino?" the woman laughed.

The giant red-velvet sofa creaked and grunted under her 250 pounds. Facing her were signal and switch levers overlooking a siding that paralleled the main track. On the bleached-out sofa was a lantern and a red flag. Proud of being the "switchman" for the railroad in the isolated area, she owed her position to her husband who was too poetic to do any kind of work. For years he had watched her from his swinging hammock, reading Dante to her, congratulating her on the way she put in a train at the siding when an express had to pass. Since the invasion, she slept on the sofa because it was his idea that she be ready at the switch when the trains were running again.

"I told you I'll pay for real eggs," said Vinci. "I've got army lire."

"Wipe your ass with it," said the husband.

"Maybe I can get some Mussolini lire."

"Wipe *his* ass with it," said the husband. "Only Victor Emmanuel lire is good."

"I have none."

"What is your name?"

"Vinci."

"Where are you from?"

"New York."

"Where are your people from?"

"Here."

"Where in Sicily?"

"Caltanissetta."

The husband was impressed. "You give me a camera and film and show me how to make pictures and I will tell you where you can get real eggs. Many eggs."

"I have no camera but I can arrange for a man to take a picture of your family."

197

"But not with a powdered camera!" said the husband. "Not with powdered film!"

Their little boy laughed. Half naked, wearing cutdown pants, he was sitting on a donkey that was hitched to a two-wheeled cart with religious pictures painted on its sides. He looked about five years old. Behind him was their home: an ancient freight car without wheels. It was sparsely furnished.

Vinci offered the eggs to the donkey. The animal refused. Vinci tossed the eggs behind the cart, washed his mess kit at the pump, folded it, and crossed the field to I Company's bivouac.

The mail clerk hailed him. "What's the matter with the guys in your Squad? They sick? None of 'em gave a damn about getting mail from home."

Vinci made no response as he passed resting dogfaces and reached the Squad. Baldy was not among the men. They were drowned in despair, weak and wet with sweat. The Sergeant understood. Appetite gutted, nerves shattered, they were reliving the assembly-line massacre in the cave. Vinci sat down. His scraped kneecap burned. He looked at the Sergeant, who was overcome with exhaustion, and saw that the letters for the men were unopened, even the four packages.

Finally Zab moved. He opened his letter and came alive as he read. He shouted, disturbing the quiet, "My mother spent the advance! She sold my book to a publisher!"

They didn't share his enthusiasm. He read on.

"She left it with some secretary and the book reached the editor and they *bought* it!" Still no reaction. "Fifteen-hundred-dollar advance!"

The Sergeant ached for a long rest. The Squad had it coming. He eased his thoughts back to the close shave. The Hermann Göring Panzers had busted through Regiment and backed the Division into the sea when those navy guns opened up. O'Brien of Cannon Company put in his licks at the right moment, too, boresighting tanks a thousand yards from the beach. It was an effort for the Sergeant to face the truth that death had come so close to the Big Red One. What if the navy hadn't—? He shuddered. What if the cruiser

Savannah decided it was insane to fight a land battle against tanks miles inland? He looked at the faces of his men and felt sorry for them because he knew that the Hermann Göring Panzer was just a starter. What faced them were two or three armored divisions and half a dozen infantry divisions. And if Hitler threw them in at the same time, the battle of Sicily would be over in an hour, and fifteen thousand men of the First Division would be dead.

"First Squad?" asked a dogface he hadn't seen before.

"Yes," said the Sergeant.

"I'm Baldy's replacement. They call me Weirdo. I'm from Washington, D.C."

Zab cleared his throat. "How're things going at the Pentagon? Those generals still tripping over colonels delivering messages in the hallways?"

"Generals are tripping over generals," said Weirdo without smiling. Brought up in the slums in the shadow of the Capitol, one of seven living in two squalid rooms, he and his family had starved while, within stone-throwing distance, the State Department worried about the etiquette of seating plans for dignitaries. He used to sit by the Tomb of the Unknown Soldier and wish his hungry body were in it because the dead do not have to eat. "My name is really Weir. W-e-i-r."

"Weirdo's not such a complimentary name," Griff said.

"I've been called that since I was a kid. It fits me. The night I was drafted I had a dream. I saw Joseph firing a rifle at Mary. Weird, isn't it? See what I mean. The name fits me."

"If you think putting on a psycho act'll get you out of the infantry," said Zab, "you're wasting your dreams on the wrong guys. You're stuck."

"I made up my mind," Weirdo said, "that the minute they put me into a rifle squad I was going to will myself to die, and that is exactly what I'm going to do right now."

He stretched out on his back and crossed his arms on his chest. Then, convulsively sucking in air, he recited,

"Now I lay me down in muck,
I pray the Lord my soul to fuck,
If I kill before I wake,
I pray the Lord my corpse to take."

His body heaved. His breath went out in a long gasp. They looked at him. His body was still. His mouth was open, eyes bulging, fists clenched, no movement of breathing.

"How come we get the Section Eights?" asked Zab.

"Oh," said Johnson, "the Sergeant'll transfer him to another squad."

"He makes sense to me," said Griff. "He'll be okay."

"Not in this war." The Sergeant felt Weirdo's neck and tried for a pulsebeat. "Give me your stethoscope, Zab." The Sergeant listened through it and returned it to Zab.

The men nervously shifted their positions. They felt cold in the blistering heat. They stared at Weirdo, knowing he was putting on an act. Then the Sergeant picked up his field jacket and covered Weirdo's face with it.

The covering of Weirdo's face electrified the men. Suddenly they realized that for Weirdo the battle was over even before it had begun. In a strange way they envied him.

"I don't buy it," said Zab, trembling. "No son of a bitch can will himself to death."

"Well," said the Sergeant, "you just saw a man who could and did."

The men stared at the covered body. The Lieutenant came over and squatted. He flapped his case open and held the acetate-covered map out in front of the Sergeant.

"The Company's sending out—" he began.

"That new man you sent me."

"Weir?"

The Sergeant nodded, glancing at the body. "He just died."

The Lieutenant lifted the field jacket. "How?"

"I don't know."

"Did he rattle off like a screwball?"

200

"Yes, sir."

"Battalion said he was pulling an act."

"He pulled it off pretty good."

"Could've been a brain hemorrhage."

"Could've."

"A German self-propelled gun's got the main road zeroed in, and air recon can't spot it. Battalion's ordered twenty patrols out." The Lieutenant dropped the field jacket on Weirdo's face. "Don't wait for his replacement." His finger made a trail on his map. "Here's the shortest way for your Squad—"

"They need rest, sir."

The Lieutenant looked at the Sergeant's gaunt face and sunken eyes.

"I'll take your Squad," the Lieutenant said gently.

His words dropped on the Sergeant like ice on a hot stove; they sizzled in the unbearable sticky heat. The Sergeant's blank eyes watched two trucks rolling behind the Lieutenant. The bivouac was suddenly silent.

"You were saying about the shortest way, Lieutenant?"

The shortest way, through vineyards and groves, was not the fastest way. Instead of replenishing their desperately needed energy, the men lost more of their meager strength after they had gorged themselves on grapes and oranges. Dropping their pants periodically not only slowed down the hunt but brought it to a halt.

The Sergeant had the worst case of the runs; he had become a glutton. He lost his drive to locate the SP's forward observer. Every man in the Squad had an ass like a blazing furnace. At first they had grudgingly accepted the discomfort, but then the uncontrollable, frequent diarrhea brought bleeding agony and rawness and a weakness that made them ineffective as combat men. Hollowed-out, sick, tourtured, they slowly followed him. Finally they reached some beehive-shaped stables, an ancient outdoor limestone stove, and a dead dog. Ten feet from the dog they collapsed in a farmhouse. Two walls and the roof were intact.

The last to trail along was Pimply Face. He stopped to stare at the flies glinting in the hot sun. He watched them feasting on the dog's entrails. He went into the house and sat down and began to writhe in pain. He looked at the dead dog and began to cry.

"P-p-poor dog—"

The men, each in his own burning hell, ignored his sobs. But the Sergeant understood the stuttering youth's need for survival and sanity after the shattering massacre in the cave. He felt sorry for him. The sobbing shook the Sergeant. He had lost command of the Squad. He hoped talk would help.

"Got a dog back home?"

Pimply Face nodded, unashamed of his tears.

"What kind?"

"Weimaraner—g-g-great huntin' dog." He struggled to his feet, went out of the house, kicked dirt on the dog to protect it, and returned. He slumped next to a wall.

Pimply Face was about to say something else when he groaned with pain and ran out again. The men continued to suffer in silence. Pimply Face returned, unbuttoning his pants, and held out a small kit. "I g-g-got this at the repple depple for VD protection." He plucked out a tube, dropped his pants, and massaged his ass with the ointment. The desperate men shared the salve to ease their own pains.

He looked at the Sergeant. "What's a S-S-SP?"

"Self-propelled gun."

"I s-s-sure'd like to be the guy who c-c-captures it."

Zab felt the burning subside. "You do that and the General'll hang a gong on you!"

"What kind of a gong?"

"Silver Star."

Pimply Face glowed. "How many m-m-medals *you* got, Sergeant?"

"None."

The Sergeant moved out of the farmhouse without a comment, trailed by the weary men. Falling in step with Zab, Pimply Face was boiling mad. "This outfit's *nuts* not g-g-giving the Sergeant any m-m-medals!"

"They did, but he said no thanks. He's allergic to 'em."

"He's w-w-what?"

202

"It's against his religion to accept a gong for gallantry in action."

"Oh." Then, after a moment, "What k-k-kind of religion is *that?*"

"What've you got against allergics?"

"Nothing! I g-g-got nothing against allergics, Zab, it's just I never m-m-met one before."

Two hours later the Sergeant maneuvered them up to an abandoned hilltop town. The tense men stood in doorways and studied the gutted buildings. Two shell-pocked structures still stood: the Banco di Sicilia and the town hall. Every man was aware that the SP's observation team, if they happened to be spotting from this town, would be on the roof or top floor of either building. The Sergeant put his ear all the way down the street for any sound. He heard nothing. Suddenly he threw his exhausted body into the job at hand. Using cover-for-cover leapfrogging, he led the Squad toward the bank and halted fifty feet from their first objective. He decided to advance another twenty-five feet. Their boots moved noiselessly through debris in the cobble-stoned street. He studied the bank, then looked at the men and they held their breath. They waited to see who would be sent.

The Sergeant tapped Vinci and pointed at the bank. The men let their breath out.

Zab grinned, whispered into Vinci's ear, "Good luck, paisano."

The Sergeant whispered into Zab's ear, "Help him make a deposit."

Zab whispered back, "My ass'll never make the roof."

The Sergeant smiled and pushed him forward.

Vinci and Zab worked their way to the bank, delicately slipped in through one of the hanging doors, and found shattered desks and debris and glass. Vinci quietly moved behind the cages. Zab enjoyed the gleam in Vinci's eyes as he hunted for money. But there was only the disappointment of finding office equipment. Vinci stared at a barred vault for a long moment. Suddenly he wheeled and went to work with Zab. They padded up the three flights of stairs, nuzzling past the wall, pressing silently into six rooms. They went up to the roof but found it empty. They threw themselves down as the scream of a shell burst behind them.

They raced down the stairs. The roof was hit.

Artillery shells falling on the town drove the Sergeant and the men scurrying for cover behind a twenty-foot-thick wall; from there they watched the roof of the town hall lift in the air. A moment later the building sagged, buckled, and collapsed in smoke and dust. A fire started.

"W-w-why all them sh-sh-shells just for a p-p-patrol?"

"They don't know we're here."

"Then who're they sh-sh-shelling?"

"They're using the town as a zeroing-in point to gauge the distance."

The Sergeant looked down the street as shells burst everywhere. Zab and Vinci hurtled out of the bank as explosions destroyed the street behind them. The bank was hit. There was a tremendous explosion, knocking both men down. Zab jumped up and ran. Vinci jumped up and ran; then he stopped, looked at the burning bank, and ran back into it.

"Crazy bastard!" said the Sergeant.

Zab also ran, reached the wall, and dived into the Squad. He looked behind him but saw no sign of Vinci in the shattered street.

"Christ, they got Vinci!"

He started back. The Sergeant stopped him. "He went back into the bank."

Zab stared at the burning bank. "He's crazy!"

Another shell hit the bank.

"Hell," said Zab, slowly dying inside, "I was just getting the hang of speaking Italian."

They watched shell bursts rolling over the town, hitting the bank again.

The men felt empty. Zab's prediction was wrong. The Four Horsemen were not going to come out of it alive.

"Look!" yelled Zab.

Emerging through smoke and zigzagging through endless thumps of bursts, Vinci ran toward them, money flying from the inside of his shirt. One fist was filled with money. He reached the wall and slammed into the men. He removed loose bills and packets of money from his shirt, from his pockets, from his helmet. They watched him in disbelief.

"I'm sending every lira home!"

The shelling suddenly stopped. The men stared at Vinci and watched him count the money, and they laughed.

"I had a hunch that big one got the vault," said Vinci, licking his finger as he counted.

"Mussolini money's no good," said Griff.

"Mussolini?" Vinci threw a bill at Griff. "Victor Emmanuel! His kisser on it makes it legal!"

"You pulled a Jesse James for nothing," said Zab. "An enlisted man can't send home more than his pay."

Vinci stopped counting and paled.

"An officer can," said the Sergeant. "I'll ask the Lieutenant to send it home for you."

Vinci shouted, "Yahooooo!", finished the count, took the bill from Griff, and put it with the rest. "Over twenty thousand dollars!" He looked at the blazing bank. *"Grazie,* Signor Hitler!" He looked at the Sergeant. "It's for my old man. He always wanted to open a bagel shop."

Zab cringed as a shell screamed over the wall. "I didn't know they had Italian bagels."

Vinci laughed. "You don't have to be Jewish to like bagels." They laughed. "The Pope eats gefilte fish on Fridays."

Then the shell landed.

50

The Schmeisser was field-stripped with scrutinizing authority by Schröder on his knees. Armin, quite satisfied with the burp gun issued to him, was sitting on a packing case watching Schröder with amusement. Not amused, as he stood there among empty shell cases, the ordnance hauptmann found his voice rising to a nervous pitch of anger as he crisply informed Schröder that the Schmeisser had been double-checked by his own men and there was no reason to field-strip it.

Schröder glanced up over his shoulder at the handsome, immaculately tailored hauptmann who looked like a Strength Through Joy leader of Hitler youth.

"Are *you* going to kill with it, Herr Hauptmann?"

"*What did you say?*"

"I said are *you* going to—"

"What's your name?"

Schröder pointed to a big ordnance truck. "It's in the record I signed for this weapon, sir, in that truck."

"Stand at attention, damn it!"

Schröder got to his feet. "I was issued a zero eight fifteen in France that almost blew my head off, Herr Hauptmann. Since then I field-strip *every* weapon I'm going to use."

"Give me your *Soldbuch!*"

Schröder pulled his service record booklet from his pocket and held it out. The officer seized it. Schröder bent over the gray blanket and placed the rear sight base among the many neatly arranged parts. The ordnance hauptmann stared at the name in the *Soldbuch*. He had heard of this much-decorated homicidal combat rebel who had shot a German officer in the back because of cowardice. He remembered hearing that Schröder was also awarded the Hand-to-Hand Clasp by the major general himself. The hauptmann returned the *Soldbuch* and strode off.

Armin smiled. "I thought you ate only panzer officers."

Schröder pocketed his *Soldbuch* and began reassembling. "I also have an appetite for bastards who shout that they want to die for the Führer and never get close enough to the fighting to get even a scratch. The bastards never use what they issue."

Three Germans dragged in a struggling pig, followed by a brokenhearted, helpless Sicilian boy. In the distance a group of women and children watched German soldiers being issued weapons and ammunition from another ordnance truck.

"Remember Major Kleink?" Schröder asked Armin.

"Wounded at Tobruk."

"Yes."

"You told me about him. Good man."

"Yes."

"You served with him in Czechoslovakia."

Schröder quickened the pace, assembling the Schmeisser with swift, precise movements. "He's where we're going. He's liaison with the Napoli Division."

"Auf Wiedersehen!" shouted an old Sicilian at a German courier mounting a motorcycle. The German waved and rode off. The old Sicilian spat after him. Schröder saw this and walked over to the old man and broke his jaw with one blow.

"You'll never spit at a German uniform again," said Schröder.

Thirty minutes later Schröder and Armin, loaded with ammunition pouches and grenades, were precariously sitting on top of shell cases stacked high behind the crew of a fast-moving tractor-drawn 105-mm gun.

There was a rumor that the First Parachute Division was being moved by air from France to Sicily and that the Twenty-ninth Panzer Grenadier Division was on its way from Calabria across the Strait of Messina. There was another rumor that all German units in Sicily would be evacuated any hour to defend the Italian mainland. Schröder was furious. The second rumor meant that the island had been written off as a loss on only the third day of the invasion! He blamed the Italians.

At Napoli Division HQ Schröder and Armin located Major Kleink who greeted Schröder warmly with, "Have you eaten?"

Armin grinned.

Major Kleink ordered them all the hot Italian food and vino they could hold and slipped Schröder a bottle of brandy. He told him he had arranged transportation for them to battalion. "They're with Schmalz's regiment, holding off the British." He smiled. "You'll be just in time to make sure they'll win."

Schröder didn't smile. "I wonder how things are going in the south."

"Let's find out."

Major Kleink led them past Italian troops to the communications truck where several Napoli men were listening to their officer shouting in Italian on the phone.

"He's getting the report right now," said Major Kleink.

The shouting officer slammed the phone down and in a rage of Italian profanities told his comrades the news.

Major Kleink turned ashen. "Things are not going well in the south," he told Schröder.

"Who was he talking to, major? A German or Italian outfit?"

"The American First Infantry Division."

Crawling through high grass, the Sergeant and his Squad heard another scream and once again didn't hear the shell land behind them. For the past hour they heard the shells passing overhead. The last time the Sergeant contacted Platoon, the Squad learned that Battalion had set a deadline by which one of the twenty patrols was desperately urged to radio back news that the gun was located. The SP had kept the Grave Registration Bureau working overtime. The Battalion CO had given a name to that SP—the Artful Dodger. The Sergeant was aware that there could be several Artful Dodgers; then again, there could be only the one they were hunting.

Reaching the edge of the field of high grass, the Squad stared at a monastery. The Sergeant studied the steeple through his binocs and slowly dipped the glasses to a statue of a saint hovering over a busted cart. There was no movement.

Between the Squad and the monastery 250 yards of exposed area had to be crossed to check the steeple.

The Sergeant had to chance the loss of one man to draw fire.

"I'll go," said Griff, reading the Sergeant's mind.

"Okay."

With their weapons aimed at the steeple, the men remained on their bellies as they peered through blades of grass at Griff walking alone toward the monastery. The new men admired him for his guts. Zab, Vinci, and Johnson couldn't understand why Griff volunteered. The Sergeant didn't look for a reason. His only concern was the steeple. It was a matter of one man's life to save many. The Sergeant had so far lost seven assistant squad leaders. He had asked Griff more than once to take the job, but Griff had refused. Griff was satisfied being a rifleman without any kind of responsibility.

Griff walked slowly. He had contempt for volunteers, but he had a reason for this display of courage. More than a reason. An obsession. He had to get over his buck fever or lose his sanity. He had to kill a German face-to-face so that he could sleep nights. He knew he was covered by the Sergeant and Squad and he also knew their cover would come to life only with his death. That was the chance he was taking and it made him walk faster. A German bullet in him would end his misery of nightmares, and *his* bullet in a German would also end it. He wasn't seeking suicide. He was seeking relief. He had about a hundred yards to go and was still alive. If a German OP *was* in that steeple, he was waiting to see how many people were with the lone American. If a German was in that monastery, Griff would soon come face-to-face with his hang-up. Having to miss killing an enemy he could see was demoralizing him: he was endangering every man in the Squad. Today he would get over that hump. Or die.

He was fifty feet from the big door when a white cloth was waved back and forth through it and the voice of a man cried out in English, "Don't shoot!"

Griff was startled.

"Come out with both hands on top of your head!" shouted Griff, aware this could be a trap: one German surrendering and his comrades opening fire. In his fear, Griff's runs returned.

The heavy door squealed open. A monk in brown habit emerged with his hands on the cowl, partially concealing his face. He advanced cautiously. He wore sandals and a cross dangled from the chain lashed round his robe. He stopped a few feet from Griff. He was short, wiry, about forty, and he was grinning. He had two gold teeth.

"Don't get trigger-happy, buster. I'm from Brooklyn. My name's Borcellino. Can I put my hands down? I'm not packing a shiv under this goddamn holy blanket."

Twenty minutes later the Squad checked the steeple, the sleeping quarters of straw mattresses in open partitions, the small library, the dining room, and the kitchen where bread was baking in the oven. There was no sign of any German radio or scope equipment.

Under the Sergeant's supervision the twenty-seven frightened monks were lined up in the chapel and searched for hidden guns. No weapons were found under their coarse brown habits.

"I told you they're the McCoy," Borcellino said to the Sergeant. "All but me. I'm no goddamn monk."

"You said you're an American? What are you doing here?"

"I was deported. Uncle Sam called me an undesirable alien."

"Hell," said Vinci, "another Lucky Luciano."

"He was a bum!" fumed Borcellino. "He had a better press than I got. I'm Salvatore Borcellino of Brooklyn. The name ring a bell?"

"Yes," said Zab. "Icepick Borcellino. Sometimes called the Iceman of Brooklyn."

"That's *me!*" Borcellino was proud.

"Yeah," said Zab, "your name rings a bell, all right. Murder, dope, girls. A two-bit gangster."

"Two-bit gangster? Five million bucks worth of gangster!" Borcellino shrugged. He looked at the dogfaces with pride. "I can't wait for you guys to make pasta out of Mussolini when you take Rome."

"You don't like Mussolini?" asked Vinci.

"He's a bastard!"

"Bullshit."

The little gangster's mouth looked like a shark. "It's no bullshit!" He opened a small bronze box that was lying near the altar, took out his alligator-skin cigar case, and selected a king-sized cigar. He observed the way Zab eyed it. "I'm Mafia here, but that bald-headed Fascist bullfrog wants all the garlic gravy for himself and for that bitch he's keeping on the side. He's got an army. I haven't. I got nothing to fight him with." He took a gold lighter from the bronze box, fired his cigar, and glanced at the monks. "These monks come in handy for my hideout. Nobody bothers us here. I feed

210

'em and they let me pass for one of 'em. Everybody's got a price, just like the cops and judges back in the U.S.A." He laughed heartily and offered a cigar to Zab who swiftly struck a match on his helmet and fired up.

"Havana!" said Zab.

"Salvatore Borcellino always goes first-class." He let clouds of smoke drift out slowly. Then he sighed. "I'd give five million bucks to be back in Brooklyn." He turned to the Sergeant. "Let me help you guys. I got to square myself with Uncle Sam."

"Seen any Germans around today?"

"Sure."

"Know what an SP is?"

"Sure. Self-propelled gun. It hits, hides, moves on its own wheels, and is goddamn hard to spot."

"Seen one around?"

"I know where they're hiding *some* kind of big gun."

"Where?"

"Uh-uh."

"What do you mean uh-uh?"

"Exactly what you know it means, Sergeant. You want to blow my head off, go on. But if you want that gun you got to make a deal with me. You listening?"

"You're doing the talking."

"Get on your radio right now. Tell your General that Salvatore Borcellino's going to help you fight the Nazis. *That* kind of front-page story'll get my ass back to the States."

"No deal."

"I'll be a war hero in Brooklyn and—what do you mean *no deal?*"

"Exactly what you know it means."

"What's wrong with it? *You* win. *I* win."

"I'll tell the General *after* you take us to that gun."

Smiling, Borcellino waved his giant cigar scoldingly at the Sergeant. "Cautious character, eh? Okay. *After.*"

"Let's go."

The men smiled. Grudgingly they liked the little gangster. "Take any Italian prisoners?" he asked them.

"Yes," said the Sergeant.

"I bet all those bastards said they were always against Mussolini, eh?"

Four miles from the monastery, carrying an empty basket, Borcellino led the Sergeant and Squad to the end of a gully running parallel to the dirt road. He motioned for them to wait. He had trouble with his robe as he climbed up to the roadside shrine and kneeled in prayer. He asked the Sergeant if he could see the big rock down the road.

The Sergeant peered over the top of the gully. "Yes."

"The gun's a couple hundred yards behind it."

The Sergeant looked through his binocs. "There's a German near the rock."

"Yeah, a corporal. He gave me food this morning for the monks. I never go back with an empty basket."

"Was he alone?"

"Yeah, they only use one joker for security, just to keep the natives away from the area."

"What's his collar patch?"

"Artillery red."

"Kill him."

"*What?*"

The Sergeant tossed up his trench knife.

Borcellino stared at the ugly weapon that landed near the shrine. "Jesus, Mary, and Joseph! What war did *that* come from?"

"Use it like an ice pick. You know how to do that."

"That ain't our deal."

"You want to go back to Brooklyn?"

Borcellino shuddered and picked up the trench knife.

"You'll get a medal," said the Sergeant.

Borcellino dropped the trench knife in his basket, crossed himself, seized the handle of the basket, got to his feet, and began to walk down the road. Waiting, the Sergeant looked at his men in silence. Then he lifted his binocs and watched Borcellino reach the German corporal at the big rock. Borcellino, gesturing, was asking for more food, then begging. The corporal waved him off and turned his back. Borcellino plunged the trench knife into his back. The corporal fell. Borcellino dragged the body behind a bush, cleaned the blade in the earth, and waved.

The Sergeant ran his Squad down the dirt road to the big rock. Still shaken, Borcellino returned the trench knife to the Sergeant and eased the corporal's body carefully around the big rock. The Sergeant saw boulders, the fallen columns of a Greek temple, and beyond them the trees.

"There's a camouflaged net under those trees," said Borcellino, "hiding five krauts and that gun."

The Sergeant studied the net through his binocs and clapped Borcellino on the back. "You'll get a medal, all right."

Borcellino grinned. "Look me up in Brooklyn."

Watching the Sergeant and Squad skillfully utilize the boulders for cover in their advance toward the fallen columns, Borcellino calmly reached under the bush for a Beretta 9-mm semiautomatic carbine. The "dead" corporal got to his feet with his Bergmann 9-mm machine pistol.

They both aimed at the backs of the men in the Squad.

51

Their first target was Ramirez, onetime farmer volunteer in the Mexican Army maneuvers of 1941. To him the brief adventure had meant enough food.

Ramirez had fled across the border, told the Times Square recruiting officer that he was Texas-born, joined the U.S. Army to eat, and was called greaser during basic. Shipped to North Africa, he was given a Red One shoulder patch outside Algiers. His judgment of Americans changed when the Sergeant reassumed command of the First Squad before the invasion of Sicily.

The Sergeant never called him greaser . . .

As Ramirez zigzagged with the Squad from boulder to boulder, getting closer to the fallen columns of the Greek temple, bullets from Borcellino's automatic carbine, traveling at twenty-nine hundred feet per second, shattered his dream of someday becoming an American citizen.

The second target was Paine, whose last furlough was spent with his sexy radical sweetheart, nineteen-year-old Laurie.

She had recoiled, called him a reactionary bastard,

213

and said that she hoped he would be killed. A German corporal's machine pistol traveling sixteen hundred feet per second made Laurie's hope come true.

The bursts from his rear made the Sergeant whirl. He saw flashes coming from behind the big rock and he saw Ramirez and Paine fall. At the same moment, the Squad, stunned by the gangster's double cross, was subjected to frontal fire coming from the fallen Greek columns and rifle fire from the flanks.

The bushwhack was complete.

The Sergeant hurled smoke grenades at the big rock, at the fallen columns to his front, and at both flanks. White clouds gathered, and within seconds he made his Squad invisible.

"Smoke grenades!" he shouted. "Every direction!"

The sandbagged Squad grenaded the compass, building up a thick smoke cocoon. Bullets zinged off the boulders, missing their steel helmets.

"Fix bayonets!" shouted the Sergeant.

A bullet ricocheted off the boulder and struck his helmet.

Six Germans, blinded by smoke, huddled behind the fallen columns and held their fire, waiting to see targets as the Squad's long knives silently moved closer and closer in a lateral crawl. The point of the Sergeant's bayonet struck a temple column, probed for flesh, found flesh, and thrust into it. Every bayonet in the Squad did the same. As the smoke began to clear, the Sergeant and his men double bayoneted every German they saw to make sure the job was complete.

Hurling their fragmentary grenades at the camouflage net, the Sergeant bellied his men toward the concealed gun, emptied clips into the net, and killed the crew. The Sergeant manned the German machine gun and, with Vinci feeding, fired bursts at both flanks, supported by the Squad's rifles. Then the Sergeant fired at the big rock. Borcellino and the German corporal were cut down by the German machine gun.

Wisps of smoke lingered. The Sergeant and Squad no longer saw any living targets. In the silence the men pulled down what remained of the net.

The Sergeant stared at the SP that was not a self-propelled gun. It was a six-barreled mortar—the *Nebel-werfer.*

He radioed the Lieutenant. "We lost two men. Ramirez and Paine. We got a *Nebelwerfer.*"

The Squad heard the boxcar sail over their heads. The men could not hear the shell land.

"That SP just got a half-track!" said the Lieutenant. "Cripple that mortar, wait at 779053 to be relieved. Another patrol's coming up to bat. You struck out!"

After putting the mortar out of commission with German potato mashers, the Sergeant and his Squad, nauseous, frustrated, and angry, headed slowly toward coordinates 779053. They had suffered the agony of the runs, lost two men, wiped out a number of krauts, and captured and destroyed a six-barreled mortar, yet were told they had struck out. They had heard of mutinies in history. Now they understood what caused revolt.

They heard a shell from the SP scream over their heads.

The men grunted. That shell was a reminder that the Lieutenant was right. The fact could not be brushed aside. They had failed to locate the SP that was making graves for the Third Battalion. Their spirits low, they dragged their feet behind the somewhat stooped figure of the Sergeant. The men shared the Sergeant's disappointment. He halted in the broiling sun and slowly sagged to the ground to rest. They stretched out on their backs and covered their faces with their helmets.

"Hell—" said Zab, "it's not the first time we didn't score."

The Sergeant agreed in silence. Often his scarred Squad had not returned victories after a patrol. But was it always the last assignment that counted, not what you accomplished yesterday or last week? He sighed. For the morning report he would have to confess his gullibility. The lives of two men had been lost because of a deal he made with a deported gangster whose loyalty to Mussolini should not have surprised him. He sighed again. The area was empty and the bend in the road a dozen yards ahead was ominously silent. He looked at his men dozing in the heat.

A few moments later, he heard a sweet song. Turning toward the bend he saw a boy of about ten pulling a two-wheel cart, quietly singing a tender Italian song. The men in the Squad lifted their helmets. The boy showed no surprise as he reached the Squad. He stopped singing. The stench from the cart was sickening. The men held their noses. The Sergeant checked the cart and found the covered body of a woman. Vinci spoke to the boy.

"His mother," said Vinci, turning his head away from the cart. "He's taking her to Gela."

"Gela?" The Sergeant also turned away from the cart. "He'll never make it in this heat. Tell him we'll bury his mother right here."

Vinci relayed the news. The boy spoke softly.

"He's grateful but no."

"She'll be decomposed before he reaches Gela."

"He's going to bury her next to his father. He's been pulling that cart since daybreak."

"Ask him about the gun."

"I knew that was coming." Vinci asked the boy. Their friendly conversation mushroomed into an argument, both of them using their hands to emphasize points. The boy had the last word.

"The little son of a bitch knows where the gun is," said Vinci, "but it'll cost."

Zab grinned. "Give him some of your bagel loot."

"It's not loot he wants. It's an ambulance. He'll take us to that gun only if we radio for an ambulance right now to haul his mother to Gela."

"No sweat," said the Sergeant.

"That's only half of it. She's got to be transported in a casket with handles," said Vinci. *"Four* handles. And it's got to be satin-lined. Or silk. He wants her to sleep in something soft."

"Tell him okay."

"What?"

"After he takes us to the gun."

"Oh, for Christ's sake, Sergeant!"

Another shell sailed over their heads.

"Tell him."

Vince did. The boy accepted.

"He says okay, but I say no," said Vinci. "I don't

trust him. He's too goddamn glib. Let him lead another patrol into a bushwhack."

The boy's big black eyes gazed at their faces and he knew they didn't trust him. He shifted his eyes and stared at the Sergeant. They stood there like two kids trying to outstare each other without blinking.

The boy spoke softly.

Vinci grunted. "The little son of a bitch got his act down pat. Now he claims his old man was hanged in Gela for fighting Mussolini. I bet the krauts got a hundred kids like him out in the hills sucking our patrols into ambush."

"Tell him we'll leave the cart in the first shade we find."

"Holy Christ!" growled Vinci and reluctantly relayed the words.

"Mia madre," said the boy, *"viene con noi o andate a trovare il fucile da soli!"*

Vinci grunted. "We've got to haul her with us or we find that gun on our own!"

The sun baked the corpse in the cart pulled by the boy and Pimply Face. Their noses covered with handkerchiefs like Western bandits, the men moved through the gorge and crossed a bleak open terrain that was disturbed only by one high mound of rocks and dirt. The Sergeant didn't like the area. There was too much exposure. Suddenly the boy darted ahead and vanished behind the mound. The Sergeant and his men jammed under and behind the only available cover—the cart.

"The little bastard!" said Vinci.

They waited for small-arms or machine-gun fire from the mound. None came. The Sergeant studied the shimmering haze shrouding the mound. The smell of the corpse above the men became unbearable.

They saw a figure in the haze. The boy emerged on the run, carrying a wooden sign. He reached the cart. The men got to their feet. The boy spoke to Vinci, giving him the sign. It read *achtung minen!* Above the words were a skull and crossbones.

"He saw Germans laying mines out there this morning. He knows a bypass up a mountain trail." He tossed the sign away, ashamed at not having trusted the boy.

Halfway up the hazardous mountain trail the men halted for a break. For the past hour they had been taking turns pushing and pulling the cart up the incline. The boy pointed at a goat crossing the minefield below. The men watched the goat step on a mine. The explosion echoed. The climb continued, the trail narrowing.

A wheel went over the precipice. The cart tipped. The boy reached out for his mother's body and his weight against the cart sent it over. The Sergeant seized the corpse. Vinci grabbed the boy in midair. The cart fell, smashing on rocks, splintering. A wheel sailed through the air and landed on a mine below. The explosion triggered three more mines.

The yellow and red flowers on the vast gentle slope were crushed by GI shoes. The corpse was carried in Vinci's shelter-half. An army of black ants carrying seeds marched. The Squad carrying weapons, ammo, and the boy's mother marched. The shoes of the GIs crushed the ants. Close to collapse from the climb and the heat, the boy led the men toward an orange grove. For the first time they heard the crack of a big gun firing.

The Sergeant and the men glanced at each other.

Trailing the boy through the orange grove, not a man picked an orange. The boy ate three by the time they reached the edge of the grove. The boy pointed as he spoke.

"The gun's in that house," said Vinci.

The corpse was placed on the ground in the shade. The Sergeant and the Squad saw women and children working in the field near the house. The big gun fired from the house. The boy spoke.

Vinci said, "A German machine gun's trained on those women and kids to give our planes a peaceful look from the air."

Through his binocs the Sergeant got a good look at the flash hider on the muzzle of an 88-mm gun where the door of a farmhouse once stood. It was not an SP 75 on a Mark III chassis. Not this one. This was a Mark VI King Tiger, and he was astonished that despite the brilliance of the idea of hiding a Tiger in a house, there was no man posted in the orange grove. Then he remembered his own lack of common sense when he swallowed Borcellino's monk act. Even as he saw in advance how he would attack the Tiger, he wondered why he hadn't checked the German corporal at the big rock to make sure he was dead. Why? Was it common sense to have trusted the boy? Was it sentiment? Emotion? *Emotion*. It was emotion. It was something he was not supposed to be capable of having, according to the women in his life.

The Tiger fired from its lair.

He slowly eased his binocs to take in the German machine gun that was trained on the women and children. The machine gunner had a stubble, wore glasses, and was smoking a cigarette. Before he would finish that cigarette he would be dead.

The Sergeant lowered the binocs. "Vinci, tell the boy to stay here with his mother. I don't want him running around out there and getting in the way. Griff, work closer to that machine gunner. When we open fire, get him before he hits those civilians with wild bursts."

Removing their handkerchiefs, the men trailed the Sergeant through the grove. Vinci told the boy what to do and then hurried after the Squad.

Griff crawled toward the machine gunner, reached no-miss distance, adjusted elevation, and waited with the German in his sights. Griff knew his sweat wasn't coming from the heat. It was coming from panic. He could see the face of the machine gunner. He could see the glasses he was wearing.

The Sergeant swiftly, silently slipped his men through the grove. From their position they were all impressed with the weird sight of the tank that had barged through the rear of the house and almost filled the room. There were only a couple of feet on each side between the Tiger and the walls. Every man had the same thought: was anybody in the house when the tank plowed into it?

The Sergeant studied the Germans outside. One on the radio and his assistant. One studying a map. One relaying the coordinates to the crew inside the Tiger.

Two of them, stripped to the waist, asleep on the ground. When the Tiger fired, the house trembled, but the two sleeping Germans were not disturbed by the deafening crack of the 88. The Sergeant saw no sign of any vehicle and assumed that the extra men and the machine gunner in front of the house were carried on the Tiger wherever it went. It still bothered him that the tank CO hadn't placed a security guard in the grove.

The Sergeant assigned his men the visible targets. They aimed. He aimed. They waited for him to fire. He squeezed slowly. His target was the radioman. He had a hair to go to complete the squeeze when his finger froze as a little girl appeared from behind the side of the house and ran in front of the radioman. She lingered for a moment, watching him.

When the 88 fired, the child ran off, clapping her hands. The noise no longer frightened her. She vanished around the front of the house.

The Sergeant waited. He had to make sure the child wouldn't run back into their line of fire. She didn't.

The Sergeant opened fire. The Squad fired.

Every bullet found its easy mark.

Griff squeezed, aiming directly at the machine gunner's glasses. The squeeze froze. Griff forced the squeeze. His finger wouldn't budge. He heard the fusillade coming from the Squad. He saw the machine gunner move his barrel toward the sound of the small arms.

Griff deliberately lowered his barrel and shot the machine gunner in the thigh. The startled German fell forward and as he hit the ground his glasses fell off. The German began to cry for help as the little girl ran to him and picked up his glasses and held them out to him, but he crawled past her to the frightened women and children who were huddling against the front of the house under the muzzle of the 88. The wounded German reached them and again cried for help.

The women and children kicked, clubbed, and hacked him to death with their picks, rakes, and shovels as the little girl ran back and forth, singing an Italian nursery rhyme, holding the glasses in front of her eyes.

The well-orchestrated killing of the visible Germans in the back of the house was followed up by the Sergeant, who clambered onto the Tiger to complete the destruction. He fired a full clip into the open turret of the Tiger. The empty clip clanged against the wall. The ringing sound was punctuated by groans coming from inside the tank. The Sergeant jammed in a fresh clip and emptied it at the crew and again the ejected clip hit the wall with a clang.

The groaning inside the tank stopped.

His aching back throbbing, his neck stiff, the Sergeant lowered himself into the tank, checked the dead crew, and climbed up. He almost couldn't make getting his remaining leg out of the hatch. He saw his men gaping at the ruins inside the house. He saw Vinci standing between the Tiger and the wall, eyes fixed on a photograph on the floor. The Sergeant glanced down. The frame was busted, the glass smashed.

Vinci picked it up very slowly and stared at the wedding couple and said, "That's my mother and father."

The Sergeant rested on the tank. The men glanced at each other, then looked at Vinci who was still staring at the bride and groom in the photo.

"This is my grandmother's house," said Vinci.

He felt horror as he looked around, dazed. Spotting a piece of black dress under the track, he fell on his knees, touched the dress, began to pull at it, tore it, stared at the piece of black in his hand.

"Good God!" he yelled. "She's under the tank!"

The Sergeant and the men watched Vinci become a madman. He dug, clawed, scraped with fingernails for her body under the tank, shouting, *"Nonna! Nonna! Nonna! Nonna!"* He ran up and down the length of the Tiger trying to get under the tank. He picked up the wedding photo he had dropped and slumped against the wall. Holding the photo close to him he began to sob, burying his head in anguish.

The men felt sick. Pushing past the men, a little old lady with white hair under an old black shawl meekly entered, moving between the tank and the wall, looking for something in the rubble, stepping over broken dishes. Reaching Vinci, she saw part of the wedding photo in his hand. She touched the photo gently, spoke in Italian in a quiet frail voice. Vinci was deaf. The little old lady tugged at the photo.

Without looking up, Vinci whacked her with the photo. She crashed against the slack track on the wheels, both lips split, mouth bleeding. But she was not angry. Only sad and scared. She again spoke in Italian to Vinci. The plea in her words meant nothing to him. Then the words themselves began to penetrate his grief, and he slowly lifted his head and looked at her. She repeated in a quavering voice, "It is my son's wedding picture. Please give it back to me."

Vinci groaned like a wounded animal. He pulled himself to her and gave her the photo and gently wiped the blood on her mouth and then he held her close and rocked her like a baby in his arms as he sobbed.

"Why are you crying?" she asked him.

52

"Let's revolt!" growled Schröder.

"We'll hang," Armin said, trying to calm him.

"We'll be decorated for mutiny against the Italians."

Armin was too hot to argue. They seldom spoke when marching in the heat, but he had been lured into mutiny talk because Schröder was right. The nightmare that kept every infantryman in Group Schmalz sleepless was no longer a nightmare. It was happening. The poorly trained Napoli Division had fled from the battle with the British, and now Group Schmalz, still under Italian orders, was probing for Americans. General Guzzoni, not Schmalz, was running the war in Sicily.

In actual command of the 186 Germans in Schröder's rifle company Tenente Colonnello Cavaleri was never without his gold cigarette holder in his mouth.

"Know what an American rifle company would do," Schröder had grumbled, "if they found themselves under command of a British lieutenant colonel who never saw combat?"

"Yes. They'd revolt."

That had launched the talk about mutiny.

Armin agreed but preferred an American bullet to an Italian noose. He knew that even though Schröder and the others would secretly be admired by Kesselring if they revolted, the field marshal would be forced to hang the mutineers to please Mussolini.

Cavaleri, who could never disguise his incapability to make a decision, was, at fifty, a small, subservient, dedicated Fascist whose god was Mussolini. The butt of jokes, he was unquestionably the most unpopular and useless officer in the Italian army.

Cavaleri was shunned by other officers and relegated to an involuntary solitude. His incompetence, bolstered by his brand of superblind patriotism, caused him to be shunted from one division to another until he was put out to pasture in the Napoli Division because he knew Sicily. He was born only a few miles from the hill on which stood the Roman columns.

The German battalion CO, in order to get Cavaleri out of his hair, agreed to the little Italian's plan to take a company of Germans out to locate the King Tiger they had lost radio contact with more than an hour ago.

As Cavaleri led Schröder's company up the hill to the Roman columns, he smelled the sweet scent of Roman glory. He had his own combat command. True, only 186 Germans, but they were battle-hardened veterans. He would restore honor to the Napoli Division, to Mussolini, and to Italy.

He climbed the hill he had played on when he was a child. When he reached the top before any of the Germans, he stood by the great Roman columns and looked down at the surrounding terrain, glowing because he knew every inch of it as well as he knew that in the end Mussolini would win.

As the Germans reached the summit they slumped to rest against the columns. Except Armin. Intrigued with the ancient wall of funerary busts, he slowly walked past the reliefs of masters and slaves.

Schröder remained on his feet, leaning against a wall, his eyes blazing at the Italian officer who was surveying the area below with the arrogance of a Caesar. Schröder raged as he glared at Cavaleri. Cavaleri represented defeat. To Schröder the critical truth was that Italians were cowards. The invasion of Sicily had proved that they retreated even on their own soil.

Even during his early infantry training, Schröder had not felt such hatred and contempt. His rage increased. Because of Mussolini, the losses in Sicily were causing the decay of the Wehrmacht morale. For Nazis, the way to preserve the Third Reich was to wage war, but how could they wage war when they were commanded by Italians spreading the cancer of defeat? Schröder feared that for Germans in Sicily to continue this fiasco called war it could mean utter annihilation.

He pictured Cavaleri as a crumpled lump of Italian uniform and blood, and the picture made Schröder feel good.

When the last man reached the top, Cavaleri pointed with his gold cigarette holder and in atrocious German assigned the sections to specific areas. Schröder was to take his rifle squad of nine men to investigate the last coordinates radioed by the Tiger in the orange grove below about five kilometers beyond the rocky area. In five hours all sections were to return to the hill.

"And where will *you* be?" Schröder challenged. "Drinking vino and singing opera on this hill?"

Every German soldier stiffened, giving each other looks of bewilderment. Armin's heart stopped. Schröder's mutiny was just a word away from becoming a reality.

Cavaleri didn't show outrage at the scathing, dangerous verbal assault that called for a court-martial. "What is your name?"

"Schröder."

Cavaleri remained calm, understanding only too well what triggered the outburst. "You hate Italians that much?"

"Yes, sir!"

"But we are allies."

"I am not fighting for Italy!"

"And I am not fighting for Germany!" Cavaleri was grateful to be placed in this position. One Italian against 186 German infantrymen. He felt good. He would show these Hitler murderers that Italians were not cowards. "I am personally taking your patrol down to that orange grove. Any objection, Schröder?"

Schröder said nothing. He was astonished that Cavaleri had taken such unexpected initiative.

"Ah, you have no objection? Good. I admire a soldier who says what he feels and you are the kind of soldier I like to lead in combat. Let's go."

Armin sighed with relief. The men started down the hill, certain that the sun had incinerated Schröder's brain. Armin looked back and again his heart halted. Cavaleri was waiting for Schröder to move, but Schröder just leaned against the wall.

"Well, Schröder?" said Cavaleri with an upbeat, then even smiled warmly.

Schröder moved. Slowly. But he moved with the rest of the men.

53

Vinci and his grandmother presented Zab with a sentimental touch for his book as Griff sketched them on V-mail. They would fit nicely in Zab's handling of blood tradition even though he revolted against that long-established custom. Zab had mixed *grappa* with Chianti and *zucco* with onions and garlic and tomato sauce and spaghetti and he was drunk and ready to burst.

He knew he'd never get Vinci to admit that there was a false note in this scene of American soldiers and Italian women eating and drinking together to celebrate the union of a grandson and his grandmother. He also knew that Vinci suspected that his granny, like most Italian grannies, was a Fascist.

Family devotion was a good literary breather for a war novel but the display was phony to Zab. He studied Vinci and granny. He knew how he would handle them in the book. They represented force and fraud.

The spectacle of family love was a fake. Zab knew that tomorrow granny would pray for Il Duce and Vinci would kill more Italians and all the hugs and kisses and tears and sweet talk were just so much bullshit. Zab laughed, wondering what face granny would wear if

225

Vinci proudly announced how many Italians he had killed.

"Ridiculous!" muttered Zab. The love between Vinci and granny was ridiculous.

But *was* it all ridiculous? Zab asked himself.

There was real sincerity in the way Vinci had busted his fingernails clawing under the tank for his grandmother. Zab admitted to himself that it had moved him though at the time the thought did cross his mind— *what's the difference if she is under the tank? It's just another body.*

Chewing his cigar Zab found himself moved once again as Griff drew the cartoon of Vinci and granny cheek to cheek.

His back felt busted from his own digging. He and the Squad had buried the Germans, even those in the Tiger. Every man tried but failed to get the tank moving. In front of the house, he watched the communal pasta joyfully served by the women from a big wooden trough. The Squad was drinking vino through needle holes in small casks.

It interested Zab the way the women—competing vigorously for the Americans' attention, and tempting the men with smiles in temporary cozy relationships— had forgotten the Tiger firing from the house, had forgotten hacking the German soldier to pieces, had forgotten living with the nightmare of sudden death by violence. There was no sign of war beneath the surface of their laughter, but now and then he detected a flash of pain behind the smiles the women wore.

"Hey, Sergeant," Zab said.

There was no response. He turned his head.

The Sergeant was asleep on the ground after three helpings of pasta and a small cask of vino. An old blanket was his pillow. Sitting next to him, holding his helmet on her lap and fingering the twigs and leaves in the camouflage net, the little girl, five-year-old Graziella, with chocolate-smeared mouth, was staring through the German spectacles on her nose, her enormous brown eyes angrily fixed on the fly that was exploring the Sergeant's sweaty cheek. The child carefully shooed the fly away.

"Sergeant."

The Sergeant opened his eyes to be blinded by the sun. "Hm?"

The radioman held out the phone. "It's the Lieutenant."

The Sergeant grunted as he sat up and took the receiver. "Yes, sir?"

"The ambulance is standing by for the minefield to be cleared." The Lieutenant's voice was in lifeless monotone. "The General got a casket for that kid's mother."

"With handles, sir?"

"Of course with handles! It's a casket, Sergeant. Not a coffin."

The Sergeant grunted. "That's good, Lieutenant." He waited for the "out," but there was a long pause, and he suspected what was behind it. "Do we move on?"

"To Hill 407."

Graziella watched the Sergeant check his map. "Yeah—about eight miles away, sir."

"Some Roman columns on it. Company'll be there in a couple hours."

"How about waiting here and moving up with them?"

"They're bypassing you to check Hill 368. Out."

The Sergeant returned the phone. "Tell Vinci the ambulance is on the way with the casket. It has handles." He stretched out on his aching back. He was too tired to kill as well as he used to. His body demanded more rest. He closed his eyes. He felt eyes on him and turned his head. Graziella was lucky. The war had passed her, and in twenty years she'd be telling stories about the Tiger in the house, the American soldiers, and the Sergeant who gave her chocolate.

The Sergeant winked. Thinking a bug had attacked his eye, she brushed away the wink. He smiled. *"Grazie,* Graziella," he said and fell asleep.

Vinci's grandmother played the accordion. The women, the old women, and the children danced with each other. Griff, Zab, Vinci, Johnson, and other members of the Squad joined in the dance. Old women dancing the tarantella with each other could not hold back their tears. The village was all female. Their men were dead . . .

When the Sergeant opened his eyes and looked at his

227

watch, he saw that he had stolen thirty minutes. Graziella was gone. He was on his feet, announcing, "We move out in five minutes."

The women and children watched in silence as the Squad buckled on cartridge belts and checked weapons and ammo. The boy thanked the Sergeant, using Vinci as interpreter, but the Sergeant simply grunted. He was annoyed.

"Who took my helmet?"

While they helped him hunt for it, Graziella marched up to him with the helmet. She had arranged red, yellow, blue, and white flowers in his camouflage net. The Sergeant smiled and put it on. She clapped her hands.

Staring nervously at the flower-covered helmet, Zab growled through his cigar, "You're not going to wear that garden, are you?"

"It's beautiful," said the Sergeant.

Graziella smiled.

Johnson groaned with the rest of the men. "Hell, you'll be spotted a mile away!"

"I like the way it smells." With a farewell wave the Sergeant was on the move.

Tearing himself away from his grandmother, Vinci caught up with the Squad. The Squad was apprehensively trailing the Sergeant's floral display. The women watched the Americans marching off. The women knew what was to come. It would be more suffering and chaos.

Granny's eyes smarted with tears as Vinci turned and waved. She looked at the faces of the children and saw their pain. Graziella kept her eyes on the flowers until they disappeared behind a big rock. Her tears clouded the German spectacles.

The Sergeant chuckled. The men kept their distance because he was a vivid target shouting to draw fire. Sweat ran down his face and dripped from his chin. He was on the verge of keeling over in the heat. The rocks were getting bigger and the heat hotter. Only eight miles. He hoped the Company would be put in reserve when they got to Hill 407. Or maybe they'd reorganize there for a forced march. Hell! That could mean another attack. No profit in bitching to the Old Man. The response was already known to him: every squad in Battalion was pulling its own weight as a work-horse. He decided not to bitch about working his men overtime.

"Sergènte!"

He wheeled with his men. Graziella trotted through the rocks. *"Sergènte!"* she called again, and on reaching him waited until she caught her breath. She kept her eyes on him as she spoke to Vinci.

The Sergeant growled when Zab said, "You've got yourself a camp follower."

Trying not to sound angry the Sergeant asked Vinci, "What does she want?"

"A kiss." Vinci grinned. "You didn't kiss her good-bye."

"G-g-go on, Sergeant," said Pimply Face. "K-k-kiss her."

The men smiled.

"Want *me* to show you how to kiss a child?" said Zab.

The Sergeant grinned, slung his rifle, lifted her up. She flung her little arms around his neck and squeezed hard. He kissed her on the cheek.

Schröder felt like keeling over. He knew it was not the heat. Cavaleri made him sick. A spaghetti soldier with courage was psychologically destructive to any German. Armin was pleased. There was no danger now of Cavaleri ending up a cadaver with Schröder's bullet in him. The German soldiers followed the Italian officer through the rocks. He had set a fast pace, moving so swiftly that he surprised them. He seemed to know every turn in the terrain.

Armin glanced at the sweat running down Schröder's face and turned cold in the heat with the fear that one day the madman with the Schmeisser would turn on him.

The drive in Schröder that made him a walking weapon only meant that *any* target would do: Italian, British, American—even German.

Cavaleri stopped, crouched behind a rock, and aimed his carbine. Schröder and Armin were the first to reach

229

him. Quickly, the others silently joined them and fell into fire positions.

"The idiot's wearing flowers on his helmet," said Cavaleri.

Schröder saw the tall American holding a child in his arms, and the flash of red worn on the enemy's shoulder brought him back to that same red flash he had spotted on Hill 607 in North Africa. Schröder stiffened when Cavaleri lowered his carbine.

"What's the matter?" Schröder demanded. He was sure the Italian had never killed a man.

"He's holding a child in his arms," said Cavaleri.

"What's *that* got to do with killing him? Shoot him!"

"*I'll* give the order when to shoot, damn it!"

Schröder angrily pushed him aside, knocking him off-balance. "Armin, show this spineless Mussolini bastard how to kill such an easy target."

"He's kissing the child," said Armin. "I'll kill him when he puts her down."

Schröder shoved Armin aside and fired his burp gun. The first bullet shattered a lens of the spectacles on her nose, the second her throat, the third missed the Sergeant as he hit the ground with Graziella in his arms. Blood spurted from her mouth and throat. The dead child stared at the Sergeant with one open eye as the Germans kept up rapid fire. Pimply Face was killed. Two men were wounded. The Squad returned the fire, covering the Sergeant as he charged through the rocks to outflank the enemy.

Hit in the fire fight, Schröder clapped his thigh wound, felt the shock, and fell into a crevice between two steep rocks.

Working his way around their flank to a high rock at their rear, the Sergeant put two bullets through Cavaleri's skull. The Italian crashed on top of Schröder, hiding him. The Sergeant fired six rounds at Armin, the bullets slamming him around like a top until he crashed on Cavaleri. The seven Germans, deafened by their exchange with the Squad, didn't see the Sergeant slapping in a fresh clip behind them. He fired seven times, each bullet killing a German. The Sergeant fired the last shot and from the top of the rock waved to his men. They ceased fire. He slapped in a full clip.

Schröder lay on his stomach with his hand glued against his thigh trying to stop the flow of blood. He felt a blow on his jaw. As the weight of the two bodies pinning him grew heavier, he became aware that the noise of the fire fight had come to a stop. He waited to hear German voices. He heard nothing. He couldn't stand the eerie silence and was about to shout that he was alive when the quiet was broken by eight fast rifle shots. In his painful, twisted confinement he shuddered. What he heard was not an exchange of small-arms fire. It was one rifle firing rapidly with precision. And it was an enemy rifle. He felt the bodies on him jerk as bullets thudded into the dead flesh. Panic seized him. A bullet at close range that pierced flesh could reach his. A madman was emptying rounds into the dead.

Silence. He waited. He had to chance the enemy or bleed to death. Waiting would resolve nothing. Crushed by the weight, panting for air, he fought the body on him inch by inch, pushing it aside, dragging himself up past the twisted face of Cavaleri's corpse. Now maneuvering into a painful position, his back against the wall of the rock, he used his last ounce of strength to shove the second body with his feet. He crawled up past his old comrade Armin's grotesque face, showed no emotion, and reached down past Cavaleri for his Schmeisser. Sucking in air until his lungs burst with heat, he very slowly bandaged his thigh wound, rested, then limped among the German dead.

The savagery of the extermination impressed him.

In the American army there was an infantryman who was as ruthless a killer as himself.

Would he ever meet him?

And, if he did, who would live and who would die?

54

That night the Company slept on Hill 407, but the Squad couldn't sleep because they had lost contact with the Sergeant who hadn't spoken since he carried

Graziella back to the women and buried her in a blanket a hundred yards from the Tiger in the house.

In his slit trench on Hill 407, the sleeping Sergeant, his head pillowed on the flower-covered steel helmet, could not end his nightmare. He hadn't heard a sound from her when Graziella was hit, but in the dream she asked him why he hadn't stopped the bullets from hitting her. Her face was as big as the black sky. In her face appeared a smaller face and a smaller face and a smaller face, as in those box-within-a-box creations, until her one staring eye became a dot and the dot became a tear.

The drone of a plane awoke Hill 407. Bedcheck Charlie was right on schedule to tuck the Company in for the night. The men covered their faces with their helmets. The plane dropped a bomb, strafed, and flew off to tuck in another company somewhere else.

The Sergeant hadn't covered his face. The child's murder had transformed him into an unprofessional dogface. He knew that to become emotionally involved in war was dangerous for a rifleman. Impersonal killing was the rule. Emotion was a fatal element in combat. He knew all this, yet he had killed in an emotional moment.

A traveling bullet had no conscience. It killed the armed soldier and the unarmed soldier with the same objectivity it killed civilians. There were no innocent bystanders. Everyone in a battle area was a target. Anyone facing the muzzle of a firing weapon was the enemy.

The Sergeant knew that it made no difference who was killed because nobody cared about a dead person, only about survival. He knew the rules in war, but he could not follow all of them—not when a German, after having killed Americans, ran out of ammunition and decided to live by throwing up his hands. Was *that* why he killed that Hun in 1918? He knew it was not.

He knew there were rules in war about noncombatants, but he also knew that since war was lunacy there could be no rules between lunatics.

He knew that in war zones men and women in uniform and those not in uniform had no sense of the future or the past, only of the terrifying present. Destruction and brutality was the order of the day, and he understood such brutality.

And yet, back at the rocks, Graziella's face was all he saw when he lost control of himself and butchered the enemy.

The haunting, sickening thought returned: had he used the child in that moment of vengeance to convince himself that he had a heart? That there was still some humanity left in him despite the brutalization of all the battles he had fought?

He shifted his helmet.

A single flower fell from its net.

In the morning the replacements in the Squad wondered why the Sergeant was the only one wearing a fading garden on his helmet. His trail of flowers began at the battle of Caltanissetta. The Sergeant took no prisoners. In the battle of Enna, nine Germans who had conjured up Graziella's face lay sprawled among three faded flowers that had fallen from his helmet. In the battle of Nicosia, Griff lunged for refuge behind a stone statue of two kissing angels and saw two Germans in death embrace, their lips touching; on their riddled bodies rested two flowers. In the battle of Cerami, Zab's shoes crushed a fallen flower near three riddled Germans. In the battle of Troina, Vinci charged into a building to support the Sergeant who had gone in alone; the Sergeant was standing over fourteen dead Germans and four dead flowers. In Randazzo, barefoot kids stripped German bodies and Johnson watched one of them sit on a faded flower and put on German boots.

The exhausted silhouette of the Sergeant moved against Mount Etna's red smoke in the night until he reached the Squad resting in the lava at the foot of the volcano.

"Light your cigar, Zab." The Sergeant's voice was music; he was himself again. "Nobody's going to take a shot at you tonight."

"Hell, I'm out of cigars!"

"Catch." The Sergeant tossed him a panatela. "The Lieutenant said it's Cuban."

"Fireworks finished?" said Vinci.

"Officially."

Zab's match struck his helmet. He puffed.

"When?" said Griff.

The Sergeant sat down in the lava. "An hour ago the campaign was over." He stretched out, placing his helmet under his head. "In thirty-seven days the Division took eighteen towns and captured six thousand prisoners."

Johnson dug his rump in deeper into the lava. "How many krauts did we kill?"

"Not enough." The Sergeant shifted his helmet. Graziella's last flower fell from his helmet.

Al Jolson sang "Alexander's Ragtime Band" in a valley that was a giant palm of the hand holding the Sixteenth Infantry as they sat on the incline of the hill, drinking vino and reaching up for almonds. Jolson was on an improvised stage erected like a boxing ring at the foot of the hill. The seven-man USO band was as thrilled to play with him as the dogfaces were to see him in the flesh. Anna Lee, the British actress, had opened the entertainment, announcing, "I don't sing, I don't dance," and the men yelled "Just stand there!" Adolphe Menjou told them about his experiences in World War I and energetically ended his speech with "You've got to kill Germans!" The actor bored the hell out of the men. The last thing they wanted to hear about was the subject of killing. Jolson was what the men wanted. He told jokes, he voiced their gripes to the General who was on the stage behind him with the Colonel. He made them forget the war.

The Sergeant and his Squad sat behind bandaged men. The steep incline didn't bother the asses of the men, certainly not Johnson's. His rubber doughnut was inflated to capacity. Zab opened a parcel from home: a box of cigars and a long loaf of bread. In the bread he found a bottle of scotch. The note read, *"Happy birthday, love, Mom."*

Zab passed the bottle. The Squad drank. Then Zab passed the bottle to two dogfaces sitting in front of him. One man had only a left arm, the other only a right arm. They drank, returned the bottle. It was empty. Zab laughed.

When Jolson finished his song the men applauded,

yelled, whistled. The dogface with only a left hand clapped it against the dogface with only a right hand.

55

Schröder limped his way to a section of his company, cut apart from battalion, that had been blitzed by American infantry wearing the Red One shoulder patch. He was horrified when the medical officer at field evacuation decided to amputate his leg. Schröder held the medical unit at bay with his Schmeisser until they promised they wouldn't chop it off but try to save it.

They saved it as Sicily fell into Allied hands hill by hill, town by town. Lying about his still-throbbing wound, painfully demonstrating that he could maintain his balance while he walked, Schröder was ferried with other men to the Ninetieth Panzer Grenadier Division in Corsica where he showed no interest in visiting Napoleon's birthplace in Ajaccio. He did show interest in the Ninetieth because the outfit had the high morale of all former Afrika Korps units. From there he was shipped with 150 men to Salerno to bring up to strength the Twenty-sixth Panzer Division's ground support. Salerno made him feel better. He knew that when Sicily fell the Allies would invade Italy. At least he was on the mainland with German strength and not on an Italian island that was crawling with Italian soldiers.

When the Americans invaded Italy, Schröder fought in the streets of Salerno with a mended bone. But the pain remained.

He poked among the debris until he rejoined his probing section and was told by the oberleutnant to stick close to the company. A moment later they were driven back, street by street, until they reached a shelled warehouse where they were relieved by the Sixteenth Panzer.

The respite was brief. Enemy mortars were lobbed in as they scrambled for cover behind a gutted hotel in the Via Roma. But his company retreated.

His battalion waited for replacements that never

came. Schröder was infuriated by the news that Mussolini, captured by anti-Fascists, was rescued by a German commando unit. Schröder couldn't understand why Hitler saved the bullfrog's life. But when news reached battalion that Italy was no longer Hitler's ally, it delighted Schröder. Now he could openly kill Italians.

He did kill them for two days until the Americans came to their rescue. Communications were cut and liaison with battalion command post impossible. Being on the constant defensive drained Schröder's stamina as he lay with his company near the river to prevent the advancing enemy from throwing down a pontoon bridge.

The young German next to Schröder came from Bremen and he knew he would never see the river Weser again unless he ran. Jumping to his feet he ran from the river. Schröder seized him by his foot and pulled him down. The young German struck Schröder who bashed him in the face with his Schmeisser barrel.

At that moment Schröder saw the red flash of an American soldier patch, a Forty-fifth Infantry Division man wearing a yellow bird against a red diamond. The American fired. Schröder was shot near the heart. The fire fight was sudden and short. The Americans pulled back from the river. The oberleutnant found Schröder still breathing and arranged for his evacuation. Because of the outstanding combat record in his *Soldbuch,* Schröder was flown in a JU-52 transport with other severely wounded men to Paris where skilled German surgeons, under Hitler's personal orders, worked round the clock to save the lives of Nazi heroes.

Twice Schröder was pronounced dead, but the chief surgeon fought to keep him alive. He could recall only one other case similar to Schröder's heart wound: an American sergeant he had operated on in Tunis.

H.M.S. MALOJA

**I'll shoot the first man
who wears the Red One patch.**

—*The General to the First Division*

56

The Four Horsemen had survived the war in one piece, as Zab had predicted. Aboard the H.M.S. *Maloja,* a British transport manned by an Indian crew, Griff, Zab, Vinci, and Johnson were relaxing on deck, enjoying the biting October breeze. Johnson was cutting Griff's hair. Sitting on an empty food crate, Griff was drawing a cartoon on V-mail of Zab posing with a grinning Indian seaman who had an aroma of cheap perfume.

Leaning on the rail watching a destroyer in the convoy, Vinci was unmoved as the *Maloja* passed a rubber raft on which lay two bloated dead German fliers. After a while the *Maloja* passed empty gasoline cans and flotsam. Vinci felt good as he rehearsed what he would tell his mother and father about his grandmother. The rumor that German subs had been spotted didn't dampen his joy. Combat was over and there was nothing more to worry about, not even subs. Vinci looked back at his war and decided it hadn't been as bad as he had expected. He was alive, he could see, he could walk, he could use his arms and hands. He had gone through two amphibious invasions, had fought in two campaigns, and he was going home.

"The way I figure it," Zab said, "from Algiers they'll ship us straight to New York. Hell, I can't wait to sit down and work on my book. What're you going to do, Griff?"

Griff smiled. He still hadn't killed a man he could see and now he would no longer have to fear or face that challenge again. He would no longer have to lie and take credit for another man's kills. "Get a job on a paper as a cartoonist."

"And you, Vinci?"

Vinci had killed Fascists to prove the difference between them and Italians. It had straightened out his fears and strengthened his faith in his own background. He now was proud to be of Italian extract. The Italians who wrote great music and painted great pictures and wrote great books. He was part of them as much as he was part of Uncle Sam.

"I'm going into the bagel business with my old man," said Vinci.

"Johnson?"

Johnson would never reveal his secret to the others. A prisoner of his own guilt, in his heart he bore the stigmata of the burning KKK cross. He had learned, in the reality of war, the irrationality of blind racism.

"I'm staying in the army," said Johnson.

"You're crazy!"

"Means a pension."

"Means living like a robot."

"I want to live like a robot."

"You're suffering from battle fatigue. When you get well you'll see what a schmuck you were saying you want to stay in the army."

Zab growled. "Why should it take such a long time for this tub to get to Algiers?"

"Who said we're headed for Algiers?" asked the Sergeant, joining them.

"That's what we heard," said Zab.

"This convoy's been going up and down the Mediterranean all day."

"It *has?*"

"Yup."

"Why?"

"To make the Germans think we're going to invade Italy."

"Where'd you pick up that news, Sergeant?" Zab asked.

"In officers' country."

"You mean to make the krauts think it's for real?"

"Maybe."

"It's *got* to be a mask! All equipment's packed and crated, that right?"

"Right."

"That means no invasion, doesn't it?"

"That could be a mask, too."

"You're kiddin'."

"The hell I am. Before we left Sicily hundreds of Italians saw Regiment pack and crate, and you know how easy it is for them to get word to the mainland. Germans are smart. They'd figure it a cover-up."

"But you don't know for *sure!*"

The Sergeant smiled. "Anybody that knows anything for sure in the infantry is dead."

"*You* think we're headed for Italy?"

"Yes."

"Why our Division?"

"Because the Germans expect a seasoned amphib outfit to get our feet wet again, that's why."

"Two invasions is enough for any man," growled Zab. "We'll revolt!"

"Even if we did get our feet wet again," said Vinci, "what's all the sweat for? You're the guy who said we're coming out of this in one piece."

"I never counted on a third touchdown."

"We stretched our luck just by hitting Sicily. There's only one way to beat the brass on this one. Mutiny."

"That kind of talk," said the Sergeant, "is going to get you stood up against the wall."

"Ah-h," grumbled Zab. "We fought in North Africa and Sicily. Who'd have the guts to shoot *us?*"

"Me," said the Sergeant.

The next day, still plowing through the Mediterranean, confusion struck every man when they were all lined up on deck. They all stood watching the Red One insignia painted off their helmets. Then every man was ordered to remove his Red One shoulder patch. No explanation was given to them by the Captain of I Company. Huddled in groups, the men tried to figure out the reason for stripping them of their identity when a dogface shouted, "We're pulling into Algiers!"

Hopes soared again. The men crowded the rail, eager for wine and women. The *Maloja* entered calm water. They stared at the tiers of white houses. And that was all they were allowed to do. Forbidden to leave the *Maloja,* the men tossed down packs of cigarettes for bottles of wine thrown up by Arabs who had rowed alongside the ship.

Still kept in ignorance, the men's hearts sank as the *Maloja* shoved off. Italy was their next stop. Every man felt it. But about two in the morning, when they learned they had gone through the Strait of Gibraltar, they whistled and shouted and pounded one another on the back. The strait meant they were not going to invade Italy. They were headed toward the Atlantic and the U.S.A.

On the night of the fifth of November, after a voyage of 3,814 miles, the Squad debarked at eleven o'clock. The Battalion was marched into a gigantic warehouse jammed with First Division men.

Facing them was the General of the Big Red One.

The men *still* had no idea where they were.

The General waited for them to quiet down.

"You are not going to invade Italy," the General said.

The men cheered.

"You are in Liverpool," he went on. "The reason you were ordered to have the Red One painted off your helmets and all patches removed is because we don't want the Germans to know that the First Division is in England. They know damn well we're a battle-hardened amphibious outfit, and right now they think we're still somewhere on the Mediterranean preparing to hit someplace in Italy. We want them to keep thinking that. The more rumors, the better we like it. One long year ago we invaded North Africa. I am sorry that our battle dead and wounded are not with us, but their job's going to be finished by you."

242

The Four Horsemen waited like prisoners expecting a death sentence.

"You're going to train like you've never trained before for the biggest job of them all. You won't like what I'm going to say—and I don't like it either—but it's got to be said. From this moment on you are not the First Division. You never *heard* of the First Division. You haven't fought in North Africa and you haven't fought in Sicily. As far as anyone, and that means *anyone*—military or civilian—is concerned, you men are all green troops just arrived from the States. That's the only way we can keep Hitler guessing what the First Division's going to do next. I'll shoot the first man who wears the Red One patch."

ENGLAND

**You Yanks have endless dollars and
endless hard-ons, bless you.**

—English girl to a dogface

57

The presence of the First Division in England was not revealed by a single careless slip by any man in the Big Red One.

Once a month for seven months the morose Four Horsemen went on amphibious maneuvers at Slapton Sands, Devon, with British soldiers on the cliffs playing the role of Germans. Real ammunition was used in practice landings to weed out faulty ammo and the new men lacking the necessary coordination for specialized teamwork. Some wetnoses were wounded, some killed in the dry runs. The replacements in the Squad were nameless, faceless reincarnations of the replacements fertilizing North Africa and Sicily; the Sergeant and his men couldn't give a damn about rehearsing with dead men who temporarily had the use of their legs and arms.

On the very first dry run of the beach exercise the Sergeant told the Squad, "There are only four exits off the beach. In front of each exit are deep barbed-wire tank traps. We'll land at Exit E-1. If our navy's failed to shell it, or our planes missed bombing it, then we'll have to blow it with the bangalore. We won't be the only bangalore relay team on the beach. You each have a number in this Squad and when I call it out you pick up a section of the bangalore pipe and you run it to the tank trap. If I call out you're hit, drop. I'll call out the next number and he picks up the pipe and runs. We're going to rehearse this maneuver until your number's part of your life."

He glanced at the Four Horsemen and saw their contempt for his instructions. He called out the numbers and when it came time for Griff, Zab, Vinci, and Johnson to exhibit their coordination, they were slow, sloppy, and uncooperative. The Sergeant understood why their bitterness affected their timing and he chewed out their asses, telling them that they were setting a shitty example for the new men. His anger created an unbearable gap between the Sergeant and the Four Horsemen who knew exactly where he stood and where they stood. Their devotion to him soured because he was, after all, regular army and First Division to the bone. They resented his lack of understanding. They were tired of the war and angry that their pride in the Big Red One was taken from them.

He sympathized with their bitterness. They had had their fill of combat and they had rightfully assumed that, as long as the army was made up of the First Division and ten million replacements, somebody else should carry the ball this time.

But sympathy could not take a beach. Battle-tested men were needed not only as morale-raising symbols but because one combat veteran was worth twenty replacements. Even when the Sergeant pointed this out to them that night on the way back to Bridport they knew that his only interest was scoring for his Squad.

"You don't give a damn about us," said Zab.

"What the hell did you expect me to do? Desert with you four bitch artists?"

"You could've maneuvered a transfer for us so we'd still be in England when the rest of the suckers hit the beach."

"I told you before. The Captain said no."

"Fuck the Captain," said Vinci. "You're buddy-buddy with the General."

"You could've pulled strings with him," said Griff.

"He's got the muscle," said Johnson. "He'd have done it for *you*."

"But you didn't want to spoil that army record of yours," said Zab. "You didn't have the stomach to tell him we four chickens wanted no part of this invasion."

For weeks they griped about everything and grimly maintained their distance from the Sergeant.

He did not seek a reunion.

The divorce was official. They never met his eyes. They spoke only when necessary. His sympathy had hardened to a resentment that matched theirs. They all were sitting on a powder keg. During a break on one of the many long marches, Zab told them that desertion wouldn't pay off. Although the army hadn't yet executed a deserter, it would be their luck to be the first to face a firing squad, as an example, because of the importance of the coming invasion, wherever the hell it was going to be.

They close-order drilled, attended classes in chemical warfare to be prepared for gas attacks, and remained armed zombies. They knew that even if they trained for seven years it would not alter one fact: in the end they would still have to hit the beach and they would still have to die on that beach. They would stand no chance of walking off that beach. Their luck could not stretch that far.

They did not let their steam out playing football or baseball with the other men. They did not bother with the local girls. They made no friends. They were marking time and there was nothing they could do about it. Every night they knew that a day after the invasion, or perhaps a week after the invasion, four new men would replace them. They knew they would be as quickly forgotten as they had forgotten the men they saw killed.

Because they were professionals, instinct made them perfect at the beach exercises. The Sergeant knew that would happen. But he made no comment that he was pleased.

They spent a cheerless Christmas pub-crawling in bleak London. Nothing interested them. The whores didn't impress them, neither did the civilians going to

249

their air-raid shelters during an alarm as calmly as they went to tea. At the Red Cross they refused doughnuts and danced with the girls. They bedded down on cots in a cold room with a score of GIs.

Their sleep was painful. They knew how easy it would be to just remain in London, get lost among the GIs jamming the city, and wait for the invasion to be over. They also knew that eventually they would be caught, and the possibility of their execution changed their minds.

London was a mistake. The noncombatant time they were spending was phony. Just a postponement. It was impossible to relax. They went back to work, back to the war.

The dry runs continued, and every time the Four Horsemen hit the beach they relived Arzew and Gela, and the more they trained for D day the more terrified they became. They began to pick arguments among themselves.

For days the four men never spoke to each other. Cigars tasted bitter to Zab. Griff refused to draw cartoons on V-mail for the others in the Squad. Johnson's ass pain heightened despite his rubber doughnut. Vinci forgot the bagel business because he felt he'd never live through the war. They felt very old.

The Sergeant was drunk. It didn't help him. He missed the camaraderie of the Four Horsemen; he missed their trust in him and their love for him. He had destroyed his relationship with them the moment they became aware that he was a professional soldier and had no room for any emotion other than what his job called for. He knew the odds against the Battalion when the first waves touched down. Too much publicity had been shouted about the coming invasion. Too much propaganda. The patriots back home and the patriots in Britain meant well, but their theatrical threats would rob the invaders of any element of surprise. The Germans would even pull field divisions off the Russian front to make sure that *this* invasion would end in the water.

He finished the bottle. He was so drunk he couldn't control himself and he got sick in his helmet. He toppled to the ground, alone in his pup tent, combat drunk and thirsting for more fighting. He was the only one with an answer to the great question that faced every combat man. He knew that he was *not* going to die on that beach.

He fell asleep and in his nightmare he was a jubilant ghoul. When he opened his eyes, his body was soaked.

"Sergeant."

He looked up. The flap was open. The shape of a man was bending down.

"We're moving out in thirty minutes," said the Lieutenant.

During the night, the Sixteenth was moved to the marshaling area, somewhere near Long Bredy in Dorset, the men were told. But nobody was really sure. They were only sure, in the light of the muddy day, that D day was close because they were ringed by barbed wire and machine guns to prevent anyone from entering or from deserting.

In the afternoon, the Sergeant led his Squad across the moist red earth into a gigantic packed tent where I Company studied a twenty-foot mock-up on which tiny white flags identified the assault teams, showing exactly where they were to touch down on the beach.

For the first time the men heard the Captain say "France."

The Squad studied the mock-up around the clock until their exhausted eyes glazed over the tiny white flags. The men became so familiar with the landmarks around Colleville-sur-Mer in Normandy that they felt they had lived there for years.

Before the Squad was trucked to Weymouth on the first of June, Eisenhower reviewed the men of the first assault waves. That morning the Red One was painted back on their helmets and the Red One patches sewn back on their shoulders.

The men listened to Ike. He told them this was the Great Crusade and he told them a lot of other things to make them feel important because the Eyes of the Free World were on them.

"You establish a beachhead for us and we'll move inland and carry the ball," Ike concluded.

Zab muttered, *"You* establish a beachhead for *us* and *we'll* move inland and carry the ball."

Nobody heard him. And he knew it wouldn't happen that way. It never had.

FRANCE

Louder!

—A deaf Frenchman to a deaf dogface

58

The men felt hidden away in the hold like mental patients in an institution, and they knew that the people back home forgot them the way they forgot madmen in their cages.

In the long line waiting to use the head, a dogface spoke. "The worst disease is to bullshit yourself you're not scared. Everybody's scared."

Griff, Zab, and Vinci came out of the head, pushed past the line, moved among the bunks crowded with Big Red One invaders, passed a poster of the grinning Ike, and rejoined the Sergeant and the Squad waiting with the Platoon near a closed door.

A new face, Lemchek, was appealing to Johnson.

"How about it?" begged Lemchek.

Johnson felt nothing for the pleader's fears. More scared of this invasion than Lemchek, Johnson found the pale, gaunt, nervous young Lemchek full of screwball ideas on how to survive. He got to know a lot about Lemchek, the dice expert, who had everything mathematically figured out. He knew the odds for every throw—but not for walking off that beach that was waiting for him. Lemchek stood out among the new young faces in the Squad because he roamed from man to man looking for a sure bet on his life. The panic that hit him on the maneuvers spread until he was begging Johnson for help in his last throw for survival.

"No dice," said Johnson. "Eleven's my lucky number. Maybe Vinci'll do it."

"Do what?" said Vinci.

"Swap with me," said Lemchek. "Number 2 for your 10."

"For how much?"

"Ten thousand bucks."

"Let me see the dough."

"My GI insurance. I'll make you my beneficiary."

"Can you do that?"

"I can name anybody I want!"

Johnson said, "You told me your mother's your beneficiary."

"She *was.*"

"Don't you love your mother?"

"Sure I love my mother but she ain't number 10. How about it, Vinci? If I get hit on the beach you're a rich man!"

"What if *I* get hit first?"

"Then your beneficiary gets the money."

"Don't blow it, Vinci," Zab grinned. "Ten thousand'll buy a lot of bagels for your old man."

Vinci deliberated. "Nah—forget it, Lemshit."

"Lemchek! My name's Lem*chek!*"

"There'll be no bangalore relay."

Lemchek was confused. "Why not?"

" 'Cause our bombs and navy guns won't leave us any tank trap to blow."

"You think so?"

"I *know* so."

"Hey, you're right!" Lemchek clutched at hope. "You been on two invasions, Vinci. You know the odds. You figure I'll make it?"

"We'll *all* make it."

"We *will?*"

256

"Sure. Only dead krauts'll be on that beach to watch us land."

The door was opened by the Lieutenant. "First platoon."

The men filed into the long room. The Captain said, "We'll begin with the Mount Cauvin OP."

"First Squad," said the Lieutenant.

The Sergeant walked up to the mural that covered the wall. It detailed what the assault teams would see when they landed on the beach. The mural was *Omaha Beach,* the left half Easy Red, the right half Fox Green. The Squad studied the other markings: three hundred yards from low water to high, two hundred yards of beach obstacles, barbed wire, tank traps, mines to the bluffs, a draw, a small stone house, a marsh, a pillbox atop the cliff, a church steeple identified as COLLEVILLE-SUR-MER, a tree on top of a hill marked MOUNT CAUVIN, four exits marked E-1, E-2, E-3, E-4. Next to the mural were photographic blowups of aerial shots of mined beach obstacles in the water and on the beach. They were all captioned for identification.

The Sergeant's finger traced the path of his Squad. "We touch down 0630 on Easy Red at Exit E-1, pass that small stone house, go up the draw to the top of the cliff, bypass the village of Colleville-sur-Mer, and fifty minutes after H hour we set up an OP on that hill with one tree—Mount Cauvin—to report enemy tank movements from Bayeux."

"Any problem?"

"Yes, sir." The Sergeant studied the mural. "We won't be able to make that timetable."

"Why not?"

The Sergeant tapped the name on the mural identifying the troops defending Colleville-sur-Mer. "Squad strength won't get past those two Schnell battalions." He paused. "Maybe a company, but not a squad."

"They won't bother you, Sergeant. They're all combat rejects."

"A reject can pull a trigger."

"They're soft and fat sitting on their asses for years."

"We could run into a company of soft and fat rejects, Captain."

"Intelligence assures us they'll cave in when the bombs drop and the navy guns spit."

The Sergeant turned from the mural and wryly looked at the Captain, who understood the look.

"Sergeant," the Captain said quietly, "by the time your Squad'll be halfway up to Mount Cauvin, those rejects'll be dead."

"Says Intelligence."

"That's right. Says Intelligence. They've done a damn good job digging up all the dope we need. And as of right now their latest information is that we don't have to sweat about those two Schnell battalions."

"And if they're wrong?"

"We'll sue 'em."

The German field marshal stood like a statue, his arms behind his back, his hands clenched as he studied the wall map of the Normandy defenses. His hands were sweating. He felt his wedding ring but did not think of his wife and family. Standing stiffly behind him was his chief of staff. They were alone in the cluttered map room in a chateau near Soissons.

The field marshal turned slowly, spoke softly. "I know you've worked hard since we lost that war. I know you've stepped over the broken bodies of your comrades, but the highest you'll reach is what you are, and that is high enough, my friend. You're a good chief of staff, but you'll never be field marshal."

"Why not, sir?"

"The Führer doesn't trust you."

"I am his most loyal supporter, field marshal!"

"There has been talk of a plot against him."

"*I* was the one who alerted Himmler!"

"That is one of the two reasons why the **Führer** hasn't ordered you to face court-martial."

"What is the other reason, sir?"

"*I* am."

"*You?*"

"Yes. I know exactly how you feel about him because he has passed other officers over you, but I also know that you haven't the courage to act against him. When he was eating his plate of rice and vegetables I convinced him that you are to be trusted." The field marshal's eye hopped back to the wall map. "Those two Schnell battalions in Colleville-sur-Mer are combat rejects, aren't they?"

"The worst in France, sir. They're fat and soft and their only exercise is with the Normandy girls."

"Who put them there?"

"*You* did, sir. You ordered them to Colleville. That was four years ago. As usual, field marshal, you were correct. The beaches are so heavily fortified with 88-mm gun emplacements in pillboxes and so heavily mined that we really don't even need any Schnell troops there. Why, a small group of blind clerks with wooden rifles could defend Colleville. It is impossible for anyone to cross the beaches there."

"Have you talked with any officer about getting rid of Hitler?"

"No! No, sir!"

"I understand the 352nd Infantry Division is being trucked to Saint-Lô."

The chief of staff began to sweat. Confused, frightened, shattered by the question, he was thrown off-balance when the subject was switched. He slumped into a big chair. He trembled. "Why do you torture me like this?"

"Tell me about the 352nd."

The chief of staff's head sagged. He glanced at his watch. His voice trembled. "They are pulling into Saint-Lô now, sir."

"What do you think of them?"

"The best field division in France."

"How long've they been off the Russian front?"

"Two months."

"Strength?"

"Full."

"Equipment?"

"Combat ready."

"Morale?"

"High."

"Alert the 352nd Division for anti-invasion maneuvers. I don't want them to get fat and soft like those coastal troops. I want them on rigorous beach exercises."

"Yes, sir."

"Move the 352nd to Colleville-sur-Mer immediately. And I want all those damned combat rejects in the Schnell battalions to participate in the maneuvers."

The chief of staff left hurriedly, not wanting to hear any more of the field marshal's suspicions about his loyalty. He was determined to prove his devotion by turning those rejects into fighting men as soon as possible.

59

The General of the First Division was seasick.

He had sweated out 210 days and nights of dry runs for this main event; he had lost fourteen pounds, increased his blood pressure, and battered his heart. Yet many dogfaces thought his job was a cinch: all he had to do was give orders and study maps. To be responsible for fifteen thousand lives was agony, although the General preferred that agony to the idea of facing a German on the battlefield. He had been a foot soldier in the other war, but in this one it was his job to wish the men good luck and to wait. He had never gotten used to waiting in North Africa and Sicily. He had never gotten used to waiting during the seven months of back-busting rehearsals in England.

Deafened by the navy guns firing from his ship and from the other ships, he held onto the rail knowing he was going to win or lose this ball game by the blood spilled by others. It did not make him feel guilty. It was a tough job. He was tough. And his men were steel in strength and confident in spirit. But they had to get on the beach, then off the beach, and they had to blunt the Germans racing from inland to support the two Schnell battalions.

He saw faint flashes as shells exploded. He couldn't hear the Eighth Air Force bombs softening up Omaha Beach. He should feel good, but a razor-edge fear made him sicker than even his queasy stomach was doing.

The fear was the possibility of a defect in Operation Overlord. Victory depended on what those navy shells and Eighth Air Force bombs were hitting. He had suspected this defect in the planning structure from the start, but he had refused to face it because he was appalled by it.

Now he faced it.

If Omaha wasn't pounded accurately, the Red One death list would reach as high as the bombers overhead.

Illuminated by gun flashes, a .pale and nauseous Brodie—top-heavy with work equipment—joined the General and his seasick staff. There were no "good lucks," no small talk as they watched Omaha getting shellacked. Brodie knew they thought him foolish for making the initial touchdown. He agreed. But this was the biggest story ever.

"There'll be nothing left by the time I get there," said Brodie.

G-3 watched the tiny explosions brighten the horizon. "We'll land without losing a man."

"Maybe," said the General.

He should not have told them there would be no resistance just because *he* was told that by men who wore more stars. He should not have echoed reports to the men who were going to do the fighting and the dying.

"Maybe?" said Brodie. "Hell, General, nobody'll be alive on that beach after that pounding. Can you imagine all the hell and noise that's going on there?"

"If they're dropping too far from shore or too far inland," said the General, "we're making one helluva lot of noise for nothing."

What if Omaha was not being hit? Brodie knew he wasn't the only correspondent making the landing. There were men with the British on the far left of Omaha and men with the U.S. Twenty-ninth Infantry Division on the far right of Omaha. But he was going in with one of the first waves of the Sixteenth Infantry, and it would be fatal to find Omaha untouched by shells or bombs.

Brodie found the seasick Colonel of the Sixteenth Infantry watching the tiny explosions. "See you on the beach, Colonel," said Brodie and pushed on for I Company in the Third Battalion area on deck.

Brodie found the seasick Captain of I Company. "I'm ready."

"Where's your Mae West?"

"I'm loaded with cameras and film and a typewriter."

"Put one on."

Brodie elbowed past more Red One patches waiting at their stations.

The Captain knew the heaving had drained all his strength. He knew he wouldn't be able to take the channel in an LCVP. He would die in the assault boat. Killed in action by vomiting. What a goddamn hell of a way to go. Had he forgotten anything? Every man in his Company was loaded to capacity with know-how. Every man wore a life belt, carried a gas mask, was equipped for killing down to the smallest detail. Every medic was ready. He had damn good platoon leaders and damn good squad leaders. He watched the pounding on the beach and pictured Germans being blown to pieces, and the picture should have made him feel good, but it didn't. He bent over the rail again.

Brodie was given a Mae West by the supply sergeant, and the Lieutenant of the First Platoon helped him clasp the life belt round his waist under the bags of film.

"The First Squad's over there." The Lieutenant pointed.

Brodie left.

The seasick Lieutenant leaned on the rail, watched the explosions, and went over every point. Had he forgotten anything? He had triple-checked his Platoon. The men were combat loaded. Their gas-impregnated clothing, stiff as frozen canvas, would be hard to move in and would weigh a ton, but it was necessary discomfort. Every man was protected against gas. His big worry was that they'd dump their masks on the beach. Hundreds of poison gas mortar shells were to be fired if the Germans used gas. His bangalore teams were ready, his bazooka teams were ready, his BAR men were ready, his light and heavy machine gunners were ready, and his riflemen were ready. He was satisfied he hadn't forgotten anything. He figured, what the hell, we've been trained for this job. The final elimination of the Schnell battalions would be taken care of by the Sixteenth Infantry because it was all figured out in detail on the masterly organized Operation Overlord timetable.

Brodie reached the Squad. The Sergeant and his eleven men tensely watched the fireworks on the horizon. Every man was seasick. Not the Sergeant. He hadn't eaten for sixteen hours.

"I took my pills," said Brodie.

"They work?" asked Zab.

"Yes," lied Brodie. He bent over the rail and belched more chicken, mashed potatoes, string beans.

"When we get into the LCVP," said the Sergeant, who didn't believe what he was about to say, "the waves hitting our faces will make us feel better."

Brodie threw up the rest of his apple pie.

Zab put a rubber over his rifle muzzle, wondering how this invasion would be written up. The textbooks would stress the same heroic garbage and omit the puke-slippery deck. He remembered the General's words booming through the ship: *"Speeches are for politicians, not for the Infantry. I'll make this short. The future of the world depends on your rifles."*

Zab's rubber broke on his muzzle. "I sure am lucky I didn't use this one in England!"

60

Major Hausen was disappointed when, returning from Russia, the 352nd was whisked out of Saint-Lô before his men could enjoy the women and wine and ordered to launch beach exercises on the fifth of June at the foot of the Cotentin Peninsula near a village called Colleville-sur-Mer. Because of truck convoy breakdown, the exercise was scheduled for the morning of the sixth of June. His men were combat ready without needing any damn exercise, but a major in the infantry was in no position to argue with a field marshal.

He admired Rundstedt and Rommel commanding the

West Wall, but he distrusted the Pétainist French holding the Loire to the Riviera. He loathed the soft fat bicycle-riding coastal defenders called Schnell battalions. *Schnell?* They were the slowest-moving combat rejects he had ever seen.

He and his men heard the night shattered by shells exploding in the English Channel. They heard the planes. They heard the bombs. They were confused. The damn exercise was not supposed to start until seven in the morning.

Madame Broban was awakened by the explosions. Her husband, a Vichy section leader, had been killed in North Africa in the invasion of Arzew, Algeria. Living alone with her eighteen-year-old daughter, Madeline, in the small, scantily furnished stone house in Colleville-sur-Mer, she was not surprised to find Madeline gone. Neither was Madame Broban surprised by the explosions and the bombers droning over the village. Ever since the German infantry division arrived from Russia there had been all kinds of preparation for the anti-invasion beach exercise.

In the small church at Colleville-sur-Mer the German lover of eighteen-year-old Madeline Broban heard the explosions, quickly rose and dressed as she begged him not to leave until she had been satisfied. But he left, cycling down the dark dirt road to his Schnell battalion. He forgot to leave her any food.

Madeline dressed in front of the altar. Tomorrow she would get food from him. She made her way down the dark road to the Broban stone house. She heard the distant explosions and the bombers overhead and the thumps deep inland. She was not afraid because her lover of four years had told her all about the beach exercise and that nobody in the village would get hurt.

French workers in their beds in Saint-Laurent, Cabourg, and Les Moulins heard the explosions and the bombers and were grateful they would have a day of rest. The Germans would be finished with the exercise sometime late in the evening and then, on the seventh of June, the forced labor battalion of Normandy peasants would have to repair beach obstacles and plant more mines.

Three miles inland, the beginning of hedgerow country—planted by William the Conqueror—was being shelled and bombed. A Normandy peasant and his two children, returning from a visit to his cousin in Bayeux, were cremated in his wagon by a direct hit.

61

The small landing craft vehicle personnel (LCVP) held thirty-two infantrymen and one war correspondent. Bombs had stopped falling; navy guns were silent. The ten-foot waves battered the Sergeant's assault boat. Visibility zero. Drenched and freezing, the men bailed with helmets, but water kept filling the LCVP as it charged toward Omaha Beach. Vomit filled the boat. Waves smashed the puke away.

Lemchek, stuck with being number 2 in the bangalore team, blew his top and began to plow, squirm, crawl, and climb over the sardine-packed dogfaces with one goal in mind: to throw himself into the water. Nobody tried to stop him. When he was halfway out of the boat a wave slammed him back. Lemchek bit his lip. What the hell was he doing holding onto his rifle if he was going to throw himself into the water? He couldn't fight back tears. Brodie watched the tears washed away by another wave.

Brodie forced himself to study the face of the Sergeant and his Squad as they were bailing. No emotion. He had seen their faces in North Africa and in Sicily and now, roaring toward the coast of Normandy, they wore the same empty expressions.

Brodie was struck by a crazy thought. Was the lack of emotion in these five experienced killers an emotion of its own? The Sergeant yelled at Griff and Zab and Vinci and Johnson to bail faster. Brodie had never before seen the Four Horsemen glare at the Sergeant the way they did now. Something had come between the Sergeant and the four riflemen who idolized him and owed their lives to him. They bailed, but they looked at the Sergeant with contempt. Or was it contempt for the business of making another invasion? Yes. It had to be that. He had seen the Four Horsemen in action. They had no room for any human emotion.

What caused this lack of emotion? Was it that the GI had gotten so used to killing that it became as natural as pissing? Was it that the fear of death calloused the men to any kind of human feeling?

Brodie knew that when they reached the beach the virgins would be cocky when they found no Germans to kill, but the veterans would feel nothing because they knew they would find Germans the next day.

How did it feel to kill? What went through the mind of a man as he killed another man? Brodie never asked the Sergeant or the Four Horsemen because it was such a cliché question. Brodie was afraid the answer would be, "Nothing."

Brodie smiled. Zab still kept a soggy cigar in his mouth. Nothing would surprise Brodie now.

But something did.

He heard a shout for help. Then every man tried to maneuver to look over the side of the boat. In the swirling mist they passed dead GIs and drowning GIs and in seconds left them behind.

Brodie knew who those men were: crews of the DD tanks that went in H-50 minutes. The first casualties were from the amphibious tanks. Brodie remembered. Thirty-two DD tanks. Brodie looked at the men with him in the boat. Most of them were stunned. They had seen the first dead in the war. Their own dead. But the Sergeant and his Four Horsemen still wore blank expressions.

Brodie understood too well why the LCVP didn't stop to try to save the men in the water. There was a timetable to keep. Those poor bastards from the DD tanks were just one tiny part of the big picture. Just like the Squad. Each small assault unit fought in their own world, would land at a defined area, would perform a specific job in reducing German strength, busting gaps in the obstacles, sweeping clear the flat section assigned to them. Swift success on the beach was de-

266

pendent on carrying out almost thousands of such small jobs which, when put together, led to the major result of opening an exit and moving up the draw to the bluff and continuing inland.

"They've got life belts and rafts," said the Sergeant. "They'll make it."

The Sergeant knew why those DD tanks foundered. Back at Slapton Sands he heard the General raising hell about the DDs in the exercise. The General wanted them to try the roughest water, not exercise water. The General said there was every chance of the struts being broken and water flooding the engine compartments.

Because he had seen the DD men in the water, Griff became conscious of the dawn for the first time. Only a half hour ago it was pitch black, and in that half hour battleships, cruisers, destroyers, and bombers threw enough stuff on that beach to sink it.

Suddenly on their right, guns were firing. The men jumped to their feet. Abreast, moving toward the beach, was a landing craft transport with two 47-mm guns firing 630 rounds. The men in the LCVP liked the noise the 62nd was making. Heavy mist obliterated the LCT. The guns stopped firing until targets could be seen. A few moments passed, then the guns of the 62nd Field Artillery Battalion fired prior to the landing.

When there was a hole in the mist the men caught a flash of other assault boats bucking the waves. It made the dogfaces feel they were not alone in this invasion. Then heavy clouds and soupy low fog swallowed the LCVP and the men barely could see each other. Zab held his hand up in front of his face but could not see it. The sea got choppier. The men knew for sure the coxswain was going to land them miles away from Omaha.

They caught glimpses through the muck of the 5th Amphibious Engineers in LCMs. The infantrymen felt secure. The special engineer task force would blow the hell out of those beach obstacles long before the touchdown.

Vinci was being pressed to death. Two men were leaning on his assault jacket's built-in pack on his back.

He tried to move, but their weight increased. He managed to get one arm free and jabbed with his elbow. He jabbed again and again. One man moved. It was the medic. Vinci jabbed the other man. He moved.

"You sons of bitches lean on me again," said Vinci, "and I'll throw you overboard."

Johnson's ribs were being smashed by equipment and heavy weapons that were fastened to life preservers so they could be floated in. When he tried to move he couldn't because he was frozen, drenched, and too weak. Immobility in the boat had paralyzed him. He didn't panic. He decided to wait until they touched down and then hope the Sergeant would get him on his feet.

The Sergeant climbed over men and reached the Lieutenant who was near the coxswain. The Sergeant waited for the mist to clear briefly and then he touched the Lieutenant who turned his head.

Over the roar the Sergeant said, "You think he'll land us where we're *supposed* to land, sir?"

"If he does I'll eat this boat!"

"I'll get you there!" shouted the coxswain. He wasn't worried about the fog. He would dump them at the specified spot and return for another load and continue ferrying them until the last dogface aboard the ship was on the beach. He felt sorry for them. They slept on the ground, fought in the rain, died in shit. Their casualties were astronomical. He wouldn't be an infantryman if they gave him a million bucks a day. "And you won't have to eat this boat, Lieutenant!"

The Lieutenant grinned.

The Sergeant looked closer at the coxswain and saw a kid of about twenty-two, not much older. The Sergeant felt sorry for the sailor. Throughout the day the kid would be subjected to German dive bombers and German strafers. The Sergeant liked the feel of earth under his feet when he was in action. He wouldn't trade places with the sailor for a million bucks a day.

"Won't be long now!" yelled the coxswain. "We're comin' to the tidal flats!"

Through a wraithlike hole in the swirling spooky muck the Sergeant was stunned to catch a flash of three

268

reinforced iron framed structures that looked like gates with support girders ten feet high. Waves covered them. The hole was plugged. He had studied photos of the Element-C obstacles. His heart pounded. He wasn't sure now whether he could separate what he had seen from what was indelibly part of his mind, but he was damn sure he saw waterproofed Teller mines *still* lashed to the uprights. He looked at the horrified Lieutenant who had also spotted the mines through the hole in the mist. Both men hadn't expected to find a single mined obstacle intact.

"We passed one of 'em a minute ago!" shouted the coxswain. "Don't blame the navy. We didn't say we'd knock out *every* mine! Bombers were in on this show, too!"

"Christ!" cried the Lieutenant. "We're going to hit *one* of 'em in this goddamn gray shit!"

The coxswain kept his eyes glued on the fog. "If we do, it'll help the infantry behind us hit the beach!"

"The hell with what's behind us!" shouted the Lieutenant. "Just get us on that beach and *we'll* make sure those men behind us don't get hit when you land 'em!"

"You got nothing to sweat about, Lieutenant! After that shellacking there'll be nobody on the beach that's going to hit anybody!"

The first explosion was forty feet to starboard.

The Squad was stunned.

"What the hell was *that?*" yelled Lemchek.

"A boat struck a mine," said Zab. "Hell, you can't expect every goddamn obstacle was knocked out."

The second explosion was thirty feet portside.

"Goddamn it!" yelled Lemchek. "I don't see no boat that hit *that* mine!"

The turbulence from the two explosions hit head on, filling the boat with water. Then they heard it as clear as a siren back home. The shell screamed at them and, as they crashed helmets in their huddle, the scream passed over them. Two seconds later they heard the explosion. Their horror that the beach strongholds had not been knocked out by navy or air was more devastating to them than the shell that was fired from the beach.

But Zab was stubborn in his optimism. "That was an 88 and all it means is that some of those coastal bastards are still alive to lob in a few shells."

"They must've heard you," said Vinci. "Here comes another one!"

The fourth shell capsized the boat, blowing the men of the Red One into the freezing choppy water.

62

Waves crashed Griff into a small knot of Fifth Amphibious Engineers trying to clear lanes through the obstacles. Subjected to machine-gun and rifle fire, the engineers took cover behind their only protection, a mined hedgehog. Seeing this, Griff plunged facedown into the water to escape the bullets hitting the iron obstacle. He dragged his weight underwater in slow motion away from the bullets when he heard the detonation. The underwater turbulence battered him. He came up for air. Coiled around the wrecked hedgehog were human intestines.

Griff's eyes smarted from salt water and smoke as they pierced the mist for a glimpse of the Sergeant. A shell hit the top of the post forty feet from him on his right, setting off four linked mines. Again he submerged. The water began to feel warmer. He lifted his head, sucking in water and air, and saw an engineer suspended in midair, palms pasted together, thumbs pressed against blood-covered chest, head bent slightly like a Hindu in salutation gracefully falling into the water. A mortar, scoring a direct hit that touched off the explosives to be used by the engineers, splattered the thick soupy air with a convulsion of men, helmets, and weapons.

Griff spotted the Sergeant. He pushed through bodies and past engineers who were fixing charges to blow lanes when a mortar shell struck the primacord. Griff plunged underwater again. The charges exploded. Griff continued to push through men, bucking waves, keeping the ghostly apparition of the Sergeant in view at all times. Griff knew he couldn't quite bring off this touchdown unless he was somewhere near the Sergeant.

Waves crashed at Zab as he hung onto the bow of his capsized boat. When it was lifted high into the air, he could see another assault boat receive a direct mortar hit. Army-Navy Special Engineer teams were trying to unload an LCM. Their buoys and poles for marking the lanes were destroyed by enemy fire. A shell hit a team dragging the preloaded rubber boat off the LCM. An assault boat caught fire and the ramp was hit as it lowered, throwing men into the water. He saw all this in a few seconds from his great height above the waves. Bullets missed his hands but he hung onto the boat. He had to spot the Sergeant. He knew he'd stay in one piece on the beach if he reached it with the Sergeant. Zab dropped into the water and fell on a drowning man. Zab's weight ended the man's life. Zab felt no emotion about the accident as he fought the waves to join the Sergeant.

Waves crashed Vinci, keeping him underwater. When he tried to surface a man kept him down. Vinci fought the dead man whose arm was caught in Vinci's gas-mask carrier. Vinci was losing the fight. With lungs bursting, he managed to release the carrier and he surfaced to stare at the corpse he had bashed in the face. He felt nothing about having hit a dead man and, under heavy fire, he pushed past engineers working on the mined obstacles. He was stopped. An obstacle was blown by the engineers. Vinci pushed on when an LCVP roared past him and crashed into an obstacle. The LCVP smashed through the timbers and set off three mines. He had to reach the Sergeant if he expected to come through this third touchdown alive.

Johnson had no idea why he was hanging onto a wounded dogface. Johnson knew that was not his job. He was no medic. He should release the screaming man and save his own ass. He swallowed salt water and the man's blood. When he released his hold for a second in order to get a stronger grip on the man, a wave car-

271

ried off the casualty and buffeted him smack into an obstacle. Sections of the wounded man came down like a shower on Johnson. Through the falling pieces of the body he saw the Sergeant and yelled but there was too much noise for him to have been heard. He hunted for the Squad. He had to find the Sergeant if he wanted to live through this invasion.

Lemchek crashed into Brodie. The correspondent saw Lemchek turned upside down, drowning. Brodie grabbed Lemchek and hung onto him, but a wave slammed them so hard that Brodie released his grip. An engineer seized Lemchek and was killed by machine-gun bullets. Brodie clutched Lemchek again and this time hung on until the Sergeant gave him a hand.

In the haze, the riflemen moved hip-deep in water behind the zigzagging Sergeant under enemy fire with two hundred yards of exposure to cross to reach the beach.

The Sergeant's calm and efficiency vanished. He was scared. The sense of disaster was the overriding emotion on Omaha Beach. He lost his balance in the uneven runnels crossing the tidal flat. His efficiency was crippled by the eastward wind battering him with brutal velocity. Through smoke, mist, and dust he caught specters of the bluffs. Smoke, mist, and dust—a godsend against constant enemy observation—made it impossible for him to recognize the stone house and the draw, landmarks identifying Exit E-1. He didn't know, and he was too exhausted to care, if he was headed for his target sector.

He sluggishly passed frozen, sick, confused, heavily laden men who had stopped to rest and reorganize. He saw others taking shelter behind obstacles and saw them fall as bullets whipped the surf. Lost men were hunting for their squads. Men tripped mines and blew up like dynamited fish.

The Sergeant was ashamed of his feelings. He had always been proud of his stamina, his endurance. That he felt too exhausted to care about hitting his target sector enraged him. *He* was the squad leader. *He* had to set the pace, achieve the goal. He sure as hell could do something about trying to keep them from getting killed. His job was to kill the greatest number of enemy, not his own men. If *he* caved in, they'd cave in.

He was angry because he was a professional soldier yet was ready to throw in the towel and say the hell with it because victory on this day seemed impossible. He did not like any part of himself.

Move, goddamn it!

He plunged into a thick mushroom of smoke, using the "blind spot" to make enemy fire ineffective. Without looking over his shoulder, he knew the Squad was close behind him. As he moved from one mushroom to another, leading his men through the covering smoke as he worked toward the beach, he felt better, and he began to like himself. On his right, officers in the thick gray fog were trying to herd stragglers across the open sand toward the seawall. Again a feeling of defeat surged through his body.

Move, goddamn it!

He suppressed the defeatism he felt and he moved, but he instinctively threw himself down when, directly in front of him, a combination of Schmeisser, machinegun, and rifle fire exploded. His men fell on their faces, some in water. The Sergeant's face landed on an olive drab *U.S.* stenciled on a black rubber carrier. Under the *U.S.* was the chemical warfare insignia with the words: ARMY ASSAULT GAS MASK.

He wasn't bothered by the wearer who had no arms or legs. He was bothered by the deadly coordination of the Schmeissers, machine guns, and rifles. Those weapons were not making the sound of combat rejects firing. They made the sound of a seasoned *field division!*

When the fire moved to other targets approaching the beach, the Sergeant pulled himself to his feet. The Squad followed him blindly.

He accepted the fact that the beach obstacles were still intact. But he was sure that when he reached the shingle bank he'd find bomb craters waiting for his Squad to give them some kind of cover. It was inconceivable that the bombs hadn't hit between the seawall and the bluff.

Their hearts bursting, their bodies battling against buckling, the Squad forced their legs to propel them until they were twenty-five yards from the shale.

The Sergeant gathered every ounce of his strength and began to run. The Squad ran. A mortar concussion knocked Griff down, and waves picked him up and carried him out. The Sergeant went after him, seized him, and pulled him to where the Squad was huddling behind the low pile of shale seven yards from the waterline.

The Sergeant ripped the condom off his rifle muzzle.

When Griff opened his eyes, the blur of men cleaning the sand out of their weapons came into focus. He looked at the Sergeant.

"I didn't drag your ass back because I *like* you," said the Sergeant. "I need that rifle. Clean it."

Griff dazedly pulled the rubber off and began to clean his rifle. When the Sergeant's words became clear to him, he smiled. The Sergeant smiled back. Gone was the gap between the two. He dug his head into the shale as bullets hit it. The Squad was getting their weapons ready to fire. Griff was in trouble. Sand got into every crevice in his piece. His fingers fumbled. Zab gave him a hand until Griff told him he was all right. Griff continued to clean his rifle.

On their flanks, Griff saw more dogfaces hit the shingle bank and clean their weapons. Many never reached the bank. The flames of burning men hit by incendiaries were quenched by waves. Bodies smoldered in the channel.

The Red One insignia on the Sergeant's helmet slowly inched above the shale and stopped when his sand-bitten eyes were level with the top of the low bank. He did not see any bomb craters between the bank and the bluff. "Jesus Christ!" he said, staggered by the fact that the navy shells and bombs had pounded too far inland and too short from the beach.

He heard a screaming shell and he ducked.

The Squad froze flat behind the shale. The shell passed and exploded in the water. Human screams mixed with the screams of more passing shells. Mortar shells blasted the shingle bank. Those landing behind it were not close enough to have their fragments hit the Squad.

A man in the Squad started over the shingle bank

274

with a loud cry. He was hit. He spun and crashed on his face between Zab and Vinci. Zab turned him over. It was Lemchek. He said, "My mother shoulda gotten an abortion!"

Zab turned to Vinci. "You just blew ten thousand bucks!"

A wave washed over Lemchek's wristwatch. It was 6:30 A.M., the scheduled touchdown in the invasion of France, June 6, 1944, Easy Red sector, Omaha Beach.

When smoke cleared for a second, the Sergeant saw the stone house and the draw, and he blessed the coxswain who landed them at Exit E-1.

He peered over the bank. It was a long haul to cross that area to reach the barbed wire in front of the tank trap. He knew the place was mined to the teeth. He looked at his watch. It was 6:40. He had little hope that the bangalore would ever get to shore as he saw gray boats destroyed before they could touch down. Waves washed up casualties and washed them back again. The men blew the minefield with bullets.

At 7:20, the time the Sergeant and Squad were scheduled to be on Mount Cauvin watching for tanks coming from the tank park in Bayeux, the men were still pinned down on the beach. The water washing Lemchek's watch had turned pink. At 8:30 the water covering his watch was bloodred. The dead and wounded of the Sixteenth Infantry—along the beach and in the water—reached a staggering number. Medics were kept busy until they too were killed or wounded. Some men defied enemy fire and plunged into the surf to rescue screaming, wounded men.

Zab saw a man in the surf holding his exposed intestines and yelling for help. Zab turned and started toward him when the Sergeant seized Zab and flung him back against the shale.

"Hell, I can get him!" shouted Zab. "He's only about twenty feet away!"

"You're no medic!"

"His guts are coming out!"

The Sergeant slapped Zab's piece. "I need that rifle!"

Zab and the men buried their faces as the mortar hit the soldier holding back his guts. Zab pictured himself blown up with the man. Zab glanced at the Sergeant, who had saved him.

"That mortar would've saved me a lot of sweating," said Zab. "Thanks for nothing!" He grinned.

The Sergeant smiled. They were close again.

On their flanks the Squad saw bangalore teams moving over the shingle bank and advancing. Three separate teams. The men tripped mines and were blown up. Other men went over the bank with their pipes. The firepower of the Schmeissers, machine guns, mortars, and rifles was devastating. The other teams were killed.

The Squad waited for their own bangalore to come.

Zab growled through a mouthful of sand, cigar juice, and pebbles, "Those combat rejects sure know how to lay down fire!"

"Rejects, my ass!" said the Sergeant. "That's *infantry* up there!"

Now it all made sense to the Squad. They listened with a different ear and a new respect to the 352nd German Infantry Division's expert distribution of cross fire raking the beach. That fire kept dogfaces pinned down while mortars hit the shingle bank and shells walked up and down the surf.

Looking behind him the Sergeant saw four men lugging a long box marked M1A1 BANGALORE TORPEDO US ARMY. He watched storms of German bullets hit waves of men staggering to the beach. The bullets brought down one of the bearers. The other three kept coming toward the Sergeant with the long box. They were hit. The Sergeant, Griff, and Zab dragged the box to the shale as a couple of medics went to work. One bearer was still alive.

The Sergeant opened the box, pulled out ten steel pipes, each pipe five feet in length and weighing thirteen pounds. Without even getting on their knees, the Sergeant and his men slung their weapons on their backs as bullets zinged the top of the shale. On his belly the Sergeant assembled three pipes laden with TNT. He looked at the nerve-racked Squad.

"One!" shouted the Sergeant.

Number 1 in the Squad picked up the three connected pipes and went over the shale. The Sergeant and

276

Squad gave him covering fire. Their target was a lone German standing on the bluff to their direct front, pointing, giving orders, arrogantly posing with his hands on his hips and watching the result of his instructions. The Squad fired at him. Griff emptied a clip at the small target on the bluff. Not one bullet hit Major Hausen of the 352nd German Infantry Division.

Major Hausen, in the throes of purging the beach of invaders, enjoyed the way his men spread terror from their dug-in safe positions with their high field of fire. The beach below was a perfect and easy target terrain for an "exercise." He was pleased that by chance his outfit had been alerted for an invasion "exercise" that turned out to be a real invasion.

Soon, he knew, his bayonets would charge down the draw and chase the surviving enemy back into the English Channel. He knew he would be decorated by Hitler himself.

Major Hausen watched number 1 carrying a fifteen-foot pole charge.

Number 1 sprinted across the mined beach toward the barbed-wire obstacle fronting the tank trap. As he ran, he knew that every man in the Squad giving him covering fire was praying that he would make it—for *their* sakes.

Number 1 stepped on a mine.

"Two!" shouted the Sergeant.

"Dead!" Zab said through his cigar butt.

"Three!" shouted the Sergeant.

Number 3, carrying two connected pipes, followed number 1's path, reached the body, connected his pipes to the pole, picked up the twenty-five-foot bangalore, and moved toward the barbed wire when a sharpshooter's bullet brought him down.

"Four!" shouted the Sergeant.

Number 4 went over the shale with a five-foot pipe and followed the same path. He kept moving forward, reached the body of number 3, connected his pipe to the pole, picked up the thirty-foot bangalore, zigzagged toward the barbed wire, and was machine-gunned by a Schmeisser.

"Five!" shouted the Sergeant.

Number 5 went over the shale with a five-foot pipe,

followed the same path, reached the body of number 4, connected his pipe to the long pole—now thirty-five feet in length—and advanced toward the barbed wire. He was killed by fragments from a mortar burst.

The Sergeant and his men were numb. Soon their numbers would come up. Griff was 8, Zab 9, Vinci 10, Johnson 11, and the Sergeant 12.

"Six!" shouted the Sergeant.

Number 6 went over the shale with a five-foot pipe and under concentrated fire miraculously ran along the safe path without getting hit. He reached the body of number 5, connected his pipe to the long pole, now forty feet in length, and moved forward, getting closer and closer to the thick barbed-wire obstacle when a German bullet went through his throat.

"Seven!" shouted the Sergeant.

"Dead!" cried Johnson.

"Eight!" shouted the Sergeant.

Griff, number 8, was the classic spectacle of paralysis familiar to every infantryman. He looked at the Sergeant, at Zab, at Vinci, at Johnson, and he knew he'd never see them again. And he knew they were not worried about him getting killed, which was a certainty in a few moments. They were thinking of their own asses. And justifiably so. Their numbers would be called next and they would die and it would be the end of the Four Horsemen. And the Sergeant, too. There would be no one left alive in the Squad to call out number 12 and the Sergeant would have to give himself the order and carry it out and he would die on Omaha Beach.

"Eight!" the Sergeant repeated.

He knew it wasn't cowardice that made Griff hesitate. It was Griff's last look at the men he had fought with since North Africa. The Sergeant should have but did not feel any emotion about the moment. He had grown to love Griff as a son. But there was no time for any kind of emotion. And yet the Sergeant was confused: if he didn't feel any kind of emotion why were those thoughts clogging his mind right now?

Griff decided to bare his secret to the Sergeant, to Zab, to Vinci, to Johnson. He would tell them he had never killed a man whose face he could see. He would tell them he was a bastard who took credit for kills scored by other men.

"I want to tell you something," Griff said as he picked up the two remaining connected pipes. "I—" The words gagged him. He couldn't say them. "When your goddamn number comes up, Sergeant, don't lose your goddamn voice!"

Griff went over the shale. He never saw the grin on the Sergeant's face. The Sergeant and men gave Griff cover fire. This time the Sergeant fired tracers but his red streaks kept missing Major Hausen standing on the bluff. The madder the dogfaces got when they missed him, the worse their aim. The son of a bitch superman was either immune to bullets or they were all lousy shots because they knew they were going to die.

Griff was only thirty feet from the shale when panic sent him crashing on his belly. He froze. He vomited. He remembered that man who willed himself to death. Now Griff was going to do the same thing. He was going to die where he fell, die by his own will and not by enemy fire. Even if he wanted to get up he couldn't because he had used up all his courage and strength. He had lost his guts and he wasn't ashamed of it.

Bullets missed him by inches. He was going to become a sieve. The bullets came closer and he realized that the bullets were not coming from the bluff!

They were coming from *behind* him!

Horrified, he looked back and saw the Sergeant aiming at him over the top of the shale. The Sergeant fired. The bullet grazed Griff's cheek. Sand and stones slammed him in the face. He touched his burning cheek. There was no blood on his hand.

"Son of a bitch!" screamed Griff, and he knew that the next round from the Sergeant's rifle would kill him if he didn't move.

He got to his feet and ran with the two connected pipes, following the path made by the dead. Bullets from the bluff made him dive on the corpse of number 6 and he found himself using the dead man as a protective sandbag as German bullets thudded into dead flesh. As he connected his pipes to the long pole, he re-

279

membered when the Sergeant used the dead dogface, Minox, for a sandbag in North Africa. Now *he* was murdering the dead.

The bangalore was fifty feet long now. He seized it and crawled away from the riddled number 6, dragging eighty-five pounds of explosives toward the barbed wire. A shell hit a mine. A chain reaction of four exploding mines hid him from view.

"Nine!" shouted the Sergeant.

Zab started over the shale in slow motion, sick and scared and angry. He was jerked back by the Sergeant who was pointing at Griff, alive and dragging the bangalore. Every man in every squad behind the shale watched Griff inching closer and closer to his goal. When he reached the barbed wire, a great yell filled the air on Easy Red. A man had reached the wire with a pole charge. He was going to blow a hole in that wire and every man on the beach would have a way to get off the beach and not be massacred.

Griff set the bangalore, inched back to a safe distance, and pulled the friction igniter.

It didn't work.

Major Hausen lost his cool and shouted for that man with the pole charge to be blown up.

Griff was startled as he watched his own hands calmly fix the igniter. Bullets missed his hands. One bullet tore through his pack. Another bullet hit so close that he was blinded by sand.

He pulled the igniter and a tremendous explosion shook the ground. As he was showered with sand and stones and the smoke engulfed him, he fainted. Bullets kept zinging at him through the smoke.

The Sergeant's eyes, glued on the smoke, watched it slowly settle. There was the breach in the wire. He kicked Zab's helmet. Zab turned, his ears ringing. From behind the shingle bank all the dogfaces were cheering Griff.

"Tell the Colonel E-1's open!" yelled the Sergeant.

Zab was sure the Sergeant had blown his top. Who the hell knew where the Colonel was and if he was on the beach or if he was still alive? And why Zab? Why should *he* be picked for the job that meant getting up on his feet?

"I don't know where the hell his CP is!" shouted Zab.

"It's *supposed* to be on our left! Find him!"

Zab looked to his left and saw the dead, dying, and living jamming the seven-yard beachhead from the shingle to the surf break.

"Move!" shouted the Sergeant.

Zab gripped his piece and ran, his shoe smashing Lemchek's wristwatch as bloodred water washed over 9:25.

The Sergeant watched Zab hurdle over men behind the shale, then he turned as a DD tank, touching down, was hit by a shell. Its gun, still operational, fired at the bluff under the direction of the Captain of I Company.

The Sergeant collected rolls of adhesive from the medics and gave them to Vinci and Johnson. He kept one for himself and chanced the run away from the shale. When he reached the Captain, he told him his plan and left. Thirty seconds later the Sergeant, Vinci, and Johnson jumped over the shale as the Captain gave them DD fire, concentrating on the mortars and pillbox on the bluff.

The Sergeant, Vinci, and Johnson began to white-tape the dead numbers of the bangalore relay team, marking the safe narrow corridor, the only corridor, off the beach. When Johnson took a step too far to the right, the Sergeant grabbed him and flung him to the ground and pointed at a mine Johnson almost stepped on.

"You're savin' a lot of asses today!" Johnson grinned.

The Sergeant smiled. The two were buddies again.

Gradually they blazed a white trail from the shale toward the breach in the barbed wire. Their fear never left them. The crippled tank's gun helped keep the enemy on the bluff pinned down, but the three dogfaces knew that at any second a bullet would find one or all of them before they reached Griff at the barbed wire. They were sure he was dead.

The Lieutenant, having regrouped his Platoon, led his men over the shale through the white-taped corridor. Up ahead were the Sergeant, Vinci, and Johnson. Soon more dogfaces from the Company were moving through the corridor.

The guns were deafening.

Vinci saw the bullets streak along the ground, kicking up stones, heading directly for the Sergeant who was about ten feet away. Vinci made a flying jump and landed on the Sergeant, rolling with him behind the dead number 6. The bullets kept moving on.

The Sergeant looked at Vinci. "You're not going to get a medal for *that!*" He grinned.

Vinci grinned. The coldness between them was over.

Zab became Major Hausen's prime target. He watched the enemy coming up the draw like ants, moving through the white-taped corridor. They had an exit now. That was disappointing, but it didn't make the major fear disaster. The 88 in the pillbox and the mortar sections in the octagonal pit behind him would take care of the enemy coming up the draw. What concerned him was the lone figure running along the beach. Major Hausen knew that man was bringing news of an open exit to his commanding officer. What Major Hausen wanted to prevent was a mass charge ordered by the enemy commanding officer. Many of the enemy would be killed, but in a charge there would always be those who got through. He had to prevent that. He wanted to keep this battle one-sided. If only a small group would try to ascend that draw, it would not be difficult to eliminate them.

But before Major Hausen could focus all his firepower on the running figure, a shell from the crippled tank burst where he was standing and sent half of his body through the air to crash into the mortar pit.

Zab knew that his hunt for the Colonel was insane. He could never get past all those dead, dying, and living who were covering every foot of the seven-yard beachhead behind the shingle bank. He tried to jump over them and he fell. He tried to move between them and he tripped. He careened into the water but the floating bodies kept hampering him. He went from the water to the beach and back to the water as he advanced, eyes on the lookout for any sign of the Lieutenant Colonel or any officer in the command post. He had no emotional reaction to stomping over dead men. He even increased his pace. The longer he remained on his feet, the longer he stayed a moving target.

He thought of just collapsing and waiting until they all started moving off the beach and then telling the Sergeant he couldn't find the Colonel. Throwing himself down between a corpse and a red-bandaged man he said, "The hell with it." But a moment later, without any explanation to himself, he was running again, looking for the Colonel.

Zab passed dazed men staring into space—nothing between their trembling fingers—thinking they were smoking cigarettes. His heart pounded furiously but he kept on running. He felt as if he had run at least five miles. But he knew he had only covered fifty yards. Or was it a hundred?

He fell crumpled like an accordion. He had to rest. He found one eye gaping at him. The other eye and the rest of the dogface's head was bandaged. Across his chest lay a dead medic. Zab spotted a soggy cigar in the sand. It was at least five inches long. He spat out his own stub and jammed the wet panatela into his mouth. He looked around with recharged interest. Who had dropped that panatela? Somewhere was a man with more of them. Perhaps someone carrying a box of cigars. A *box!* Zab hunted, stepping over men, dropping when bullets came like tornadoes, crawling among the bodies. Who the hell was the cigar smoker?

He saw him. Less than thirty feet away was the Colonel hugging the shale. In his mouth a dead panatela. Zab flew the thirty feet and fell on the Colonel, knocking the cigar out of the mouth of the regimental CO.

Prone on their bellies behind the shale were the shreds of the command post. Only two officers. Zab didn't wait to catch his breath. "Exit E-1's open!" he panted.

"Who blew it?"

"Griff, sir. First Division."

"Take it easy, son. We're all First Division in this son of a bitch place."

"First Squad, First Platoon, I Company, Third Battalion."

"What's your name?"

"Zab, sir." He picked up the panatela. "Can I have it, Colonel?"

"It's a lousy stogie I use only for invasions." The Colonel reached into his bag and pulled out a box of twenty-five cigars. "Enjoy 'em." He readjusted his helmet. "They're Havanas."

Then the Colonel got to his feet. His act stunned every man who saw him standing. The Colonel had gone nuts. He was *standing* on the beach. He wanted to get hit!

"There are two kinds of men on this beach!" said the Colonel. "Those who are dead and those who are about to die. So let's get off this goddamn beach and die inland!"

He went from man to man and kicked them to their feet, ordering them to get up, cursing them, until his action forced the dogfaces to make themselves vertical targets for the bullets that were flying everywhere.

"We'll follow you, Zab!" said the Colonel.

Shit! thought Zab. Do I have to make that goddamn run all over again? He couldn't repeat the stomping of the dead and wounded.

"Yes, sir!" said Zab as he got to his feet.

He lost no time moving. And he knew they all had to move damn fast. The Colonel followed him, trailed by the others.

"Is your Sergeant still in one piece?" asked the Colonel.

Zab hopped between two men, but an upright rifle barrel tripped him and he crashed on a body. "He sent me, sir!"

The Colonel helped him up. "Did Griff make it?"

"No, sir."

Under fire coming from the bluff, the sight of the Colonel inspired dogfaces along the narrow strip of the First Division–held beach to follow him on the double along the seven-yard beachhead to Exit E-1. On the way the Colonel shouted orders to officers to get their men on their feet. After fifty yards of the agonizing run through dead and wounded, it was no longer necessary for the Colonel to give an order. Officers and men jumped up, some forced themselves up, and others dazedly got to their feet. All of them followed him. Several of them fell but the men continued to remain on their feet, ignoring the bullets, mortars, and shells.

The Colonel was hit. He seized his arm. "Flesh wound!" he told a medic. "Make it a temp!"

The temporary bandage took exactly eleven seconds. The Colonel was on the move again. He could see the Captain directing the crippled tank's gun. Even as Zab led the Colonel and the men to Exit E-1, they all saw the tank's gun hit the pillbox on the bluff. The DD tank kept lobbing in shells all over the top of the bluff and behind it.

The Captain standing next to the tank watched swarms of Red One men moving from the left and from the right over the Squad's sector of the shale and, with the Colonel following Zab, moving across the mined beach through the adhesive-taped white corridor. Men were hit but they continued, single file, staring at the adhesive, running from one dead man to another and another.

When Zab reached the breach in the barbed wire he saw no sign of Griff. At the base of the bluff Zab met up with the Sergeant, Vinci, and Johnson. Griff was alive and still in a stupor.

Zab pointed. "That's Griff, Colonel."

The Colonel looked at Griff without a word, then his eyes brightened when he saw the Sergeant. Still without a word the Colonel kept moving up the draw, followed by men who knew that when they reached the top they would have to fight the Germans waiting for them up there.

The Sergeant looked at Zab's fly. It was covered with blood.

"You're doing pretty good," said the Sergeant, "for a man who lost his cock."

"It's still there." Zab looked at his red crotch. "I *think*." He felt his fly and grinned. Then he slumped next to them.

The Sergeant, Griff, Zab, Vinci, and Johnson rested against the wall at the base of the bluff. Above them was the pillbox. The 88 was not firing. They heard the fury of battle increase on the bluff between the First Division and the German 352nd Infantry Division. They watched exhausted dogfaces climbing up to join the battle. They looked down and saw Red One patches filing through the breach.

285

Zab spoke to Griff without looking at him. "I guess the Colonel'll hang some kind of gong on you."

Griff watched the ants coming up from the beach, forming a giant *T* as they moved through the Squad's white-taped corridor and filed through the wire breach that had been blown by him. "Yeah—I guess he will." He looked at the Sergeant. "Would you have put a bullet in me if I hadn't moved?"

"Uh-huh."

The men glanced at each other.

A young lieutenant, with the face of a nun, stopped. He was with another battalion. He glared down at the Sergeant and four enlisted men sitting out the fight on their asses.

"The fight's up *there,* Sergeant!" said the officer.

The Sergeant said nothing. Johnson rearranged his rubber doughnut. Griff gave the wetnose officer five minutes of life on the bluff. Vinci closed his eyes. Zab opened the box of cigars and jammed a Havana into his mouth.

"Our job," said Zab through the cigar, "was to establish a beachhead. We did it. Got a match, sir?"

The lieutenant's face turned beet red. "Move your goddamn asses!"

"Move *yours!*"

The lieutenant spun angrily. The grimy Captain of I Company came up behind him.

"You're holding up the war," said the Captain.

The lieutenant moved on. The Captain flicked his Zippo and held the flame for Zab, who puffed.

"The Colonel wasn't bullshitting. It's Havana."

"We haven't established a beachhead yet, Zab," the Captain said, moving on.

With a grunt the Sergeant got to his feet and started up the bluff. The Four Horsemen followed without a word.

63

Schröder enjoyed the cigar and cognac even more than the massage. Stretched out on the long table, he gazed through his cigar smoke at the Parisian dusk. He was naked. The French girl, who was in her early twenties, was tall with jutting breasts and dark brown pubic hair that didn't match the golden hair on her head. Her hands were firm as she worked on his flesh.

"You speak good German," said Schröder.

"That's because since 1940 I've been good to the Germans."

"Your hands have a nice touch."

"Thank you."

"They don't have hate in them."

"Only stupid people hate the victors."

"You are intelligent."

"*And* alive *and* well fed."

"And happy the Americans are in Normandy."

"No."

"*No?*"

"No. If they come to Paris—"

"They'll never get past Saint-Lô."

"I hope not."

"You mean that?"

She hesitated. Then she said, "If they come here it'll mean fighting in the streets and in buildings and in this apartment. I'll lose everything I've worked so hard for. Everything."

"What did you lose when we took Paris?"

"Nothing. There was no fighting. Pétain thought about us, about people like me and instead of causing the death of Parisians he swallowed his pride and gave Hitler Paris."

She pressed down hard. His prick flattened on the table.

"If I were French," said Schröder, "I'd have killed Pétain."

"*Why?* He agreed with Hitler, didn't he? He hates the Jews, too."

"He's a fraud, a coward, a shithole. He'd have collaborated with any powerful army to save his own French ass."

"He's an old man. He had nothing to gain."

"His age made him afraid to die. He's a hyena. There are traitors like him in every country Hitler took. They don't give a damn about the people. They just give a damn about hanging onto their lives, their homes, their bank accounts, and their positions. You think Hitler would kiss the ass of the enemy and hand over the Reich so he could sit on a puppet's throne?"

She gently touched his wound. "I'm sorry."

"It didn't hurt."

"Where did you get hit?"

"Kasserine Pass."

"Where is that?"

"North Africa. A stupid German—"

"A *German* shot you?"

He grunted. "Nobody guarantees where a bullet lands in a fight. In the Kasserine a stupid German shot me from his tank."

"And that wound in your thigh?"

"Sicily." Smoke filled his face as he remembered. "He wore flowers on his helmet, the idiot. Such an easy target—but the bastard moved his head."

"And that scar over your heart?"

"Italy." He moved his head to one side and stared at the photo of a French soldier on the wall. "Your husband?"

"Yes."

"Killed?"

"Yes. He refused to surrender."

"A stupid man."

"He was a good soldier."

"No. A *good* soldier should surrender when he is defeated so he can live to kill the enemy another day."

64

Zab was bitter. Drunkenly he questioned where Intelligence's brains were when Overlord was planned. Surely, he reasoned, at least one brass head must have been helped by the local French underground. The brain-trust boys in London, playing toy soldiers for months, had accumulated a mountain of OSS (oh so secret) information—right down to the geographical location of Normandy outhouses. But there was not a goddamn bit of information in the report about a new kind of enemy more demoralizing than the German soldier: it was the rows of thick hedges with tangled roots that separated Omaha Beach from Saint-Lô.

Crouched in the dark, thick, impenetrable patchwork that fenced in each field with solid ramparts of earth, and still only a bullet's trajectory from the beach, Zab, in the tangled mass of brambles, painfully shifted his stinging foot that had dozed off. Noiselessly he pulled the cork and took another swig of calvados that had been liberated from the abandoned Happy Cottage Bar in Colleville-sur-Mer.

Zab didn't particularly enjoy the potato fire trickling down his throat, but the futility of his situation made him drink. Drunk, he convinced himself, he wouldn't dwell too much about the possibility of ending up dead in this terrain after all the dangers he had survived on the beach. He looked around, his glassy eyes studying the hedges whose tangled roots bound each row into a natural fortification for the Germans.

What day was it? D plus two? Plus three? Plus four? Was it yesterday or the day before when the Squad followed the Sergeant from the Omaha bluff fight, into Colleville, right into the muzzle of a German tank's 88 that did not fire at them?

It's dead or a dummy, the Sergeant had said, and it turned out to be a dummy. And not the only one. A Frenchman who lived in Colleville, and who had led them to three Germans he killed with a shovel, pointed out four more dummy tanks between the church and the schoolhouse. The phony tanks meant that Hitler was short of or had run out of tanks. The news electrified I Company: it meant the war would end in France.

But night brought more enemy bombs and the war did not end. Dawn brought the order to move. The Squad trailed a Sherman Crab mine-clearing flail tank that was cleverly fitted with extending whirling chains that took the brunt of the explosions, its containers spitting powdered chalk to mark the cleared path for the Company. Then the Crab penetrated the *bocage* country that those bastards in London had never warned the footsloggers about. An AT gun knocked out the Sherman Crab just about the same time Schmeissers and Mausers drove the Squad down the sunken road past

289

bloated cows into bramble tunnels to face a new enemy
—the hedgerows of Normandy.

The mass of ugly growth looming all around was
based on dirt parapets twelve feet high and four feet
thick. They rose up to fifteen feet to mark the limits
of ancient fields and had developed as shields to crops,
animals and inhabitants against the ocean winds. Zab
discovered that the hedges were infested with beetlelike
snipers whose rifles' close coughing sounded as loud as
thunder. Along with the others, he found himself
scrapping from hedge to hedge, fighting, or *trying* to
fight, the hidden enemy that had turned each Norman
field into a disastrous battleground and each hedge
into a dangerous obstacle. The close-range fighting with
the elusive Germans turned the dogface hunters into the
hunted. Less than an hour ago Zab had learned that
of the nineteen men who were killed in K Company, not
a single one was shot by the Germans.

When tanks did try to penetrate the hedges, their
bellies became easy targets. When blades were attached
to their fronts as hedge-cutting tusks to crash the thick
barriers, the tanks were stopped and there they died. It
was up to the dogfaces to fight through the hedgerows.

Zab took another sip of calvados. He couldn't recall
the exact moment when the radioman on his right
caught the sudden blast of a German rifle from five
feet away.

"Why don't our tanks fire point-blank in these hedges?" Zab had asked the Sergeant, who gave the radio
to another new face to carry.

"Too many of us trapped in 'em."

"Then why don't we haul our asses back to where
we came from?"

"Because Germans are behind us, too."

"I thought that was the Third Squad."

"The Third Squad's wiped out."

The Sergeant zigzagged through the foggy bower of
brambles again, but enemy fire drove his men back.
When two charging Germans were downed point-blank
by the Sergeant and another man, Zab was impressed.
The other man, a new face, was Private Lilienthal,
who spoke with an Austrian accent. Zab liked him be-

cause Lilienthal had rifled both bodies in the road and come up with four cigars. He gave them to Zab. "I know you like them," Lilienthal had said.

The sting of calvados became more pleasant to Zab. They had made progress since the loss of that radioman. Two hundred yards. Or was it three hundred? In what? Twenty-four hours? Forty-eight hours? Somewhere a night was lost. Zab sipped the calvados, watching the Squad pretzeled together, eating, crapping, pissing to the sounds of scattered fire fights in the hedgerows. The walkie-talkie confirmed that I Company wasn't the only company embalmed in the hedges that had no coordinates. It was impossible to tell Platoon exactly where the Squad was; impossible to find a hole off the road; impossible to join up with Company for reorganization of the scattered squads slowly being reduced by snipers.

He guardedly nursed what remained in the bottle, his mind veering and tacking through his heavy thoughts. Oh, he'd write about these goddamn hedgerows someday, he said out loud, the way Dumas wrote about them. No, it wasn't Dumas. Zola. No, it wasn't Zola . . .

"Balzac!" Zab announced.

"I said keep it down!" said the Sergeant.

"Balzac," Zab repeated. "Balzac's the guy who wrote about the Chouans. They were the smugglers who fought against the Republic after the French Revolution."

"Fuck the French Revolution," said Vinci.

"They sandbagged the Republicans the way the krauts are sandbagging us in these same goddamn hedgerows."

Johnson leaned close. "When did all this happen?"

Zab moved the bottle away. " 'Bout 150 years ago."

"You're drunk."

"Sure I am, but that don't change facts. It happened."

"*Here?*"

"*Here!*"

"These hedges been here that long?"

"Been here over a thousand years."

291

"I'll be a son of a bitch."

The Sergeant leaned closer. "You mean you read about people fighting in these hedgerows?"

"Damn right I did. Haven't you ever read Balzac?"

"What did he write?"

Zab killed the bottle. "The Chouan leader got himself trapped in these hedgerows like we are and he got himself shot because he was wearing his rebel clothes. If the poor bastard had changed clothes with the Republican he killed, he'd have made it through these hedges."

He tossed the bottle. It missed one of the two dead Germans in the road. An instant later the bottle was hit by a German bullet.

The Sergeant's eyes riveted on the two dead Germans. He turned to Lilienthal, who read his mind. When a heavy fog cloud engulfed them, the men dragged the two corpses, their Schmeissers and helmets, into the hedgerow arch. The dead were stripped. The Sergeant donned a German uniform, turned to Lilienthal, and pointed. Lilienthal put on the other German uniform.

"How do we work it?" Lilienthal asked the Sergeant.

"We got lost, that's all you've got to tell them." The Sergeant pulled out the German's first aid kit and rubbed the gauze in the blood of the man he killed.

"What outfit are we with?" asked Lilienthal.

"Schnell Battalion."

"You speak German, too?"

"I got hit in the mouth." The Sergeant tapped the sticks in their belts. "We use their potato mashers first. Johnson, Griff, hook our grenades on the back of our belts to pull off fast. Zab—no. You're drunk. You carry our rifles. Vinci, bandage my mouth."

"*Ja wohl, herr* Sergeant."

Private Lilienthal loathed the uniform he was masquerading in. Ironically, Lilienthal's father was in the German Sixteenth Infantry Regiment in the Great War, just as now the son was in the American Sixteenth Infantry Regiment in this war. His father's regiment was made up of Bavarians. One of those fellows was Pfc Adolf Hitler, regimental courier, who suffered a nervous breakdown when he learned that the adjutant was a Jew named Gutmann. In September 1916, when his wound had him evacuated to a hospital, he was deposited next to Lilienthal's father. When Hitler found himself next to a Jew he threw himself on the floor and raved until he was moved to another bed at the end of the ward.

Lilienthal's father regretted often that he hadn't driven a knife into the Jew hater's heart. Later, when Pfc Hitler rejoined his regiment, he fought in the battle of Soissons against the First U.S. Infantry Division. The son, now with that same First U.S. Infantry Division, glanced at the bandaged Sergeant walking beside him. They both carried Schmeissers. Before joining the Squad on D plus two, Lilienthal had heard many stories about the legendary Sergeant.

"Did you fight in the Great War at Soissons?" he asked the German-uniformed Sergeant.

"Yes and shut up."

Lilienthal suddenly felt cold as he gazed at the man who could have killed Pfc Hitler in combat.

Acting Corporal Langewiesche, 352nd German Infantry Division, enjoyed the slaughter of the lost Americans in the hedgerow.

He heard the sound and caught a glimpse of a figure in the sunken road. He aimed his Mauser and squeezed, but the shape of the helmet halted the squeeze.

"Halt!" shouted Langewiesche. "Who goes there?"

Lilienthal halted. "Schnell Battalion! We're lost! We have prisoners!"

"Advance alone!"

Langewiesche and four Germans tensely kept their weapons aimed at Lilienthal as he advanced, carrying his Schmeisser. Four other Germans watched from the left flank.

"Just stand right there," said Langewiesche.

Lilienthal stood erect, unafraid.

"How many are you?" said Langewiesche.

"Only one more. He caught a bullet in the mouth."

"How many prisoners?"

"Three Americans."

"Advance with the prisoners."

Lilienthal shouted over his shoulder. "It's all right, Otto! Boot their Rosenfeld asses, make them move!" Langewiesche watched Griff, Vinci, and Johnson approach, their hands on their helmets. Behind them came the German-clad Sergeant, his mouth bandaged. He was carrying a Schmeisser. Langewiesche noticed the Red One patches on the prisoners.

"You taking them to battalion?" said Langewiesche.

"If I can find the CP," said Lilienthal.

"Why take them anywhere?"

Lilienthal grinned. "That's what I've been thinking."

Langewiesche grinned. "Bunch them over there." He pointed.

Lilienthal and the Sergeant prodded Griff, Vinci, and Johnson away from the group of Germans.

"Did you search them carefully?" Langewiesche asked. "Any cigarettes or extra food?"

Lilienthal's response was to dive into the brambles as the Sergeant hurled the first potato masher at the Germans. Lilienthal hurled his. Griff, Vinci, and Johnson hurled theirs. From the flanks Zab and the other survivors opened rapid fire that was supported by the Schmeissers in the hands of the Sergeant and Lilienthal. Leaving nine dead Germans behind them, the Sergeant and Lilienthal repeated their masquerade again and again, slowly working their way through the hedgerows, leaving no German wounded, taking no German prisoner. The Squad totaled thirty-three enemy dead before Lilienthal was shot by a dogface.

The Sergeant caught a flash of the Red One insignia on an American helmet.

"Hold your goddamn fire!" the Sergeant shouted. "We're not krauts!" He hurled the bandage to the ground.

The voice from the hedgerow was from New England. "What's your outfit?"

"I Company!" The Sergeant advanced alone. He was not carrying the Schmeisser.

The stomach of the Boston dogface flipped as he recognized the Sergeant. His humor was forced. "You shouldn't be walking around in that uniform."

The Sergeant spoke quietly. "You killed one of my men, you bastard."

294

The dogface's stomach coiled into a ball. "I saw a *German!*"

"Sleep with it!"

"Wait a minute, Sergeant! Don't you try making *me* feel like a shit!"

The Captain emerged with a small group of men. The dogface turned to the Captain. "Why the hell should *I* feel any guilt, Captain? I saw a kraut and I—"

"Who was it?" the Captain asked the Sergeant.

"A wetnose who spoke German."

"Did you score?"

"Thirty-three dead, sir."

The Captain gazed at the dead Lilienthal.

The Sergeant walked back and checked the corpse's dog tag. "Lilienthal, sir."

"Shit, Captain!" said the Boston dogface. "I didn't know—"

"Forget it," said the Captain.

"*Forget it?* Christ, I killed an American."

"I said forget it, goddamn it!" The Captain turned to the Sergeant. "We'll keep using your masquerade until we make physical contact with L Company."

"We're low on ammo, Captain."

"So are we."

"Anything good from Battalion?"

"If we can hold off from getting wiped out we'll get air support in a day or two. Tweny-five hundred planes are going to bomb the way open for us through Saint-Lô."

Johnson growled. "That's a hell of a long beachhead—from Omaha to Saint-Lô."

"What's that, Johnson?" said the Captain.

"Nothing, sir."

"If you've got a beef," the Captain said, pointing at the thick hedges, "the chaplain's in there—somewhere."

65

The American planes came. The Eighth and Ninth Air Force bombs dropped, thousands of them, on hedges, fields, roads, farmhouses. They dropped as close as they could to the American lines. Some Americans were killed and wounded. An American general was killed. When the planes left, hundreds of Germans emerged through the smoke from the hedgerows and fields. Shaking, vomiting, bleeding, they were the dazed victims of concussions, more dead than alive. Eyes filled with terror, staring blankly, the Germans raised their hands above their heads, formed a grotesque, disorganized ballet of men desperately searching for someone to surrender to.

The men of the Big Red One moved toward the shuffling Germans, herding them together. No words were spoken. The Germans offered no resistance, no tricks. The heavy bombardment had destroyed their last hopes of standing fast against the Americans.

That night the Sergeant knocked the flame out of Zab's fingers. Zab's cigar and the match fell to the ground. The Sergeant tried to sleep, but the danger of what lay ahead kept him awake. Beyond Saint-Lô were more roads and fields created for panzers. Six, maybe eight panzer divisions, pulled off the Russian front, backed by Göring's bombers and fighters, could drive the First Division back into the channel in twenty-four hours. It could be a repeat of Kasserine Pass, only this time there might not be any survivors at all.

The next day Battalion was given a twenty-four-hour rest break. I Company bivouacked in front of a château. The Squad had been replenished with new men. Zab threw a volleyball to Griff who tossed it to Vinci who tossed it to Johnson. The Sergeant was asleep on the ground, his head on his helmet. Dogfaces in the area were taking it easy, some playing baseball. Others lined up for coffee and doughnuts served by two Red Cross girls in a truck.

A dogface sitting on the ground, his back against the wall, played the harmonica. Two French kids stood without moving, watching him. Two dogfaces, wearing the 2nd and 29th U.S. Infantry Division patches, had trouble riding bicycles into the area. They had come to visit friends in the First Division. A dogface dropped a basketball through a hoop made of barbed wire.

When Zab missed the volleyball it rolled past a one-legged French World War I veteran, and headed toward two new faces in the Squad. They were Coop and Edwards. They had been watching the veterans with admiration. Soon they would be fighters like the Four Horsemen. Retrieving the basketball, Zab noticed the green paperback Coop was reading. It was the armed forces edition of his mystery novel, *The Dark Deadline.* Thrilled, Zab watched Coop's face for reaction. Then Zab removed a bottle of scotch from under his pack on the ground, opened it, and offered it to the surprised Coop.

"My mother sent it to me in a loaf of bread," said Zab. "Take a belt now that you're a member of the First Squad."

"Thanks!" Coop took a swig and passed the bottle to Edwards. "You guys sure know how to live."

Edwards hesitated. Zab nodded. Edwards drank.

"You replacements timed it on the nose," said Zab, not showing any eagerness to retrieve the bottle. "Patton's tanks are racing across France. How do you like the book?"

"Pretty good."

"*Pretty* good? That all?"

"Yeah—why?"

"That's my book."

"*Your* book?"

"That's right."

"That's very interesting." Coop didn't want any trouble with one of the combat veterans.

"You think I'm bullshitting you, don't you? Hey, Vinci, come here!"

Vinci joined them.

Zab plucked the book from Coop's hands and shoved it at Vinci. "Tell him who wrote that book."

Vinci, just as thrilled as Zab, showed no sign of elation as he turned the pages. "I don't know." Vinci tossed the book back. "I can't read."

Zab couldn't get Griff or Johnson to back him up. Even when he asked for the Sergeant's support, he found none. He took the ribbing with a smile. Actually, he was surprised that the armed forces edition had come out before he received a copy of the hard-cover.

Bathing in the safe sunlight of the rear area, Zab carefully read his book. When he finished, he couldn't

297

help but think of his life before the war. He didn't long for the good old days before Pearl Harbor. Looking back was not pleasant. He had no interest in reliving the past or reproducing any moment of it. He was aware that nostalgia was more than homesickness: it was a cop-out. After the war the survivors would look back at those good old days in the First Division and over beer and pretzels the horrors they had lived through would be replaced by a memory. Commandos and adventure. The whole fucking war would be reduced to a myth. Even the Sergeant had filled them with myths about the Doughboy in France.

But the men Zab killed: they were not myths.

He killed every German automatically. He still remembered his first in North Africa. The act didn't bother him then. Neither did its repetition.

He was sane enough to know that unless one was a born madman one had to feel something when one killed. Even in war. But he felt nothing. He felt no torment, nothing haunted him.

If he lived, would he be nostalgic about the men he killed in battle? Would he even remember them at all?

An interesting question, Zab decided. He would have to stay alive until the war was finally over to find out the answer.

66

The Squad was in high spirits in the rumbling 2½-ton truck. Sitting between Coop and Edwards was Johnson. Across from them the Sergeant, Griff, Zab, and Vinci. Edwards was looking angrily at a black soldier on a machine gun mounted on the cab. His name was Woody. When the truck passed French peasants, the GIs waved. The peasants waved back. Edwards resented the way Woody waved at a white girl.

"Next stop—Paris!" shouted Zab. He thrust his arm out rigidly. "This convoy has the longest hard-on in history."

The men laughed as they reached the intersection: one arrow pointed to Paris, the other to Corbeil. The trucks followed the lead jeep on the road to Corbeil.

"We're bypassing Paris!" yelled Zab.

Slowly he lowered his rigid arm and let it become limp. The men groaned. "The longest hard-on" went limp with disappointment. The convoy rolled through the countryside. The men were depressed. When the peasants waved, the men did not wave back.

Johnson observed Edwards's anger. "What's eatin' you?"

"It's that nigger."

Johnson glanced at Woody. "What about him?"

"Hitler makes sense. Those niggers are mongrelizing the white race."

"Knock it off," said the Sergeant.

Edwards grunted. "I got a right to say anything I want, Sergeant."

"Sure you have," said Johnson.

Edwards suddenly blurted, "A horse can't go with a cow!"

"A cow can't go with a hog!" said Johnson.

"And black can't go with white!" they said together. They laughed.

The Sergeant, Griff, Zab, and Vinci were stunned. They had never suspected Johnson was a racist.

"Man," said Edwards, "that sure sends me rarin' to klux."

"Me, too."

"I'm Edwards."

"Johnson."

They shook hands as if they had just met for the first time. Edwards clapped him on the back.

"Alabama?" asked Edwards.

"Tennessee."

"Me, too! Nashville!"

"Pulaski."

"That's where the Klan was born!"

Johnson grinned. "My old man was a big wheel there."

"Johnson? Hell, yes! Giles County Junction. Hell, man, he was the grand dragon!"

"He sure was!"

"Well, I'll be! I'm sittin' with the son of the grand dragon of Giles County! Well, I'll be!"

"Sure 'nough."

"And in the same Squad!"

"Right!"

"Johnson, I sure am going to enjoy this war!"

"You sure are."

"I wish I knew your old man."

"Yeah."

"He's a real Kluxer!"

"He sure is," said Johnson. "One night he brought home a nigger whore and carried her right into the bedroom. My mother screamed, and when I ran into the bedroom he was on top of the whore telling her she tasted finger-lickin' good. He told my mother he'd bang her next. I went crazy and began beating up on him and would've killed him for sure, but my mother stopped me and she told him she'd let me whip him into the grave if he didn't own up and tell me the real truth about the Klan. Ma-a-an! I never knew how much she hated the Klan till that minute. He was bleeding, he was naked, he was whimpering like a scared pig and he 'fessed up and told me the Klan was nothing but a big red, white, and blue racket."

"That's a goddamn lie!" cried Edwards.

Johnson cracked him across the face. "Don't you call my pappy a liar!" Now he cracked both palms against Edwards's cheeks, shifting the Klansman's ringing head from hand to hand like a basketball. "Y'heah?" He suddenly snapped Edwards's head back as if throwing the ball. "He told me he'd raid niggertown with a bunch of Klansmen to rape the girls, and next morning in church he'd make a speech how niggers were mongrelizing the white race. He told me it was easy to make loot selling Hitler and America and Jesus. He said every Ku Kluxer was a goddamn ignorant sucker. He's in the mental hospital right now. He thinks he's the Pope!"

Before Edwards could hit out in defense of the Klan, two German planes strafed the convoy. The trucks roared to a stop. The GIs jumped out, dived into ditches on both sides of the road. Woody brought down

300

the first plane. When his machine gun jammed he jumped from the truck and found Edwards standing in the middle of the road, paralyzed with fear. Woody seized Edwards and pulled him toward the ditch. Suddenly Edwards struck Woody.

"No nigger lays a hand on me!"

The Sergeant and the Squad watched Woody fall as Edwards jumped into the ditch. The second plane's bullets tore up the road and hit Woody in the stomach. A machine gun from another truck brought down the second plane. The men piled out of the ditches.

Coop propped Woody's knees up to stop the stomach bleeding. The Sergeant and Squad watched Woody gasp and choke and plummet into the painful death reserved for soldiers with stomachs torn open by bullets. The men looked at Edwards. He showed only contempt for the black man who had saved his life.

"Edwards," said the Sergeant quietly, "straighten his legs."

Edwards looked at the Sergeant and decided his next move was the right move if he wanted to live. He bent over and straightened Woody's legs.

"Pick him up," said the Sergeant, "and put him in the ditch."

Still wary of the look in the Sergeant's eyes, Edwards obeyed and placed Woody in the ditch. The men got back into the trucks. The convoy moved on. Woody's body in the ditch was covered with a shroud of dust from the passing trucks.

The convoy pounded the road. Edwards sat four men away from Johnson. The dogfaces in the Squad sat silently, motionless, tense with anxiety. Now and then their eyes glanced at Edwards who stared blankly at the shoes of the men sitting across from him.

Johnson agonized for thirty minutes of silence, ignoring the old men, women, and children waving at the passing Americans.

"Sergeant," Johnson said, "are you going to keep that prick in the Squad?"

The Sergeant felt sorry for Johnson; that was one hell of a messy legacy left by his father.

"If he stays," added Johnson, "I'm finding a home in another squad."

The Sergeant also felt sorry for Edwards. The Sergeant had met Kluxers in the army but unlike Edwards they masked their hatred. He was the kind of racist the First Division was killing and by rights *he* should be killed. But Edwards was a rifleman wearing the Red One patch, and in his hands was an M-1. That was all that counted to the Sergeant.

"He won't be with the Squad long," said the Sergeant.

That night the convoy was stopped by the river. The Colonel struggled to maintain his equilibrium. Several days before, he had fallen into a crater and the fall had resulted in an inner-ear injury; now he felt the dizziness again as he phoned the General the bad news. "The Germans blew up that bridge with some of their own people on it, sir. We can't cross until we knock out their 88. Their flares keep the river in constant daylight."

"I've got a trick, Colonel. A trick the Sergeant and I pulled in 1918. It'll take about fifty rubber boats."

"You want the Sergeant to pull it off, General?"

"Yes. And tell him not to forget the red flare."

Shortly after midnight some fifty rubber landing craft, propelled by outboard motors and carrying stuffed sacks that looked like men, began to cross the river in the glare of the German flares.

Beyond the glare a single rubber boat carrying the Sergeant and his Squad stole across the river as the decoys were being blown out of the water by the 88. The General's ruse paid off with the loss of most of the decoys. Moving along the German-held riverbank, the Sergeant's objective was the 88, its gun flashes easy to follow.

The Sergeant halted. "Edwards—"

The Kluxer moved closer. "Yeah?"

"You did a lot of night prowling with the Klan, didn't you?"

"*Prowling?*"

"That's right."

To Edwards it had never been just prowling. It had been real good American fun. Staring at the Sergeant, he suddenly felt like crying. He missed his family. He

302

longed for his friends, their laughter, their jokes, their community closeness. Now he felt alone, the outsider in this Yankee Squad filled with nigger lovers. He had counted on being shipped to the Pacific to kill Japs. Not Nazis. Their enemy was his. If Roosevelt had any red, white, and blue blood in his veins he'd put every kike in the gas chambers. He hated the idea of fighting for the Jews in the name of patriotism.

"What if I did do some night prowling?" he asked.

The Sergeant pointed at the 88 firing. "Prowl out there. Find out how many people are between us and that gun."

"You're setting me up because of that nigger."

The Sergeant said nothing. The men watched Edwards. He knew exactly what they were thinking.

"I'm not chicken-shit," said Edwards.

To prove it, he vanished, sweating every step he took through the brush, trying to be quiet, his hatred for the Sergeant reaching the boiling point. About three hundred yards away a flare was fired. He saw a couple of decoy boats hit by the 88. He went forward about a hundred feet and froze. He didn't have the guts to take another step toward that flare. He waited a few minutes so that his story would ring true. Then he turned and ran back into the Sergeant's fist. He crashed on his back. The Sergeant jerked him to his feet. Behind the Sergeant was the Squad.

"Prowl!" said the Sergeant.

"*You* prowl!"

The Sergeant hit him again. On his back again, Edwards felt his nose. He was sure it was broken. Again he was jerked to his feet.

"Prowl!" said the Sergeant.

Edwards turned and advanced alone, forcing himself to take those steps. He was sure the Sergeant was close behind, anxious to take another swing at him. He slowed down when he heard German voices. He could see two Germans. One selected a cartridge from an open box and tossed it to the other who loaded the signal pistol and fired a flare. The river illuminated showed another decoy boat hit by the 88.

Edwards turned, expecting to find the Sergeant. Edwards was alone. He ran back and found the Sergeant.

"Two of 'em with flares," said Edwards.

"Why didn't you kill them?"

Pushing him aside, the Sergeant led the Squad about 150 feet and with his trench knife killed the first German as Vinci bayoneted the second. After making sure no other people were in the flare-gun area, the Sergeant moved along the riverbank, followed by his Squad, with Edwards bringing up the rear.

They reached the 88. Its crew numbered eight.

Whispering, the Sergeant pointed out the targets to specific men. On his signal the Squad grenaded the Germans. Then the Sergeant placed satchel charges in the 88. Griff and Johnson placed the taped blocks of TNT against the stack of shells. Zab and Vinci and Coop gathered up German stick grenades, removed the heads, and tied ten of them into a bundle around the eleventh, making it a demolition charge.

From across the river the Colonel watched the explosion of the 88 being knocked out, followed by the chain reaction as the shells exploded like balls of fire.

"That 88's knocked out, General," the Colonel phoned. "I'll get the engineers started on the pontoon bridge.

"That's good, George," said the General.

There was a long pause.

"What's wrong, George?"

"There was no red flare, General."

"Look again."

"I *am* looking."

"You're sure?"

"Yes, sir."

In his command post the General aged twenty years. He fought shock. He was tired. Slowly he hung up and turned away from his staff. They knew the bond between him and the Sergeant. There was silence in the usually noisy CP. The General sat in the corner of the room that was the mayor's office in the small French town. He kept his back to his staff. He felt the strength draining out of his body. It was as if he had lost a part of himself. He regretted okaying the Sergeant on that mission. In 1918 that red flare meant the Sergeant

was alive. Now it was 1944 and there was no red flare.
The phone rang.

"Danger Forward," answered G-3. He listened and
smiled. He hung up. "General—"

The General turned.

"The Colonel reports a beautiful red flare in the sky."

The Colonel smiled as he watched the red flare hanging in the sky.

The General more than smiled; he laughed the laugh
of a young man. He felt he was going to make it, that
they all were going to make it.

The Sergeant had saved his ass again.

67

Schröder dragged the German corpse through the
mist to the front escape hatch of the disabled Mark VI
tank and gave an order. From inside the tank two
hands pulled the dead man halfway in, feetfirst. Schröder arranged the corpse to appear as if the man had
been killed attempting to get out through the hatch.
Schröder crossed the area that was bristling with German
soldiers placing dead Germans on the ground. He as-
cended the high mound, climbed the rope ladder behind
the support, passed the crossbeam, and reached the arm
and footholds made for him. A small radio hung from a
nail. From a bigger nail hung Schröder's Schmeisser.
Settled in a comfortable position, he pulled up the rope
ladder and checked his position, his eyes level with
Christ's two gaping holes. The mouth of Christ sagged
open. Strands of 1944 American and German telephone wire formed the crown of thorns. From his
position on the high mound, Schröder observed the Germans unloading the last of the dead Germans and
placing them in position to give the appearance of the
result of a battle. Then the two trucks pulled out and
the live Germans took their places among the dead . . .

❖ ❖ ❖

The Sergeant moved through the mist with his Squad. They came upon a First Division monument. Under the stone-carved Big Red One patch were the names of the men killed in action. The men in the Squad stared at the names.

"Holy smoke!" said Johnson. "They don't wait for a body to get cold! Look how fast they put up the names of guys killed in our Squad."

"That's a World War I memorial," said the Sergeant.

"But the names are the same!"

"They always are."

The Sergeant moved on. Trailing him, the men looked back at the monument, each man seeing his own name on a World War II memorial. The Sergeant halted, peered through the mist, and stiffened. Behind him the ghostly figures of his Squad stared at the Christ on the Cross on the high mound. The Sergeant was thrown back to 1918 and the Hun.

The Sergeant turned to Edwards. "See what's on the other side of Christ."

"You're after my ass because I'm KKK."

"You going?"

"No. And you can coldcock me again, but when I see the Lieutenant I'll take my chances with a court-martial."

"You were just killed in action," the Sergeant said very quietly.

Edwards stared at the Sergeant's cold eyes.

Schröder, standing behind the hollow eyes of Christ, watched Edwards advancing alone through the mist. "Enemy scout coming," Schröder whispered into his phone. "Give him a round-trip ticket."

The four German noncoms he spoke to on the radio whispered their acknowledgment.

From his high perch behind Christ, Schröder observed Edwards tensely passing the dead Germans, approaching the Mark VI, and staring at the body halfway out of the escape hatch. Then Edwards climbed to the turret, looked in, and saw the three dead Germans. Jumping off the tank, he found more enemy dead in the area. Schröder smiled as Edwards lost his fear and began to whistle "Dixie" on his way back to the Squad, his walk faster, his bearing unafraid. Edwards vanished in the mist.

"When he returns with his patrol, hold your fire," Schröder told his noncoms. "We wait for the whole company."

❖ ❖ ❖

Waiting in the mist, the Sergeant and his Squad heard Edwards whistling "Dixie" as he came toward them.

"Scouting is for kids," Edwards said cockily. "Nothing but dead Germans all around Jesus. There's a knocked-out tank and an armored car that's going nowhere."

"See any dead Americans?"

"No."

"How many in the tank?"

"Three dead Germans."

"You went into the tank?"

"I looked in. Hell, they're dead. Everybody there's dead."

The Sergeant led his men through the mist, slowly passing the German bodies, passing the crippled armored car. He looked up at Christ on the Cross. Part of the left crossbar and the left hand had been blown off by a shell. The hollow eyes gave him the same shudder in the same grayish haze of World War I. He cautiously approached the disabled tank. He looked at the body halfway out of the escape hatch. He pulled the body out of the hatch and crawled into the tank, his eyes on Christ.

"You're wasting time," said Edwards. "I told you, I checked in there."

Inside the big tank the Sergeant smelled the brandy and the cheese. He looked at the pink piping on the collar patches of the two corpses flanking the dead noncom whose collar patch piping was white. Edwards poked his head in through the hatch.

"See?" said Edwards. "I told you three dead ones in here." Then he added with sarcasm, "You sure got big

307

Yankee balls when it comes to tangling with dead guys."

Edwards's eyes popped as the Sergeant clapped his left hand over the mouth of the first corpse and drove his trench knife through the soldier's heart.

"What the hell you sticking a knife into a dead man for?" asked Edwards. "The war's got you loony."

The noncom came to sudden life. His scream was smothered by the Sergeant's hand, and the trench knife was plunged into his heart. His gurgle was muffled as he died. Edwards froze as the Sergeant repeated the same safety measure on the third man. That one was already a corpse.

Finding the noncom's bottle, the Sergeant took a swig of brandy, then tapped the piping on the collar patch.

"What color is that?" said the Sergeant.

Edwards was still too stunned to reply. The Sergeant seized him by the throat and pulled him in. "What color is that piping?"

"White."

"White is infantry." The Sergeant pushed Edwards out of the hatch and whispered to the Squad, "Live ones watching us. It's a bushwhack. Act normal. Don't panic." Aloud he said, "Found some brandy. Get me the Lieutenant."

He crawled out of the tank and tossed Griff the bottle. "Hang onto it for me, Griff. The rest of you jokers find your own brandy."

"I got the Lieutenant," said the radioman.

The Sergeant took the walkie-talkie. "This is Sergeant Possum, sir."

"Possum?"

"I'm at Point 33—a big Christ on a Cross."

"Can you see any of those possums?"

"No, sir, but their smell's loud and clear—dead krauts, a knocked-out Tiger, a crippled six-wheeled heavy armored car. The shit must've hit the fan here, Lieutenant."

"You're in one piece because they're waiting to sandbag the Platoon or even the Company. Try to pull back. We're on the way. Out!"

The Sergeant spoke loudly into the dead radio. "Why

can't they meet us *here*, Lieutenant? What? What's that, sir?—okay, Lieutenant—*okay!*" Tossing the radio over his shoulder he maintained the act, his eyes glaring at the Squad. "Goddamn it, we've got to go back and escort the Company through here or they'll get lost, goddamn it! Let's go!"

He led his men back past the dead Germans, knowing he and his men were in gunsights.

Schröder smiled.

The tension increased as the Squad walked through the human minefield. Every step they took tore at their guts.

Edwards glanced down and slowly passed the open eyes of a corpse staring at him, and when he glanced over his shoulder the eyes of the corpse were still staring at him, following him. Edwards cracked. He fired at the corpse, fired at the armored car, even fired at Christ on the Cross. As the Sergeant and the men dived to escape Edwards's wild bullets, the "dead" Germans among the corpses opened fire.

A noncom under the armored car sprayed Edwards with his machine pistol. Coop grenaded the armored car. A Schmeisser fired from the Christ. Through the mist the Sergeant zigzagged his men back to the tank for cover. He climbed in through the escape hatch and bellied over the three dead Germans. Trying two mounted machine guns that failed to fire, he found the third one next to the driver's seat operational and emptied a belt. His bullets thudded into corpses and into the live Germans among them.

Coop crawled in through the same hatch. Loaded with grenades he stepped up to the platform of the open turret, popped his head up, threw two grenades, and ducked. He repeated this action as the Squad behind the tank fired into the bodies that littered the area. Germans rose from the dead with portable flamethrowers and hurled stick grenades. But the tank's machine gun stopped all charges, and when enemy survivors continued to advance Coop grenaded them.

Still behind the Christ, Schröder was enraged because he had no targets in the thick mist. When he managed to spot anything through a hole, he saw Germans assaulting both flanks of the tank.

The fire fight was swift. The Sergeant continued to spray the area with the tank's machine gun. His bullets splintered the Christ, hit the radio, and hit the crossbeam.

Suddenly it was silent. Schröder knew his well-planned trap had failed. He was too good a soldier to try another burst. He would surrender only if discovered. He remained as still as the figure he was hiding behind, clutching his handholds, keeping his boots frozen in the footholds. He heard the Americans' victorious yells. He saw four of them emerge from behind the tank. The mist cleared long enough for him to see the Red One patches on their shoulders. For one very grim moment he congratulated the Sergeant who led this patrol. Keeping carefully hidden, he watched one of them checking for their dead or wounded.

The Sergeant emerged through the hatch. Coop jumped down from the tank.

"We lost four," Griff said. "Kaiser's still alive."

"Make sure dead krauts are dead," said the Sergeant as he watched Johnson check Kaiser's wound. Griff, Zab, and Vinci moved out. The Sergeant was surprised by the way Johnson's hands treated the wound. A professional job. A sudden downpour hit them. They pulled Kaiser under the tank.

"You belong in the medics," the Sergeant said.

"I was one in the States," said Johnson.

They heard Griff, Zab, and Vinci firing, making sure the dead enemy was dead.

A clap of thunder deafened Schröder. The rain came in torrents. His left boot slipped off the foothold. He regained his balance and watched Griff, Zab, and Vinci return to the tank. Then he saw the Sergeant slowly walking toward the Christ. The Sergeant stopped and looked up at Christ.

Schröder fell. He hung onto the rain-slicked handholds, his boots dangling for a grip. Trying to pull himself up, he dropped his Schmeisser. He watched it fall and, as if in slow motion, his life fell with it. It crashed on a German helmet next to a corpse, but the clang was drowned out by another clap of thunder. He slowly regained his foothold.

The Sergeant was still staring through the rain at Christ . . .

The Sergeant and Griff heard a sound and dived behind the mound. A French civilian was drunkenly riding a three-wheeled motorcycle through the pounding rain. He fell off. Driverless, the cycle weaved toward them, then hurtled into the mound.

The Sergeant and Griff ran to the man. A bloody makeshift bandage was wrapped around his chest. He opened his eyes and choked on his words. The Sergeant put his ear against the man's mouth, tipping his helmet to get closer. As the man spoke, water from the helmet ran into his mouth. He coughed and died, his mouth and eyes still open.

The Sergeant went to the tilted sidecar and lifted out the soaked blanket. A woman screamed. Thunder cracked. Lightning flashed. The Sergeant lifted her out of the sidecar and carried the screaming big-bellied woman toward the tank. Griff trailed behind him.

Schröder lowered his rope ladder, descended, picked up his Schmeisser, plunged down to the mound of German corpses, and vanished north in the rain.

The Sergeant gently lowered the screaming woman under the tank. "She's having a baby, Johnson. Deliver it."

"*Me?*"

"You're qualified." Then the Sergeant yelled. "Get those krauts out of the tank. Get her in!"

The three dead Germans were hauled out. The woman was lifted up. Her belly became wedged in the hatch.

"She's stuck," said Griff. "Don't pull."

"I'm not pulling, goddamn it," said the Sergeant. "Don't push that hard."

"I'm not pushing."

Gently the Sergeant worked the belly through the hatch, slowly moving it left and right as though he were trying to free a child's head caught in an iron fence. Johnson lifted the rain-soaked blanket. Her

311

shriek reverberated off the steel walls of the Mark VI. Griff climbed into the tank. They lifted her. Her foot knocked over one of the stacked 88-mm shells. They maneuvered her around in the driver's seat. Her feet hit gears. She cursed in French.

"How the hell do you know she's going to have it now?" asked Johnson.

"Her labor pains were five minutes apart when the farmhouse was hit. The doctor was killed. Her husband's dead out there. Give me that brandy, Griff."

The Sergeant poured brandy on Johnson's hands, on Griff's hands, on his own hands.

"I don't deliver no baby without rubber gloves," said Johnson.

"Break out your rubbers, both of you," said the Sergeant. He blew up the condoms.

"Hold your fingers out, Johnson."

Johnson did.

"*Stiff!*" said the Sergeant. "Like a cock."

Johnson obeyed. The Sergeant fitted the condoms on Johnson's fingers, two to a rubber.

A rubber broke.

"That's the damn U.S. Army for you!" growled the Sergeant. He tried another. It did not break.

"I'm getting a hard-on," grinned Johnson.

"Get to work."

"I need a mask."

"I'm not going to breathe germs on the baby."

"You crazy? This Tiger's loaded with germs!"

"I won't deliver the baby without a mask, goddamn it!"

"We've got no time for that bullshit!"

"No mask. No baby."

The woman shrieked in pain. The Sergeant looked around the tank, took out his trench knife, and used it to peel off the thin cotton loose-weaving cloth covering the big wheel of cheese. He poured the brandy over it, fitted the cheesecloth over Johnson's nose and mouth.

"Diaper pin, Griff."

Griff unfastened one from his wet bandolier. The Sergeant secured the back of the cheesecloth. They

312

looped the machine-gun belts over the overhead pipe, securing the ends to the gears, reinforcing with bandoliers.

"Prop her legs up high," said Johnson. "Higher!" They fitted her feet into the "stirrups," making sure the bulletheads in the belt pointed away from her. They lashed her kicking feet with their belts. Johnson bent between her widespread propped-up legs. She cursed them in her pain. She groaned and grunted and screamed. Her French never let up lashing them and God and the world and the war. She struck the Sergeant. She struck Griff. They pinned down her hands.

Johnson pressed down on her belly. She moaned and moved her body from left to right.

"Push—push! Poooosh!" urged Johnson. "Come on, lady. This is tougher on me than on you. I know you got to push. Come on, lady, pooosh! Goddamn it, Sergeant, she's not pushing hard enough. I can't pull this off alone. She's got to give me a little muscle. How do you say push in French?"

"*Poussez.*"

"Pussy!" yelled Johnson. "Pussy! Pussy! Pussy!"

"Not pussy," growled the Sergeant. "*Poussez.* Poo-*say!*"

"That's what I said!"

"You said pussy. It's poo-*say.*"

"Pussy!" yelled Johnson, pushing down on the woman.

"*Poussez!*" yelled the Sergeant.

They both pushed.

"Pussy!"

"*Poussez!*" The Sergeant slapped his hands away. "I'll do the pushing! Pussy—no—*poussez! Poussez!*"

"I'll be a sonofabitch!" cried Johnson. "She's pushing! Poo-*say,* poo-*say!* Come on, more, more, that's it, lady, don't stop, poo-*say*—poo-*say*—that's it! That's it! Poo-*say!* Poo-*say!* Poo-*say!*"

Griff mopped her brow, kept her hands down. "Pussy! Pussy!"

"Poo-*say!*" yelled Johnson.

"Poo-*say!*" yelled Griff.

313

The Sergeant kept pushing.

"I see it!" yelled Johnson. "I see it, goddamn it! Push! Push! Push! Push!"

He clawed deep, his condom-covered fingers pushing away blood and flesh as the top of the red bloody head appeared.

"You really see it?" Griff had trouble saying the words.

"Goddamn right I see it! Look!"

"Let me see!" Griff moved his position, bent over. The Sergeant yanked him back. "Hold onto her!"

"Don't stop," yelled Johnson. "Push! Poo-*say!* Push! Poo-*say!* More! More, more, more, more! A little more! Don't stop, lady, Christ, don't stop now! I got hold of its head. You're doing great. It's coming out, it's coming out. Jesus Christ! It's a boy! What a pecker!"

The Sergeant quickly ordered "Leggin' lace, Griff!"

Griff unfastened his lace, poured brandy on it. The Sergeant grabbed it, gave it to Johnson who tied off the umbilical cord.

"Cut it," said Johnson.

The Sergeant cut the cord with his trench knife.

Johnson slapped the baby. There was no sound other than the mother's great moans of relief. He slapped it again and again, but still no sound came.

"He's dead," said Johnson.

"The hell he is!" The Sergeant took the baby and, holding it upside down, began to slap it. Then he slapped it harder and harder. The mother held her breath, knowing the baby was dead. She began to stifle her moans. There was no life in the baby.

Suddenly the baby let out a manly howl. The grinning Sergeant placed the baby on the mother's belly. Johnson pulled off his mask and grinned. Griff grinned. The Sergeant gave Johnson the brandy. Johnson took a swig, gave it to Griff who took a swig. Both vomited. The Sergeant crawled out of the tank and told Zab and Vinci that Johnson just delivered a baby boy.

BELGIUM

Why are you crying?

—An insane child to a burning tank

68

Four civilians, three men, and a young woman lay dead as their blood slowly changed their white armbands red. Schröder turned and rejoined a group of German infantrymen.

"You didn't have to kill the woman, Schröder."

"She was one of them."

The day was as cold and gloomy as the face of the young German. He stared at Schröder with disappointment. "I thought only the SS killed like that."

"She had gun oil on her hands."

Schröder grunted as he walked down the road. The men trailed him, passing smashed German transport in the wake of retreat. He glanced at the bombed, charred remains of panzers and Germans. He was exhausted. From the moment he had run through the rain from the Christ on the Cross, his animal instinct had kept him from being spotted or captured by the Americans. Hiding in a barn he saw the result of four years of German occupation. The Free French Interior had executed seventeen Frenchmen and three women for collaboration. He saw a public ceremony where six women, one holding an infant, were having their heads shaved for fraternizing with the Nazis. He saw four of the "master race" kicked to death by men, women, and children.

He slept in the daytime and moved only at night, believing that all that happened was temporary. Soon, he knew, Hitler would reorganize his strength and return. The counterattack would drive the Americans back to the channel and wipe out every Frenchman and Frenchwoman who had stomped on, spat on, pissed on, and murdered German soldiers.

As he walked down the road with the German infantrymen, Schröder wanted to throw himself to the ground and sleep, but his determination to catch up with his retreating outfit kept him putting one boot in front of the other.

❖ ❖ ❖

"Take ten," said the Lieutenant.

The Platoon grunted. Men and weapons sagged to the ground. The Sergeant and his Squad sat. Some men pissed. Griff removed his helmet and scratched his tingling head. Vinci readjusted his legging lace. Zab chewed on a dead cigar. Johnson was too weary to blow up his rubber doughnut but his aching ass forced him to. As he hunted for a level piece of ground to place his doughnut, he felt something.

"What the hell!" he said, carefully maneuvering his ass in the doughnut. "There's some dead people under this tree, Sergeant."

Zab investigated. "Civilians. Four of 'em."

Nobody paid attention. With morbid curiosity Coop checked them. "Three men and a woman." He held up a bloodstained brassard. "They're all wearing white armbands."

The Sergeant's eyes remained closed. "Means they were underground terrorists. They're called the Belgian White Army of Resistance."

"You mean we're in Belgium?" asked Griff.

"According to the Lieutenant."

"I guess," said Coop, "they did a pretty good job."

"They all did," said the Sergeant. "Blew up trains, bridges, munitions works."

Coop sat next to Zab and struck a match for his cigarette. Zab whacked the match and cigarette out of Coop's hand and mouth. "Want to get our heads shot off, Coop?" said Zab. "Don't *ever* make a light at night!"

He grinned. The Sergeant, his eyes still closed, smiled.

The Lieutenant joined them. "They want you at Battalion, Sergeant."

The Sergeant sat up. "What's up, sir?"

"They didn't tell me."

"On your feet," the Sergeant told his men as he got up.

"Not them, Sergeant," said the Lieutenant, "just you."

The Sergeant stared at him. "What about my Squad?"

"I'll drop 'em off in the ditch at Point 96."

"I don't know anything about Point 96, sir."

"About four miles from here. Supposed to be the Angel of Mons, if it's still there. Ring a bell?"

"Yes, sir."

"Rejoin your Squad there. Wait here for the jeep."

Griff, Zab, Vinci, and Johnson moved off with the Squad. The Sergeant watched the Platoon trail the Lieutenant past the smashed German transport. Alone under the tree, he stared at the four dead civilians until the jeep pulled up.

On the ride back to Battalion, the Sergeant remembered a Christmas Eve in Paris after the war—Christmas and Mons . . .

He had met a British soldier in a bistro and they drank together. The Tommy, one of the men indebted to the Angel of Mons for its supernatural aid to his trapped outfit in the battle against the Huns, had called it a miracle. The Sergeant had laughed. To prove his point the Tommy took the Sergeant to a dank walk-up on the Left Bank and introduced him to a freak born without arms or legs. The girl, urged by the Tommy, told the Sergeant that she had prayed to the Angel of Mons and a miracle happened. From her shoulders

319

grew two formed hands and from her hips two feet. "The angel gave my fingers the strength to feed myself," she said. "Mons is the capital of faith and if you have faith the angel will perform a miracle."

The Sergeant thought about the three men and the woman under the tree. They had had faith in God, in Belgium, and in their cause. Either their faith had come apart at the seams or the Angel of Mons was on furlough.

Zab chewed on his cigar as he and the Squad waited in the ditch for the Sergeant. He chuckled to himself. How would he handle this in his novel? Tell it the way it was? Twist it to make it more dangerous, more melodramatic? Play it up the way they do in war books?

Not a single reader would believe the last twenty-four-hour snafu. The Platoon was not in Belgium, but in France. The Company had been near the border since yesterday. The actual invasion of Belgium was taking place right now in the ditch, and the invaders were the snoring members of the First Squad.

Zab checked his watch: 6:30.

It was September 3, 1944.

An hour ago the Lieutenant had radioed the Squad that the Platoon was on their left rear in France. There had been some kind of a geographical fuck-up coming out of Maubeuge. Wait in the ditch for the Sergeant, was the crisp order. Don't probe for trouble.

Zab could not shrug off the humor of this invasion. Once the Squad realized there was no danger, despite the scream of shells passing them, the men went to sleep. Everything about the approach to Belgium had been absurd. The enemy on the run and not a single rear guard to stub Division's toes. A group of lost Germans, captured by the Company cook, swore they were still in Belgium. They thought Maubeuge was in Belgium.

They peered over the top of the ditch and saw the jeep coming down the road. They knew it was the Sergeant. The jeep was about four hundred yards away when a shell landed a hundred yards on its flank.

The jeep made a sudden U-turn. The Sergeant

jumped out and dived into the ditch. The jeep started back. The fourth shell scored. The Sergeant reached the Squad. A coiled lasso was slung across his chest. They watched the blazing jeep.

Zab felt the lasso. "Who're you going to rope?"

"That gun's OP," said the Sergeant. "I know where he lives."

He set a backbreaking pace for them through the deep winding ditch, surprisingly surefooted for a World War I retread. The hearts of the young men almost burst as they forced themselves to keep up with him. When he finally came to a stop it was not to catch a breather. He had reached his objective. He crawled up to the crest. They joined him.

Less than a hundred yards away was a building with an onion-shaped tower. It was on high ground surrounded by trees and thick bushes. Some of the trees made it impossible for anyone in the building to spot the men in the ditch. Rolling up from a long smokestack was heavy black smoke. There was a twisting dirt road about a hundred feet from the ditch and it led to the building.

"He parks his ass in that onion tower," said the Sergeant.

"Why don't we drop a couple bombs on it?" asked Zab.

"It's an insane asylum."

"So?" said Vinci.

"Killing insane people is out," said the Sergeant.

Johnson was confused. "It *is?*"

"Yes. Bad for public relations."

"Oh," said Griff. "But killing sane people is okay."

"That's right." The Sergeant tied his loose legging lace. "The SS have taken over that asylum."

"That what you learned at Battalion?" said Griff.

"Uh-huh. A priest saw the SS throw two nurses and a doctor and a cook into the baking oven. That's their black smoke coming up from the oven."

The men stared at the smoke rolling up from the smokestack.

"The SS let the priest go so he could tell Battalion that all fifty-one inmates will be butchered if we fire one shot at the asylum." The Sergeant paused and sucked in a deep breath, the first sign that he was winded.

"Is that gun racking up a lot of casualties?" asked Vinci.

"It's knocked out fourteen Shermans. Got two roads zeroed in. We can't move until they run out of shells."

"What the hell," Zab said angrily. "So we bomb fifty-one nuts. So what? That's a pretty good swap for saving the asses of eight hundred men!"

"I *told* you," said the Sergeant. "Killing insane people is out!"

"Then what the hell're we doing here?" demanded Zab. "We going to pull this job off with that rope and a goddamn miracle?"

The Sergeant grinned. "That's right. There's a goddamn miracle in that nut house. She's a Belgian underground fighter who's hiding there from the Gestapo."

69

Her underground code name was Walloon. In 1940, on the day the Belgian armies, after eighteen days of fighting, were ordered by King Leopold III to capitulate to Hitler, Walloon had a heart attack that was not caused by the German invasion. She discovered on that fatal May 27 that her husband, a publisher of children's books, liked having sex with little boys. After two months she emerged from the Namur Hospital—a pathetic, emotionally crippled woman. It was her forty-first birthday. And then she survived another great shock. She shot her husband in his office during a White Army raid on the Rex—Belgians for Hitler. She had not known that her husband was a Rexist. Immediately she captured the loyalty and respect of the Belgian underground.

At first, every German and Rexist she killed was her husband. In time he became a blurred memory and gradually she found herself sharing the underground's reason for fighting the German conqueror—patriotism. Her courage and cunning as a saboteur made her one of the most wanted Belgians on Hitler's list. In

1942 four women members of the underground were strangled to death by the Gestapo for refusing to divulge the identity of Walloon. In 1943 she derailed six German troop trains; she was wounded twice dynamiting an ammo dump in Huy; and she blew up a hospital in Charleroi, killing forty-seven wounded German soldiers in order to eliminate three powerful Gestapo chiefs who were visiting the casualties. She impersonated a maid in a hotel in Brussels to slash the throat of a German general while he was in the bathtub, and she masqueraded as a nun to halt a four-truck German convoy carrying high explosives that were swiftly seized by her colleagues. Later she posed as a nun in the cathedral in Liège to shoot a high-ranking Wehrmacht officer and his aide.

By 1944 her record as a killer had boomeranged. To the men in the underground she was harder than crystal. Despite her beauty, the men did not bust down doors to go to bed with her. They respected her, but not a single man had the courage to lay her. They were afraid of her. Something about her coolness in killing made them limp when it came to sex.

Despite her loneliness, she continued to kill key Germans and detonate key installations. Surrounded by men, she slept alone. Masturbation only frustrated her.

On D day she led a commando operation that failed. She eluded the Gestapo and found refuge in Verviers until a Rexist divulged her sanctuary to the Germans. She escaped during a grenade duel and was hidden by underground cells across Belgium until she found safety in the insane asylum near Mons.

Helped by the priest, she became the fifty-first inmate.

Watching and studying the other lunatics, Walloon found herself envying their world. They knew nothing about Hitler and murder and betrayal and fear.

When the SS moved in to use the asylum as their OP for a big gun, Walloon went back to the same business of war. The SS lieutenant found the forty-five-year-old Walloon amusing when she flaunted her dancing talent, announcing that she was the most famous ballerina in the world. The priest had dug up a two-foot ballerina doll with the classical tutu to help Walloon in her insane act.

On September 3, on the roof of the asylum, Walloon danced, her ass transparent through her knee-length nightgown. Performing *The Beauty of Ghent* ballet with her partner-doll, Walloon executed graceful arabesques as she floated among the insane men and women who were sitting around the smokestack. Ranging from catatonics to grinning gargoyles, they paid no attention to her. As Walloon moved about among them, an SS machine gunner's barrel was trained on the inmates. The gunner was engrossed in a German magazine. Next to him on a small table were a hand-crank phonograph and a bottle of brandy. Seated by the table was the SS lieutenant enjoying his cigar and brandy, his eyes glued on the light-footed Walloon creating an awkward *pas de deux* with her doll. She had offered to exhibit her talent if she had music. He supplied the music. She danced a circle around him and the machine gunner. Lifting the doll on her left shoulder, she stared over the front ledge of the roof, waiting for the appearance of the priest on the dirt road below.

In the onion-shaped tower, the observer on the scope and the German on the radio were at work. The job was monotonous. The observer said, "Two degrees right," and the radioman repeated it to the railway gun in the tunnel. The observer watched Red One men and their vehicles being shelled. "Fire six more for effect," said the observer. The order was repeated by the radioman.

Through his scope the observer saw a movement on the dirt road. It was the priest on his bicycle, his black cassock flapping in the wind. The observer descended the spiral stairway to the roof and opened the door. "That priest is coming back!" he shouted, and then he returned to his scope.

The SS lieutenant finished his glass of brandy, allowed his hand to brush Walloon's pirouetting ass, then left the roof by a gray door. Going down the stairs he hummed the ballet music.

Dancing behind the machine gunner, Walloon pulled out a straight razor from inside the doll and slit the gunner's throat. The inmates paid no attention to her. She ran past them to the rear ledge, tossed the doll into the air, and caught it as part of her performance. She watched the Sergeant and his Squad work rapidly through the thick bushes to get to the rear of the building. The Squad formed a human pyramid against the wall. The Sergeant climbed to the top man, stood on his shoulders, and threw the coiled rope up to her. Walloon caught the lasso and lashed the rope around the base of the smokestack. The inmates watched with blank stares as she dropped the rope over the ledge.

As the priest pedaled toward ten inmates who were sitting on the ground in front of the asylum, his only fear was for their lives. They didn't know they were being used as human sandbags for two German machine gunners and two German riflemen covering the entrance. The priest reached them and dismounted. The four Germans eyed him with contempt.

The Sergeant pulled himself up the rope to the roof and followed Walloon to the tower door as Griff, Zab, Vinci, and Johnson climbed up to the roof. The Sergeant trailed Walloon up the spiral stairway to the tower where they silently killed the observer and the radioman. They descended. The rest of the Squad in the rear of the building worked their way through the bushes and trees toward the front of the asylum.

The SS lieutenant appeared at the front door and smiled at the priest. "You delivered my message?"

"Yes."

"You were stupid to return."

"The Americans gave me a message for you."

"What can they say that will alter the situation?"

"You have five minutes to release all the inmates and to march out with your hands on your heads or the building will be bombed and shelled."

"They must be smoking opium."

"Five minutes, they said. A telescopic sight is trained on us right now."

The lieutenant laughed. "A weak threat! Everyone knows Americans don't kill civilians, especially insane men and women. I've exposed the lunatics on the roof so that any plane can see we are not bluffing."

"I was ordered to wait here for five minutes."

"You think they will shell you, too?"

"I *know* they will."

The lieutenant smiled. "If they don't, I'll shoot you myself for bringing me such a stupid bluff."

Walloon led the Sergeant and the Four Horsemen down the stairs to the dining room where she danced with her doll in front of two SS soldiers and five inmates. When the Germans turned to watch her ass, they were knifed and bayoneted by the Sergeant and Zab.

She repeated the action in the kitchen for the benefit of more SS soldiers and inmates. During the attack, a German entered through a side door and immediately opened fire with his Schmeisser. Griff saw his face. Instead of firing, Griff felled him with his rifle. Zab finished him off with his bayonet.

When the SS lieutenant heard the Schmeisser bursts, he charged into the building. Outside, the priest threw himself down on the inmates as Coop and the rest of the Squad killed the four Germans. The dog faces charged into the building, trailed by the priest.

In the kitchen an inmate called Rensonnet had observed the same men in action. He also observed the way the German had fired the Schmeisser before being knocked down by Griff. With the rest of the Germans now alerted to the attack, the Squad left the kitchen to fight the remaining enemy.

Rensonnet picked up the Schmeisser. He had a lucid moment. Before losing that moment, he knew what he had to do: he would do what sane men did until he blacked out again to his normal state of insanity.

Rensonnet fired bullets at the walls, the pots and pans, and the dishes, and he was delighted with the destruction. He ran out of the kitchen firing the Schmeisser wildly.

Griff threw Walloon to the floor and covered her body with his to protect her from bullets and ricochets.

Rensonnet killed the SS lieutenant. Then he killed the priest. Then he killed Coop. Then he killed three inmates. Rensonnet knew he didn't belong in this place. He was as good as the sane people now. He wanted to be complimented. He was killed by the Sergeant.

The battle moved into the laundry room, through the ward, and up to the roof. The inmates watched dogfaces and SS shoot at each other.

During all this Griff remained on Walloon. He was excited by the warmth and pressure of her body. It had been a long time since he had been so close to a woman. His cheek was pressed against hers. She felt his prick become as hard as his rifle barrel.

The sudden silence that followed a fire fight filled his ears. He heard footsteps. Zab stood over him, grinning. Slowly Griff got to his feet and helped her up. Zab told him the bad news. "The Squad's down to the four of us again and, of course, the Sergeant."

"How many people did we kill?"

"Sixteen."

"And inmates?"

"The Sergeant's making the count now."

That night the onion-shaped tower was silhouetted against the moon. Zab entered the ward. Some of the inmates were staring at the ceiling, others were asleep, others talked to themselves. He saw Griff sitting on the edge of a bed. Moonlight streaked through the barred windows.

"Did you score?" Zab asked.

"No."

"She likes you."

"I know."

"How do you feel about her?"

"I like her, too."

"What're you waiting for, you schmuck?"

"She's too old for me."

"I'm glad Benjamin Franklin ain't here."

"What the hell's Benjamin Franklin got to do with this?"

"You never read that famous letter of his?"

"What letter?"

"He wrote a letter to a young schmuck with your problem."

"You pulling my leg?"

"You want to hear about it, or you want to jerk off?"

Griff forced a grin. "I want to hear about it."

"Well—Ben sat down and wrote that young punk many reasons for hitting the sack with an older woman. First of all she wouldn't saddle him with a kid. She wouldn't give him a disease. She'd show him tricks he never heard about and she'd give it everything she

327

could as if it was her *last* lay—" Zab struck a match on his helmet and puffed slowly, turning the cigar end over and over above the flame. "He ended up advising the young Romeo that if he couldn't stomach the old Juliet's face or moustache to cover it with the American flag and shoot for Old Glory."

Griff smiled. "But I *like* her face! I like everything about her!"

"Then stop being a schmuck!" Zab left, a cloud of cigar smoke trailing him.

Griff slowly walked past the inmates. When they were sleeping he couldn't tell the difference between the sane and the insane. He reached the corner bed and sat down on it. Walloon's hand reached for his and placed it on her bare breast. She spoke softly.

"Hello—Benjamin Franklin."

Griff didn't think about her age or Ben Franklin as he caressed her breasts, kissed her lips, and held her to him. In her, he was a man, not a soldier. He was happy. It was as if the war had stopped.

"Benjamin Franklin," whispered Griff, "was never in a rifle squad. He didn't really know the score." His hand, used to the grip of his rifle, gripped the back of her head as if to crush it. She reacted to the iron strength in his fingers and felt the danger in them. They shot fireworks through her body. Burying his mouth on hers, he gently pushed out the ballsy promise. *"I'll* show you tricks you never heard of." He became the aggressor, much to her surprise and joy. What started as a gentle lay supervised by a woman exploded into uncontrollable passion dominated by a man who knew that he could stop a bullet tomorrow. He bit her ear. "And I'll give it everything because this could be *my* last lay."

70

The Battalion CO studied the simple sentence in I Company's incredible morning report: the Sergeant and his Four Horsemen were once again the only survivors in the asylum attack. In his command post in the small brick building near the steelworks outside Charleroi, the Battalion CO's face wrinkled as he read. He glanced up from the report. His expression was picked up by the Captain of I Company. In the shadows, an officer and a noncom were working on a map.

"That's the story, sir," said the Captain. "The inmates were killed by another inmate. He—uh—he went crazy with a Schmeisser during the fire fight. Killed the priest, too."

"An insane man went *insane?*"

"Yes, sir."

"Do *you* buy it?"

"Yes, sir."

"Regiment won't."

"Division will, sir. That report was made by the Sergeant himself."

"The plan was not to lose a *single* inmate. Seven were killed."

"Yes, sir." The Captain began to grow nervous; he didn't want to get in the middle of this incident. "I'll pick up my replacements now, sir. Okay?"

"Hm?" The Battalion CO was still studying the report.

"My replacements, sir."

"They're out there, about fifty yards to your right."

"Yes, sir." The Captain started out.

"Peel off twenty-nine of 'em, Captain."

The Captain turned slowly. He had expected to be shortchanged, but not that much. "I need thirty-eight, sir."

"You'll get 'em when *I* get 'em."

The Captain did not move.

"Everybody's hurting," said the Battalion CO. "Peel off twenty-nine men."

"I remember after Kasserine you threatened to blow up Danger Forward if you didn't get the specified amount of replacements *you* requested, sir. And I also remember that you got them."

The Battalion CO smiled. "They *had* them, Captain. I don't have them. Peel off twenty-nine men."

The Captain left. A half hour later he faced his four platoon leaders. "Peel off sixteen men for the First Platoon," he told the Lieutenant of the First Platoon.

"I need twenty-four sir."

"You'll get 'em when *I* get 'em."

"Before you went to Battalion, sir, you told me—"

"Sixteen men, Lieutenant."

The Lieutenant left the school that housed the Company CP and shortly after distributed twelve men, then personally delivered the remaining four replacements to the Squad in the abandoned coal shed. The Sergeant waited for more. The Lieutenant told him there were no more.

"I need seven, sir," said the Sergeant.

"You'll get 'em when *I* get 'em." The Lieutenant left.

The Sergeant looked at the four new faces. "I'll get your names later."

"This is the First Squad, isn't it, Sergeant?" asked one man.

"Yes."

"First Platoon?"

"Yes."

"Can I say a prayer?"

"Sure, you can say all the prayers you want before we get into a fight."

"I mean can I say a prayer now—for the Squad?"

"Suit yourself," said the Sergeant.

The new man closed his eyes. "With justice He judges and wages war. Guide and protect the safety of the First Squad. Amen." He opened his eyes. "Thank you, Sergeant."

"What's your name?"

"Matthias O'Hanlon."

Johnson's neck stretched to a kink as he pivoted. *"Matthias?"*

"I was named after Saint Matthias."

"Never heard of him."

The Four Horsemen expected to hear a long history about Saint Matthias but the new man remained silent.

That night, in the glare of the Coleman lantern that Johnson had liberated from Service Company, the three other new men became chatty with the Four Horsemen.

"You know what we saw when we landed in Normandy where you guys landed?" said one. "We saw 'em making a big cemetery for the Omaha Beach memorial. That's right. The cemetery's right there where you landed."

"German PWs are hauling the dead and digging graves—and you know who's guarding the Germans? Negro soldiers with rifles." The second new man lighted a cigarette.

"But," said the third new man, "get this! They got no ammo for their rifles."

"Who told you that?" said the Sergeant.

"*They* did. They told us they're scared shitless for fear the Germans'll learn their rifles are empty."

"I don't swallow that," said Griff.

"I do," said Zab.

"Why?" said the Sergeant.

"They got a KKK officer and he just doesn't trust any nigger with a loaded piece."

"Makes sense," said the Sergeant.

"You ought to know it makes sense," said Johnson.

The second new man said, "We heard all about you, Sergeant, at Division."

The Sergeant said nothing. As he stretched out on the floor, resting his head on his helmet, the three new men looked at the legend of the First Division.

"At Division," the second new man went on, "we heard that many sergeants tried to imitate you, but you outlived all of 'em."

Vinci opened his eyes and grinned. "Tell 'em how we take care of you, Sergeant."

The Sergeant smiled.

Matthias paid no attention to their conversation. Off in a world of his own, he stared blankly and in silence. Matthias never spoke about his past. In fact, he never spoke at all, even when he pulled night security with Griff. When he went on combat patrols, he kept his mouth shut.

A devout Roman Catholic, born in Providence, Rhode Island, he was taught that war was always wrong. But Hitler had made this a right war, a war that had to be fought. Matthias knew he was at his country's most crucial moment of history and that his faith in his righteous cause was about to be tested when contact with the enemy would be made. He was not

331

scared. He never brooded, never griped, never showed any sign of exhaustion.

The Sergeant, Zab, Vinci, and Johnson were up ahead on point. Griff was acting squad leader. Walking alongside him was Matthias, and Matthias knew that the smartest thing he could do was to stay close to this veteran and do exactly what he did when he did it. The countryside looked like any other countryside. The low distant hills were half hidden by patches of trees. Birds could be heard exchanging good-mornings. The Squad passed a farmhouse. In front of it three kids waved at the dogfaces.

Matthias was bewildered. "I thought they evacuate civilians before a fight."

"They do," said Griff, "but when it's quiet for a day or two they go back to their farms." Then, as an after-thought, he added, "Where the hell are they going to go when they evacuate? All over Belgium the Germans got rear guards. You heard what the Captain said. They're going to tear up this country before they pull back to Germany—*if* they pull back."

"*If?*"

"That's right. They like to make it look like they're running scared—then from nowhere they counterat-tack. It's a trick you'll get used to—if you make it."

Matthias never doubted that he would outdistance death in the war. "I'll make it."

The burp of a Schmeisser sent the men flying to the ground. On their left a fire fight erupted. It was swiftly followed by a fight on their right. Griff zig-zagged the Squad to the trees and spotted the Sergeant, Zab, Vinci, and Johnson fifty yards away, exchanging fire. Griff maneuvered through the trees, deploying the men with arm signals. Matthias stuck close to Griff. He and Griff came face-to-face with a lone German. Griff tensed in that moment of familiar anticipation of a bullet. The three men matched lightning glances. Matthias should have been electrified. Instead he logically and instinctively fired point-blank when Griff's rifle obviously jammed. The startled young member of the Wehrmacht fell sideways on his cheek. There was elegance in the manner in which Matthias fired two more rounds. Griff watched the replacement from Providence use his rifle with the precision of a diamond cutter. Griff realized that the enemy's blood had spattered his M-1 as well as Matthias's shoes. The entire action lasted a breath over a second. But it was enough time for the Squad to have lost Griff or to have killed a German.

Griff spotted a movement in the trees and caught a flash of the enemy helmet. The figure was far enough away for him to kill and close enough not to miss. He aimed and squeezed. He was astonished. His goddamn rifle jammed on him.

Matthias, never one to be slowed by indecision, scored a bull's-eye. The figure of the German collapsed. But three more Germans on his flank opened fire. A man in the Squad, hit in the shoulder, spun but remained on his feet. He staggered toward Griff and Matthias who were returning the fire. The wounded dogface passed Matthias as seven bullets spun him round again and he crashed backwards on Matthias, dead as he collapsed.

Darting from tree to tree, Griff and Matthias flank-worked close enough to cross-grenade the three Wehrmacht. The third German in the gut of the explosion rose to one knee in the smoke. As the smoke cleared his other splintered leg, he held his burp gun in his right hand. His left arm had been blown off clean. He looked like someone had spilled a can of red paint all over him. He lifted his burp gun.

Matthias kicked the Schmeisser out of his hand and crushed his face in with his rifle butt.

"They are animals," said Matthias. "They must be destroyed. Any animal that condones the gas chambers and the crematoria must be destroyed."

"A hell of a time for you to make a speech." Griff beckoned. Four men in the Squad joined him. He stared at a strange face. "You're not in the First Squad."

"Third Squad," said the strange face. "I got lost in the fight."

"You men hurting?"

"A hell of a lot."

The enemy rearguard action ceased as suddenly as it

had started. Company had forty-seven German PWs, eighteen wounded. German dead: twenty-one. I Company box score: fourteen dead, nine wounded.

Matthias fed kids and the elderly with chow stolen from a headquarters company truck. He gave blood to a casualty at battalion aid after he learned plasma had run out. As he cradled a dying dogface in his arms he prayed for him. Zab dubbed him Saint Matthias. Soon the men called him the Saint. The name stuck. In I Company he was the Saint.

It was impossible for the Sergeant to pinpoint precisely when Matthias began to mystify him. Matthias fought as if he had a personal vendetta with the Germans. When questioned on this, Matthias said it was not a vendetta; it was a thing that had to be done because the Germans had betrayed Christ.

Griff watched the Saint's conditioning as a rifleman and saw no change. Matthias fought with a self-punishing ferocity.

The Saint's eyes intrigued Zab, who felt that Matthias's lack of emotion mirrored the passion with which he fought. Matthias deliberately kept out of the mainstream of the Squad's life, yet in action he asked nothing of the men and took his own risks without endangering any of them.

Vinci wasn't at all certain how to figure out the Saint. Both were Catholics, but Matthias refused to discuss religion. Yet everything he did had the stamp of a religious man.

Johnson had clearly observed him under fire and concluded it wasn't reckless or false heroism that the Saint displayed. Johnson couldn't detect a single flaw in the way Matthias killed with calculated design.

Matthias's saintliness had a strange effect on every man in the Squad. Zab knew that profanities were not growled by the men because of limited vocabulary; they simply expressed their feelings of the moment. However, by the time the rifle-bearing Battalion's pinpoints on the landscape were south of Namur, the men in the Squad had stopped blaspheming in the presence of the Saint.

Matthias was in deep thought on the march. The

way death worked disappointed him. He was disappointed that dying men—and he had seen so many—never mentioned mother, wife, father, child, sweetheart, corner drugstore, hamburgers and Coke, or the Yankees before becoming corpses. *"Oh, no!"* was their usual final gasp. Once, cradling a dying man in his arms, he was sure the soldier would say something touching. But the soldier mustered the strength to say, "My wife's a cunt. I hate her," and he died with hatred. Yet he had also seen men die unafraid, pleased they had done their jobs well, each death adding honor to a humanity that was cherished. These men proved the capacity of man to hold fast to God. It proved to him that beautiful things could be made by monstrous weapons. Their principles survived bloodbaths.

Every step he took brought him closer to the Nazis he was trained to demolish. The weapon, ammo, grenades, and combat pack he carried felt as light as smoke. He didn't believe in the merciful God of the New Testament. The word *rabbi* was used by the apostles to address Christ. He liked the ring of the word *rabbi*. When he prayed to Christ, he prayed to his Rabbi.

He knew that emperors who led persecutions against any sect, Christian or Jew, came to horrible ends. But Hitler would survive unless he was killed. And to bring about Hitler's death it was Matthias's job to kill Hitler's defending angels. Many nights Matthias fell asleep with the same vision: Hitler crucified in Berlin, hung on the cross head downward.

He felt good. He was on the way to crush the vermin of life, the betrayers of Jesus.

71

The Sergeant's spine felt worse as he crouched behind the high, damp embankment, his binocs hunting for K Company's patrol scouting the riverbank. He knew it wouldn't help to see the regimental surgeon about that pain. He would be told he was over the hill,

335

and ruddy, chubby Doc Tegtmyer would recommend transfer to Division HQ as a clerk. Spotting no movement, he angled slightly left to L Company's patrol. He saw only many draws, a lot of brush, many trees, and a sniffing hound. He kept his eyes on the hound for any sign of sudden movement. The hound lifted a leg, then went on sniffing. The Sergeant eased the binocs right and saw life. He stared without blinking. Only one man. The Sergeant held his breath and when he spotted the Red One patch he let his breath out. It was Stockwell of the Intelligence and Reconnaissance Platoon out of Regiment. He wished he had Stock in his Squad. The tall, quiet pig farmer from upstate New York was one of the best scouts in Division. Behind Stock came his eight-man patrol, each one a seasoned hunter. They were returning and that meant there were no people on the right.

He must remember to keep his men out of those draws. German mortars zeroed in on them. He made a mental note to ask for more grenades for the rifle launcher. And more frag grenades. He was overstocked with white-phosphorous and concussion grenades. He sensed that Matthias could become a damn good sniper and decided to try him out with a Springfield '03, but there was something about Matthias that bothered him.

"Matthias," he called out.

Matthias climbed up the embankment and crouched next to the Sergeant.

"It's your digging—" said the Sergeant as he lowered his binocs. "Your fighting hole's never been six feet deep. It's been five, but never six. Any argument about that?"

Matthias shook his head. He was alert and worried. He had never seen the Sergeant so grim faced.

"When we cross the river," said the Sergeant, "their tanks will steamroll over us to stop us from getting to the German border. If you're not six feet deep their tanks'll crush you. Six feet. Understand?"

Matthias nodded, grateful that that was all there was to it.

The Sergeant read his mind as easily as he read a map.

"There's more," said the Sergeant. "Last night on outpost with Zab, was he smoking a cigar?"

Matthias, feeling better, smiled.

"If he does," said the Sergeant looking through his binocs again, "knock the match out of his hand." He paused. He could feel Matthias still smiling. "I caught you on the BAR when that man was killed. You did fine, but forget the bipod. Takes too long to set it up. Another thing, I'm going to try you out sniping with a Springfield. And what I'm going to tell you is personal. When you fired at tracers last night you didn't wait for my fire order and if you didn't hear me your mind was elsewhere. That German pumped tracers from a high point. He had other guns on grazing fire that got the two men next to you." He lowered his binocs and looked at Matthias and spoke very quietly. "You drew that fire, Saint."

The Sergeant's painful descent was made alone.

Pale, his heart going like a wild drumbeat, Matthias watched him reach the Squad.

"Sergeant," said a new face, "what if I freeze and can't shoot in a fight?"

"Chances are you'll be dead."

"I told him," said Griff, "to hit for cover if he's going to freeze."

"No man in my Squad freezes," said the Sergeant. "I only buy buck fever when the man is alone. Otherwise he weakens the Squad's firepower and is responsible for one of us getting killed."

"How about hypnotizing *me,* Sergeant?" asked the new face.

"Who the hell gave you that idea?"

"Zab. He told me you always hypnotize the Squad before going into action."

"Oh, he did, did he? Well, Zab's the best hypnotist in Battalion." The Sergeant smiled at Zab. "Work on him, Zab. If he's not hypnotized before we move out, I'll send you out on point every working day—and no overtime."

The Sergeant left. The new face turned eagerly to Zab who ignored him and gave his attention to Vinci.

"Like I was saying, Vinci, I'm dedicating my novel

337

to those who shot and didn't get shot." He puffed slowly, then examined his cigar's long white ash. "Know why?"

"You told me why," smiled Vinci, "but tell me again."

"Because corpses don't buy books."

"How about it, Zab?" said the new face. "Start on me right now!"

"Well—first I've got to know what to call you."

"Spider."

"Your nickname?"

"No—my real name."

"You're kidding."

"No, I'm not."

"Okay, Spider, I'll make a deal. When you come up with a box of stogies for me, I'll hypnotize you into another Sergeant York."

Going past the rest of the Platoon, the Sergeant shifted his rifle to his left shoulder. His back felt a little better by the time he reached the Lieutenant who was cleaning his carbine. He told the Lieutenant he had spotted I and R coming back.

"I know," said the Lieutenant. "Just talked to Stock. No booby traps or mines out there. And not a sign of any people at all."

"Our Piper Cub must've seen troops before he was shot down."

"That's what Regiment figures."

"And *you,* sir?"

"I smell rear guards out there somewhere to stub our toes."

"What about plastering with heavy stuff?"

"The Old Man put in a request, but Division artillery's helping Second Battalion cross the river about ten miles south of us and Cannon Company's been shanghaied by First Battalion for extra muscle. They're in a helluva fire fight."

"K and L patrols?"

"Found no people. Shit!"

"Shit? No people out there's good news."

"It's this goddamn carbine. Couple grains of dust and it's stopped up."

"I wouldn't trust my ass with that peashooter."

338

"That why you turned down bars?" The Lieutenant smiled. "Officers don't look like officers when they carry an M-1." His smile slowly faded as he observed the Sergeant's familiar grim expression.

"Got a beef?"

"It's Weapons Company, sir. Something's happened more than once."

"They never fucked up giving you support."

"Worse. They got a bad habit of moving up with us."

"They like your personality."

"I like theirs, too, but not when their heavy machine guns draw mortar fire and get pinned down so they can't give us support. They've got to get word from the Old Man to keep in *back* of us and fire over our asses."

"He got the same beef from the Second and Third Platoons."

"There you *are,* sir!"

"Their beef took a nose dive, Sergeant."

"Dead end?"

"Yup. He told them when those .50s move up alongside riflemen it's time for riflemen to keep moving ahead of them."

The Sergeant grudgingly changed the subject as he glanced at the steep hill about a thousand yards to the right. Pockmarked with trees and bushes, it towered over a long valley beyond it. The Lieutenant caught the glances and also looked at the hill.

"Still bug you?" asked the Lieutenant.

The Sergeant nodded. "I'm not running down the Third Squad, sir, but they checked it out too fast for my blood."

"I'll make you a happy man, Sergeant. Take your Squad up there and hang onto the summit for observation while Company crosses." He placed his carbine against his crotch. "There'll be no room for about twenty men. They'll have to get their asses wet."

"Their balls'll turn blue." The Sergeant laughed, then frowned. "How will *my* men get across?"

"I'll leave a rubber raft for you."

Platoon Sergeant Hanson joined them. A regular army rifleman who worked his way up to become regimental sergeant major, he was busted for breaking the jaw of an enlisted man in a crap game. Reduced to

T/Sergeant, he was given the First Platoon because he had already proven himself capable of handling the key infantry job in line action.

But Hanson kept one secret to himself. He was sapped. He had the know-how and the ability, but he was physically incapable of fighting a platoon. He was good only for paper work now.

He admired and envied the Sergeant. And he was grateful because the Sergeant was his lifesaver. The Sergeant made the First Squad, and the First Squad made the First Platoon the best fighting unit in Battalion. And Hanson shared the laurels. He knew it wasn't the Sergeant's favoritism that made the young Four Horsemen old veterans. It was observation, intelligence, cunning, and speed—learned from observing the Sergeant.

Old soldiers never die was a proven fact to Hanson because combat-wise men knew how to stay alive. Replacements were killed, wounded, or missing because they never got over their initial fear and froze under enemy flare drops instead of taking intelligent cover from bombs and shells. Or they were patriotic heroes who, in their stupid show-off eagerness for the Silver Star, forgot caution. Or they were rebels who hated discipline and were deaf to combat orders. Or they were so pessimistic they just didn't give a damn, an attitude that cost them their lives. Or they were mentally slow and lacked the coordination to kill and not be killed.

"Did he talk you into it, Lieutenant?" asked Hanson.

"Yes. He's going to check the hill himself."

To Hanson the Sergeant was more than just the best fighting man he had ever seen. When Hanson watched him in action it was like watching Death carrying an M-1.

Hanson wondered if such a soldier as the Sergeant existed in the German army. What would happen if the Sergeant met his enemy other half? What would happen if Death fought Death?

340

72

Schröder led his sullen men through the long valley, deployed a hundred of them to the draws, and took twenty-five up the steep hill facing the river. His face reddened and his muscles strained but he forced himself up the slope. Trees helped for handholds, but sheer rock and thorny bushes infuriated him. Suddenly he lost his balance, fell sideways, and wrenched his back.

Now, as he forced one boot up the slope in front of another, the pain in Schröder's back deadened, but his rage increased. The German army's pulling back was incredible and stupid. A stupid retreat bordering on military insanity. A retreat ordered by blinkered officers safe in their Berlin bunkers playing with their overrated logistics and their pricks. He would like five seconds alone with the general who had convinced Hitler's staff to retreat.

He was having difficulty breathing and, as he heard himself panting, one thought drove him mad. They should have left panzers, infantry, and artillery on the other side of the river to stop and destroy the enemy attempting to cross it. He was told the brass didn't want to lose their troops to American planes and this he could not understand. He knew that American planes would spot them near Liège as easily as on the banks of the Meuse.

Oh, he understood the importance of massing defensive strength at the border, but wasn't it more logical to mass the strength at the Meuse? Logic! *He* was using logic. *They* didn't know the meaning of the word. He stumbled again and fell. His back pain grew worse. He got up and continued the ascent. He had been promised fifty Rexists to support him at this hill, to help him short-cut any possible getaway because they knew the area. But not a single pro-Nazi Belgian bastard had appeared. He knew why. They were like so many false followers of Hitler who had deserted him in the fight they now assumed lost because of the presence of Americans in Belgium.

He stopped for a breather. He knew the young men behind him were laughing at him and the way he climbed the hill, but to hell with them. It would be their last chance to laugh. Oh, they would delay the enemy for a moment, but then they would die. Only the wounded would be able to watch the Americans crossing the river on the way to Germany. Unless . . .

Maybe the German general staff actually *had* a foolproof plan. Perhaps even now troops were speeding from Russia across Germany to the Belgian border while at the same time troops were speeding south from the Netherlands to the Belgian border.

He brushed past a rock, continuing his backbreaking climb. Then another thought made him even more optimistic. What about those troops stationed in Poland, Czechoslovakia, Hungary? And those spit-and-polish troops garrisoned in Stuttgart, Nuremberg, Dresden, Leipzig, Berlin?

Yes! That had to be the plan! They would all mass at the border and form an impenetrable steel wall and then—*then* enemy morale would collapse as Hitler's massed buzz-saw juggernaut would send the Americans running to their death the way the Ivans ran when Hitler blitzed Russia.

Again he rested, grunting at the responsibility he had, knowing the officers were clever and cowardly to have put him in command. Why should *they* lead a doomed rear guard into oblivion? Pick Schröder, he could hear them say. Schröder had outlived all the men in his section. Schröder was the perfect sacrificial lamb.

"Psst!"

He stopped, turned, saw that a few of his soldiers had gathered over a fallen man. Schröder cursed as he awkwardly descended fifty feet that he would have to climb again.

When Schröder reached the group, a young German pointed at the fallen man. "I think he broke his leg. He fell on that rock."

Schröder squatted. The casualty looked about nine-

342

teen and his face distorted when Schröder examined his leg. It was broken.

"When the Americans find you," Schröder told the casualty, "they'll take care of you or shoot you." On the rise he added, "Either way you're out of action."

He sighed and continued to climb the hill.

But when he reached the summit he felt he had just scaled Everest. He sank to the ground and rested as the young men struggled up to him. He watched them closely. He felt better. They were all exhausted.

From the valley, as the sun came up, he had observed the enemy scouting party climb the hill for a security check. He saw one American trip and fall. He was still curious why they had bypassed checking the valley. They would never have found his men because he worked too well to conceal them, but the enemy should have investigated the valley.

Now, waiting for his normal breathing to return, he watched the 160 Americans below. Through his binocs he could plainly see the Red One patches. It was a patch that annoyed him, a patch that had fought him in North Africa, Sicily, and France.

His pulse suddenly throbbed. What if they sent up men to use the hill as an OP during the crossing? He got to his feet and set his mortars and machine guns and riflemen, telling the men to hold their fire until he was certain every American was in the water. It would be easy to kill them in the river. Even as he spoke, he was aware that their delaying the enemy would be brief. The hill would eventually be shelled and mortared, then a fixed-steel ascent, perhaps at battalion strength, would swarm up the hill. He had decided against laying mines because enemy shells would trigger a chain reaction. He thought about the possibility of the enemy below spearheading a regimental crossing. He wouldn't be surprised if the whole damn Red One American division would cross at this point.

Checking the position of every one of his men, he noticed with a smile how they posed behind their weapons like the golden-haired heroes on the propaganda posters, and he hoped these young Germans were the killers they appeared to be. They were no longer sullen. They knew they were going to massacre the enemy in the water from their high field of fire. Their gnawing terror vanished and each one was suddenly eager and in control of himself and his weapon.

He also noticed the glitter in their eyes. The river butchery was going to be exhilarating. He was surprised that he even felt sorry for them. Soon they would be corpses. In their arrogance none of them realized that after the slaughter began, it would be *their* unscarred young bodies that would end up rotting blanks because their job was to remain on the hill until they were dead.

He arched his body to ease the pain in his back when he heard the first shot and felt the bullet glance off his helmet. Lunging behind a tree, he heard the clockwork bursts of the Squad's weapons and saw a flash of the Sergeant directing devastating fire. The young Germans, caught in the surprise attack, were torn apart by bullets, blown apart by grenades.

The action was over. Using his old possum trick, Schröder played dead after smearing his chest with the blood of a German corpse. He kept his eyes closed and held his breath as he heard the Sergeant calling for a count of his Squad. Schröder didn't have to understand English to know that the Sergeant was counting his own dead and wounded as well as the number of enemy dead. Soon someone would check him.

He gritted his teeth, froze, and waited. A man's shoe moved against his body. Someone was bending over him.

"Forget the others," said the Sergeant. "We'll let the medics check for wounded. Let's go."

Schröder heard them descend. Except for the sound of their shoes scraping past brush and rocks, the Americans were as silent as the Germans they had killed. When he thought it was safe, Schröder opened his eyes. He had lost every man on the hill. He knew that during the bursts of the attack, his men below had suffered the same result from the Americans. He wondered how many of the hundred men he had sent to the draws were wounded. He figured only a few.

He watched the men with the Red One patches

cross the river in rubber boats. Hearing men coming up the hill, he hid behind a tree to watch the medics hunt for GI and German wounded. They carried down the casualties. He saw more men below with Red One patches and he knew it was the rest of the battalion. He watched them cross the river. It was getting dark. He had a plan and now went to work on it. He moved past dead Germans and found two dead Americans.

He placed his Schmeisser on the ground, swiftly stripped one of the bodies, and put on the American uniform. He was now wearing the Red One patch. He fastened the GI cartridge belt around his waist, slung the bandoliers, picked up a GI steel helmet with the Red One insignia on it. Seizing an M-1, he took the man's dog tags and put them around his neck.

In the dark he worked his way down the hill. When he reached the bottom he saw many Americans waiting to cross. He fell behind two of them, walked through a group, and joined about seven of them who were following a noncom.

Schröder got into the rubber boat. It was packed with silent men. He felt their tension as they crossed the Meuse.

When they reached the other side he joined them as they moved through the brush. He waited with them as more Americans were ferried across the river. He knew he was watching the battalion and he kept close to the men but not close enough for anyone to start up a conversation with him. Twice an officer said something to the group he was with and he followed the men and joined another group.

They started a forced march and Schröder walked with the enemy. When a dogface asked him a question, he growled and turned away, hoping the sound and gesture would work. It did.

When some of the dogfaces pulled out to crap, Schröder did the same but didn't return. He slipped off into the night and made his way through the countryside. He fell asleep under an overpass, but, being a light sleeper, controlled himself to wake before dawn. It was still dark when he heard tanks and trucks rumbling past him on the right. He reached the road and watched the enemy pass. Howitzers rolled by. Daybreak brought the end of the convoy. He waited. There was no sound. He began to walk down the road, his M-1 slung, when he heard the stuttering engine. He turned, flagged down a jeep, and jumped in beside the American driver.

"Gotta take a piss," said the driver. He got out and unbuttoned his fly and began to piss when Schröder slammed him on the back with the M-1 barrel. The driver fell, his helmet tumbling off a few feet. Schröder stomped the driver's head with the rifle butt, producing a report like a muffled gunshot, dragged the body into the brush, and drove off in the jeep after cursing the three minutes it took for him to get the hang of it. He covered at least twenty miles, using side roads and lanes, keeping away from the convoy road, when the jeep came under rifle fire. He jumped out from the moving vehicle, dived into a gully, and yelled that he was a German.

But the rifle fire coming from behind a deeper ravine kept reaching for him. A bullet filled his right eye with dirt. He saw a figure, killed him with his first shot, slowly walked to the body, and stared at the Belgium Rexist who had just died for Hitler. When Schröder turned he caught a glimpse of the runaway jeep crashing into a bomb hole. He kept to the ravine until sunset and then he slept. Rising before dawn, he watched American troops on foot in the distance until they were blotted out by dust churned up by tanks. He ran across the field, putting more miles between him and the convoy. Reaching a bombed farmhouse, he clawed among the debris for food, found nothing, then rested. Two hours later he came upon an abandoned warehouse and swept up the grains, but he did not find enough to eat.

He grew weaker.

Essentially, he knew, he was untouched by the loss of his men, untouched by his own situation. If he came across Germans he would be shot. If he came across Americans he could be unmasked and then shot for wearing their uniform.

The spatter of gunfire started him scrambling. He was on the edge of collapse.

"You alone?" yelled an American.

Schröder whirled at the burly corporal who was

crouching behind the tumbled remains of an ancient rock wall. The corporal didn't wait for a reply but pointed at a big heap of manure a hundred feet to the left. "Work your way to that horseshit. Two krauts behind a rock. Too far for grenades. We'll lay it on, you get 'em in cross fire."

Even as the corporal barked the order, Schröder saw three Americans firing rifles over the wall. German bullets zinged off the wall. Schröder dutifully worked his way to the manure and poked round it. Six Germans were on their Mausers behind the rock.

Schröder worked his way back, maneuvering behind the corporal and three Americans. Four rapid shots were squeezed off by Schröder. He waited until the confused Germans held their fire, then exposed himself, shouting that he was German and that he had shot the four Americans in the back.

Challenged by one of the Germans for proof, he dug his own identification tag from his GI pocket, hurled it at the rock. Two Germans emerged slowly as the other four kept their weapons on Schröder. The first German picked up the identification tag. The second German found the four Americans dead with bullets in their backs.

Both Germans smiled.

"I'm hungry," said Schröder, grinning back at them.

73

Zab gorged himself on the variety of fire fights the Squad was in. There were more than enough incidents to use in his book. The Platoon struck a slaughterhouse with massed momentum. The abattoir was as big as a hanger, the smell deadening, the action sickening. The first thing he noticed was the way the dogfaces kept their heads low, breathing close to the ground the way the pigs did. Moving past rows of loins and hams, using live and dead pigs for cover, the Squad bellied toward the thirty-odd SS soldiers. Within minutes the blood of the Platoon and the blood of the SS mixed with the blood of the pigs. Zab spotted Griff finding refuge in a cloud of his own vomit between the carcass of a white pig and a trapped black pig that was grunting in panic.

The squealing of swine, the burst of machine guns, the crack of rifles was like music made by a drunken organist. Zab found himself in the heat of fire. Disgust began to dominate his feelings about writing of the locale. Faces of pigs and faces of men exploded in a swirl of hideous masks. And still, he found a nightmarish beauty in the rot that was suffocating him. It was a dream that could not be shaken off because there was no dream to shake off. This was realistic in an unreal world.

When the slaughtering was over, the winners and the losers and the dead pigs were motionless. After a while Zab saw someone move. It was the Sergeant climbing over carcasses of swine and SS, making sure that no wounded enemy soldier still had the energy to squeeze a trigger. Then Zab spotted Platoon Sergeant Hanson checking casualties. The Platoon had taken half the punishment. The SS, with the exception of one live soldier with his intestines exposed and another holding onto what was left of his shoulder, were dead. Griff rose to his feet, sick and trembling. Vinci staggered between pigs. Johnson got to his feet drunkenly. Matthias was an exhibition of a miracle infantryman: he didn't look exhausted or sick. Zab was sure that the slaughterhouse fight would never haunt Matthias.

Two hours later the Squad was told by the Sergeant, "You're not off the hook altogether." There were more areas to probe for German troops left behind as rear guard to delay and confuse the advancing Americans.

One part of that hook was the hill. The enemy, dug in hard, made enough noise to sound like a company; and the taking of the hill chewed up so many of them that it was named Hamburger Hill. The Squad had also been chewed down to the Sergeant, the Four Horsemen, and Matthias. The Sergeant was sent only four new men. While he sized them up at the base of the hill, one overlooked German, his leg bleeding, worked his way down the Hamburger slope close enough to hurl a single potato masher. The four new faces were killed, but no fragment struck the Sergeant. Matthias shot the wounded German, who got up, holding a second potato masher high above his head. He was shot in the chest and he got up again, still holding the grenade. Suddenly it blew him apart.

By noon the next day the Squad was up to full fighting strength again. Not a man in the Big Red One had to be told that enemy resistance was increasing by the hour.

Zab was bitter. The wetnoses passed on rumors they inherited all the way down from Division that the Germans were demoralized and scattered in their retreat. It also embittered the others in the Squad, for such rumors, started by optimistic brass safe behind army HQ, made the man with the rifle feel like a horse's ass. The mounting number of GI dead and wounded was proof that it would be one hell of a long time before the German soldiers would show any sign of being demoralized.

What made Zab really bitter was an incident with a beautiful young woman whose voluptuous measurements threw him off guard. From her isolated house, firing through the window of her bathroom, she sniped at him, missing his ear by an inch. Matthias's third bullet scored above her heart. They found her still wet from her bath, cursing them as she lay dying. A pale-faced wetnose was horrified. When he joined the army he knew that he would have to shoot and kill men, but now he stared at the woman, who looked like a sex goddess. And it was a GI had shot her!

The Sergeant understood her last words. She was a pro-Hitler Belgian, a member of the Rex. She spat at them and died. Bitter, Zab was furious with Matthias. Zab wanted to question the girl. What made such a beautiful specimen want to die for Hitler?

"You could've wounded her," Zab growled. "You didn't have to put her out of action for keeps."

"He saved your goddamn ass," Vinci said to Zab.

"He cost me a goddamn character for my book."

"It's your own fault," said the Sergeant.

"Mine?"

"You were daydreaming when she missed you."

Zab shrugged, agreeing with him without a word. As they came out of the house the Sergeant said, "If you'd have been on the ball you would've kicked her yourself. Then you could've asked her why she had a hard-on for Hitler."

Matthias's face was barren of emotion. "She was a Judas Iscariot. She had to be killed."

"Zab." The Sergeant pointed at a group of houses some five hundred yards away. "It's your turn up at bat." He indicated the pale-faced wetnose. "Show him how."

"Come on," Zab growled.

The pale face fell in step behind Zab like a shadow. Zab set a fast pace down the road. Suddenly he stopped and struck a match on his helmet. He puffed.

"An American soldier," said the pale face, "should never shoot a girl. It's downright un-American!"

The cigar was dry. Zab resumed the fast pace. As they reached the outskirts of the small village he slowed down and became tense. He led the way, padding into the deserted village, showing the pale face how to approach a house, how to check it by keeping away from windows, how to kick a door in without exposing yourself. They went from house to house and the suspense lessened. Many houses were in trouble. They found the church intact and there they saw a horse hitched to a glass hearse. The church door was open. Zab eased his head in, saw four women and two men in mourning with bowed heads. A priest in a black cassock was praying over four infant coffins. Behind him was a crude crucifix overhanging Christ's tomb.

The pale face's rifle struck the doorway. The four women and two men turned, glanced at the two uniformed intruders, then turned their heads and bowed them once again in prayer. From the doorway Zab beckoned okay with an arm signal and saw the Sergeant and the Squad, who had been covering him all the way, appear from behind some trees. They joined him and the pale face to jam the doorway and to peer inside and to listen to the mass. Matthias slung his rifle, took off his helmet, walked in, and sat down on a wooden bench. He bowed his head and prayed.

While the Squad watched, each of them moved by the sight of the four infant coffins, eight German soldiers appeared from behind drainage ditches and opened fire at the bunched dogfaces. One fell. The

Sergeant and the rest dived into the church.

Suddenly the priest, flattened behind the four coffins, seized a hidden Schmeisser, and his first burst killed two more new men.

The Sergeant and the Squad, on their bellies between benches, were caught from the front and the rear. The Sergeant managed to drive his fourth bullet through the top of the priest's head when he found himself subjected to fire coming from the four women and the two men who had ducked behind the bench. In the exchange of fire, bullets chipped benches, ricocheted off walls, splintered the coffins, and peppered the crude crucifix.

Grenades were thrown wildly. Smoke began to fill the church. Through the smoke the eight German soldiers dashed in, firing, but before they could shoot the Squad, fifteen Belgians wearing red, white, and blue armbands avalanched through the smoke and wiped out the eight Germans with point-blank machine-gun fire.

The pale face saw one of the women aiming and he chopped her nose, cheekbone, and one eye from her face with a bullet. At the same time the Squad and the Belgians blew apart the remaining three women and two men.

The fight was suddenly over and as the smoke settled the panting leader of the Belgians pointed at the AB inscribed on his armband. *"Armée Blanche,"* he said. "White Army. Belgian underground. My English is better when I catch my breath." He stepped over dead Germans and pointed at the riddled bodies of the four women and two men. "Rexists—Belgians for Hitler." He kicked one of the demolished coffins. It was empty. He booted the dead priest, then ripped off the black cassock, revealing the German uniform. "They like to put on fake funerals in abandoned villages to ambush American patrols. My name is Guinle. I am a notary."

They followed him out of the church.

"What about the white armbands?" asked Johnson.

"All are Belgian Maquis."

"You worked like professional soldiers," said the Sergeant.

"The professionals in our army never surrendered to

the Germans in 1940. And amateurs like us joined them and *became* professionals."

Two of his men began to argue. Threats were exchanged. He had to separate them. "Sometimes," Guinle told the Squad, "their different languages endanger the trust our alliance is based on. You see, our country has two languages. We have Dutch-speaking Flemings and French-speaking Walloons."

"Walloons?" asked Griff.

"Yes."

"Ever met an underground fighter who calls herself Walloon?"

"Yes."

"We met her."

"Where?"

"In an asylum near Mons."

"She belongs in that institution. A wonderful Maquis, but she has no normal feelings."

Griff smiled.

When the Sergeant radioed Platoon that the village no longer held any Germans, he was told to tie in with the Company at Reference Point 34, a windmill seven miles northeast of the church.

At the windmill, I Company dug in for the night. Guinle and his Belgians had hot chow with the Squad. In the morning the Belgians had vanished. Guinle, learning that K Company was sending out a patrol, volunteered the services of the underground. By eleven o'clock, I Company was on a forced march to support K's right flank. On their left they could hear the fighting escalating. There was a spatter of gunfire from the right. The Lieutenant sent the Squad to investigate. The Sergeant spotted enemy bursts at a distance, observed the random fire, and at the distance read the Germans' minds. He ordered every man to fire at the bushes between themselves and the enemy bursts. He was right. Bullets hit mines. Detonation tripped detonation. Four Germans stood up and surrendered. The Sergeant beckoned, shouting for them to advance. They remained as statues, their hands on their helmets. They had given up, but the Americans would have to come to them to take them. The Sergeant grunted, admiring their plan and their courage. "We didn't hit all their mines," he said. "They're waiting for us to blow ourselves up."

"Goddamn crazy standoff," said Zab.

"Standoff, hell." The Sergeant opened fire. The Squad emptied clips. The four Germans were killed and the rest of the mines exploded. "They could've planted 'em for a mile," said the Sergeant.

"Do we bypass?" asked Vinci.

"Uh-huh. Got to reach K Company."

"You need a guinea pig," said Matthias.

The Sergeant didn't stop Matthias, who advanced through the exploded minefield. At safe distance the Sergeant followed in his footsteps, the Squad trailing. Very slowly, lifting each foot as if it weighed a ton, Matthias crossed the field. Only a few yards from the bedrock, he tripped an AP mine and vanished in the explosion's smoke. By the time the Sergeant reached him, the smoke had settled. Matthias was a gory splash of blood. He had only seconds of life left.

"Was I a good replacement?" asked Matthias.

"Yes," said the Sergeant.

"Saint Matthias replaced Judas," he whispered, and he died.

GERMANY

What took you so long?

—A dead Jew to a dead dogface

74

The Sergeant was lost in the morning fog. At first the patrol was no sweat because I Company had eight of them probing to make physical contact with the Germans. E Company on the left contact and C Company on the right assured the men of complete support. But what started as a normal recon hunt became a loser's patrol when the thick fog closed in and made it impossible to see more than a few inches away.

Inching forward, not knowing whether they were groping straight ahead, left, right, or in circles, each man held the shoulder of the man in front of him. Since they had not touched a single German, the men were sure there were no Germans left in Belgium; they were also sure that the enemy was now racing across Germany to battle with the Russians who were probably invading Germany right now on the eastern front.

Ordered to maintain radio silence, the Sergeant broke it to learn that his flanks couldn't identify where or how far from him they were. Every patrol was bogged down to a standstill. He asked about runners. Four were lost in the fog.

He halted for a break, making sure each man's body was glued to the next man. He didn't want any MIAs because of the fog. A young black man grabbed his arm.

"Sergeant?"

"Yes?"

"I sure hope you don't get into a mess on my account."

The Sergeant vaguely made out the blur talking to him.

"On whose account?"

"Me. Spencer. QM."

"What mess are you talking about besides this goddamn fog?"

"Letting me fight with your Squad."

"You haven't been in a fight yet. Now work your way back to the man you were holding onto."

"I've been holding onto you all the time, Sergeant. We're lost, ain't we?"

"Yes."

"Like I was when my truck hit that mine."

"You're lucky."

"I'm sure glad I was hauling rifles and ammo. I'd feel silly fighting Germans with a .45."

"You're sure you can handle that M-1?"

"Hell, Sergeant, we all learned how to handle all kinds of weapons at basic, but then they shoved us behind wheels or in rear camps to unload. I got an ulcer counting the notches of nigger insults that cut me up. Hell, man, I just squeaked through not coldcocking the red-necks. They made me feel I'm a slave to a truck. Hell, we got eyes, we got fingers, we got balls, we can fight, man. I don't know where the brass got the idea we're all chicken. Bet they wouldn't call Joe Louis chicken."

"No, I don't think they would."

"My CO's a nice guy, a white guy, and he gives us a lot of patriotic jabbering about how the war's coming along just fine—as long as we don't do any real fighting in a rifle company."

The blurred black face started the Sergeant thinking about the General visiting Battalion, handing out a couple of D.S.C.s, hunting down Griff, and thanking him for the cartoon the General kept tacked on his battle map. Before returning to Danger Forward, the General had walked alone with the Sergeant for one of their rare get-togethers.

"You look fine, General."

"That's because we're getting close to Hitler's stamping ground."

"Think they'll throw in the towel?"

"Not while that bastard's alive. They'll bounce off the ropes and come at us swinging. Look, Sergeant, I know it's a waste of time, but at Regiment I told the Colonel I'd take another crack at you. He wants you to fight with B Company."

"You know the score, sir."

"Of course I know the score, otherwise I'd commission you right now as acting CO of that company, but I want you to *want* it."

"All I want is what I requested."

"How many men are you shy this time?"

"Two."

"You'll get them if I have to send down a couple of my clerks to keep you up to strength."

"Your two stars can make sure I don't get any cream from your clerical pool."

"That's showing favoritism."

"Nobody'd have the guts to call you on it, sir."

"You'll get them."

"How about Negroes?"

"I'm for it."

"The ones I talked to since North Africa are pissed off being called gutless. All they ask is a crack to fight in the infantry."

"I know—but the order to integrate has to come from upstairs—way, way upstairs."

"Now and then I've come across a black straggler—give me the okay to use any of them I find, will you, General?"

"It's your Squad."

"That's all I want to hear."

"That's not all, Sergeant. You can get away with it in a fight, but when the shooting's over and he's still alive, it's back to the QM for him."

359

"Even if he puts up a hell of a scrap?"

"Even then—it's back to the truck or the dock or the warehouse for him. That's the picture, Sergeant."

"A shitty picture, General."

"It sure is."

The Sergeant suddenly realized that Spencer was saying something to him. "What did you say?" said the Sergeant.

"If I score with this rifle can I stay in your Squad?" The Sergeant felt lousy. "We'll talk after I see you in action. Let's go."

He plowed through the wall of fog, Spencer gripping his shoulder. The ghosts followed. The Sergeant was for the first time overstrength. He had a thirteenth man and he didn't have the guts to tell Spencer that no matter how much he scored in action he couldn't stay on.

The Sergeant blindly led his Squad single file in the fog between invisible blunt-headed pyramids.

"Zab," said Johnson.

"Yeah?"

"What's the name of that new guy who speaks German?"

"Kaiser."

"Kaiser—" said Johnson, raising his voice.

"Yeah?"

"What did Hitler say on that radio last night?"

"The same Nazi bullshit that no one but a German soldier'll ever set foot in Germany."

Johnson grunted. "I know *we* won't."

"How do *you* know?"

"Ike'll pull us out long before we reach Germany."

"Ike? You mean Eisenhower?"

"That's right. Back in England he told us all we gotta do was establish a beachhead in Normany. Who ever heard of a beachhead from Normandy to Germany?"

It was 5:45 A.M. on September 12, 1944 when the men groped past the concrete conical dragon's teeth of the Siegfried Line without knowing they had just invaded Germany.

75

They hit the city of Aachen brutally. For the first time the First Division fought in a battlefield of buildings and paved streets with signs and sewers and electric lights. They killed Germans in cafés, hotels, hosptials, offices, and apartments.

The defenders of the Third Reich desperately sold and bought death. For the first time they were fighting on German soil, fighting in the streets of an ancient city where they had made history since Charlemagne. Every German knew that if Aachen fell, Germany would fall. So they fought with a fury to mask their panic, a fury that turned the battle into confused slaughter on both sides. In the frenzy, dogfaces killed dogfaces, Germans shot Germans, and many civilians were shot in the haphazard cross fire.

Blood drenched the city because the German CO refused to surrender. The General of the First Division had sent word that unless Aachen capitulated it would be reduced to rubble by bombs and artillery. But the German in command, Colonel Wilck, rejected the ultimatum. Aachen was bombed and shelled and still Colonel Wilck and his garrison refused to capitulate, so finally the Big Red One was sent in to wipe out the city in which thirty-three kaisers had been buried.

The only dogface in the Squad not wearing the Red One patch was Spencer: he zigzagged down the street between the Sergeant and Kaiser, covered by the Platoon's fusillade. Snipers fired from sewer holes, windows, doorways, and the rubble of shops and roofs. Approaching an intersection, Spencer was waved left by the Sergeant who sped to the right with Kaiser to hunt down Germans hiding in a four-story building.

Spencer ran into a small boy bouncing an invisible rubber ball and incoherently singing a German song.

The child was insane from the bombing and shelling.

Spencer carried him over the rubble into a half-demolished flag shop where a German, hiding behind a stack of swastika flags and banners, shot Spencer and

361

spat at the corpse, cursing him for fighting for Jew money.

Two mortar shells hit, blowing the child, Spencer, the German, and the flags out to the street where a passing Mark VI Tiger tank ran over them, its 88 firing.

Civilians huddled in shelled shops as the Sergeant passed them, leading the Squad into the department store to clash with the fleeing Germans on every floor. He reached the top floor—the mirror and chandelier department where reflections glittered in the debris of broken glass. When Griff spotted a German's three images in a triptych, he shattered the mirror. Fragments from the grenade explosion reached the flesh of the German who was hiding behind a counter. He appeared to be not too greatly surprised as he collapsed in death on the shards.

Checking the roof, the Squad picked off six snipers on other roofs. They fired rifles and tossed grenades into the windows of the building across the street, making it secure for the Platoon to race below to hit Germans supporting an army 75-mm howitzer.

Before descending, Zab was confronted by a German on the roof. The German waved a white cloth in surrender, and when Zab motioned him to advance, the German aimed his Luger and squeezed the trigger, but it jammed. Zab clubbed him with his rifle and tossed him off the roof.

Using the back stairway, the Sergeant reached an alley. He led the Squad into a sausage shop where three Germans were killed. Back in the street the Squad came under fire and took cover in a real estate office, only to be driven from it by 20-mm guns blasting from the paint shop on the corner. The Second and Third squads wiped out the guns, giving the Sergeant's Squad the chance to dash past bombed streetcars, shelled buses, and blazing vehicles into the cathedral, where Vinci killed the enemy at Charlemagne's marble chair, whirling to fire point-blank at a German trying to conceal himself behind the remains of Charlemagne's body in its shrine. The assault on the city swept the Squad from a fire fight in a dentist's office into a hardware store and into the switchboard room of the telephone office.

Joining up with the Platoon, the Squad came face-to-face with women and children being used as cover by Germans firing from behind them. The men in the Platoon were picked off.

"Oh my God!" cried the Lieutenant.

Not a dogface in his Platoon had the guts to shoot at the civilians. Only the Sergeant would do it. Before the eyes of the horrified GIs, using every desperate cover, he fired rapidly, carefully wounding two women, one child, and killing five Germans. Even as his ejected clip flew through the air to carom off Griff's helmet, the stunned Germans scattered. The Platoon opened fire, killing the rest of the German troops.

Around the corner, surrendering German soldiers were shot down by their own snipers who were concealed in a gas station. A bazooka from K Company hit the pumps, blowing up the snipers. The Platoon's battle on both sides of the street was halted by a German mortar. Seizing a rifle grenade launcher dropped by a dead Third Squad man, Griff bellied behind rubble, slammed the rifle butt on the ground to give the grenades a high angle of elevation, and lobbed in rockets to silence the mortar. From around the corner of the bank, a Mark III appeared and opened fire.

The Sergeant, spotting an unmanned enemy infantry howitzer near an alley, led his men to it. They lifted the end of the carriage and pushed the gun down the alley. Using the gun's shield for cover against the tank's machine gun, they gave a Fourth Squad bazooka the range to cripple the Mark III.

Assaulting the still-intact public library, the Squad found the building bristling with die-hard defenders. Heavy Weapons Platoon paved the way for the Sergeant and his men to enter the library where Zab passed many corpses, observing that the majority of Germans had had their hands blown off. As the Squad swept through rows of shelves to kill the enemy, Zab had a strange thought: the army should take footprints of dogfaces to identify the dead. Most corpses still had their feet. Their shoes protected them. If dog tag and hands were gone, the footprints would tell the Grave Registration Bureau the name of the dogface. Zab's idea of identification was forgotten as the fight took the Squad down to the cellar where thousands of compulsory reading books provided a battlefield.

Filled with the stench of the city, the Squad hunted for the enemy and spotted some of them vanishing into a movie theater. Going inside the theater, the Squad walked into darkness. Suddenly a blinding beam of light from the projection booth hit the white movie screen, illuminating the house. Every dogface hit the floor and squirmed under the seats as German bullets filled the air. The window in the booth next to the whirring projection machine was busted by a German who fired through it at the seats below.

The Sergeant dashed out of the theater and ran up the ancient narrow circular iron stairway outside the front of the building. He charged into the booth, killed the German, and saw a one-man army named Johnson wiping out the enemy between rows. When Johnson used up all his clips in front of the blinding white screen, he tossed his grenades. He astonished the rest of the Squad by the way he massacred fourteen Germans. The theater became a tomb. Johnson slowly walked up the middle aisle, looking neither to his left nor his right for living enemy, and left the building. The Sergeant and Squad found Johnson, covered with enemy blood, standing in the outside open lobby staring at big movie posters of coming attractions. One poster hypnotized him. It showed two actors in a fistfight as a horrified girl looked on. Johnson was a great movie fan.

"That's a movie I got to see," he muttered. "I love action movies."

Twenty minutes later, in what remained of a delicatessen store, the Captain's radioman gave him the walkie-talkie. "First Squad, First Platoon, sir."

The Captain, sure the news was that the Lieutenant was KIA, knew he could order the Sergeant to lead the Platoon. He would do exactly that, damn it. The Sergeant wasn't going to talk his way out of that responsibility this time. "Yes, Sergeant?"

364

"The Lieutenant said for me to get the okay from you, sir. He's in a fire fight in a clothing store."

The Captain was relieved. At least the Lieutenant was still alive. But he was puzzled. "Okay for what?"

"We've got a civilian here who talks English. He used to work in the garrison's ammo dump. It's underground. A Tiger's in front of it. We can't get close enough to bonfire a bogie, but we've got a Toonerville that could do the job."

"A *what?*"

The Sergeant grunted, remembering the Captain's age. "A trolley car, sir. If you get me TNT and HE, I'll load it up. The tracks go downhill smack into the Tiger at the intersection."

"Great! You don't need my okay to pull that off."

"I need men out of Company to draw fire on the street to my left."

"Is it 88 fire?"

"Yes, sir. Got to keep that 88 pointed away from my trolley."

"How many men?"

"At least ten."

"Shit!"

"It's a swap, Captain, ten wetnoses for an ammo dump and a Tiger. Okay?"

There was a long pause. The Captain would have given his right arm to be working behind a desk at army. "Okay, goddamn it!"

Fifteen minutes later the Sergeant and his men helped load up the outdated little trolley with ammunition brought by Company, then they waited until they got word that ten men were drawing fire on the street to their left. The Sergeant poked round the corner, saw the 88 pointed away from his steep-graded street, and he and his men shoved the loaded trolley around the corner. Griff had drawn a cartoon of Hitler on it.

The trolley picked up speed as it rolled down the tracks toward the intersection. As it crashed into the Tiger, the giant explosion rocked the city, sealing the fate of Aachen.

The ten wetnoses were scraped off the street into canvas bags by the Grave Registration Bureau.

365

In front of the cathedral, the Colonel of the Sixteenth Infantry faced defeated German soldiers and civilians, all ringed by dogface guns from windows and roofs; then the Colonel turned to what was left of the Third Battalion, some five hundred dogfaces. "Every word will be translated from English to German, and from German to English, and will be heard throughout the city of Aachen by loudspeakers. Colonel Wilck has a few words to say to his men."

Wilck spoke movingly in German, his words, translated by the interpreter, echoing through the city: *"Dear German soldiers, I am speaking to you at a painful moment. I was forced to surrender Aachen because we ran out of ammunition, food, and water. I saw that further fight was worthless. I was acting against orders; I was supposed to fight to the last man. At this time I have to remind you that you are German soldiers, and please, behave as such. I also wish you the best of health and a fast return to your Fatherland after the ceasing of hostilities. We need you to help rebuild Germany."*

The Sergeant thought about the end of World War I and the time he spent in the army of occupation in Germany.

The German officer turned to the Colonel. "May I give a *Sieg heil* and *Heil Hitler* to my men?"

"No."

The German officer turned to the Germans. *"I was refused to give a Sieg heil and Heil Hitler, but we can still do it in our minds."*

"Finished?" asked the Colonel.

"Yes."

"And now," said the Colonel, his voice booming in German over the city as he spoke in English, *"we're going to give every man of Hebrew faith the chance to hold Yom Kippur services for the Jewish High Holiday, the Day of Atonement, and those services are going to be held in this cathedral—now."*

He waited. His words made every German want to tear out the throats of the dogfaces.

"The Jewish chaplain," said the Colonel, "is busy giving the Twenty-sixth a hand at burial service. I need a man to replace him. Is there a Jew here who knows how to conduct the Yom Kippur services?"

A small, wiry dogface stepped forward. "Private Army Archerd, sir, K Company."

"Army? What the hell kind of name is that?"

"You try growing up in the Bronx with a handle like Armand, sir, and you'd change it in a hurry, too."

"You don't look Jewish to me."

"I may not look Jewish to you, Colonel, but two of my cousins looked Jewish enough to have been buried in Dachau."

"Okay." Then the Colonel's voice boomed thruout Aachen: *"Every man of Jewish faith in the Third Battalion who wants to take part in the Yom Kippur services follow Private Archerd into the cathedral."*

The defeated Germans contemptuously waited to see just exactly how many Jews were fighting men. Led by the Sergeant, five hundred dogfaces—the present strength of the Third Battalion—marched into the cathedral.

76

Brodie and Hank Wales of the *Chicago Tribune* filed their copy from Army Hq. "Ever see so many patches from fighting divisions?" asked Wales.

Brodie had never seen such a rainbow of patches all gathered at one place. The 4th Division, the 5th, 13th Airborne, 17th Airborne, 26th, 28th, 29th, 36th, 78th, 104th . . . The only patch missing was the Red One, and Brodie spotted it when the General's jeep pulled up.

"Where's the First Division now, General?" asked Brodie.

"Resting in Germany's most romantic hunting grounds."

In the Hürtgen Forest, every man in the Squad read his letters, except the Sergeant, who never got any mail. The biting cold, age, and exhaustion were taking their

367

toll on the Sergeant. He lay on his back, his woolen-clad head resting on his helmet-pillow. He was drowsy, and he knew he was falling into a deep, restful sleep. But he struggled to keep awake. The chills came with severe frequency.

Zab read his letter. "I'll be a son of a bitch! My mother sold my book to Hollywood for fifteen thousand dollars!"

The men looked at him, awed.

"What're you going to do with all that money?" the Sergeant asked, not because he gave a damn, but talking would help keep him awake.

"Blow a thousand on a Squad party."

"When?"

"At the next rest camp. I'll have my mother send a money order to Division."

Plitt spoke up. "Am *I* invited?"

"Who're *you?*"

"Plitt. I joined the Squad last night."

"Sure. Everybody's invited, only you better come up with the wildest thing to do with a girl if you want to come to *my* shindig."

"I'd like two girls at the same time."

"How about you, Sergeant?"

"I'll come up with something."

Kaiser spoke up. "I want a big plump girl to press her big plump ass against an ice-cold window and hold it there till it freezes."

"Who're *you?*"

"Hell, Zab, I fought with you in Aachen. I'm Kaiser. I got hit in France, near that tank."

"What're you going to do with that plump frozen ass of hers?"

"Thaw it out." Kaiser leaned against the tree and lifted his eyes, grinning at the murky sky. "It may take a while."

"You're invited."

Plitt tried again. "What if I ride horseback on a naked girl?"

"Forget it. You lack imagination and originality. Griff?"

"Working on it."

"Vinci?"

"I'll come up with something to top you all."

"Johnson?"

"I got an idea. I just want to work it out in detail."

"I knew a girl—" the Sergeant said quietly, "one of those intellectuals. We were in the sack and she turned iceberg on me—hated my uniform—hated all uniforms —said soldiers were lazy, dull, illiterate—she said she was afraid I'd poke her pussy with the end of my rifle barrel. She said a grenade in my hand, not her tit, would make me come. Man, she sure hated the military."

He smiled. The words made him feel warmer.

The men waited for him to continue.

"Tell you what, Zab, I want a girl wearing a uniform, and a pack, and a helmet, and a cartridge belt, and bandoliers with ammo, and then I'll give her the goddamnedest intellectual bang she ever had."

"You're in, Sergeant!"

Plitt was persistent. "I want to break a dozen real eggs on the belly of a beautiful girl. And I want to scramble 'em. Then I'll eat one egg at a time."

The men were impressed.

"You're in, Plitt," said Zab.

That night the Sergeant, blanket-wrapped like a mummy, smashed out the flame and cigar in Zab's hands.

A shell burst above them, hitting the tree. They all buried their heads in their helmets in the ground. Several bursts later the Sergeant slowly raised his head in the darkness and saw the forest explode with tree bursts and heard the splinters as they bounced off helmets. A man yelled that he was hit. The Platoon medic checked him and shouted that the men should take cover—not from the shells but from the tree splinters.

On the radio, the Sergeant told the Lieutenant that the tree bursts were making hundreds of thousands of splinters.

"I know," said the Platoon leader. "Company says Battalion's getting clobbered by 'em. If we don't knock out those 20 millimeters, we'll all wind up dead porcupines." He paused again. "They don't give a damn about firing at us; all they have to do is hit a tree."

369

The Squad ran to escape the rain of splinters, but there was no escape. Illuminated by flashes of bursting trees, the Sergeant tried to corral his men, but panic drove them fleeing in all directions. No tree was safe to hide behind or under.

The Sergeant fell on his face as splinters flew. He felt his muscles weaken, his blood vessels harden, his bones grow brittle. He shot up, enraged. They were the signs of becoming an old man, of senility. He was not old and goddamn far from being senile. He was simply helpless. He was trying to make logic out of an illogical way of fighting. Never before had anyone thought of using trees to kill and wound the enemy. He felt his career as a soldier was finished. He could not combat those tree bursts. It was time for him to retire and let someone else save the ass of his sacred Squad.

"Sergeant!" yelled Plitt. "I'm hit!"

"Medic!" shouted the Sergeant.

Plitt was hit and yelling for him and he didn't do a goddamn thing but lay on his belly.

"Sergeant!" cried Plitt. "For Christ's sake, help me!"

"Griff!" yelled the Sergeant. "Check Plitt!"

"You check him!"

"What?"

"I'm no medic!"

"Zab!"

"Fuck Plitt!"

"Vinci!"

"You bring him to me, I'll check him!"

"Johnson!"

"I'm deaf!"

"Kaiser!"

Kaiser didn't bother to answer.

"Sergeant!" Plitt yelled again.

"Where the hell are you?"

"Find me!"

The Sergeant heard more men shout for the medic. More men were hit by splinters. For a long sixty seconds he heard a flood of 20-mm shells bursting. Splinters bounced off his helmet, and several hit his right heel. He found himself bellying, then suddenly he was on his feet, running.

"Plitt!" he cried out.

"On your left!"

He found Plitt covered with splinters in his back and one six-inch splinter resting near his heart.

"Patch me up, Sergeant! Pull 'em out—patch me up! I got to break a dozen eggs on the belly of a girl and eat—"

Plitt was dead. The Sergeant saw it in the light of the tree bursts. Once again he was the Sergeant, moving swiftly, gathering up his Squad, urging them to move behind him, to keep up with his search to find the 20-mm guns.

He didn't chew out their asses for refusing to check Plitt. They were scared. They had the right to tell him to go to hell about Plitt. He forgot all about Plitt. Plitt was dead, and nobody cared about a dead man.

He tracked down four German 20-mm guns and wiped out their crews by simple, uncomplicated head-on charges with half the Squad firing, the other half grenading.

At dawn, Company I was still hunting for 20-mm guns that were still barraging them with the splinters. Spotting a movement through the trees on his left, the Sergeant squeezed off three rounds. Suddenly he heard, "Hold your goddamn fire," and he saw the Second Squad leader emerge through the mist, gaunt, wide-eyed, spittle running from his mouth.

"Did I get any of your men?" said the Sergeant.

"Goddamn it, didn't the Lieutenant tell you the Second Squad's on your left?" Behind him several grim members of his squad appeared.

"That was last night," said the Sergeant.

"It *was?*"

"You're supposed to be on our right rear this morning. Did I get any of your men?"

"Two dead," said a Second Squad man.

"Y'know what happened?" said the Second Squad leader. "A guy put a live grenade in my pocket and asked me for a light."

The Sergeant moved closer to get a better look. "A couple of you better take him back to battalion aid."

The Second Squad leader cracked the Sergeant across his face. "You sayin' I'm ready for Section Eight?"

A tree burst drove the men flat. All but the Second

371

Squad leader, who walked toward the sound of the 20-mm. firing. "I told you krauts to stop makin' all that racket, didn't I?" he yelled at the trees. "Now you stop it right now, y'hear? That is an order!"

"Griff," said the Sergeant, "put one in his leg. Bring him down."

Griff aimed carefully. He was calm. He knew he was the best shot in the Squad. All he had to do was hit him in the leg to save his life. Griff squeezed. The bullet tore through the right thigh of the Second Squad leader without hitting the bone. He dropped. Before the Sergeant could reach him, the tree bursts stopped him. When the bursts died, the Sergeant found the Second Squad leader pierced by hundreds of splinters. He checked him.

"I got bleeding ulcers," said the Second Squad leader. "You got to stop 'em from making all that noise. It's bad for sex." He smiled up at the Sergeant.

He coughed for a few seconds, then died.

An hour later the two squads found the 20 mm and silenced it. Two hours later, on their own again, the Squad was down to eight men: the Sergeant, his Four Horsemen, Kaiser, a radioman, and a tall redheaded youth. They wolfed down their C rations, then, following the Sergeant's order, they took off their shoes and, sitting in a circle, rubbed each other's frozen feet to keep the blood circulating. There was the crack of a Mauser. The tall redheaded youth fell forward on Zab's feet. As the men scattered for cover and jammed feet into shoes, the second crack of the Mauser lost the Squad its radioman.

The Sergeant deployed his men through the forest toward the single Mauser. Sniffling from a cold, he pierced the wispy fog curling round the trees and moved into the shadows like a mirage. Every man stalked the Mauser waiting to pick them off one by one in the Hürtgen.

Zab started thinking about the book he was going to write and asked himself, what can I say that is new? That hasn't been said better by others? In the last analysis, he convinced himself, he had the Squad party to look forward to. It made him feel good thinking about it. It would be lusty, exploding with wildness. He

372

looked around and found himself alone. He stopped, heard the sound of steps, and, without turning his head, advanced. The footsteps were Griff's.

Griff was tired of trying to overcome the rain of splinters in the Hürtgen. It was time he was killed. He glanced to his left and saw a blur in the fog that was Zab. He knew it was Zab without keeping his gaze fixed on the blur. The blur walked on his flank. Griff had a strange thought. If Zab stopped a bullet from that Mauser, would it mean the charm was broken and the other three Horsemen would end up fertilizing the forest?

Vinci felt safe. He knew he was completely invisible in the damp fog. The chilling air seeped through his body as he advanced slowly, maneuvering like a ducking fighter. He was fully aware that only a stray bullet could kill him, and, since a sniper never wasted a bullet that could become a stray, his only prayer was for the fog to remain thick all day.

Johnson hungered for even a five-minute break to ease the throbbing pain and to stretch out, using his rubber doughnut to protect his ass. He could easily stop walking and rest. He could not be seen by the others, and he would not be missed. But it was asking for additional trouble to lose contact with the men even though they couldn't see one another. Without questioning, he knew that the Sergeant would not stop for a rest until the Mauser was smoked out and eliminated.

Kaiser put his money on the million-dollar wound. He counted on the sniper hitting him in the knee or elbow.

The Sergeant heard the crack of the Mauser, followed immediately by the crack of a Garand. Then there was silence.

"Griff?" the Sergeant called out.

The overlapping echo of Griff-Griff-Griff-Griff rang through the forest.

Finally, Griff shouted, "Ho!"

"Zab?"

Again the echo, then Zab shouted, "Ho!"

"Johnson?"

A silence, then Johnson shouted, "Ho!"

"Kaiser?"

373

Silence followed the echo.

"*Kaiser?*" the Sergeant yelled louder.

The echo reverberated as the fog suddenly began to thin out and the wisps that remained were whipped away by a strong freezing wind.

"Sergeant—"

The voice was Kaiser's, and it was weak.

The Sergeant found Kaiser still alive. A dozen feet from him was the German with the Mauser. He was the first the Sergeant checked to make sure he wouldn't get his head blown off while examining Kaiser. The sniper was dead. The Sergeant dropped on his knees next to Kaiser, who was cold and unmoving. The blood had swiftly coagulated on his cheek and chin like a ball of powdered butter on a hot griddle.

"Think I'll get to thaw out that big plump ass?" said Kaiser.

The Sergeant felt the wound. "No."

"Did I kill the man that killed me?" asked Kaiser.

"Yes."

It was Kaiser's final word. His body trembled, he farted, and he died.

77

Schröder showed the strain of battle as he and a small group of Germans, supervised by a bayonet-spined major, planted concealed explosives in the German castle. The woman watching them was tall, attractive, and just what a German countess should look like.

"Make sure the fuses are very long," the major told Schröder. "When you have finished, rejoin your company." Without waiting for any "yes, sir," the major kissed the right hand of the countess. "You are very courageous."

He left. His men followed him out of the room, leaving Schröder alone with the countess. She vanished for a moment and reappeared with brandy and two glasses. She poured. They drank.

"How fast does the safety fuse burn?" she asked.

"Ten feet per minute."

"How much time will I have to get away from here?"

"Ten minutes." Schröder shrugged. "If you run."

It amused her that Schröder never addressed her as countess. "You look exhausted."

He said nothing, kept on preparing the fuses.

"My bed," she said, "is very comfortable."

An hour later, while the Sergeant and his Squad with new replacements were approaching the castle, Schröder and the countess were resting. The bed was huge. Schröder was fully clothed, his Schmeisser a foot away from his hand. She was naked, a blanket half covering her.

"You *were* exhausted," the countess said.

"*You* were not." Schröder smiled.

The countess sighed. "Hopeless—"

He grunted. "With a good night's rest I—"

"Not *you*. This war."

"There is nothing hopeless when a woman of your rank will blow up her castle for the reich."

"Nothing is gained. So an American general and his staff are blown up. We will still lose the war."

"Hitler will live for one thousand years."

"Oh, no! Not *that* quote!"

"They were your husband's famous last words on the battlefield. He died a hero."

"He died a shit."

It took a moment for Schröder to swallow her words. He looked at her.

"We were in this bed," she went on, "when he told me about his plot to kill Hitler. We were winning then and I was a Nazi, so I shot him. Hitler gave him a state funeral and personally eulogized him as a hero who died in battle." She stroked Schröder's hand. "You will come out of this war if I shoot you. Not a serious wound, of course. I will tell the Americans I shot you to save their general. They will take you prisoner. They will not confiscate my castle or my money. After the war I will give you $100,000." She smiled. "Alive and rich."

"When did you begin to hate Hitler?"

"From the first day he dined here, but like so many

375

others I *had* to go along with that fanatic to keep my castle and my money. It was unbearable to tolerate that impotent Austrian peasant."

Schröder stared at her. She smiled.

The Sergeant and his Squad were surprised to find the door unlocked. They cautiously padded into the castle when the bursts of Schröder's Schmeisser sent them to the floor. The Sergeant dashed up the stairway. Schröder was halfway out the bedroom when the Sergeant's bullet, hitting the door, drove him back. He heard men running up the stairs. He smashed the big window with a chair and dived under the bed just as the Sergeant charged in, firing. The Sergeant ran to the smashed window. Griff, Zab, Vinci, and Johnson came in like a wave.

"Who'd you fire at?" asked Griff.

The Sergeant at the window could see no trace of anyone below. "Wehrmacht."

"Jesus Christ!" said Zab.

The Sergeant turned. The men were staring at the corpse on the bed.

Under the bed, inches from their GI shoes, Schröder heard them.

"You're sure?" asked Zab.

"Yes," said the Sergeant, "I caught a flash of his uniform. He was Wehrmacht, all right. The bastard's probably moving through those woods with a busted leg. It's two stories to the ground."

"He must've put a dozen rounds in her," said Vinci.

"Yeah," said Zab. "Looks to me like a crime of passion."

"Maybe," said Vinci, "there's more than one kraut here."

"What're you waiting for?" said the Sergeant.

"You heard him," said Johnson. "Let's take a look around."

Schröder watched their shoes vanish, all but the Sergeant's. Schröder began to sweat.

The Sergeant didn't leave. The Sergeant stared at the bullet-riddled body, trying to figure out what could have driven the German soldier to such brutality. Then he left.

Schröder waited a good five minutes before he

crawled out from under the bed with his Schmeisser. He didn't waste a second even looking at the countess. He had a plan and he had to carry it out. Destroy these men. It was more important. He maneuvered from room to room, lighting the fuses, barely missing the dogfaces as they hunted for Germans. He was almost detected in the hallway, but he managed to slip out through the rear passageway and run from the castle into the woods. He felt good as he ran. Every fuse was burning.

When the men reported to the Sergeant that the castle was clean, they made themselves comfortable and tried the brandy and whiskey. The fuses burned as the Sergeant and his Squad rested.

"Maybe," said Zab, "he got word she was cheating on him and he came back and blew her apart."

"Maybe," said Vinci, "she worked here and he was her boyfriend and they had a beef."

"I bet," said Johnson, "the Colonel uses this place for his CP."

"You mean the General," said Zab. "He'll grab it for himself."

"Not *him*," said the Sergeant. "He never would set up a CP that would be such an easy target for bombers and shells."

The radioman's voice came up the stairs from the main entrance. "Sergeant! Hey, Sergeant!"

The Sergeant appeared at the head of the stairs. "What is it?"

"Just talked to the Lieutenant."

The Sergeant hurried down the stairs. "What kind of trouble's the Platoon in now?"

The radioman grinned. "Happy trouble, Sergeant! It's back to Belgium for us to a rest camp in Herve! The Ninth Division's relieving us. We're being pulled off the line for good!"

"Come on up and have a drink."

"Not me, Sergeant. My liver kicks like a jackass when I drink. The Lieutenant wants you guys at Platoon on the double."

Two minutes later the Sergeant and Squad were moving among the trees, and the explosions shook the earth. The men hit the dirt. Behind them the sky was black-

377

ened with smoke, now and then punctuated by red balls of fire erupting from the castle.

"What the hell was *that?*" said Griff.

They all turned and followed the Sergeant back through the brush to the clearing and they watched the castle in flames, each man knowing how close he had been to death.

"That bastard never jumped out the window," said the Sergeant. "He was lighting fuses while we were hunting for him. He was on the run while we were guzzling brandy." He turned and made his way back to Platoon, followed by the men. "I think they rigged the castle for our brass, but we fouled up the fuse lighter when we dropped in."

"Maybe," said Zab, "that woman on the bed tried to warn us. Maybe that's why she was killed." He left a trail of cigar smoke as he grunted. "Nah—I still think it was a crime of passion."

78

Madame Marbaise blamed Wagner for the war.

"Hitler," she told the four dogfaces as they sat in her huge, immaculate, warm kitchen, "was a cheap plagiarist, but Wagner was the king of thieves. He stole ideas of other men and wrote loud, bad opera. He was a Nazi before the word was created!"

Waiting for them to comment, she grunted impatiently. She was talking to Americans. What would they know about Wagner—in French yet? When she laughed, the walls trembled. She spiked her coffee with brandy, then spiked the coffee in the hands of the Sergeant, Griff, Vinci, and Johnson. The Squad was clean-shaven, rested, and amused. Only the Sergeant caught a word or two when she spoke French like a machine gun. The kitchen was the warmest room in her small hotel near the railroad tracks. It was the toss of a snowball from the German border. Because Madame Marbaise had stashed away a heavy supply of booze and wine, she was the only person in Herve, in fact in all Belgium, who had a surplus of steaks. The village butcher was a drunk.

She never showed despair. It made her popular with the neighbors and it used to irritate the Germans. She had no patience with defeatists. She hated gloom. To her, life was never empty, never dark, even during the Kaiser's War.

She knew the Nazis would lose this war. The day Belgium fell, she stood behind her long wet marble bar —a fifty-year-old human being, 250 pounds of woman who loved life—and announced that Hitler would lose. She called him a cockroach that would be forgotten in five years.

Now, fifty-four and still huge, her future was bright. She loved human beings, particularly the American soldiers. A lusty woman, she ran a lusty hotel. Sinners would use her rooms. When Herve was chosen as the GI rest camp, she was drunk for two days, the news made her that happy. She encouraged virgins—and she had found them among the young GIs—to lose their innocence in Belgium. She ran the only bar in Herve. GIs would spend the night in her hotel with the neighboring girls, or they would just hang around and play the piano and sing songs.

The street door opened and slammed shut.

"Sergeant?"

"In the kitchen, Zab."

Zab marched in wearing his GI overcoat, swept the long big table with a big canvas bag, and sent the cups shattering on the floor. As Madame Marbaise protested in French, Zab opened the bag and dumped the money on the table.

"Fifty thousand Belgian francs—beautiful! Count it. One thousand bucks for one night in your hotel for the party for my Squad. Count it, Madame Marbaise!"

She did, muttering to herself.

"You must get," said Zab, peeling off the coat, "*les femmes pour mon* party."

"Ah, *les femmes! les femmes!*" She scooped up money in both hands.

"Now listen to exactly what I want . . . *Je désire une femme avec une* plump—a *grand derrière—*" He

379

cracked her giant ass. "Against *la fenêtre. Comme ça!*"
He pressed his ass against the window. "Like this! But
bare-ass! *Compris?* Bare-ass! Show her, Griff."

Griff drew a woman's bare ass on one of the Belgian francs.

She stared at the drawing. *"Pourquoi?"*

"Never mind *why! Et la femme* stays *comme ça* until
her *derrière* gets *beaucoup froid*—frozen—*compris?"*

Her voice was low, husky, wary. *"Pourquoi?"*

"Come on, Sergeant," said Zab, "you know more
French than I do. Tell her the score."

"It's *your* party, *you* tell it."

"Êtes-vous fou?" asked madame.

"Huh?" said Zab.

"She wants to know if you're crazy," said the Sergeant.

"Hell, beautiful, *pas pour moi*—*pour mon ami*—for
my friend, *compris?* Not for me. He's dead—*mort*—"

"Fou! Fou! Fou!"

"She's right," said the Sergeant. "You're crazy wanting a frozen ass for a guy who's dead."

"One of you can pinch-hit for Kaiser."

"Why don't *you?"* asked Vinci.

"I'm a tit man." Zab was mad. "How about you,
Griff?"

"I've got my own request and you okayed it."

"Scratch Kaiser from the party," said the Sergeant.

"Like hell I will."

"You going through with every request in the
Squad?"

"Goddamn right I am!"

"Five dead men won't show up."

"I'll get replacements for 'em."

"You're going to have a rough time asking anybody
to thaw out a big frozen ass."

"I'll do it," said Johnson.

"You see!" cried Zab. "I'll dig up four guys to take
their places!" He turned to Madame Marbaise. "Now
I've got to tell you what the other requests are. I want
you to find a girl who'll let a guy break eggs on her
belly and, oh, hell, Sergeant, give me a hand. Tell her
for me!"

The Sergeant sighed. In his pitiful French he told

380

Madame Marbaise he fought in the Kaiser's War, fought in the Ardennes—in Belgium. As he spoke quietly, explaining why it meant so much to Zab to give the party for the dead men, she began to feel that he was unlike any soldier she had ever met. There was the beauty of life in his eyes. And in his eyes she also saw the death that was his life. It frightened her, yet she found herself moving closer to him as he told her the crazy but humorous requests made by the corpses and by the living.

Her boom of laughter drowned the kitchen. She loved the originality of the requests.

"Formidable!" she boomed.

An hour later Zab was still hunting for the four replacements, moving through the jammed bar where "Roll out the Barrel" was sung by GIs and the local girls while a corporal banged the piano. Zab looked for some GI who would be turned on by busting a dozen eggs on a girl's belly, then eating one egg at a time. He was turned down until finally he hooked a sad-faced pipe smoker who agreed, nervously. With three more wetnoses to convince, Zab tried the next morning's hot-chow line and was consistently turned down. All afternoon and into the night he made his pitch in the crowded bar where "Don't Sit under the Apple Tree" and "White Christmas," sung by GIs and girls at the piano, drowned out his words. Then he concentrated on new faces sitting alone in corners, and he managed to corral the replacements, promising each one fifty dollars as a bonus.

In the kitchen Madame Marbaise, after some difficulty, convinced the suspicious girls that they would be doing their duty as Belgians in honor of the United States of America.

And it would be a great sexual experience.

The Closed, Private Party sign nailed on the street door assured, in French and English, complete privacy and no disturbance. Zab bought the hotel for the night.

The Squad party began to warm up in the bar. The Sergeant was pleased with the girl in the GI uniform, with pack, helmet, and bulging bandoliers. The pipe smoker's ear was nibbled by the girl with the eggs. Griff and Vinci had seven girls between them. Johnson was holding onto the girl with the plump ass who looked forward to it being frozen, and thawed out. Zab, using Madame Marbaise's tape, was measuring the tits of six girls and finally admitted they were the biggest he had ever seen. There was no shortage of brandy. The guests began to get horny.

"Okay," Zab announced. "Every man's accounted for, every request's going to be carried out. We all got a hill to take tonight so let's take 'em!"

They drifted out, vanishing into rooms, leaving Madame Marbaise alone with a bottle of brandy. She sat at the piano and, in groping English, tried to play "White Christmas" as she sang the words.

A half hour later the platoon sergeant, forced to break into the hotel when he got no response to his pounding, found Madame Marbaise drunk at the piano. He investigated several rooms with increasing astonishment. Finally in the beam of his flashlight he found the Sergeant on a mattress on the floor. He was fucking a dogface! The platoon sergeant was speechless. The dogface was still wearing helmet and pack!

The Sergeant looked up. "Something bothering you?"

Shattered, the platoon sergeant forgot why he was sent to find the Sergeant. Finally he found his voice. "I'm a broad-minded guy, Sergeant. I think a guy should dip his wick any way he wants to, but the Lieutenant wants you and your Squad—"

"Beat it."

"The Germans busted through, Sergeant! They're in Belgium!"

79

The Squad huddled behind a snowbank. The clanking roar never let up as they listened to the passing German tanks. It sounded like a whole division of thickskins was on the move. The Sergeant was killing mad. He and his men had been promised white camouflage coverings. They never arrived. The men in their GI clothes stood out against the snow like waiting targets. Zab was sure the white camouflage had been shipped to the Pacific.

When the last tank passed, the Sergeant waited for panzer grenadiers or German infantry, but no thinskins appeared. There was a promise from Battalion that when the weather broke the sky would tremble with planes that would bomb the panzers. But the sky remained dark and muddy.

"Christ," said Zab, "if they keep on coming like that we'll have nothing but tanks all around us!"

"That's the idea of a breakthrough," said the Sergeant. "They've got a good chance of busting right through to the English Channel!"

"Where the hell are *our* tanks?" said Johnson.

"Caught with their goddamn tracks down."

"Is it true the panzers barged through two of our infantry divisions?"

"How the hell do you think they got this far? Of course, it's true."

"What the hell are we supposed to do? Just wait until they run over us by accident?"

"We've got a small piece of real estate to worry about, that's all. We're not supposed to let any of their grenadiers or their footsloggers get past us."

"What difference does it make if their tanks are on their way to Normandy?"

"Pins on maps aren't moved when tanks take ground, only when the man with the rifle takes it and holds it."

"What happened with those guys at Intelligence? I thought they're getting good pay to warn us about these damn breakthroughs?"

"Like they warned us about that German field division waiting for us at Omaha Beach?"

"What do we do now?"

"We stomp our feet to prevent frostbite."

They all rose and stomped except for one man.

Griff shook him, then leaned closer. "He's dead."

"I don't remember him getting shot," said Vinci.

The Sergeant examined the new corpse. "He wasn't hit. It's his heart."

A new man said, "You mean guys die in war without getting shot?"

"Sure," said the Sergeant.

When the Second Squad relieved his, the Sergeant and his men trudged through the snow back to Madame Marbaise in Herve. The Lieutenant had okayed the hotel for their rest area since the Platoon's action of defense covered an area only a few miles away. They found Madame Marbaise and some women making white coveralls for them out of bed sheets and tablecloths, and helmet coverings from white pillowcases. She counted them as they entered. The Squad was shy one man. She said nothing. For the next three days, wearing the white coverings, the Sergeant and Squad guarded their roadblock without incident. But on the fourth day nine dogfaces approached, waving, exchanging a few words with the Squad. Then the nine dogfaces opened fire, killing five new faces before they were shot down by the Sergeant and his survivors. The Sergeant ripped the GI clothes off, found a *Soldbuch* on one man and German dog tags on another. He had them stripped down to their shorts for other identification. He turned the service book, along with the dog tags, in to Platoon.

On the fifth day a lone GI approached the Sergeant's roadblock.

"How do I know you're a GI?" said the Sergeant.

The lone American growled, "You crazy? I'm a goddamn dogface. Here's my dog tags."

"Proves nothing."

"Hell, I know everybody's touchy with these goddamn krauts infiltrating our lines, but ask me anything you want."

"You mean about the Yankees and the Hollywood stars?"

"Sure."

"Take down your pants."

"What're you guys? Queer or something?"

"Drop your pants or you'll get a round in your mouth."

The soldier dropped his pants. The Sergeant stared at his shorts and shot him in the chest. Then he rifled the pockets and found German dog tags inside a pack of American cigarettes.

"He wore his shirt *inside* his shorts," the Sergeant

384

explained to his men. "We wear our shirts *outside* our shorts."

The sixth day gave them their second fire fight with German infantry dressed as GIs. When the Sergeant halted their advance and called out the sign, waiting for the countersign, the white-clad GI enemy opened fire. Several rifles in the Squad failed to function. When the fight was over, thanks to Griff's grenading, the Sergeant had the men piss on their rifles to thaw them out, and those men who couldn't piss had to eat snow until they *could* piss.

"I still can't get used to shooting at dogfaces," said Johnson. "Gives me a funny feeling, aiming at a GI helmet."

The Lieutenant was swamped with complaints. Other men in the Platoon wanted to shack up in Madame Marbaise's hotel; they resented the favoritism. But the Lieutenant told them to knock it off. As far as he was concerned, Madame Marbaise had made it plain that she preferred the Sergeant's Squad to any other.

Every night when the Sergeant and his men trudged in, half frozen, there waiting for them were brandy and steaks with eggs on them, Belgian style. They would sit at the long table in the kitchen and eat, their rifles herself over to one of the GIs' cartridge belts hanging on nails. Some of the men carried .45s on their belts. They would discuss what was happening at nearby Monschau, at Bastogne, at Malmédy. They talked about the 78th Lightning Division, the 101st Airborne.

Like a mother Madame Marbaise watched them, intrigued every time by the way they handled their knives and forks American style. One night, after a day of bad news for the Americans, with more Germans slipping through and raising havoc with supply dumps, Madame Marbaise noticed that one of the new men in the Sergeant's Squad was using his knife and fork European style.

She watched him closely, then slowly maneuvered herself over to one of the GIs' cartridge belts hanging from a nail on the wall, and removed the .45 from the holster. As the others devoured the steaks with eggs on them, she inched close to the man she suspected.

She leaned over and spoke to the new man: *"Hat ihre*

385

Mutter Ihnen nie ein Bifsteak mit einem Ei darauf gegeben?"

Caught off guard, the new man said, *"Nein, sie hat mir nie se otwas—"*

Holding the .45 in both hands, Madame Marbaise shot him. The Sergeant searched the body, found a map showing the location of a Sixteenth Infantry ammo dump between Herve and Monschau.

Before the Sergeant could calm Madame Marbaise, who had begun to sob, the Lieutenant came in and looked at the dead man.

"Infiltrator?"

The Sergeant nodded. He held out the map.

"Forty-seven men out of the Company," the Lieutenant said as he studied the map, "were taken PWs behind the barn near the Second Squad crossroads. We're all linking up with K Company to find them and get them back. Let's go."

"At night, sir?" asked Zab.

"They were taken at night."

The barn, as they expected, was deserted. Moving through deep snow, fighting the icy wind, I and K companies spread out, hoping to find the captured dogfaces. There were no tracks to follow because of the heavy snow that had been falling all night. Several times men fell out because of frostbite of toes and fingertips, and they were left behind for the medics to treat them. The men had huge gauntlet mittens, with one finger for the trigger finger, but still the cold seeped through.

By dawn more than twenty men were down with frostbite. One man in the Sergeant's Squad stared at his toes. They were reddish. Before the eyes of the Squad the toes turned pale white with a yellowish hue. The Sergeant felt the man's toes.

"Numb?"

The man nodded. "Don't feel a thing, Sergeant."

"No pain?"

"None."

"If they get you to a warm place and treat 'em, you'll be okay."

"What if they don't get me to a warm place?"

"Gangrene. Your toes'll have to be chopped off."

The hunt continued. In a vast field of blinding snow

a dogface shouted and waved his rifle. White-clad ghosts stumbled toward him from all directions. The snow came down hard by the time they reached him. The Sergeant and Squad counted the dogface corpses, each man with his hands tied behind his back and a bullet hole in the back of his head. The lashed hands were frozen, some of them already covered with snow.

By three in the afternoon all forty-seven bodies had been found.

By five o'clock the Sergeant's Squad moved to Monschau, where they learned that a German called von Rundstedt was in charge of the breakthrough, which looked like it had a chance to succeed. In many outfits, cooks and clerks were given rifles to fight the advancing enemy. The Sergeant was given the job to secure the Platoon's right flank, and to do that he had to probe through the snow with his men to find out if any Germans were holed up near a village that had been abandoned by the civilians.

By midnight the Squad made its way to about three miles from the village. Spread out, they made slow headway. As they gradually closed in, they heard singing. The Sergeant halted his Squad and listened. From somewhere in the village, a Christmas carol was being sung in German.

Zab was the first to spot the three Germans on guard. They were huddled in a circle, sitting Indian fashion, rubbing each other's bare toes to prevent frostbite. One of them hummed along with the singers. Using his trench knife, the Sergeant killed the hummer as Vinci and Johnson bayoneted the other two.

The Sergeant slowly led his men into the village. The voices coming from a darkened church grew louder. The Sergeant sent Griff and three men to check the house across from the church as well as the rear of the church. As Griff's group plowed through the snow, the Sergeant deployed his men to the church door. The singing was loud, filled with the fervor of the birth of Christ. The Sergeant silently jammed a shell into his flare gun, whispered to each man, then kicked the door in and fired.

The yellow star slammed into the altar and, as the singing Germans were illuminated in the blinding yellow light, the dogfaces opened fire. The Sergeant shot a second yellow flare point-blank at the devout Germans. Several of them burst into flames.

Christmas for the Squad was spent in white blankets and bed sheets as the men were subjected to artillery and mortar fire while they hunted down German patrols. Zab heard from a man in Battalion that the minute the sky opened up not a panzer would escape an American bomb. Zab grunted, not buying it. He was sure the sky would never open up. At night, Division artillery kept firing on enemy outposts and strongpoints. During the day they directed their big guns and mortars on reported enemy convoys, on reported tanks, on reported enemy personnel who had exposed themselves. For the first time Zab was certain that, despite all the support, the Four Horsemen would end up gangrenous corpses in the snow. Fatigue had made it almost impossible for him to move. His sluggish circulation slowed him down. He couldn't understand how the Sergeant kept up his pace. Zab kept pressing his fingers together, horrified when numbness made it impossible for him to feel them.

Johnson broke into Zab's thoughts. "Your fingers frozen?"

"Why?"

"I hear when gangrene gets 'em they just drop off."

"Can you feel your fingers?"

"What fingers?"

Griff said, "I can't feel mine."

"Neither can I," said Vinci.

"Let me feel 'em," said the Sergeant. He felt their fingers. "Hell, they're hard. Just superficial frostbite. When you get blisters, let me know."

"Merry Christmas, Sergeant," said Zab.

"Merry Christmas, Sergeant," said the others in a chorus of sarcasm and despair.

"Merry Christmas," said the Sergeant.

Then I Company was hit hard by the SS.

The Sergeant spotted several SS on the far right flank. Within minutes the fire fight was in full blast among the entire Company front. For a moment, it looked like the regimental front would collapse if the

388

SS broke through. The fight developed into hand-to-hand combat in the snow, white-clad ghosts bayoneting white-clad ghosts. The road became a no-man's-land: dogfaces on the left and the SS in the ditch on the right. The SS began to gain until three U.S. tanks, flanked by infantry, filled the ditch with HE and machine-gun fire.

The Colonel of the Sixteenth ordered a full-out attack and the Squad approached Faymonville, a German strongpoint. They watched Division artillery lob in shell after shell. Suddenly a hole opened up in the sky and an American artillery liaison plane flew over the Squad. The men forgot their frozen fingers and frozen toes and waited for Faymonville to be leveled, until German shells started pounding dogfaces.

"Goddamn it!" said the Sergeant. "That American plane's being flown by a German!"

Even as they all opened fire at the liaison plane, the hole in the sky closed and the plane could no longer be seen. The Squad watched the Sergeant who was watching Faymonville through his binocs. He lowered his glasses. His face was filled with defeat.

"They're using our stuff," he said quietly. "Our trucks, our tanks, and our uniforms."

"Shit," said Zab. "Yesterday the Twenty-sixth had a break in the sky, too. They were strafed and bombed by our planes and by British planes."

"I'd shoot the sons of bitches down," said Johnson, "even if they *are* our planes."

"You think our pilots *like* it?" growled the Sergeant. "It's tough for them to spot the Germans when we're so close to 'em. Those pilots are goddamn sick about it."

"Sick isn't like being dead," muttered Vinci.

That night Battalion moved a strong patrol to the rear of a German outpost north of Faymonville. The patrol, out of First Battalion, using knives, killed eleven. They captured six and sent them back to Battalion for interrogation. The following night Germans executed the same kind of knife patrol on a Second Battalion outpost. The seesaw raids on outposts continued, as did accidental shelling of dogfaces by American artillery.

When the Squad, on patrol, came under friendly artillery fire that killed two men and wounded one, Zab blew his top and ran, aping the others whose minds had snapped, shouting at the Germans to stop their shelling because they were making too much noise and interfering with his beauty sleep.

Zab finally collapsed.

When the Sergeant reached him, Zab was okay. He got to his feet. "How're we doing?"

"How're *you* doing?" said the Sergeant.

Zab grinned. "I'll take heat in Sicily or eat sand in Africa any day."

"You blew your stack, you know."

"Bullshit! How can I blow my stack if I'm going to write about guys blowing *their* stacks?"

Five mornings later, the Squad had no idea what day it was, or month, or year, and not a man gave a damn when the Third and First battalions attacked Faymonville. By nightfall they all knew the box score: the Third Battalion had lost seventy men.

A place called Schoppen was next, according to the Sergeant, who, like his men, really wasn't interested in the name of any village or town that had to be taken.

"We still in Belgium?" Griff asked him.

The Sergeant shrugged. "Company's going in with K abreast."

The attack was launched in the most vicious weather endured by the Sixteenth since the invasion of North Africa. In knee-deep snow, whipped by wind that slashed their faces, the Squad first had to fight the blizzard. Observation was out. Small-tracked weasels and Belgian horse-drawn sleds were used for observation. No other vehicle could move. When the Squad inched past Weapons Company, Griff couldn't understand how those dogfaces could carry their heavy machine guns and heavy mortars through the deep snow. He was grateful that he was a rifleman.

"This weather's the best thing that happened," said the Sergeant. "We can't see the Germans and they can't see us. But we got the edge because they don't know we're attacking."

He was right. Surprised, the Germans holed up in the houses, and cellars caved in after the second assault by the Company. The victorious dogfaces, in their wet clothes and wet socks, were hit by trench foot. Even when snowplows opened the road for chow jeeps, the victorious dogfaces looked like they were the ones who were whipped. Many men died from frostbite.

Town after town was attacked, and new faces kept replacing the dead faces in the Squad. The Four Horsemen were still in one piece.

"We'll make it all right," Zab said. "We'll come out of this northern corner of the Bulge in one piece."

"What the hell is the Bulge?" said Johnson.

"I don't know. I heard some guy call this fight the Bulge."

"I hear the Eighteenth and Twenty-sixth are hitting the Siegfried Line," said the Sergeant.

"Why?" asked Griff.

"What do you mean *why?*"

"The Siegfried Line means Germany, doesn't it?"

"Yes."

"Why don't a couple regiments out of another division hit the Siegfried Line? Why the First Division?"

"Why ask me? Ask the General."

"He's *your* friend! You ask him!"

"No," said a voice. "*You* ask me."

The Squad turned. The General was waiting, his eyes fixed on Griff. "Well?"

The Sergeant grinned. "Hello, General."

"Sergeant." The General kept his eyes on Griff. "I still think you made my goddamn schnozzle too big."

Griff was speechless.

"Well, Griff," said the General, "I'll tell you why the First Division's always getting its ass worked to the bone. Because we're experienced. Experience means better. And better means fewer dogfaces dying in combat. That's why the Big Red One's the army's workhorse. Hell, anybody can get into a fight, and a lot of men want to get into it. But to come away from a fight with the fewest casualties and leave behind a lot of enemy dead—that's what this is all about. You've been in scraps since North Africa. You're worth a dozen new dogfaces—hell, *two* dozen! And the sooner we get this goddamn war over with, the sooner we can go home."

80

The sun glinted off his snow glasses as the Captain of I Company was jeeped to the regimental command post. The respite—after smashing back into Germany under Allied air bombardment—had been short-lived. The briefing awaiting him meant going back to the line. He passed old men and women sitting on the stone wall ringing what was left of a statue of Martin Luther. Kids were playing in the rubble. He was deposited in front of a small church that two weeks ago had been battalion aid. From the jeep to the church he ran a gauntlet of children bombarding him for chocolate and chewing gum, but not for cigarettes, the way the kids in North Africa used to pester him.

In the church he slipped into an aisle seat in the third pew and exchanged a few words with other company COs. The Colonel was studying a big map of Bonn. S-3 told the Colonel that all the officers were present.

The Colonel faced them. "Our objective is Bonn, but there will be no artillery preparation or bombing."

The Captain of I Company didn't like it; neither did any of the other company COs.

"There'll be no fire fights," said the Colonel, "unless absolutely necessary. We're going to sneak into Bonn. Our new tanks have 76-mm muzzle brakes, giving the appearance of the high-velocity weapon used by all panzers. We're banking that in the dark, on the moonless night, those tanks'll be mistaken for panzers. You company commanders will be given specific streets in which your men will march behind a tank. The plan is quite simple: I want the Sixteenth to be in Bonn before the enemy can alert the SS panzer division on the other side of the Rhine."

The Captain of I Company warmed up to the idea. All he knew about Bonn was that Beethoven was born there and that it was on the Rhine. He would have something to celebrate if the infiltration worked according to the Colonel's plan.

The Colonel pointed at the map. "At first daylight we'll hit the post office where some three hundred Germans are sleeping. All you men have to do is to make sure that we secure our bank of the Rhine."

On the way back to his Company, the Captain thought about the plan. Bonn was a job for the Forty-fifth Infantry Division. He was sure there were still enough Indians left in the Thunderbird outfit who were better trained, by instinct, to sneak into Bonn the way their forefathers sneaked into the camp of an enemy tribe. It amused him that, long before Hitler, the shoulder patch of the Indian Division was a swastika. After Hitler, the patch became the thunderbird. They couldn't use the head of an Indian because that was worn by the Second Infantry Division.

The Captain faced I Company in the big shattered factory building. The men had been served sandwiches and coffee. The Company was at full strength, some 180 men. Now and then they glanced up at the detailed street map of Bonn that the Captain was studying.

"Since we crossed the Roer, the people in Bonn have put up a hell of a defensive barrier of automatic weapons, ack-ack guns, clip-fed 20-mm guns, 75s, and 88s. They sure as hell know we're coming, but they don't know when and where or how. We've got to pull this off without firing a shot unless we have to. We're going to walk into Bonn, spend the night there, and in the morning open the fireworks."

In the silence that followed, Johnson said, "You're kidding."

The Captain shook his head. "I know it *sounds* like I'm kidding, Johnson, but it's on the level! *Without firing a shot.*"

"But with all that stuff waiting for us, sir, those people aren't going to be asleep."

"We're going to walk right past 'em."

"We *are,* sir?"

They did. The night was moonless. The Company marched down the road in a column of twos, the Lieutenant leading the Platoon of four medium tanks and one assault gun. Bringing up the rear were 57-mm anti-

393

tank guns. An engineer team with minesweeping equipment rode the lead tank.

Enemy sentries at intersections were disarmed, and the astonished Germans found themselves marching with the American dogfaces. Turning into a street, the American tank that could pass in the dark for a panzer lumbered slowly, its clanks bouncing off the walls. Walking alongside the tank was the Sergeant. Behind him was his Squad. Behind the Squad, the Lieutenant had hung back to make sure every man in the Platoon was proceeding according to plan. As they passed a panzer lurking in an alley, some fifteen Germans watched the dogfaces file by with the tank.

Using their common sense, the captured German sentries, walking alongside the Sergeant, did not alert the Germans in the alley. An alert would erupt into a fire fight, and the sentries knew they would be the first to have their heads shot off their shoulders by the dogfaces. Now and then a German they passed would greet them warmly, and the captured sentries would respond just as warmly.

When a German squad fell in with the Platoon and several of the enemy moved ahead to walk with the Sergeant, one of them raised his voice above the clanking in the street so that he could be heard. He said something to the Sergeant.

"*Ja,*" said the Sergeant.

The German continued to talk.

Again the Sergeant said, "*Ja.*"

The German laughed. The Sergeant laughed.

The German squad peeled off at a narrow intersection. A hundred feet away in the blackness stood a Mark VI with 88, and beyond it, on the flank, were the 20-mm guns with crews. They watched the American tank lead the Platoon. Behind them was I Company.

The Squad walked through the human minefield in the streets of Bonn. The eardrum-shattering boiler-factory noise of the tank rumbling through narrow alleys bristling with enemy guns mesmerized each man. To the Four Horsemen, all this was a dream. It was hard to believe that they had actually penetrated the city of Bonn without a single shot being fired, without a single German discovering the Trojan horse in their midst.

The Sergeant sensed a trap. He was sure the people he passed were smiling in the darkness, waiting not only for the Company but for the Battalion to be sucked into a trap and bushwhacked by tanks.

"What panzer division is this?" a German shouted. The Sergeant saw that only a couple of feet separated them as the German fell in step. Taking advantage of the lead tank's noise, the Sergeant shouted, making sure the words *Hermann Göring* were heard. He had picked the wrong outfit. The big German seized his arm, stopping him, and in the darkness his words challenged the Sergeant. What was the Hermann Göring doing in Bonn?

The Sergeant drove his trench knife into the German and swung him up onto the moving tank, dumping him behind the sandbags. More Germans fell in and marched side by side with I Company down Koln Strasse. When Platoon reached Rosental Strasse, the dogfaces, according to plan, turned left, and the Germans continued down Koln Strasse.

The Lieutenant led his Platoon down Bonngasse, halted in the alley-street, and told the men to get some sleep, to get off the street. The men tried doors, noiselessly forcing stubborn ones open, and vanished. Zab and Johnson tried a door, pushed in until it gave, and went in. Under the number *20* was a plaque: *BEE-THOVENHAUS,* stating that in this museum Ludwig van Beethoven was born.

In the Beethovenhaus the two dogfaces probed through the blackness, felt a rope slung in front of them, crawled under it, and went to sleep. The dawn's weak light through the alley window made Zab open his eyes. He saw the velvet rope above him and he turned his head. He and Johnson had slept next to a piano. Zab saw the light focus on a framed manuscript on the wall. The title *Bonaparte* was crossed out by a thick gray stroke and in its place was the word *Eroica*. At the bottom was Luigi van Beethoven's signature. Zab remembered. Beethoven, whom he idolized, had a sense of humor, and when he wrote that music in Italy he had called himself Luigi instead of Ludwig. Then Zab saw more pieces of music framed on the wall, and there were busts of Beethoven and framed letters and paintings. Electrified, he realized where he was. He shook Johnson to share his discovery and passion for Beethoven. Johnson seized his rifle.

"Beethoven was here!" said Zab.

"What outfit?"

"Aw, come off it, Johnson! You must've heard of Beethoven!"

"I don't know, Zab. So many guys come and go in the Squad, it's hard to keep track of names."

By the time more light began to fill the streets, the few civilians that appeared were unaware that the column working its way through Bonn was not a friendly column. When the post office was taken, most of the Germans threw up their hands rather than be killed. The Platoon worked its way down to the river's edge. The bridge across the Rhine was still intact.

Camouflaged German SP guns opened fire, driving the Platoon into the buildings. Moving to the Rosental-Romer intersection, two American tanks returned the fire. Enemy infantry in support of the SP guns advanced. The Platoon, from windows and doorways, wiped out the assault. German trucks and cars attempted to reach the bridge, but they were knocked out. All German traffic coming from the north came to a halt when news spread that Americans were in Bonn. The Sergeant's Squad was given the job to houseclean all buildings on Rosental Strasse, then they were ordered to hit the cemetery where German machine guns were hidden among the gravestones. M Company's mortars moved into position and shelled the gravestones. A twenty-minute lull followed. The Sergeant was radioed to join the Company assault on the Agricultural Institute of the University of Bonn. K Company had been driven back, caught in heavy cross fire, but they had hurt the enemy somewhat. As the Germans licked their wounds, I Company picked up the attack, but the Platoon was driven back by firepower coming from the classrooms. Both sides of the big brown building kept the dogfaces from advancing.

Johnson shot the driver of an approaching enemy truck. The truck slammed into a sandbag barricade. Swinging round the truck, a German light armored car fired two machine guns at the Platoon on the flank.

Griff zigzagged through the smoke to the truck, threw the dead driver out, climbed behind the wheel, and rammed the German light armored car with the German truck. The crew of three surrendered to Vinci, who appeared from behind the barricade. The Sergeant worked his way to the armored car, followed by Zab as Johnson gave them cover. Griff hopped out.

"Griff, drive!" said the Sergeant.

Griff, the Sergeant, and Zab got in. With Griff at the wheel, the light armored car charged the institute, smashed through the two giant doors, and moved down the long wide corridor. The Sergeant was firing one German machine gun into classrooms on the left, and Zab was firing the other German machine gun into classrooms on the right. Reaching the end of the corridor, Griff put the armored car in reverse and again the machine guns riddled Germans in the classrooms as it rode by.

When the Squad rejoined the Company they had 150 POWs.

Preparing to cross the bridge that night, the dogfaces watched it blown by Germans. By morning, the Squad, along with other squads, began to mop up the city. They met last-ditch resistance near the Beethoven statue. Zab was the only man to enjoy the names of the streets: Haydnstrasse, Brahmsstrasse, Bachstrasse. For the hell of it, to rankle four Germans they captured in a stationery store, Zab printed *Chopinstrasse* on the back of a piece of wood and lashed it on the street post, covering Humboldtstrasse with it. He grinned, knowing how the Germans hated anything Polish.

The night capture of Bonn a success, Regiment now concentrated on the only other bridge across the Rhine. It was at Remagen, a short march for I Company.

81

The Squad was far beyond the great Ludendorff Bridge when the bridge collapsed at Remagen. Rumors were exchanged when the men heard the news: American planes knocked it out. The Germans blew it. It simply caved in and died.

The Sergeant didn't give a damn. He and the Four Horsemen had made it all in one piece up to now. The air was filled with rumors of surrender. He paid no attention to the rumors. He had been through this before, in the other war, where every hour word came that the Kaiser had thrown in the towel and scratched his name on that magic piece of paper—the Armistice agreement.

It began to rain as they rested.

The men paid no attention to the rain. They covered their faces with their helmets, but the rain kept hammering the Big Red One insignia on their steel pots. The Sergeant moved away from the small brook that was now spilling over and stretched out on the small plank bridge spanning the brook. Motionless, the men looked like corpses battered by rain.

Zab was thinking about Marlene Dietrich and Rötgen. It had rained then, too, when the Company was pulled out of the line to see a show in the village they had taken five days before. Mud and rain had slowed down the trucks that were pulling up in front of the Stadtstheatre in Rötgen, and within minutes the theater was jammed with soaked dogfaces anxious to see, in person, the one woman who represented all women to them. She came out on the stage in a flaming red gown, but she didn't show even an inch of her famous long legs. She told them she was born a kraut and she knew how many krauts the Red One killed and she wanted the men to look at her as an American, not a kraut. She told them she would feel better if she could hear their pieces hit the floor, and Zab knew right then that some man had coached her to say pieces instead of rifles. The pieces made a clatter as they were placed on the floor, but she said she wanted to hear more, and it amused Zab the way she waited until the last M-1 finally hit the floor. She asked for a dogface to volunteer to go up on the stage and Zab and Johnson pushed a new face, Fitz, on the stage and Dietrich asked the nervous red-faced Fitz his name and from that moment on she called him Fitz. "We're going to play a game, Fitz." She helped guide him to a small table, told him to

398

sit on it, then she moved in between his legs and the dogfaces watched in silence. "This is a mind-reading game, Fitz. What is on your mind?" The dogfaces broke up and cheered. She didn't do much after that, just was a kind of mistress of ceremonies, introducing the different USO acts. When it was over Zab asked the driver of his truck how long it would take for the truck to turn around in the mud. The driver told him a good twenty minutes. Zab went backstage but was stopped by a special service officer who said it was off limits. Zab insisted he wanted to speak to Dietrich. She heard them arguing and opened the door. "It'll only take a minute, Miss Dietrich. I've got to speak to you." She invited him into the bare, cold, damp, dirty dressing room, the only light a weak naked bulb dangling from the ceiling. A picture of Hitler was still on the wall. "I'd like you to take a message for me back home, Miss Dietrich." She was kind but firm. Impossible. She met so many soldiers who wanted her to phone their families and girl friends. She just couldn't promise him anything because it would be quite impossible. He knew he stank of filth and urine; he had a beard and looked like hell. His eyes were red. But so were hers. He felt sorry for her. She looked so goddamn cold. "My message is easy, Miss Dietrich. One word. *Cigars.* Just say cigars to Charlie Feldman in Hollywood." She stared at Zab for a long, long moment. "The agent?" she said. "Yes, Miss Dietrich." She gazed at him for some time, speechless, until she said, "How do you happen to know Charlie Feldman?" "He's my agent, too, Miss Dietrich. He sold my book to Hollywood." She gave Zab a drink of brandy, then gave him the bottle to keep, and she was laughing all the time. She said she'd be glad to deliver the one-word message to Charlie Feldman. Zab told her it was unnecessary for her to know or try to remember his name. "Just say cigars, Miss Dietrich." Before he left with the bottle, she asked him if she could do anything else for him and he said yes, he would like her to write a few words on paper for certain members of his Squad, four men to be exact. They tore out small pieces of paper from an old program and he told her what to write and she wrote down the exact words and she signed the four pieces of paper, laughing as she did. He said "Thank you, Miss Dietrich" and left, climbing onto his truck, just making the turn in the mire. When he told the Squad he was with Marlene Dietrich and it was she who gave him the brandy, Zab knew the men wouldn't believe him. He checked the four pieces of paper and gave them out to the Sergeant, Griff, Vinci, and Johnson. When they read them there in the rain they laughed. Her few words to Johnson referred to his aching ass and his rubber doughnut. The Sergeant's read "To the Sergeant," but the rest of the words were being washed away by the rain. He, Griff, Vinci, and Johnson held their helmets over their scraps of paper and enjoyed what Marlene Dietrich had written. They were all very brief personal notes.

Zab smiled as he thought about it, his helmet pounded by the rain. He had never met such a woman in his life. Then he laughed, remembering Johnson's face when he read in the truck, "You'll find another frozen rump to thaw out."

The Lieutenant approached, followed by the rest of his Platoon. "Let's go," he said, and as he watched the Sergeant and his Squad get to their feet, he had no words to describe the stamina in every man in the Platoon.

The forced five-mile march was one long frustration, but not a single man dropped out. He watched the tall figure of the Sergeant, who had taken point the last mile. It astonished him the way the soldier from World War I set such an easy pace for the men despite the rain. The Sergeant was more than a soldier with rare courage and fortitude. He was the symbol of the Red One, and every man marching behind him knew this. They would plow through anything as long as he was up there moving one foot in front of the other. They would fight, outnumbered, as long as he was up there doing what he did better than any man in the army.

It intrigued the Lieutenant that there was always a wall between himself and the Sergeant. Brodie, the newspaperman, had asked questions the Lieutenant couldn't answer about the Sergeant, the oldest rifleman in Division and the best scout in the army. To the questions, all about the personal background of the Sergeant, the Lieutenant had no answers. Never questioned was the Sergeant's policy to always kill the enemy, taking prisoners only when necessary to gather information.

The Lieutenant could not explain what kept the Sergeant winning his gamble to stay alive, a gamble that had begun in the other war.

The Sergeant wore a bulletproof halo. He was a man who thrived on crises—without mourning for dead dogfaces, without talking about the enemy he had killed, without even a hint of any kind of emotion. Still, there was something almost colorful about the way the Sergeant cast his net for Germans and always came up with a fat catch. He never talked about the fish that got away.

Watching him plod ahead, the Lieutenant believed that the Sergeant was in a race he was running against himself.

Since the Sergeant had no fear of death, did he have the lust for death? The enemy's death, of course, not his own. To the Lieutenant, a soldier who never showed shock or pity or pressure in combat was a soldier that belonged in Section Eight.

But the Sergeant was far from losing his sanity. He was always in complete control in every action. He had survived without ever thanking God. But he also never thundered against God. He was a man of violence but only when violence was the order of the day.

No, the Lieutenant grunted, he sure doesn't belong in Section Eight.

As he moved down the mountain pass, Zab was preoccupied with the book he was going to write. The sky was clear, the air brisk. He wasted no time wondering why the Squad was told to check what was in the rubble of the German castle. If Battalion suspected it to be an OP, a few well-placed shells would remedy that. It was their job. He thought about those men who turned down the job, who refused to be drafted, and who, as conscientious objectors, did six months in the federal pen. He admired them for their stand. In fact, he not only understood them, he agreed with them. When he wrote his big war novel he would write about the C.O.s

401

with respect because they were right. If a man didn't believe in war, he certainly should not have an M-1 thrust into his hands. He, personally, was one dogface who loathed war, but he had to admit that he was proving something to himself in combat, even though his reason for being a dogface was to get material for his book.

Before reaching the ancient fortress with its high tower, he observed the way Griff hung back in the approach. He had never seen Griff so nervous. When they had investigated the ruins, again he had noticed Griff hanging back. He figured Griff was beat, that's all. Just beat. And why not?

Griff was more than beat or edgy. He was unable to avoid the chilling realization that his jangled nerves had run their course and that he was on the verge of once again losing his reason and ending up in Section Eight. When he was examined in North Africa, he was just a wetnose. He no longer was one now. He had killed many people; in fact, more than the average infantryman in the war. He got over the hump of killing, all right, but not of squeezing the trigger when looking into the enemy's face in the target. His frustration, born on the beach at Arzew so long ago, became a dangerous desperation. He had heard and, when lucky enough to get copies of *Time* and *Newsweek,* he had read enough about the horrors that were going on in the extermination camps. He knew about the ovens and the crematoria and the mass slaying of men, women, children. Yet he still hadn't reached the point of such anger and disgust that he could shoot a man he could see close up and then try to forget his face.

The Sergeant moved around the bend. Blocking his advance were dozens of giant pictures of Hitler. Holding the posters were some 250 old men and old women, most of them armed with shovels, picks, sticks, brooms, and mops. Several gripped butcher knives. They all wore armbands reading *Volkssturm.* When the Squad rounded the bend the men saw the Sergeant attempt to move past the old people, but not one of them budged. Instead, they lifted their "weapons" to show they planned to fight to the last man and woman.

402

The Squad felt sick. The old ones were grim, their faces lined with hatred but not defeat. The only dogface not sick was the Sergeant. He showed no sign of being nervous.

Without turning his head, the Sergeant said, "What's the name of that man who speaks German? Switsomething."

A new face moved forward, shifting his rifle nervously.

"Switolski."

"How good's your German?"

"Polish, with a New Jersey accent. My aunt's German. I picked up a few words."

"All you'll have to say are a few words." The Sergeant looked over the side of the long drop and in the distance he could see their village below. It looked like a picture postcard. Peaceful, old, surrounded by mountains. "Tell 'em to let us pass. We don't want to hurt 'em. Make sure you use the right words. We don't want to hurt 'em."

Switolski relayed the words in German. An old man wearing a heavy green shirt and holding a shovel proved to be the spokesman as he barked out words loud and very clearly.

Even as the man was speaking, the Sergeant muttered over his shoulder, "Hitler sure scraped the bottom of the barrel for his last-ditch stand." Green Shirt finished his speech.

Switolski translated. "He says he and his friends are the *Volkssturm*. It means the Peoples' Army. He says they're ready to kill for Hitler. He says they got orders from Hitler not to let one American get through these mountains. He says every mountain pass is defended by the *Volkssturm*."

The Sergeant sized up Green Shirt, concentrating only on him. Then he looked at the others. Nothing but guts and hatred in their aged faces. The Sergeant glanced over his shoulder at the Squad, and his men knew that all he had to do was give the command to fire and they would fire. They prayed he would not give that command.

"Tell them I'm going to count to three." The Sergeant pointed at Green Shirt. "And if they don't move out of our way Herr Green Shirt'll get the first bullet."

Switolski relayed the words, slowly and loudly. There was no reaction from the old people. Only Green Shirt moved just close enough to spit at the Sergeant.

"Heil Hitler!" shouted Green Shirt.

The old men and old women waved their big blow-ups of Hitler, chanting, *"Heil! Heil! Heil! Heil! Heil! Heil! Heil!"*

Their chant froze the Squad, the dogfaces showing a hell of a lot more fear than the old civilians.

"Griff," the Sergeant called out.

Griff swallowed the lump, stepped forward.

"Show Green Shirt how big your muzzle is."

Why *me?* thought Griff, but he moved in front of the Sergeant and aimed his rifle between the cold blue eyes of Green Shirt. What Griff dreaded in North Africa, Sicily, France, and Belgium was about to happen in the Harz Mountains in Germany, and he knew that now, on this mountain pass in the middle of nowhere, he would finally have to shoot a human being whose eyes he could see—an old man, a civilian, without a goddamn weapon in his hands, armed with nothing but a beat-up shovel. Griff was scared, sick, and ready to vomit. He was going to be ordered to commit cold-blooded murder. He knew it.

"Switolski," said the Sergeant.

"Yeah?"

"Tell the people that rifle is aimed between Green Shirt's eyes."

Switolski told the people. Still they didn't budge.

"One!" shouted the Sergeant.

"Eins!" shouted Switolski.

"Two!"

Switolski died inside. *"Zwei!"*

"Three!"

Switolski was speechless.

"Three, goddamn it!"

"Drei!"

The German wall of aged defiance didn't give an inch.

"Heil Hitler!" shouted Green Shirt.

The old ones chanted again. *"Heil! Heil! Heil! Heil!—"*

"Shoot him, Griff!" yelled the Sergeant above the chant. *"Shoot him!"*

Bathed in sweat, Griff began to squeeze the trigger. Shouting *"Heil Hitler!"* Green Shirt kept his blue eyes on Griff's trigger finger without fear. Griff felt halfway through the squeeze, or was it two-thirds? In the flash of a part of a second he would send a .30-caliber bullet between those angry blue eyes, right through the old man's head. Green Shirt's eyes slowly raised to meet Griff's, and Griff knew it was a matter of which one would break first.

Griff's finger stopped squeezing. He slowly lowered the rifle. The old ones kept chanting *"Heil!"* Green Shirt laughed with contempt.

Suddenly the Sergeant squeezed off three fast rounds, the bullets grazing the top of Green Shirt's head and puncturing the giant blowup of Hitler. Then the Sergeant aimed at Green Shirt. Green Shirt dropped his shovel and fell on his knees.

"Nein! Nein! Nein! Nicht schiessen! Bitte! Bitte! Bitte! Nicht schiessen!" He broke into tears of fear.

His panic broke the dam of resistance. The old men and old women, unable to maintain their wave of defiance, cracked. They lowered their "weapons," then dropped them and slowly made a path for the Squad. The Sergeant led his men through the silent people, their helmets brushing past the big blowups of Hitler. Griff looked at the faces of the old men and women. Most of them were still filled with hatred, but some were now filled with tears.

82

Zab plucked one of the remaining bottles out of the case of schnapps. He was drunk, but still thirsty. The Sergeant and the Squad had bedded down in what was left of the village. The full moon lighted up the jagged walls around them. The broken stones and chunks of wood didn't bother them. The vacation from marching and fighting was far more important than physical misery and the smells that came with it.

Many of the men had their own bottles. When they talked, they were incoherent. They faced another typically wretched night, only this time, thanks to Switolski, they had inherited all those beautiful bottles.

"You're a good man, Swit," said Zab.

Switolski grinned, his wet chin glistening in the moonlight. "Hell, the shop was burning, and I didn't want all that schnapps to go to waste."

"*I* got a confession," said Griff suddenly. "I never killed anybody if I could see his eyes. Never."

"Never?" said Vinci.

"Never. Know why? 'Cause I ain't really mad enough to knock him off that way. Hell—I'll kill a thousand of 'em if I don't have to see their faces. How about you, Sergeant, you got a confession to make?"

The Sergeant finished his bottle, opened a new one, and took a heavy swig. "I murdered a soldier."

"You told me we kill in our business," Griff went on, leaning closer to the nodding Sergeant. "You told me we don't murder."

"Ah," said Zab, "what's the goddamn difference? It's the same goddamn thing."

"*Like hell it is!*" boomed the Sergeant.

"A man's dead, goddamn it," said Zab. "What's the big deal how you say you knocked him off? You murdered him or you killed him. What's the big deal? It all depends on one goddamn thing—is he alive or dead? If he's dead, he's dead no matter what the hell kind of word you use."

"Bullshit," said the Sergeant. He took another swig. "All depends on a watch—a piece of paper—and a pen—" He drank slowly, draining almost half the bottle. "And when that second hand of the watch calls the shot and the Kaiser scratches his name on that piece of paper with the pen, you got to call it quits. That scratch of the pen makes the difference—kill all the Huns you can before the scratch of that pen but not after—not after—never after—" He took another swig. "He came at me four hours after the scratch of that pen."

"Who came at you?" said Griff.

406

"He came at me four hours after that goddamn shell-shocked horse stomped my rifle and tried to kill me. He came at me with that war-is-over bullshit, and I murdered him." He took another swig. "Remember that goddamn Christ on the Cross in France, where we delivered that goddamn baby in the Tiger tank? *That's* where I murdered that Hun four hours after the scratch of that pen."

The Sergeant promptly fell asleep in a crooked position. In the silence, now slightly sobered, the men listened to his irregular, heavy, strained breathing. Griff propped the Sergeant's head on his helmet as Zab, Vinci, and Johnson gently straightened out his body and legs. They stared at him. They had no idea of exactly what he was talking about, but they sensed the pain in him when he had made his confession.

"Killing or murdering a German," said Zab, "still means the same thing."

The men agreed and went on with their drinking and toasting. But not Griff. He sat like a statue, staring at the Sergeant asleep in the rubble. Everything seemed unreal except the words about Jesus and the Hun and the four hours. Those faltering words began to make sense, and Griff suddenly understood the cross the Sergeant had been carrying since the Kaiser War. The admiration he felt for the old soldier overwhelmed him. He understood now the difference between killing and murdering.

"It's not the same—murdering and killing. I know what he means now."

"Ah, you're too goddamn drunk to know what anything means," Zab said.

"To a professional, it's not the same," said Griff. "That's what makes him a professional. He only kills enemy soldiers. Murder is when you shoot a civilian."

"You're drunk."

"You're right." Griff smiled. "And I'm going to get drunker."

The Sergeant watched the rest of the Platoon veer right as he led his Squad left toward the castle that looked like it was hatched out of the side of the mountain. Battalion was on its way and the pockets had to be cleaned out. For three days snipers had held up the advance. Passing rapids that roared under the castle, the Sergeant studied the mammoth cave above the weird structure. The men were impressed by the grandeur of the cave castle.

"They got a soup at Battalion," said Switolski, "that all you got to do is turn a key and it gets hot."

"What kind of soup?" asked Vinci, impressed.

Switolski was shot just as he said, "Vegetable."

They hit the brush for cover. Chancing the run when he saw Switolski still moving, the Sergeant dived from his concealment to check the wound as his men poured it on, firing at the cave above the castle and at the more than twenty narrow windows facing them. The Sergeant dragged Switolski into cover.

"Pour it on!" he yelled. Switolski was dead.

They did, giving him rapid covering fire as he zigzagged toward the castle. A bullet glanced off his helmet. He didn't know whether it came from the sniper or from his own men. He dived behind a brick wall at the end of his run and opened fire, covering his men as they took turns zigzagging to reach him. Leapfrogging the advance, the Sergeant waved for them to spread their fire. A dog, frightened out of the brush by the noise, ran alongside the Sergeant, snapping at his shoes. A sniper bullet killed the dog.

The Sergeant and his men reached the entrance. One of the two massive wooden doors was ajar. The Sergeant made a gesture and swung the door wide open as his men fired blindly into the dark stone maw.

Their luck was bad. They had no idea of how many snipers there were in the castle. As they moved cautiously toward a bleak light coming from above, they heard the crack of a Mauser, the bolt action, and another crack. The bullets caromed off the stone wall. Moving past the gray-white stone that was streaked with moisture, the Sergeant found the source of light—a hole on top of the castle, on top of the cave, a hole that showed the sky right through the top of the mountain.

The sniper, or snipers, had the edge. The Sergeant shouldn't have maneuvered all his men into the cold trap. The sniper, and for the moment the Sergeant took it for granted that there was only one, knew this place.

He could, with patience, pick off one man after another. There were stone steps leading up to the left and a narrow iron circular stairway up to the right. He heard the sniper's running footsteps. Then there was silence. It was hard to figure out where the footsteps had come from. The echo was loud and deceiving.

Again the footsteps were heard, but this time the Sergeant was sure they came from the circular stairway. He crouched behind a stone parapet and slowly raised his head. A bullet missed his helmet brim by an inch. He ducked. He wondered why riflemen weren't issued small periscopes.

Waving half his men to climb left, he gestured for Griff, Zab, Vinci, and Johnson to blast the circular stairway with bullets. They each fired three clips. Then the Sergeant ran up the iron steps. The pace made him dizzy. He stopped, fired up at nothing but stone walls, then waved. Griff and Zab bolted up past him. They halted and fired, then Vinci and Johnson ran up past them. By the time Vinci and Johnson had each used a clip, the Sergeant reached the top of the stairway. The walls of the castle turned out to actually be part of the mountain stone.

His back began to bother him again. He knew he had wrenched it coming up like a mountain goat on that circular stairway. He moved toward a wide opening and in the shadows studied the grotto.

The sniper fired again, the bullet reverberating beyond the grotto. Griff, Vinci, and Johnson joined him. They checked the grotto and found a wide slab of stone suspended over a drop into a black cavern. The rapids roared below. As they crossed the slab, each one maneuvering the other, they discovered a wooden door about four feet in height and they swung it open. A hole stared back at them. The Sergeant leaned over, saw nothing but blackness, and fired into the hole. They heard his bullets zinging off stone walls deep below them.

From another part of the castle they could hear the rest of the Squad firing their Garands. They ran back across the stone slab. Forty feet above them a dogface shouted, "We think we got him cornered!"

"Finish him off!" yelled the Sergeant.

Another dogface appeared above them. They were both crouching on a stone promontory. Above them was the hole in the sky.

"False alarm!" yelled the second dogface.

The Sergeant deployed the Four Horsemen, each man finding different stone stairs going up. Zab was sure the castle went back to at least the thirteenth century. It intrigued him that part of it was the mountain wall itself. He passed several deep drops as he climbed. Vinci investigated a bare stone room. Johnson found another slab bridge and crossed it as he spotted Griff below, crawling along the edge of the drop that went down the middle of the castle.

Griff stopped when he heard the sniper's bolt action. Slowly he inched forward along the stone slab, surprised how unafraid he was. He didn't even stop when he heard the sniper fire. Griff knew he was not the target. He heard the bullet ricochet below.

Griff continued to crawl until he found a wet rock that he climbed over; below him, hiding behind a jutting parapet, was the sniper with the Mauser.

Griff aimed. He couldn't see the sniper's face. He would get this over with quickly. His finger stopped the squeeze as the sniper moved into the light that came from the opening above them.

Griff kept his aim, but his finger stopped the squeeze.

He heard scraping behind him but didn't turn because he knew it was the Sergeant. When the Sergeant reached him, he waited a moment to catch his breath.

"Spot him?" The Sergeant's words were hardly audible.

Griff nodded.

The Sergeant was confused. He moved closer, whispering, "What the hell are you waiting for?"

Griff pointed below.

The Sergeant painfully forced himself into position to fire. He aimed, but he held the squeeze because he sensed Griff's horror. The Sergeant turned. Griff's expression begged him not to fire.

The Sergeant worked his way across the stone ledge until he was fifteen feet directly over the sniper. To jump down on that parapet was too dangerous. It was also ridiculous for him to remain there, an easy target if the kid looked up. Griff scurried backward, making enough noise to trigger the sniper to fire three rounds —enough time for the Sergeant to work his way to a seven-inch ledge. The Sergeant lowered himself slowly, then dropped, falling on the kid who was jamming another round into his chamber. The wind knocked out of him, the kid still had the strength and guts to reach for the Sergeant's eyes with clawing fingers. The Sergeant belted the kid across the face with the back of his hand, seized the Mauser, and flung it down into the black pit.

Followed by the rest of the astonished Squad, he dragged the kid all the way down the narrow spiral iron stairway.

The little Nazi with the face of an angel was furious. *"Ich bin Soldat des Dritten Reiches! Hitlerjugend! Ich bin ein Hitlerjunge! Ich verlange, als regelrechter Kriegsgefangner behandelt zu werden, von euch Scheiss-judengesindel! Heil Hitler!"*

The Sergeant hurled the sniper to the ground in front of the castle. The ten-year-old kid wore a *Hitlerjugend* armband with swastika. He wore scuffed black shoes and short pants with suspenders over a dirty blue short-sleeved shirt. His hair was dirty blond and his angry blue eyes were filled with murder. When he jumped to his feet, the Sergeant cuffed him down. Again he got to his feet and attacked the Sergeant. Again the Sergeant cuffed him, this time harder, drawing blood from the kid's mouth.

"Imagine a little weasel like that," said Johnson, "killing Switolski."

Vinci saw nothing but a miniature Hitler lying on the ground as he spoke. "What do we do with the little son of a bitch?"

"Shoot him," said Zab. "We're supposed to kill any bastard that kills us."

"He's a goddamn kid," said Griff.

"Makes no difference how little the finger is on a trigger," said Johnson. "I say shoot him."

The kid sensed what they were talking about and, to show that he wasn't afraid to die for Hitler, he told them in German that he was a soldier of the *Hitler-*

jugend and that he must be treated as a prisoner of war.
"Heil Hitler!" he shouted.

"We'll use his carcass as a warning to all Hitler's kids," said the Sergeant, "that we kill 'em if they kill us."

"That makes sense," said Zab.

"All agreed we shoot him?" said the Sergeant.

They nodded. All but Griff, who was dazed by what the Sergeant said. Again the kid sensed what they intended to do. This time he slowly got to his feet, talking fast in German, telling them he wanted to be executed like a German soldier, not shot down as he groveled in the earth. He wanted to be on his two legs and he didn't want any blindfold. He was honored, he told them, to die for Hitler and the Third Reich.

"Heil Hitler!" he shouted again.

He gave the salute.

"He's all yours, Zab," said the Sergeant.

"Why *me?*"

"You said shoot him."

"But why *me?*"

"We've got no time for a goddamn firing squad, Zab, shoot the little son of a bitch."

Zab didn't make a move.

"Vinci?" said the Sergeant.

Vinci didn't shoot the kid.

"Johnson?"

Johnson didn't shoot the kid.

"Griff?"

Griff turned away.

"No volunteers?" said the Sergeant.

No one moved.

The Sergeant lifted his rifle and Griff gasped at the same time the kid gasped. But the Sergeant tossed the rifle at Griff, who caught it. Then the Sergeant began to yank the short pants off and the kid began to yell protests, struggling like a wildcat. Enraged, he knew what was going to happen. But he was helpless and the Sergeant now tore off his underpants to expose the kid's bare ass.

The kid cursed him.

The Sergeant propped the kid across his knee and began to spank him. Each crack sounded like a rifle shot. The infuriated kid took the punishment without a

412

whimper and his rage increased as his ass began to turn pink. He frothed at the mouth in anger; he was being treated as a child instead of as a soldier of Hitler's army.

"*Nein!*" the little Nazi yelled. "*Sie dürfen mich nicht wie ein Kind behandeln! Ich bin doch deutscher Soldat!*"

The Sergeant kept whacking the boy's pink ass.

"*Hören Sie sofort auf, Sie Schweinehund! Sie beleidigen den Führer! Sie beleidigen Deutschland! Ich bin ein Hitlerjunge! Ich bin Soldat! Heil Hitler!*"

The Sergeant kept whacking the flesh that turned red and the two little Nazi cheeks began to show welts. Griff looked at the kid's distorted face and thought about what he had read back at the rest camp in Herve. It was a story about kids in Russia playing on a snow slope, using the frozen bodies of German soldiers as sleds.

Suddenly the little Nazi began to whimper. Then he screamed "*Papi! Papi! Papi!*" Now the little Nazi totally reverted, his tears the tears of a child being spanked by his father for having done something naughty.

The boy cried in the rubble that was all that was left of Hitler's thousand-year reich.

CZECHOSLOVAKIA

Who won?

—A dogface basket case to a German basket case

83

Their despair was disturbed by a new sound that brought their gaunt faces to the filthy window of the concentration camp barracks. The sound of distant rifle shots and Schmeisser bursts threaded its way through their bodies until a sparkle of life glimmered in their eyes. These living dead—who were tortured, beaten, and experimented on—heard in that sound of death their first hope of life.

Liberation seemed unreal. Any whisper of hope had long died. Victims of hunger, TB, and a variety of other fatal diseases pressed closer to the only window in the barracks. Standing on dirty bare toes, they stared like zombies; but they could not see anything.

Bursting out from his small neat building, the kommandant checked his Luger, then checked the positions his SS guards were taking to defend their leader, their country, and their jobs. They wore the death's-head killer's insignia of Himmler's pride and joy. They ran to their defensive posts while the kommandant himself marched briskly toward the giant swastika that was suspended over the main gate and silhouetted against the bleak morning light. SS guards on watchtowers, above tightly drawn high-tension double barbed-wire fences, shifted their eyes from the direction of the rifle shots to the kommandant himself opening the gate. The sign above the gate read: KONZENTRATIONSLAGER FALKENAU.

The Wehrmacht was on the run.

More than seventy-five German infantrymen, firing as they fled, swarmed into the concentration camp, some of them killed at the gate. The last German, about a hundred yards behind them, did not seek refuge in the camp to take advantage of the SS guns. He was firing his Schmeisser at pursuing dogfaces. He knew better than to box himself in behind that wire fence and to rely on the SS firepower. Schröder had not lived through the war for nothing. He fled into the nearby woods.

He watched men with Red One patches fly past him. He did not fire at them.

At the helm of I Company the Captain led the grenade barrage that was supported by seven bazookas that knocked down the two front watchtowers and blasted the main gate. The First and Second platoons grenaded the high-tension wires. The Company charged into the camp at exactly 6:30 A.M., April 28, 1945, and the battle of Falkenau, Czechoslovakia, was on.

To the Germans fighting on soil *east* of their Fatherland, complete and total defeat was a reality. And yet they fought because there was still in each heart the hope that from out of nowhere Hitler would put the broken pieces back into place and the loyal diehards would be the first to share victory with him.

The Captain's carbine sent three rounds into the face of the kommandant as the Lieutenant of the First platoon emptied two carbine clips at Wehrmacht and SS troops. The rest of the enemy scattered, many fleeing into the barracks and outlying small buildings. The men in the Platoon pursued the enemy as the rest of the Company, hungry to bring this fight to an end, charged after the fleeing soldiers.

The Sergeant and Griff grenaded SS and Wehrmacht who were firing from behind a bulldozer as Vinci and Johnson fired at a command car that exploded into a flaming mushroom, incinerating the SS who were trying to escape in it. Zab ran into a small building, flinging himself behind a mound of teeth wrenched from dead prisoners. He tossed his grenade. He moved around the teeth, reaching a large pile of toothbrushes, shaving brushes, spectacles, and artificial limbs. Zab heard a sound behind him and turned. Griff burst in and flung himself down alongside Zab. Zab pointed, then showed he was out of grenades. Griff threw a grenade in the direction Zab had pointed. They waited until the explosion's fragments were spent, then climbed over the teeth and saw three dead SS.

For the first time Griff saw the teeth.

He ran out.

In the compound, the Sergeant and Vinci, covered by Johnson, whipped to a big wagon that was loaded with naked corpses of men and women. Moving under the limp arms and feet that were dangling from the back of the wagon, the Sergeant and Vinci killed four Wehrmacht who were firing at Johnson's bursts.

Griff spotted four SS on the run, brought down one of them, saw the second man run into a stone hut, but lost sight of the other two. Griff ran to the hut, tossed in a grenade, ran in after the explosion, and saw the shattered sections of the SS men sprawled against naked corpses of men and women piled like cordwood.

He stared at them, then ran out.

A bullet hit the hut behind him. He threw himself down, rolling with incredible speed. The stock of his rifle missed the ground by an inch. He found cover behind a blazing truck.

From behind the rear wheel of the truck he saw the German rushing him firing his Schmeisser. Smoke from the truck blotted out the German, giving Griff the chance to duck behind the barracks. When the German emerged through the smoke, Griff saw the Sergeant cut him down with two rounds fired point-blank a foot from the German's face.

Griff spotted an SS man running into a small building. He bolted after him, hugged the side of the building with his back, pulled the pin, kicked in the door, threw the grenade in, and waited. Smoke from the explosion drifted out past the sign on the door that read *Desin-*

fektionsbraum. He entered to find the room bare but for tins of Zyklon B gas on the shelf. There were no chairs, no tables, no windows. And no body of the SS. He saw a rear door, opened it, and caught a flash of the SS dashing into the crematorium.

Griff repeated his action, kicking in the door of the crematorium, and tossing in his last grenade. When he burst in, smoke from the grenade still filled the room. But there was no sign of the body of the SS. The smoke finally settled. Griff stared at the ovens. One door was open. He was drawn to the oven and he looked in it and saw the remains of a cremated body. He vomited. He started to leave, but again he was drawn back to the ovens, and he opened the door of the second one and saw another cremated body. For a long moment he stood as if hypnotized, unable to believe what he was staring at. It was impossible. A human being had been actually cooked in the oven. This time he did not vomit. He was deaf to the outside sound of the fire fight slowly coming to an end. Then there was silence, followed by many shouts of dogfaces herding prisoners. Suddenly there was the burst of a Schmeisser followed by the crack of several M-1s.

Then silence.

Griff opened the door of the third oven and stared into the frightened eyes of the SS who had crawled in backward, his body locked with the remains of a cremated body. The SS was frozen with fear. The Schmeisser in his hands was useless. He simply stared.

Griff fired point-blank at the eyes of the German. He emptied his clip. It zinged against an oven. He jammed in a loaded clip and emptied it, firing the eight shots as fast as he could. He jammed in the third clip, squeezing off shot after shot into what was left of the German's face.

The Sergeant, drawn by the shots, advanced, watched Griff grimly squeeze off rapid shots into the oven. The Sergeant looked into the oven. When Griff's empty clip zinged out, bouncing off the Sergeant's helmet, Griff looked for another clip. He was out of ammo. He looked at the Sergeant. The Sergeant untaped his own emergency clip from his rifle stock, tossed it. Griff caught the full clip, jammed it in, continued firing into the mess of what was the face of the SS as the Sergeant turned and left.

Checking other buildings for stubborn diehards, the Sergeant entered a room. It was suddenly quiet. The dripping of a faucet disturbed the quiet. He passed shower stalls. He caught a movement in the corner stall and fired, but he was such an experienced killer that he raised the barrel of his rifle even as the bullet tore out of the barrel. The bullet ricocheted off the damp wall an inch above the frightened eyes of a girl.

She seemed to be about twenty. It was hard to tell. She could have been older. Her big black eyes were frightened. He pulled the rags away and helped her to her feet. Fragile and underweight, wearing rags, her face paled with panic. She retreated among the rags like a cornered sparrow. Then she collapsed. He slung his rifle and picked her up. She seemed weightless. He saw a number tattooed on her bony forearm.

He carried her across the compound, passing the Company moving out with the PWs, and heard the Lieutenant tell the Platoon they were to remain to make a clean sweep of the camp for diehards. He passed Griff, Zab, Vinci, and Johnson without a word. They watched him carry the girl into the kommandant's quarters.

There were picture blowups on the wall of three naked women running past grinning SS guards; of four naked women attacked by dogs as SS guards watched with grins, some of them eating. The Sergeant gently placed the girl on the kommandant's bed under the blowups. He put his canteen to her lips but she remained unconscious. He hunted for something stronger, found a bottle of brandy, and that made her open her eyes. She looked up at him, then her eyes shifted to the blowups above her, then back to him, and she recoiled again. He read her fear and threw the pictures out of the room into the street. He ripped a picture of Hitler from the wall and held it out in front of her and tossed it out to the street. He could see that he was confusing her. He stared at her emaciated face, gently touching it. She jerked it away. He opened a can of C rations, dumped the food into a pan on the small stove, and hunted for a match. He opened a small box near a

421

picture of the kommandant's wife and three handsome smiling children. It was a music box. He gave it to her and smiled. She listened to the music. He found matches and lighted the coal stove. While he waited for the food to heat, he spoke softly to her.

"Jewish?"

She stared.

"Polish?"

She stared.

"Czech?"

She stared.

"Russian? French? Belgian? Dutch?"

She stared. The music wound down. He rewound it and placed it on the bed near her hand. "You'll be okay," he told her. "We're going to be here a while until they make up their minds if we go on or it's all over." He smiled. She suddenly looked closer to thirty. "I'm going to put some beef on you, get some color in those cheeks."

Zab poked his head in, stared at the dying girl.

"Rustle up some milk, Zab," said the Sergeant. "And vegetables. And meat. Kill a cow."

He spoon-fed her.

According to the Lieutenant, there was talk among the Russians and the Americans and the British as to who was going into Berlin. Until they decided, the Platoon's ass was to be parked in the camp. This gave the Sergeant the chance to bathe the girl in the kommandant's tub and to massage her with oil he got from the regimental surgeon who was busy separating the malnutrition cases from the TBs. The Sergeant played the music box for her for four days until he was convinced that her dead eyes were beginning to show life.

On the fifth day the girl was about to be moved from the camp with the other emaciated cases, but the Sergeant pleaded with the regimental surgeon to let him take care of her.

"I'm putting beef on her, sir."

"She's got a slim chance to make it, Sergeant. All we can do is try our best."

"I don't want her swallowed up with all those other

422

cases. Hell, major, I'm getting color back to her cheeks."

Major Tegtmyer was regimental surgeon because he owed a lot to the General: and he knew how close the Sergeant was with the General.

"If the General okays it."

"He'll okay it, major."

"Then I better see to it that you feed her more than that dog food you pack."

"Thank you, sir."

"The General told me you weren't much of a ladies' man, Sergeant. What's that girl got that the others didn't have?"

"Nothing like that, sir."

"Then what is it?"

"I'm tired of killing people." The Sergeant paused. "I'd like to keep one alive."

For the next few days the Sergeant fed her the best that the regimental surgeon could dig up for him. She had steaks and milk and vegetables and fruit. He took her into the woods on a picnic and she seemed to like it. Day after day he massaged her and at night he slept on the floor next to her bed. When she had nightmares he would comfort her and give her warm milk and play the music box for her. To him, very slowly, her dead eyes began to show a speck of life.

Griff, Zab, Vinci, and Johnson watched two Red One men bringing in seventy captured Germans, their hands on their heads.

"So they've finally got you Third Squad jokers working overtime," said Zab. "Where'd you pick up your friends, Stock?"

"Lotta diehards are still in the woods. They cry uncle only when they're out of ammo."

Alone in the woods, Schröder moved through the trees with his Schmeisser.

The next morning Griff, Zab, Vinci and Johnson watched a group of ninety German prisoners herded by two Red One men.

"That's the Second Squad doing there homework," said Griff. "Vacation's over. We'll be sent out into those woods next."

"Hey, Collura!" Vinci yelled at one of the dogfaces of Second Squad. "Paisan! What's new?"

"You tell *me*, Vinci!"

"Hitler knocked himself off."

Collura was unmoved. "That's gettin' *you* no stripes!"

The German prisoners moved off. About thirty yards behind them the Sergeant was crossing the compound with the girl. The Sergeant waved at his Four Horsemen. They waved back. He was carrying his picnic bag.

"He thinks she's putting on weight," said Griff.

"Somebody ought to tell him," said Zab.

"Why don't *you* tell him she's dying?" said Vinci.

"Me?" said Johnson.

"Yeah, you."

"I don't want my head blown off."

The Sergeant reached them. The girl was emaciated and dying, but when the Sergeant looked at her he saw her as beautiful, putting on weight, close to being radiant. They watched him leave the compound on his daily picnic with her.

"You think it's true, what the Lieutenant said?" asked Zab. "That Hitler's dead?"

Johnson grunted. "He wouldn't say it if it wasn't true."

"If the Russians are fighting in Berlin that means the war's over," said Vinci.

"Maybe," said Griff.

"What do you mean maybe?" said Zab. "If that piece of paper the Sergeant talked about is signed, the scratch of that pen'll mean Division fought the last battle in Europe."

"What about the Russians fighting in Berlin?" said Vinci.

"You said *if* they're fighting in Berlin," said Zab.

"Yeah, I guess that's what I said."

"It'll mean," Zab went on, "that Division fought the last battle in Europe, right here in the Sudetenland."

"Is that where we are?" asked Johnson.

"Yes, the Sudetenland, right here is where Hitler started the whole goddamn mess back in 1938."

"Where the hell did you get that from?" said Vinci.

"From the Lieutenant." Zab grinned. "He told me a reporter—guess who—"

"Brodie—"

"Right. He told me Brodie sent word out that the war was over and he got his ass chewed out for jumping the gun."

"Shit," said Griff. "Nobody around here knows anything."

"Well, I know one thing for sure," said Johnson. "I know this is the goddamned longest beachhead in history, all the way from Normandy to Czechoslovakia!"

EPILOGUE

"See. You're gaining."

The Sergeant felt her legs and thighs and arms and stomach. For the last few days she had worn a pink dress he had managed to get her from the mail clerk who was saving it for a girl he met in the town of Falkenau. She loved the dress and the dark-brown shoes with full soles. They had eaten their chicken sandwiches and he made her finish the apple and the milk. When the music box died, she rewound it. She smiled.

He had never been happier in his life, and he was sure she shared his happiness. He caught her looking at his uniform. She touched it gently, then touched the Red One patch on his left shoulder. "I'm going to tell you something," he said. "I know you hate uniforms— but sometimes it's a uniform that stops people from doing to people what was done to you. Understand?" She smiled, as if she understood. He helped her to her feet. "Time for more leg exercise."

They picked flowers and walked through the woods, and when they reached a brook he lifted her in his arms and carefully stepped from one rock to another.

When he almost lost his balance, she laughed. He laughed. He stood on the flat rock in the brook, enjoying the beauty in her face. Her arms were around his neck and she hugged him. Then she kissed him. It was a tender kiss and during the kiss her left arm began to slip down. Then he felt the other arm falling limply and he knew and he silently cried out for her not to leave him but she did. As he felt the dead weight in his arms he removed his mouth from hers and stared at her dead lips and the dead eyes that were still open. She had died with a peaceful smile. He remembered another girl telling him that what he represented was war and the only girl war could have was death.

He carried her back across the brook, her eyes still open and her smile still on her face.

The night was chilly. Sitting alone on a fallen log in the woods, the Sergeant rewound the music box and listened to the music. He had made the coffin. He had dug the grave. And he had buried her. Griff, Zab, Vinci, and Johnson had been the only ones there and they said nothing when they saw him cry.

He paid no attention to the sound of the plane. Several leaflets fluttered down. He ignored them.

The music died. He began to rewind it when he thought he heard a sound. Slowly he turned, saw nothing, only blackness and ghostly trees. He finished winding and listening to the same tune when he heard, *"Ist vorbei—ist vorbei—"*

The words automatically made him freeze, and with the instinct he was known for, he reached out, without looking, for his rifle, but it wasn't there. It was propped against a tree some fifty feet from him. He couldn't understand how he could have been so careless. He couldn't remember a moment when his rifle wasn't his third leg. He reached for his trench knife and turned.

Schröder, without his Schmeisser, was advancing with a leaflet he was waving. *"Der Krieg ist vorbei. Nicht schiessen."*

The Sergeant saw the dead girl with the dead open eyes and the peaceful smile and he blew his top, dropped the music box, and lunged at Schröder with his trench knife.

"Der Krieg ist—"

The Sergeant was on him. They battled, rolling over the music box, crushing it. The Sergeant drove his trench knife into Schröder.

"Sergeant!"

The Sergeant turned and rose. Griff repeated the cry. The Sergeant scabbarded his trench knife as Griff, Zab, Vinci, and Johnson came running toward him.

"Where the hell've you been?" said Griff.

Zab lighted a cigar with a match. The Sergeant knocked the match and cigar to the ground.

"How many times do I have to tell you no goddamn lights at night?"

"It's okay now, Sergeant," said Zab. "The war's over. Look!"

Stepping backward, Zab struck another match on his helmet and held up the flame. Before the Sergeant could knock the flame to the ground, Vinci and Johnson and Griff struck matches and a cigarette lighter; they held up the flames and even waved them.

"See?" said Johnson. "Nobody's shooting at us! The goddamn war's over!"

"The pen was scratched on that piece of paper one minute after midnight, Sergeant," said Griff.

"The war's been over for four hours!" said Vinci.

The Sergeant caved in without falling. He could feel himself reel.

"It's official," said Zab. "Where the hell did you knock my cigar?"

Zab hunted for it. The Sergeant remained a zombie. Zab stumbled over Schröder's body and felt it.

"Holy smoke! A dead kraut—and still warm."

The Sergeant's voice was barely audible as he spoke. "I murdered him again."

Zab forgot his cigar. They all stared at the Sergeant, and dimly his words during the drunken confession now began to make sense to them. They suffered for him.

"You didn't know it was over," said Griff.

"He did," said the Sergeant.

He lumbered away slowly, like a blind man. Griff heard a moan and went to check Schröder.

"His heart's still pumping!"

431

Like a bull the Sergeant whirled and rushed at Schröder. With his trench knife he cut away the uniform to get at the wound. The men struck matches to give him light. The surrender leaflet Schröder dropped was used by Griff as a torch while the Sergeant sprinkled the wound with sulfa powder, shoved sulfa pills down Schröder's throat, forced water from his canteen down Schröder's mouth. The flaming leaflet in Griff's hand was in English and in German. It said: "The war is over! Germany surrendered!" ALL SOLDIERS CEASE FIRE! This surrender leaflet guarantees every German soldier his life. Dwight D. Eisenhower, General, Supreme Headquarters Allied Expeditionary Forces."

Tearing open his first aid kit, the Sergeant bandaged the wound. Schröder opened his eyes.

"Alles kaput!"

The Sergeant whacked him across the face with the back of his hand. "The hell it is!" He lifted Schröder to a sitting position. It was as important to the four riflemen as it was to the Sergeant to keep Schröder alive. "You're going to live, you son of a bitch. You've *got* to live or I'll blow your goddamn head off!"

He lifted Schröder across his back and they marched through the woods toward voices of GIs yelling—toward flashlights and flickering lamps and all kinds of lights popping up in the woods.

The Sergeant quickened his pace, and his Four Horsemen quickened their pace to keep up with the war horse. Zab scraped a match on Griff's helmet, fired a fresh cigar. Griff, who never liked Zab's cigars, grabbed this one from Zab's mouth and puffed on it. Zab lighted a second cigar which Vinci seized and puffed on. Zab took out a third cigar but Johnson plucked it out of his hand, lighted it. Zab took out the fourth cigar, his last one, and jammed it into his mouth and fired it. The Four Horsemen marched behind the Sergeant who shifted Schröder's weight.

The woods filled with matches struck for smokes. Cigarette and cigar ends were glowing like sputtering fireflies.

A FEW WORDS
FROM THE AUTHOR

Ante bellum. Copy boy on the New York *Evening Journal* for the great editor Arthur Brisbane who taught me the drama of facts. Crime reporter on the New York *Evening Graphic* for editor Emile Gauvreau whose religion of facts became my Bible.

Bellum. 16th Infantry, 1st Infantry Division. North Africa, Sicily, France, Belgium, Germany, Czechoslovakia. Baptized as rifleman, emerged Corporal with Bronze Star for D-Day in Sicily and Silver Star for D-Day, Omaha Beach in Normandy.

Post bellum. This book took shape, but battles, tactics, strategy, movements on maps of the 15,000 dogtags that made up the Division was for military historians. For years the book changed shape. Too close. Discrepancies. Memories blurred. The book was like taking a hill. Once taken, it had to be held.

Facts were eclipsed by emotion. Personal, private, the heart exposed, the brain bared. Thus this became the rifle bore's human approach to war told through a combat veteran Sergeant and four young dogfaces in his rifle squad, each doggie an amalgam of fictional characters.

But the place, the fight, the date and death are factual.

A war novel's objective, no matter how emotional, is to make the reader feel war. But war means casualties. To take the reader into reality, one page in the book should be booby-trapped. Since it is against the law to kill a reader, and because it makes unsound business sense to be wounded-while-reading, it became much safer when turning back the combat clock to live backwards than to die backwards.

When *The Big Red One* movie of my outfit became a fact, and Lee Marvin said he would play the Sergeant, I went on location hunts checking actual battle sites.

They no longer had "the feel" of reality; their handwriting in the sky of TV aerials spelled negative for World War II.

Israel was pictorial for the North Africa sequence. Gradually the Holy Land incredibly became Sicily, France, Belgium, Germany and Czechoslovakia.

Jews played Nazi soldiers. Israeli soldiers and civilians wore German helmets over yamulkas, the skull-cap of the Orthodox Jew. Even a 10-year-old boy portraying a Hitlerjugend gave the Heil Hitler salute wearing his skull-cap under an oversized German steel helmet.

The concentration camp in Falkenau, Czechoslovakia was filmed in the heart of Jerusalem. Israeli Cabinet Ministers watched the scene of Mark Hamill finding an SS soldier, seeking cover in a firefight, on charred skeletons in one of the still-warm, ash-piled ovens. The Ministers watched, as did the crew, in factual silence and factual tears.

Jewish concentration camp survivors played the People's Army fighting for Hitler, grimly holding up his picture with their tattoo numbers covered.

To make a real war movie would be to occasionally fire at the audience from behind the screen during a battle scene.

But word-of-mouth from casualties wouldn't help the film sell tickets. And again, such reaching for reality is against the law.

Anyone seeing the movie or reading the book will survive.

"A MUST-SEE EVENT. LEE MARVIN'S PERFORMANCE MAY BE HIS FINEST."
— David Ansen, NEWSWEEK

"A MUSCULAR MASTERPIECE. BETTER THAN JUST ABOUT ANYTHING ELSE TO HIT SCREENS THIS YEAR."
— A.O. Scott, THE NEW YORK TIMES (10/2/04)

AVAILABLE ON DVD MAY 3, 2005